Tilly Tennant was born in Dorset, the oldest of four children, but now lives in Staffordshire with a family of her own. After years of dismal and disastrous jobs, including paper plate stacking, shop girl, newspaper promotions and waitressing (she never could carry a bowl of soup without spilling a bit), she decided to indulge her passion for the written word by embarking on a degree in English and creative writing. She wrote a novel in 2007 during her first summer break at university and has not stopped writing since. She also works as a freelance fiction editor and part-time lecturer.

Hopelessly Devoted to Holden Finn was her debut novel; published in 2014 it was an Amazon bestseller in both the UK and Australia. In 2016 she signed to the hugely successful Bookouture and is currently working on her fifteenth Tilly Tennant novel. She also writes young adult fiction as Sharon Sant. Find out more about Tilly and how to join her mailing list for news and exclusives at www.tillytennant.com

D0238583

The Christmas Wish

TILLY TENNANT

sphere

SPHERE

First published in 2018 by Bookouture, an imprint of StoryFire Ltd.
This paperback edition published in 2019 by Sphere

1 3 5 7 9 10 8 6 4 2

A CIP catalogue record for this book
is available from the British Library.

ISBN 978-0-7515-7801-0

Printed and bound in Great Britain by
Clays Ltd, Elcograf S.p.A.

Papers used by Sphere are from well-managed forests
and other responsible sources.

Sphere
An imprint of
Little, Brown Book Group
Carmelite House
50 Victoria Embankment
London EC4Y 0DZ

An Hachette UK Company

www.hachette.co.uk
www.littlebrown.co.uk

For Mel, who kicks me up the bottom when I need it!

Chapter One

The front door was scuffed and scratched and it wore a faded version of the same bottle-green paint that had been slick and smart while Granddad had been alive. The honeysuckle that had once prettily garlanded the frame was burdened by the husks of dead flowers, with tendrils that stretched and crept and snagged, like the thorns in *Sleeping Beauty* that kept the prince from Aurora. Two empty milk bottles stood on the scrubbed grey doorstep along with a note in a spidery hand that read: *One extra please.* Esme shook her head with a small smile. Who even saw milk floats out on the roads these days? She'd been away for three years, but while her life had changed beyond recognition, it seemed that nothing much had changed here in the sleepy village of Little Dove Morton. But that was OK; it represented reassuring familiarity and that was what she'd come for.

Her attention turned to the windows. All looked quiet within – not that she'd expected anything else. But something nagged at the back of her mind – all wasn't as it should have been. Her grandma had always been so fastidious about the whiteness of her nets and yet today they had more than a hint of grey about them. Esme's gaze went back to the honeysuckle that badly needed pruning, the peeling green paint of the front door and the weeds on the path beneath her feet. Perhaps Grandma was struggling of late. Perhaps she'd welcome a little help around the place and some company in the evenings. Esme raked her teeth over her bottom lip and hoped all that would be true. Now that she was here, she wondered if she ought to have phoned ahead. You couldn't just turn up at someone's house in a state, even if that someone was the grandma who'd always told you they loved you most in the world.

But she was here now and she didn't have anywhere else to be. She raised her hand to the knocker and took a deep breath. Before she'd touched it, the door was flung open and her grandma stood on the step, cheeks pink with delight, her silver hair still cut into the same cute bob pinned on one side with the diamanté grip that Granddad had given her the Christmas before he died. For a moment, Esme was ten years old again, standing on the doorstep with her overnight bags ready to be spoiled with home-made chocolate puddings and snuggles in front of the television with her granddad. Except she wasn't, and that girl had been gone for a long time.

'Esme!' Grandma cried. 'What a lovely surprise!' But then her smile faded. 'What on earth is wrong?'

The reply got caught somewhere in Esme's throat, and suddenly she couldn't see for the tears she'd sworn she wouldn't shed. She threw herself into her grandma's open arms and breathed her in, the smell of lavender soap and talcum powder and the safety of childhood.

She was in the only place she wanted to be right now.

She was home.

Chapter Two

Esme opened her eyes. The autumn sun streaming in through a chink in the curtains was mellow, like apples aged in a hayloft, illuminating the dust that spun in the beams. She took in the details of the old bedroom, so familiar and yet rendered strange by absence: wallpaper patterned in delicate florals; the old sheepskin rug covering the floor and worn flat by years of bare feet; the antique dressing table she'd once been mortified to spill blue nail varnish over, layered by generations of polish and the stains of her accident still visible; the old iron bedstead creaking as she shifted. In that bright moment, all her troubles seemed distant. She was safe and warm in the arms of the past, a place where Warren didn't exist and couldn't hurt her. How wonderful it would be to stay here forever so she wouldn't have to face the present again. As for the future, she barely had any interest in that right now either.

There was a faint tap at the door and then it opened, the swollen wood dragging on the carpet. Her grandma appeared with a chintzy cup and saucer that rattled as she carried it to the bedside table.

'I thought you might like tea,' she said, setting it down.

Esme pushed herself up and reached for the drink. 'How did you know I'd be awake?'

'The sun always comes round to this window at this time of the morning and it's hard to stay sleeping when it fills the room.'

Esme's smile was a faint, brief shadow. Of course it did – how could she have forgotten all those teenage weekend visits when she'd complained about not being able to stay in bed because of where the spare bedroom was? A peculiarity of Thimble Cottage's location that had always been a natural alarm clock to wake Esme for a day of fun with Granddad during her prepubescent years had become a torture to be endured when she'd wanted to sleep the day away during her teenaged ones. And Esme had made no bones about how much it annoyed her. She coloured at the memory. God, she'd been a royal pain in the butt at that age. It was a wonder her grandparents hadn't put a stop to her visits entirely. More than a decade had passed but she felt like that much of a pain now, though the reasons were very different.

Her grandma gave a strained smile as she sat on the edge of the bed. 'Do you feel like telling me what happened now?'

Esme shook her head, eyes burning again. After the previous night, how could there be any more tears? She'd lost so much, so many of her dreams had been shattered – the wedding that would now never happen, the life she'd mapped out for herself that she'd now never have. She'd wept so much for those things that there couldn't possibly be anything left. And yet, the mention of what had driven her back to Little Dove Morton after three years away tightened her throat once more. Fat teardrops spread dark pools on the bed sheets.

Grandma rubbed a gentle hand over Esme's. 'When you're ready; there's no rush at all.'

'I'm sorry,' Esme whispered.

'Whatever for?'

'That I haven't been to see you in so long.'

'You're here now, that's the only thing I care about.'

'You're not angry? I didn't give you any warning…'

'How could I be angry with my best girl? I'm happy you chose to come here to see me instead of suffering in silence alone – I couldn't bear to think about that. Whatever ails you, I'm glad you chose me to help. And when you're ready to receive that help, I'll be ready to give it.'

Esme gave a jerky nod. Words of gratitude and love whirled in her head, just out of reach, and even if she could grasp them they wouldn't have been big enough or profound enough to express what was in her heart for Matilda Greenwood, the grandmother who would never let her down, who would always make space in her life for Esme, no matter what.

Matilda took the cup and saucer from Esme's shaking hands and placed it back onto the bedside table.

'It's a little hot right now,' she said, her understanding instinctive. Esme's fragile mental state would be all the worse for anything drawing unnecessary attention to it, making it an issue they would have to discuss sooner rather than later. Her grandma understood – she always understood – that Esme would talk when she was strong enough, and that time wasn't now. 'I'll leave you to finish up when it's cooled. And if you like, have a lie down afterwards – the sun will move round the house soon enough and you look as if you need some extra sleep.'

Esme didn't need a mirror to tell her that her eyes were gummed and swollen from hours of crying. It didn't matter because there was only Grandma here to see and she'd never judge.

'There's a lovely pack of bacon in the fridge from the farm shop,' Matilda continued. 'For when you feel hungry. I can easily get some eggs.'

'Don't go out on my account. I don't think I'll be able to eat much today.'

Matilda patted her hand again. 'Get some rest.'

Esme nodded shortly again and turned onto her side, tears soaking the pillow where she settled. Her grandma rose slowly from the bed, her steps across the room stiffer and slower than Esme remembered, and closed the door, the wood dragging on the old carpet as she left the room.

It was mid-afternoon by the time Esme felt able to go downstairs, too late for a bacon breakfast but her grandma cooked one anyway. Esme had asked her not to, knowing she'd struggle to eat any, which would only add to the list of reasons her arrival was bad news for her grandma, but the remarkable woman who was Matilda Greenwood, née Smith, the woman who had brought up Esme's father practically alone while her husband, Stanley, travelled the world as a merchant sailor, would have none of it. The villagers had gossiped and wondered why he stayed away, and they hadn't stopped until he'd finally come home to stay, but Matilda hadn't given it a moment's attention. And as the salty smell of frying bacon drifted through the house, and the old radio babbled in the corner with the silken tones of Matilda's favourite presenter, Esme sat at the table and sipped hot, sweet tea, and it was like salve for her soul. The future lightened by degrees, so that the long tunnel of hopelessness she'd constructed for herself shrank before her eyes, and she could almost see the pinpoint of light beckoning her to something better.

'Do your parents know you're here?' Matilda spooned beans onto a plate next to two crisp rashers of bacon.

Esme shook her head. She had refused to discuss much of what had brought her back to Little Dove Morton and, so far, Matilda had seemingly been content to wait for explanations. But this time, Esme knew she wanted an answer. 'Would it make any difference if they did?'

'I think so.' Matilda turned back to the stove, adding a golden-yoked egg to the plate.

'They made their feelings clear the last time we spoke.'

'It takes two to have a fight.'

'It wasn't a fight… it was a difference of opinion.'

'A difference of opinion?' Matilda wiped a hand on her apron. 'Hmm. A difference of opinion so strong that it's stopped you going home when you're in trouble?'

'I'm sorry.'

'For what?'

'For landing on your doorstep like this.'

Matilda waved a vague hand as the pan hissed and spat. 'You know I'd never turn you away. I do think your mum and dad would want to know what's going on though.'

'Trust me, I don't think they're as bothered as you imagine.'

'I'm not sure they know the full extent of the situation you were in.' Matilda stopped and paused, her back still showing to Esme. 'I suspect none of us really do, and if they did know perhaps things could be sorted. All it would take is a phone call—'

'Sorry... Maybe some day, but not yet. I can't...'

'Stubborn as the day is long.'

'That's Mum, not me.'

'And where do you think you get it from?'

Esme tried to smile but it wouldn't come. 'Maybe. I can't phone them yet and that's that. It's just too complicated for me to think about.'

'But you *will* think on it?'

'Yes.'

'Good.' Matilda turned to face her. Slowly, with that same stiffness Esme had noticed before, she brought a plate loaded with bacon, eggs, black pudding, beans and fried bread to the table. Esme suppressed a groan – there was no way she could eat even a fraction of that.

'Grandma, I...'

'I know,' Matilda said, plonking the plate down in front of Esme before lowering herself into the opposite chair. 'You don't need to eat it all, just take what you can.' She reached for the teapot. 'Would you like a top-up?'

Esme nodded, the world looking warmer and brighter by the second. Returning here had been instinctive, but now she knew this was the only place that could heal her. She watched as tea spilled from the spout of the old chipped pot that her grandma would never part with, its lid stained from years of use, and she took comfort in the fact that whenever she wondered if she'd made the right decision in leaving Warren, she would only have to think of this moment to know that she had.

Chapter Three

The kitchen in Thimble Cottage was warm, the air scented with dark sugar and rich fruit and spicy sherry. The autumn that Esme had spent with her grandma was making way for winter, and the hills outside the village were crisp with frost in the mornings now, the sunlight bright and clean as it cascaded down into the valleys. It was too early to decorate, but the house was transforming, gradually, falling into the yuletide festivities by deeds and chores, sights and smells and discussions. Christmas was still six weeks away but it felt imminent as Matilda began to get ready for it in the same ways she always had.

'I should have started this earlier,' she said now, shaking her head as she laboured over a huge mixing bowl.

'I'm sure we don't even need a Christmas cake this big.' Esme brought over the dried fruit she'd just weighed.

'We do if we're expecting guests.'

Esme didn't reply, but returned to fetch a net of oranges from the pantry.

Matilda stopped mixing and looked up. 'Are you nervous?'

Esme put the oranges down. 'Not nervous, exactly. I'll admit to being apprehensive.'

'And you're telling me the truth when you say you haven't heard from that man this week?'

Esme made the sign of a cross over her heart. 'Not a peep. A whole week… perhaps he's finally given up. It has been over two months since I left, after all, and I would imagine that's enough time for anyone to get the message.'

'You could have gone to the police,' Matilda said, returning to her task, 'nipped this in the bud before he'd had time to upset everyone. He might have been in prison by now and it would have served him right.'

Esme frowned. This wasn't a new conversation. It was hard to understand why her grandma hadn't been able to let it go since Esme had first made the admission. Esme had almost come to terms with her broken engagement. The future she'd planned and longed for as Warren's wife had been snatched away from her but she was putting it behind her now – at least she was trying to. She supposed her grandma was probably more devastated on Esme's behalf for all that she'd lost than Esme herself was. It was hard to see injustice done to those you loved, harder than bearing injustice yourself. If things had been the other way around and someone had hurt Matilda in that same way, perhaps Esme would have been just as angry, just as reluctant to let it go. 'And say what? Warren hadn't done anything criminal.'

'He intended to,' Matilda said tartly.

'Well, we can all intend things but unless we do them they're only intentions, and you can't be arrested for an intention.'

'I'm quite sure you can—'

'Warren's not a terrorist, Grandma. Just a pain in the arse.'

'He's an idiot – did he think he'd never get found out?'

Esme took the wooden spoon from Matilda and started to mix. 'Sit down, you look shattered.'

'I'm alright.'

'You're stubborn. This is making *my* arms ache and I have sixty years on you.'

'Don't remind me,' Matilda said, taking a seat and wiping a handkerchief over her brow. She looked pale today, and even though Esme had asked repeatedly if she was feeling under the weather, Matilda had stoically denied any problems, claiming only that she had too much to do.

'There's plenty of time to get things ready, and for all the things you don't have time to make, there's a Waitrose in Buxton; I'd have been happy enough to drive you there. Honestly, Mum and Dad would barely be able to tell the difference.'

Matilda looked sternly at her granddaughter. 'I've never bought a factory-made pudding in my life and I'm not about to start now.'

'So you'd rather be in bed the whole of Christmas Day because you're exhausted than suffer a perfectly decent pudding from a supermarket finest range?'

'This is too important – everything has to be perfect.'

Esme stopped mixing and smiled. 'It's perfect that this Christmas is even happening and you don't need to stress on my account. We'll work things out, and whether we do or don't isn't on your head.'

'I wouldn't want to…' Matilda paused and Esme waited. It wasn't often her grandma couldn't find exactly the right words for a situation but she seemed to be stuck now.

'I want things to be right,' she said finally. 'I would hate to think I was leaving you in a mess with no support.'

'Leaving me?' Esme gave a little laugh. 'Where on earth would you be going? If there's a world cruise on the cards you'd bloody well better take me with you.'

'I'm not getting any younger.' Matilda's tight smile came and went. 'Every morning I wake to see the sun rise I count as a lucky extra these days.'

'Don't be daft! You've got more energy than anyone I know.' Esme tapped the wooden spoon on the side of the bowl. 'Stop it now, you're freaking me out.'

'I'm being practical. One day you'll reach the age where these thoughts occur to you too, but you won't be scared, you'll just be mindful of all the things you'd like to see done before you go.'

'Like getting me and Mum and Dad talking again?'

'Yes.'

'But that's not your responsibility.' Esme pushed the bowl to one side. 'Where's the recipe book?'

'Here,' Matilda said, brushing her hand across an old leather-bound tome. 'But I don't need it to tell you what comes next.'

'OK, what comes next?'

'Nothing for now; let it sit. Come and talk to me.'

Esme stood the spoon in the mixing bowl and sat across from her, hands folded over one another on the table. Her cheeks had the bloom of health and she'd put on weight in the weeks she'd been living with her grandma, but, as her grandma had commented, she'd been so thin when she'd arrived back that it was almost dangerous. Esme had rubbished the assertion, of course, but what she hadn't said was that Matilda had been closer to the mark than she could have imagined. Esme had often felt weak and ill before she'd come back to Little Dove Morton. Warren had been the one constantly telling her she was too fat, even when she'd lost so much weight at his insistence that she weighed less now at twenty-eight than she had as a gangly fifteen-year-old. But he was so pleased each time she'd announced the shedding of another pound and he'd kept telling her how much sexier she'd be, how he'd love her more and how proud he'd be to show her off to the world. What would he say if he could see her now, full of her grandma's home-cooked dinners and jammy puddings?

'What do you want to talk about?'

'You,' Matilda said firmly.

'I've already told you everything.'

'Sometimes I wonder if that's true.'

Esme held in a sigh. 'Why wouldn't it be? There's no reason for me to hide anything now.'

'I can't help feeling you're still suffering from that dreadful episode.'

Esme reached across the table with a smile and took Matilda's hand in hers, sensing hollow bones beneath paper-thin skin, tendons and veins and frailty, and it suddenly struck her, though the evidence was always in front of her eyes, that her grandma was very old. 'I'm getting there,' she said, trying not to think of Matilda's mortality and, selfishly, of what that might mean for her own future. 'Thanks to you. I don't know what I would have done without you.'

'I hope you would have found a way to get away from him, even if I hadn't been here.'

'But nobody would have kept me safe like you have. I'm sure I would have ended up back there, if not for you.'

'It's lucky we live in the back of beyond.'

'It is.'

A cold shudder of doubt crept over Esme at the thought of Warren finding her now. If he knocked at the cottage door today, what would she do? She could sit smugly in her grandma's kitchen, where the air was warm and spiced and full of hope and say it wouldn't change a thing, but he had a quality that was like witchcraft, a power over her she couldn't explain or even understand, and she wasn't certain that she would be able to resist if they were face-to-face right now. She shook off the thought. Grandma would keep her safe, as she'd always done.

'So, you see, we'll be just fine here in our little cottage.'

'I'd feel happier if your mum and dad were part of your life.'

'And they will be, as soon as we've met up and sorted things out.'

Matilda gave a tight smile. 'Just see that you do.'

Esme looked towards the window. It was easier said than done, but she was hopeful too. She'd never wanted to be at loggerheads with her parents in the first place – it was a situation she'd been forced into. At least, from where she stood she'd been forced into it. They'd say she'd been the stubborn one, but perhaps there had been a reluctance to compromise on both sides. At least there was dialogue now, and that was a huge development.

She turned back to her grandma with a smile. 'Remember when you always used to say to Granddad that you wanted to go to that place in Lapland to see the Northern Lights?'

Matilda blinked. 'What's that got to do with the price of eggs?'

Esme laughed. 'But he thought it was the daftest idea he'd ever heard, didn't he? Couldn't understand why you'd want to go somewhere so cold.'

'He said it was cold enough here in the Peaks and to go somewhere worse was madness.'

'He might have had a point there.'

'And I never did get to go – miserable old sod.'

'You loved him really.'

'More than my own breath. But that didn't mean he couldn't drive me mad from time to time and it didn't mean we always saw eye to eye.'

'I suppose that's what true love is about.'

'It's certainly what marriage is about. You learn to compromise. I'm not bitter that we didn't go – we just compromised.'

'What did you get out of the compromise? He got to stay out of the cold, but what did you get?'

'A quiet life,' Esme's grandma said with a smile. 'That was good enough for me.'

Esme paused. And then she grinned. '*We* should go.'

'Where?'

'To see the Northern Lights in Lapland. Next year or something. It should be our Christmas present to each other.'

Matilda stared at her. 'I'm far too old to go traipsing around the North Pole now.'

'You don't have to go to the North Pole then. I'm sure there are other places you can see them.'

'It would still be freezing.'

'You'd be fine – I read about it. They have sleds to take you out into the snow where it's perfectly dark and you can sit covered in furs so you'd be plenty warm enough. It would be just like a scene out of *Doctor Zhivago*.'

Matilda shook her head. 'You've gone mad!'

'I haven't!' Esme laughed. 'I just think we should go – make some serious memories. I want to take you; please say yes.'

'I'm far too old for that sort of thing.'

'You're only as old as you feel.'

'Which is very old these days.'

'I don't believe that for a minute. You never stop buzzing around the house. Come on, you know deep down you'd love it!'

'Is this because *you* want to go?'

'If it will make you agree then, yes, it's because I want to go. But I won't go without you so if you want to make me happy then we have to make it a definite plan.'

Matilda let out an exasperated sigh, but it hid a smile. 'It's lovely to see you so much happier. It's good to see you making plans too – it means you're really on the mend.'

'So that's all the more reason to say yes. Just imagine how disappointed I'll be if you don't – and I'm sure you don't want that on your conscience.'

'That sounds like bribery to me.'

'Think of it as encouragement rather than bribery.'

Matilda eyed her warily now, pulling the mixing bowl towards her and taking up the spoon again. 'I'll think on it, and I can't say fairer than that.'

It had been three years since she'd spent Christmas with any of her family, and while it had been easy to slot back into her grandma's life, Esme's parents, Dennis and Coral, were an entirely different matter. Esme had never figured out why, but they'd hated Warren from the start. She'd put it down to silly, old-fashioned ideas about the age gap – Warren was ten years older than Esme and she was an only child who'd been doted on as she'd grown up on the outskirts of the spa town of Buxton, where her dad had moved to for work, just a few miles from her grandma's home. They'd told her that the age gap had nothing to do with it and it was as simple as the change they'd seen in her as soon as she'd started to date Warren, that she was neglecting her friends and family, that she pandered to his every whim, that she was always where he wanted her to be whenever he called. As far as Esme was concerned, this was love – you made compromises when you were in love, didn't you? You put yourself out to make your partner happy and you were there for them. Sometimes your life had to change in unexpected ways to make it work. Dennis and Coral didn't quite see that and couldn't get past their dislike of Warren.

Esme had eventually hated that they'd hated him and, in the end, when she'd let them down once too often on his account – not turning up for family meals or days they'd arranged to meet, borrowing money that she couldn't pay back because of some bill he hadn't been able to manage – things had come to a head. Esme had tried to explain that Warren loved her and needed her and she couldn't just up and leave him and, besides, she was in love and couldn't they respect her choice of partner? But her pleas had fallen on deaf ears. They couldn't show Warren the tolerance and patience Esme was asking for – more to the point, they simply didn't want to. Things had escalated and before long there'd been bristling animosity on both sides and a chasm too vast to bridge. With vigorous encouragement from Warren himself, Esme had reacted in the only way an inexperienced, gullible, headstrong young woman could react – she'd cut herself off from a support network that she'd later desperately need. Not that it would have been easy to do anything else. Somehow, Warren was certain that he and Esme were always too busy to go and see her family and friends when she'd asked, and when she'd mooted the idea of going alone he'd reminded her of the reasons she'd cut ties in the first place and he'd said that to build bridges with her parents was to betray him. Esme would have to take sides – him or her parents.

None of it was Warren's fault, she'd reasoned. He wasn't the one laying blame, he hadn't asked her parents to hate him, so why should he be the one to suffer? Her parents had each other but Warren needed Esme and he needed her more. If she left him she was certain he'd come to the most terrible harm and all that guilt would weigh on her for the rest of her days. He'd said as much. But that had been before the discovery that would change it all. It turned out Warren had more than just Esme to worry about his well-being.

As these thoughts filled her mind, Esme waited in the car outside Matilda's house, the engine idling while the heater worked to warm the interior. The thoughts seemed to have come from nowhere, though, in truth, they rarely left her, secreted in the dark places of her consciousness and creeping into the light when she least expected or wanted them. But they were banished again by the sound of tapping at the window and she turned to see her grandma waiting to be let into the car.

'It's open,' Esme called, smiling inwardly. Matilda had had a lifetime to get used to the idea of central locking but apparently the concept had never sunk in. 'Everything alright?' she asked as her grandma climbed in, a little breathless. 'We don't have to go right this minute. In fact, we don't have to go today at all if you'd rather put it off.'

'Oh, I want to go. Better to get it over with. I just had to top up the bird feeder – they go mad if there's nothing in there.'

Esme raised her eyebrows. 'Those birds eat better than we do.'

'I like to do my bit. There's not much in the hedgerows this time of year.'

'Can't they find worms like all the other birds have to?'

'I expect they've got used to not having to.' Matilda pulled the door and it shut with a dull clunk.

'Better keep on top of it then,' Esme said. 'You don't want to lose a star on Birdy TripAdvisor.'

'On what?'

Esme chuckled. 'Never mind. You're all good to go now?'

'Ready when you are.' Matilda settled in her seat, arms wrapped around the hefty leather handbag on her lap. 'It's been ages since I went to Bakewell. I think the last time was when your granddad fell into the river. What year was that…? I think it must have been 1989.'

Esme let off the handbrake. 'Blimey, it's been that long? I wish I'd been there to see that! Every time I hear about it I just think it must have been hilarious.'

'Oh, he was livid. He was just about ready to march after the cyclist who'd spooked him and throw him in the river too – bike and all. He never found it hilarious, even when the rest of us did.'

'To be honest, it's been a while since I was there too and I'm looking forward to seeing it all lit up and Christmassy. I'm looking forward to bringing a couple of Bakewell tarts home too.'

'Dear Lord, don't call them tarts in the presence of a local! They're *puddings* – you'll get us thrown out of the town by saying it wrong.' Matilda clicked her tongue on the roof of her mouth. 'And you born in Derbyshire too!'

'Sorry,' Esme said with mock penitence. 'I know they're puddings and I won't forget. It's just that I've got used to living in places where nobody would know what the hell a Bakewell pudding is. More to the point, tarts, puddings… they wouldn't care which it was.'

'They might not care in London but they do in Bakewell. These things are important round here.'

'I know.' Esme steered them through the junction that took them onto a broad A road bordered by wild grasses and shrubs and fields left to fallow. 'It's hard to believe really that somewhere like Bakewell is in the same country as London – they're so different that they might as well be on different continents.'

Matilda brushed an imaginary speck of dust from the catch of her handbag. 'You can keep London as far as I'm concerned. I went once, and only because I had to, because of something to do with a commission for your granddad on a new ship. He left me in a café while he went to see them. He was gone for hours; I'd got to my fourth cup of tea and nobody spoke to me once in all that time.'

'It's a busy place. I suppose it was back then too. People don't always have time to worry about what anyone else is doing. I expect they weren't being deliberately rude; they probably just didn't notice you.'

'Well, I didn't like it. I couldn't wait to come home.'

Esme cranked the heating up in the car. 'I liked living there, but it's very different from being out here. For one thing, it's hard now for me to get used to the fact that pretty much nothing happens after dark.'

'Plenty happens – it's just going on behind closed doors, quiet and private, as it should be.'

'I wasn't thinking of a lock-in at The Rock Face,' Esme said with a chuckle, her mind going back to evenings in the company of the landlords of that establishment, Tony and Jim, who'd both been known to leap onto the table and do impromptu impressions of Shirley Bassey if they'd had enough of the guest ale. Which was more often than not, because almost everyone who ordered a drink in the pub offered Tony or Jim a couple of pounds out of the change with the instruction 'and have one yourself', an instruction they were only too happy to follow.

During her teens when her granddad had first taken her in for pop and crisps while he had a pint, he would tactfully usher Esme out if it got too rowdy in there, but when she'd started to visit as a lawful adult, they'd had some great evenings and Esme had been allowed to stay, no matter how rowdy it got. Tony had since died and Jim retired to the coast and The Rock Face had a new landlord now; Esme hadn't yet ventured in there since she'd arrived back in Little Dove Morton, but now that she thought about it, perhaps she would. It was yet another thing to go on the list of things she'd do with her new freedom.

'There are other things to do, you know.'

'I know. You just have to know where to look I guess. In London you can walk down any street and there'll be something going on – a parade or a demonstration or a party or just someone playing music. Whatever it is, something will be happening.'

Matilda looked beadily at Esme. 'Do you miss it?'

'It was fun, and for a while I liked it, but I don't miss it. You can't think with all that stuff going on sometimes.'

'I should think not. Still, there's not a lot in Little Dove Morton for young ones.'

'I'm not that young!' Esme laughed. 'In some eras I'd have been considered middle-aged.'

'Young enough to want the company of people your own age – not an old hen like me.'

'I'm happy enough right now. I quite like spending my time with an old hen, even if the old hen can't quite believe that I'm perfectly content helping her bake and dig the weeds from the garden.'

Matilda gave a sage nod. 'Perhaps for now it's for the best. I know you lost a lot of your old friends when you started courting that man, but perhaps, in the months ahead, you might want to look them up again?'

They passed a field of cows, faces impassive as they lifted their heads from the grass to watch Esme's car roar away. Esme understood that her grandma's comments were made in an attempt to steer Esme's life back to some kind of normality. The problem was, Esme wasn't ready for that – not just yet. The Peaks were a world away from her old life in London but, right now, she rather liked it that way.

Chapter Four

It would be a few hours until dusk fell and it would be dark enough to really appreciate the coloured lights and twinkling Christmas displays that festooned the little town of Bakewell. It had taken time to find a parking space too, and while Matilda had muttered about how it never got any better and didn't Esme think the council would do something about it, and how the last time she'd come with Esme's granddad back in 1989 it had been exactly the same, Esme nodded mildly and persevered. And her patience was rewarded when a space was vacated just as she'd done her second circuit of their third car park and she drove right in, content that she'd rather keep the quaint and unspoilt town and have to wait for a parking space from time to time than have it developed into somewhere faceless and cloned and full of multistorey car parks.

The town was comfortingly familiar to Esme, who hadn't been here since she'd fallen out with her parents, but it seemed tiny in comparison to the metropolis she'd been calling home for the past three years. Even though it was bigger than Little Dove Morton, it still felt small. It had been raining that morning but the sky was clearing now, pockets of sun in a still heavy sky bouncing blinding rays onto wet pavements. The cottages that crouched over narrow roads were squat and sturdy, built from local stone, some of them converted into shops with wonky doorframes and windows like keen eyes in old faces. The town seemed to Esme to be old-fashioned, rooted in days long gone, and yet there were stores lit by bright displays of colourful modernity – radios and kitchenware, trendy toiletries and designer clothes. Imposing Christmas trees, dressed in pearls of yellow light reflecting on slick cobblestones like stars on a black sea stood sentry at their thresholds, the doors wreathed in scarlet holly.

'Isn't it gorgeous?' Esme said, but more to herself than to anyone else, as if she needed to somehow reinforce what her eyes could see, convince herself somewhere so pretty could be real.

But then she turned, aware that her grandmother was no longer at her side, and saw that Matilda was flagging, even though they'd only just left the car park.

'I'm sorry,' she said, walking back to offer an arm for her grandma to hang on to. 'I'm walking too fast for you? I'm used to rushing everywhere and it's hard to stop doing it.'

'Not a bit of it,' Matilda said stiffly, though Esme could hear the wheeze in her voice. 'I've just been distracted by all the lovely decorations.'

Esme said nothing. Matilda was as practical as ever and she'd never let herself get distracted by such trifles as fairy lights when there was a list of Christmas presents as long as her arm that needed to be bought. It wasn't that she didn't enjoy the beauty of a town adorned in red and gold, and she was as fond of a spot of Christmas cheer as anyone else, but there was a time to appreciate such things for Matilda and that was after the job in hand was done. But Esme knew better than to air these thoughts.

'We could stop awhile if you like,' she said instead. 'I wouldn't mind a lazy shopping day if I'm honest. We could take our time; there's no need to rush.'

'I wonder if the little teashop is still by the river…' Matilda gave her head a tiny shake. 'What's the name of it again…?'

'I don't think I've ever been to it.'

'I don't suppose it's still open now. It's years since I went there.'

'We could go and see? It might be open, even if it's not under the same management?'

Matilda paused for a moment before giving her head a firm, final shake. 'Not yet. Later, when we're done.'

Just as Esme had suspected – her grandma would always be practical to the last. But she couldn't banish the growing, nagging concern that day-to-day living was not quite as easy for her grandma as it had once been, and it saddened her that she hadn't been around to help Matilda through this change in the years it had been creeping up on her.

'It sounds like something to do with gardening…' Matilda murmured, as if the name of the teashop being so elusive to her caused her some distress. 'It's…'

'Gardening?'

Matilda clicked her fingers with a triumphant look. 'Capabilitea Brown's! Oh, such a dear little place. Granddad loved the scones and clotted cream.'

'I could definitely eat a scone,' Esme said with a smile. 'I'm up for walking along to see if it's still there when you're ready to take a break.'

'That's if we have time. I've got so much to do it'll likely be dusk by the time I've finished.'

'Where do you want to go first then?' Esme asked.

'I'll get your gift first.'

'But I thought we'd agreed that I didn't want a gift because I've been living with you rent free—'

'Nonsense! We agreed to no such thing! You said it and I didn't reply.'

'But I thought that meant you'd agreed!'

'Well, that was a daft thing to think. Do you make every decision in life based on the lack of a reply of anyone else involved?'

Esme blinked. And then she started to laugh. 'You're such an infuriating pain! Anyway, you can't buy a gift for me when I'm with you.'

'That's easily remedied. I presume you'll be wanting to buy one for me today?'

'Well, yes, but—'

'Then we'll have to part company at some point or it will all get a bit silly.'

'Ah, but Bakewell is a small place. You can guarantee we'll bump into one another at some point and it might be just at the moment one of us is buying the other's gift!'

Matilda smoothed a prim hand down her coat, but when she looked up at Esme her eyes were full of mischief. 'Then we'll just have to pretend we haven't seen anything.'

'OK.' Esme laughed. 'I suppose we could do that. You're sure you'll be alright on your own?'

'I've been alright all the other times I've shopped alone so I expect I will be this time.'

'Meet back here then? Say around twelve? We could go and see if that teashop is still there and get some lunch?'

'That sounds lovely,' Matilda said. 'Let's do that.'

Finding the perfect gift for her grandma was always going to be a struggle. Not only was she a practical woman who had neither time nor patience for beauty regimes or creams or lotions or potions, or make-up or perfume or expensive clothing, but the only one indulgence she did allow herself – jewellery – was party to the same practicality. The only things she really wore were the few pieces Esme's granddad had bought for her during their years together. But Esme felt the weight of a gratitude that she needed to show in a way greater than any words she had, and the perfect gift seemed like a good way to show it. If not for her grandma, there was no telling where Esme might be right now. Matilda had taken her in at a moment's notice, with no argument, no reproaches, no need of an explanation and wanting no thanks. She'd been ready to listen and not judge when Esme needed to talk and ready to fill hopeless silences with exactly the right words to banish them. When Esme had only been able to cry, Matilda had sat quietly with her until she was done, and when Esme had been tempted by Warren's silky promises and words of remorse, Matilda had shaken the sense back into her. Warren had been very persistent with texts and phone calls and if Esme had been living with anyone else she was sure he would have won her round. But she was coming out of the other side of that long tunnel now, she could feel it, and it wouldn't be long before even Warren's most fervent pleas would leave her unmoved. She'd loved him when she'd left him, and she still loved him a little even now. Her grandma understood this and, unlike Esme's parents, she didn't judge Esme for it.

She had gifts to buy for them too – they would be visiting soon in a bid to put the past behind them and make friends again, and although Esme was pleased by this, what did you get for the parents you'd barely spoken to for three years? It had been Esme's fault really – looking at it now she couldn't say anything else. Being with Warren had driven all common sense from her and when he snubbed someone – as he had her parents – she snubbed them too. That was how she'd come to lose not only family members but friends as well, until she'd had nobody left, nobody to turn to, nobody to rely on but Warren. Perhaps that was how he'd wanted it, but Esme tried not to think about that possibility. She believed him capable of many things, but that kind of manipulation seemed a cruelty too far. And now all that turbulent water was under the bridge and her parents were ready to welcome her back. But how could a simple Christmas gift even begin to rebuild such a broken relationship? Esme had no idea what the right thing would be, but at least that was one problem her grandma would be able to help with. She put those gifts out of her mind for the moment. First, Esme had to use her time alone to find something perfect for Matilda.

Esme perused the shelves of a craft shop, pored over swanky kitchen goods and expensive china (both of which would probably end up in a cupboard as 'best', meaning they'd never see the light of day again), sniffed at various toiletries and tested out make-up, despite knowing that those gifts weren't right at all. After coming away from each establishment empty-handed and frustrated, Esme's gaze was drawn to the travel agents. It sat in a long row of stone-fronted shops, huge posters of Caribbean beaches with sugary sand and turquoise seas in the window. It was open but the staff within looked faintly redundant as they sat at desks and chatted, each with a mug in front of them, while a pack of biscuits lay open between them. Esme supposed it wasn't a busy time for travel agents when everyone was thinking about Christmas gifts. But it had her mind racing. Would her grandma really dismiss the idea of that trip to see the Northern Lights? She might have been half-joking when she'd suggested it before, but Esme knew her grandma had always wanted to go – she could recall in vivid detail conversations between her grandma and granddad about it over the years. They had been full of banter, good-natured and witty sniping, but, ultimately, even Esme had been able to sense the very real longing in her grandma, despite the cool retorts and laughter. Matilda hadn't asked for much in life and Esme could count on one hand the foreign countries her grandma and granddad had travelled to together. Suppose Esme booked it right now – they couldn't possibly go *this* Christmas, could they? Could her grandma be ready? And more to the point, would it be fair to expect her to break with her annual traditions, to part with the age-old routines and timetables that had been a feature of her Christmases for the last sixty years? Perhaps such a trip would be less of a gift than Esme imagined; perhaps all it would do was throw Matilda into turmoil, not knowing how to reject a present that really wasn't something she felt up to doing at all. Not to mention the impending reconciliation with her parents, who might not see it as much of a reconciliation at all if Esme upped and left just when she was meant to be putting things right with them.

With a faint pang of regret, Esme quickly dismissed the idea of the Lapland trip. Maybe next year, when they'd had time to plan and talk about it. And maybe not during Christmas at all. She'd approach her grandma over dinner later, suggest it again as something they could do together when they could both be ready for it.

Instead, her gaze turned to a jewellery and fancy goods shop across the street. Taking advantage of a gap in the traffic, she rushed over to take a closer look at the window display and her eye was immediately drawn to a beautifully gilded silver photo frame. Only the previous week the old mother-of-pearl one that housed Matilda's treasured wedding photo had fallen from the wall as she'd dusted it, the rusted hook finally giving way, and it had cracked beyond repair. It sat on the kitchen dresser now, propped up by a pile of cookbooks while Matilda wondered what kind of tradesman she'd need to find to repair such a thing when everyone, she said, threw things away now once they'd broken. Esme didn't want to add that no tradesman she knew would make the journey out to them for such a tiny job and she'd never heard of a shop that took in repairs like that.

The silver frame in the shop was expensive, but it was stunning and Esme had planned to spend a lot, despite her grandma's warnings about overspending on her. Besides, Esme was due to start a new job at the local farm shop after Christmas, once their current sales assistant had retired, and her savings would soon get topped up again. Not that they'd been paltry to start with – after all, she'd been saving for a wedding. It had never happened in the end, but the way she saw it, she might as well spend the money on something else that would make her happy – something just like this.

The shop had a bell that chimed as she pushed the door open and went inside, and a young man looked up from a newspaper spread out over the counter. He smiled, folding it away.

'Anything I can get you or would you just like to look around?' he asked.

He was fair, the kind of blond where even his eyelashes looked like spun gold, and his eyes were a startling aquamarine, and perhaps if her heart hadn't still been quite battered, Esme might have fancied him. It was hard to tell his age but he looked younger than Esme. Old enough, though, she decided. Then she noticed the chunky wedding band and shook away the silly daydream. Instead, she returned his smile and pointed to the window display.

'Could I look at the silver photo frame?'

'Certainly – just let me get it for you.'

'Thanks.' Esme stepped aside to allow him access. The shop was tiny and crammed with shelves of delicate-looking items that made it difficult to get around but at least it was just the two of them. If it had been full of customers she might have walked out again and tried to come back when things had calmed down rather than risk knocking a display unit over getting out of people's way.

'Here we go.' He pulled a duster from his pocket and gave the frame a gentle wipe before handing it to Esme. 'Christmas present?'

Esme nodded, the cold, solid frame oddly tactile and satisfying beneath her fingers as she traced the delicate rosebuds embossed into the metal.

'It's heavier than it looks, isn't it?'

'It's lovely quality,' he said.

'But would it be too heavy to stay on a wall? My grandma's old one fell and broke and I don't want the same thing to happen.'

'Even if this did fall off I doubt it would break. I doubt it would fall off either – it's got quite a sturdy hook. Good workmanship. We get it from a craftsman down in the Welsh valleys – none of your mass-produced rubbish.' He tucked the duster back into his pocket. 'We can engrave a message on the back too if you'd like. Free of charge, while you wait – doesn't take too long.'

Esme handed him the frame. 'I'll take it.'

'You want me to engrave anything on it?'

Esme looked at the frame. It could be so much more perfect with the right message, and yet how could she possibly conjure a single phrase that could encompass all that was in her heart?

'Yes,' she said uncertainly.

'You want a minute to think about it?'

'If you don't mind.'

He gave a slight nod. 'Be my guest. Would it help if I left you alone while you pondered it?'

She looked at the frame again. Perhaps the simple approach would do just as well. Her grandma was hardly one for pomp and fuss anyway, and words straight from the heart would hold just as much meaning to her as flowery prose. In fact, Esme had to wonder if a simple expression wouldn't mean more to her grandma than flowery prose, because it *was* straight from the heart. She looked back at the shopkeeper.

'If you could engrave: *To Grandma, with more love than I can ever express, from Esme*, that would be perfect.'

'Esme,' he said, taking it to the counter. 'You don't come across many Esmes.'

'Don't you?'

'Well, I don't recall the last time I heard it.' He gestured to an old, deeply varnished, high-backed seat standing against a wall. 'Take a load off if you like; it'll be about ten minutes. Unless you have somewhere you need to be, then you can come back and pick it up later if it suits.'

'I'll wait. My grandma is shopping for my present somewhere in the town and this way I won't bump into her until I've finished.'

'Let's hope she doesn't have the same idea and come in here then,' he said with a smile. 'At least, not until you've gone.'

'I don't think we need to worry. Knowing her, she's probably buying me a vacuum cleaner as we speak.'

'Doesn't everyone dream of owning a vacuum cleaner?'

'Possibly,' Esme replied, laughing.

She sat down and watched as he lifted a heavy piece of machinery onto the counter and put on some safety goggles. Out of habit, she pulled her phone from her bag and swiftly checked for messages. Nothing, and the odd feeling she'd had for the whole of this week persisted. Warren had finally given up. She should have been relieved… she *was* relieved. But there was also a sense of closure that she hadn't been ready for. This was it – she was on her own. When she'd left Warren this was what she'd wanted, wasn't it? His constant messages had brought her nothing but misery and distress. But instead of being happy, she now felt somehow unloved, as if something about her was unlovable. While Warren had kept trying to get her back, at least she'd felt desirable; she'd felt as if she meant something. But now?

Esme hadn't told her grandma any of this, of course. Maybe she ought to – Matilda would shake some sense into her. She always knew how to get Esme back on an even keel. She'd call it first-night nerves – Esme was making her return back into the world of dating and she was bound to be jittery and uncertain. Sometimes, when people said *better the devil you know*, what they were really saying was *I'm too scared to find out what else there might be*.

'How is your name spelt?' the shop assistant asked.

Esme blinked and looked up. He was smiling at her. He really was very good-looking indeed.

'Oh. Of course. It's E. S. M. E.'

'Great.' He bent back to his work, the engraver emitting a tinny whine as he pushed its point along the metal. He made it look so easy and graceful.

'You do this a lot?' Esme asked.

He looked up, the engraving machine falling momentarily silent. 'We get a few requests.'

'And you work here full-time?'

'I do.'

'Seems like a nice job.'

'I can't complain. But then I am the boss.'

'You own the shop?'

'Yes.'

He glanced down at his work, and then back up at Esme. A polite way of saying that he really needed to get on.

'Sorry, of course,' Esme said. 'I'd better let you finish. I expect you'll be getting busy again soon.'

'It is an unexpected lull right now,' he said, snapping the goggles back into place. 'But then if I'm not busy at this time of year I might as well give up.'

Esme nodded, and he turned back to his work, long lashes blinking over his blue eyes, forehead creased into a vague frown as he concentrated. Esme wondered what his wife was like. She couldn't help but feel that whoever she was she was a lucky woman.

The frame had been re-polished and wrapped in layers of scarlet tissue paper and a gift box printed in a holly motif. Esme stepped back out onto the street, a small smile lighting her face, box clutched in her hand. She couldn't wait to see Matilda's expression when she opened it on Christmas Day. She was tucking the box into a tote bag so her grandma wouldn't see it when her attention was caught by a small group of people gathered across the street, only a few feet from the travel agents. Some were looking down at something and others were standing about them with anxious faces. One man was on his phone, pacing up and down, arms flapping madly as he tried to explain something. It could be a bus party, Esme reasoned – a lot of bus companies put shopping trips on at this time of year and Bakewell was a popular destination. But when she drew closer and saw that two of them were bent over something on the ground while others looked distraught, she knew that this was no bus party. Or if it was, something had gone horribly wrong for them. She could help, but then it looked as if there was a lot of help there already. Grandma would be finished with her shopping soon too and they'd arranged to meet – Esme didn't want to be late. After a moment's deliberation, she opted to leave things be. One more body might be more of a hindrance than a help.

She started to walk. But then she turned back and looked again at the crowd. Grandma would understand if she was a bit late when she explained it, and her conscience wouldn't let her leave if there was something she could do here. A second later she'd made her decision and she dashed across the road.

'What's happened?'

The closest woman turned to her. 'Someone's collapsed.'

'Oh God! Are they alright? What can I do?'

'There's enough people here already helping. It might be sensible for you to go on your way; if too many people keep joining us it's going to turn into a right circus.'

'But I know some first aid,' Esme insisted, desperately trying to recall now techniques she'd learned a couple of years ago but never had cause to use since.

'Somebody's already having a go.'

Esme's eyes widened. 'Do they know what they're doing? Do you want me to call an ambulance?'

'We've just done that too. I think it's all under control. You should give the poor lady some space.'

'Right. But if they need help with the first aid, I could…'

She began to squeeze through a gap in the crowd. But as she broke through to see what was happening at its centre, she halted and managed to breathe only one more word.

'Grandma!'

Chapter Five

The days in between Esme leaving the hospital alone to Matilda's funeral had been a mess of hours that stretched endlessly into the distance without meaning or purpose or shape. Esme did things because they needed doing and her thoughts were not of her tasks, only of the new void in her life. Thimble Cottage had always been cosy, but now it was vast and cold, and even though the same welcoming shabby furnishings decorated the rooms and Grandma's old umbrella still stood in the rack in the hall, and the Christmas cake they'd baked together was still in the tin waiting to be eaten while her cookbooks still propped up the old wedding photo of her and Granddad, it felt like solitary confinement without her grandma in it. People had visited, of course, lots of people from the village. So many, in fact, that Esme tired of trying to smile and be brave for them. She didn't want to show a stiff upper lip, and she didn't want endless cups of tea in stilted, awkward silence. Being alone in the cottage was miserable, but it was the only alternative and sometimes, on her lowest days, it was an alternative she welcomed.

She was curled on the sofa now, a cold coffee by her side, looking once again at the travel tickets she'd found in her grandma's handbag the day she'd died out on the street. Her grandma had booked the trip only moments before she'd collapsed, and with the tickets was a receipt for payment in full and details of the travel party:

Mrs Matilda Greenwood
Miss Esme Greenwood
The Magic of Lapland – seven-day tour

Esme had been wondering what to do with the tickets since Matilda's death. She could have taken them right back to the agent and explained and they would have given her a refund, but somehow that didn't seem right. Her grandma had clearly meant it as a Christmas gift, a special, once-in-a-lifetime trip for them both and, really, it had been Esme's idea anyway. She had no doubt that her grandma hadn't booked the trip because she herself had wanted to go – she'd booked it because Esme had wanted to go. Besides, what would Esme do with the money? She could hardly give it back to her grandma and it wasn't hers to keep. Matilda's estate was yet to be settled officially but Esme and her mum had found a will, tucked in a dresser drawer, newly amended to leave Esme a half share of Thimble Cottage and including a clause that said Matilda wished for her to be able to live there as long as she wanted, regardless of only having half ownership. The other half was to pass to Esme's dad – Matilda's son – but Esme guessed that with the clause – and her dad would never contest it – the other half was hardly any good at all because he couldn't do a lot with it unless Esme agreed. Esme's mum had merely pursed her lips and they'd carried on going through the rest of Matilda's papers.

In fact, the only aspect of the whole situation that had forced Esme to focus had been the reintroduction of her mum and dad back into her life. It had been meant to happen anyway but it wasn't meant to be like this. They were talking again but nobody was saying anything of comfort. Now, the blame for Matilda's heart attack was being laid firmly at Esme's door – at least, so it seemed to Esme. Nobody said it, but there were comments about unnecessary stress and extra pressure and twice as much work to do, and if Esme hadn't already been burdened with the weight of her own guilt for the part she'd played in events, then the guilt her parents had now placed upon her would have done the job nicely. It didn't matter that Esme had done her fair share around the house, that Matilda had enjoyed her company and had said many times she was happier with Esme there than she had been in years, or that the doctor had said at the hospital that Matilda had probably been on a sticky wicket (his words, and not entirely appropriate Esme had thought) for some time, because the truth was Esme had arrived at the cottage and shortly afterwards Matilda had died and any idiot could join the dots and find the connection.

Esme had wanted to ask her mum what to do with the travel tickets but they'd had no time for such trivialities. There were solicitors to instruct, banks to contact, house deeds and insurance documents to find, distant relatives and long-lost friends to inform and a funeral to arrange. Esme had gulped, eyes hot with tears, as her mother had plonked the newspaper in front of her at breakfast one morning, the announcement of Matilda's death succinct and heartless in bold black type upon the page – because these things had to be done in the proper manner – directions to the funeral service equally precise. Matilda had been a living, breathing person, a wonder of nature, and now she was simply five lines in a newspaper finished by a postcode.

Esme was still looking at the tickets now, chin resting on her hand, and wondering what to do with them once again when the screen of her phone lit up. Warren. Knowing that to read it was a bad idea, she read it anyway.

> *Are you alright babe? I heard about your gran. I know we're not together now but I'm always here for you.*

Esme pushed the phone away, nausea washing over her. It had been inevitable that Warren would find out, but still she'd hoped he wouldn't. She didn't know how, but people talked to people and it was constantly surprising how these things got to those you'd really rather they didn't. Social media, tenuous links, random acquaintances – they all played a part. And Warren would have been keeping an ear to the ground where Esme was concerned, of that she had no doubt. He'd done a good job of cutting Esme's friends from her life, gradually and stealthily, but he'd made it look like a natural drifting apart. And he had charm by the bucketload – he knew where he could find Esme's old friends and he'd know just how to tease the right information out of them. He'd already worked out where she'd been living, and she hadn't been able to figure out how he'd done that either, except knowing that if you really wanted to find out where someone was, there was usually a way. Apparently, Warren had *really* wanted to know. At least he hadn't got the exact address and Esme knew this because he'd bombarded her with text messages and calls but he hadn't actually turned up in person. If he'd got an address, he would have come, circling like a vulture around a dying gazelle.

Her phone bleeped again and she glanced at it to see Warren's name flash up once more. Why hadn't she deleted him from her contacts? It would have been the sensible thing to do – delete him, block the number – and yet she'd done neither of those things. She closed her eyes and tried to pretend there was no message waiting to be opened, and she tried to picture her grandma sitting across from her, scolding her for even thinking about a reply. She needed someone to keep her on the straight and narrow and at this point even one of her parents would have done, but soon after the funeral they'd packed their bags and gone home, telling her that they had too much to do to stay and babysit a grown woman and promising to check on her once in a while, but essentially leaving her to fend for herself.

Esme reached for the phone, even as she cursed herself for it. She flicked open the message.

By the way, I've left Shelly.

Esme closed her eyes again. Why now, just when she was at her lowest? She'd been doing so well, thinking of him less and less, building her life anew and rediscovering the person she'd been before Warren had walked into the café where she'd worked one fateful day with a cocky smile and chiselled jawline and had left with her phone number.

'Don't reply,' Matilda would have said. 'Don't give an inch.'

'I won't, Grandma,' Esme whispered to the empty room. 'I won't.'

More messages came. Over the following days the bombardment that had almost dried up before Matilda's death began again. Esme deleted some and some, in moments of weakness, she read. They all promised he'd changed. He wanted to love and support her and it was tempting, an easy path to rebuilding after the earthquake of her grandma's loss. She didn't have to do this alone, he said. But she never replied, afraid of where it might lead.

Her thoughts stayed with him though. Had he really been that bad? Had she been the unreasonable one, judging him too harshly for a mistake anyone could have made, the mistake of falling in love with the wrong person at the wrong time? If Esme was really objective about it, the person who ought to be complaining was Warren's wife, Shelly, because she was the real injured party in all of this. Not that it was Esme's fault, of course, because she'd been blissfully unaware of Shelly's existence until the day she'd been out with Warren and someone who was a mutual friend of both Warren and Shelly had rumbled him and the messy truth had finally been revealed.

So now he was telling her he'd left Shelly and he only wanted Esme, to love and protect and keep safe from the rest of the world. It was all he'd ever wanted and for Esme to think anything else broke his heart. Maybe Esme had got him wrong after all? Even as she thought all this, it left her uneasy. Was it right to be glad Shelly had lost? Hadn't she loved Warren too? Hadn't he once told her he wanted to be there for her, to love her and keep her safe from the rest of the world? Part of her wanted to talk to Shelly, to find out for herself whether it was true, whether Warren had left her, but she hated herself for such a callous desire.

There was only just over three weeks left until Christmas but there was no tree up in the cottage, no streamers hanging from the ceilings or wreaths of holly at the front door, no rows of cards across the mantelpiece and no lights around the window frames. Esme's gift to her grandma still lay in the box on Esme's dressing table and her grandma's gift to her, the tickets to Lapland, lay next to it. The Christmas cake they'd made together was still untouched in a tin in the pantry alongside the tins and jars of pickles and preserves and cooked meat Matilda had bought as extra in anticipation of more family in their little home than it had seen in a good many years. Whenever Esme's gaze fell on any of this she was reminded, like a jab to the gut knocking the air from her, that it was almost Christmas and yet she had no reason to celebrate and nobody to celebrate with, even if she'd wanted to.

Pulling on her coat, she grabbed Matilda's old house keys and headed for the front door. The walls were closing in and the house that had once felt like a sanctuary felt more like a mausoleum these days. A walk in her beloved hills and valleys might be just the thing to clear her head and the afternoon was as crisp and bright as any she'd seen in weeks. The cottage door slammed behind her, echoing on the deserted street, and she headed for the road out of the village.

*

The hills were dark masses of green, patches of exposed rock showing the flinty grey of their spines, and the sky was clear and cold, the outlines of distant peaks beginning to glow saffron and pink as dusk crept over them. Out here there was peace like nowhere else Esme knew. As a child, she'd go out walking the hills with her granddad on a Sunday and it was one of her earliest, fondest memories of him hauling her onto his shoulders when her little legs got tired, explaining with endless patience what each craggy outcrop was called and the legend that had given it a name, showing her different plants and looking out for elusive wildlife that Esme could try and photograph with her little instant camera – though not one of them ever turned out any better than a tiny dark blob against a green-grey landscape. He'd loved the hills – they'd been like a piece of his own soul and, by association, Esme had grown to love them too. Now, they gave her peace and room to think, and they made her simultaneously more isolated than ever and yet at one with the world. Here, it was possible to be apart from humanity and yet to be connected, treading in the footsteps of generations of peak dwellers who had walked these hills before her. She'd never really appreciated any of this, just how much the hills meant to her until she'd moved to London. Back then she'd been all wide-eyed and hopeful, fresh from a provincial college and off to university in the big city to change the world. But university had not been all that she'd dreamed it would be, and she'd ended up taking more and more hours at the coffee shop she'd originally worked at part-time to provide an income while studying, until she was working there full-time. Quietly, without ceremony, life at the university ceased and the little job at the coffee shop became a career. Hardly a career at all really: there were no prospects of promotion and certainly no prospects of a raise, but it was steady money and she liked the work. She'd continued to live in the student house she'd shared with three other girls until they graduated. A new group moved in to take their place, and seeing them start where she'd been three years previously only served to make her feel like more of a failure than she had before. By the time the second bunch had all graduated, Esme was living with Warren. At first they had really *lived* too, drinking every night, out at clubs and pubs and the wildest sex Esme had ever had – anywhere and everywhere whenever the fancy took them. He was so much older than her, so much more experienced, handsome and funny and confidence oozed from him – it was hard not to be awed and completely spellbound. And at least her education, or lack of it, didn't matter to him. In fact, he always seemed pleased that she was less qualified than he was. He only cared that she was there for him. Esme's failure at university had been the first hammer blow to the relationship with her parents. They'd been disappointed, even though they'd tried to understand. And then she'd met Warren when things had already been fragile with them, and somehow her relationship with him made things a hundred times worse.

But he was here for her now – his messages proved that – and maybe everyone was doing him a grave disservice by doubting his intentions.

Tucked in her coat pocket, her fingers traced the outline of her mobile phone. She'd heard it ping some time back and hadn't

looked, because she knew it would be another message from
Warren. But now she sat on a boulder and took her phone out.

> *I'll make it right this time, babe. I'm divorcing Shelly. You
> and me can get married this time, all above board. Please
> come back – I need you and I think you need me. We're meant
> to be together, babe. You know it.*

Esme slipped the phone back into her pocket and gazed around
at the darkening hills, her breath spiralling into the air. Solitude
could be tranquil and beautiful, but it could also be cold and bleak.
Suddenly, she was sick and tired of being alone. Hadn't it only been
Shelly keeping them apart before? Hadn't they had plenty of good
times as well as bad? Like the day trip to Brighton where they'd
got so drunk they'd skinny-dipped in the sea once dusk had fallen
and had laughed so much they'd completely missed their last train
home. They'd had to sleep at the station because they'd run out of
money for a hotel and they'd snuck into a toilet to have sex and it
was scary and exciting and rebellious and it had made Esme feel
totally alive in a way she never had before. And the fancy-dress
party where he'd gone as Tom Cruise in *Top Gun* and she'd dressed
as Kelly McGillis and he'd sang 'You've Lost that Lovin' Feeling' to
her on the karaoke and they'd won a booby prize for the cheesiest
costumes. Every relationship had ups and downs, didn't it? He'd
made a mistake and he'd strung her and Shelly along but he saw
that now – the fact that he was trying to comfort her showed that.
What was the point of struggling alone when she didn't have to?
He wanted to make things right, and if he was divorcing Shelly
then he was serious about that, wasn't he? They *were* meant to be

together, because they did both need each other, and, in the end, wasn't that the only thing that mattered?

Esme took the phone out once more, and this time she sent a reply.

Chapter Six

It seemed sensible to leave the keys to Thimble Cottage with her mum and dad so they could come in and check around from time to time. They wouldn't like it considering the clause in Matilda's will stipulating that Esme should live in the house, and she tried to convince herself that had Matilda been alive, she would have understood. For now, at least, Esme focused on packing the essentials. She'd have to arrange to come back and get the rest once she'd settled back in the flat in London she'd once shared with Warren and she'd have to phone the little farm shop down the road too and let them know that she wouldn't be able to start her job after all, and she hoped she'd be able to get work in London again without having to wait too long.

As for her grandma's house, she'd need to work out what to do with that too. She didn't want to sell it, but she didn't want to leave it empty for years on end either. It wasn't a problem she was in a place to solve right now, and it would take her parents' input too – something they wouldn't be keen to give when they found out where she was going.

Outside, darkness had now cloaked the hills beyond the village. There were hardly any streetlights near the cottage, not like it was in London. On quiet nights with her grandma, Esme had liked that because the moon would seem so much brighter and closer and she could see more stars than she'd ever seen in London. But tonight, she only longed for saffron streetlights illuminating the dark corners of the lane, bright windows and noisy bedrooms overlooking hers. Little Dove Morton was a lonely place without her grandma.

Her phone bleeped as she stuffed underwear into her suitcase and she rushed over to check it.

Can't wait to see you, babe. You won't regret it.

Esme smiled and then returned to her task, a slight frown creasing her forehead as she inspected some less-than-glamorous undies before shoving them back into the drawers. She'd left a lot behind when she'd left Warren, including her sexiest underwear – something she certainly hadn't planned on needing for a long time. There was going to be a lot left behind here at the cottage too that she'd have to sort, but it would wait for a while at least. It wasn't like anyone else was going to move in. And who knew, maybe she'd even persuade Warren to leave London and settle for life at an easier pace in the Peaks once they were married? In which case, it made sense to leave things here for her return. It had been more than a pipe dream since she'd made her decision to take him back, and she felt sure that if she went about suggesting it in the right way he'd be willing to hear her out. After all, the house was half hers and there was no rent to pay – unless her parents suddenly decided to charge it, but even then it wouldn't be as much as she'd pay in London – and Warren was always complaining about money, so it made perfect sense. Although, she had to accept that she might have to wait a while for that eventuality when he still had to divorce Shelly before they could even think of marriage and moving house. Esme didn't know Shelly at all – apart from the few things Warren had told her – but she could only hope that Shelly wasn't the type to make things as slow and painful as possible by dragging her feet. Part of Esme wouldn't have blamed her for that, and part of her felt guilty for being the other woman – no matter that she hadn't been aware of her part in the betrayal – but when all was said and done, Esme reasoned, Warren's relationship with Shelly couldn't have been right when he'd been looking for comfort and love elsewhere, could it? Did that make Esme the villain of the piece for being the one he ran to? She didn't want to think so, and so she tried not to think of it at all.

Her stomach growled impatiently but she ignored it and carried on with her packing. She had to lose all this weight she'd put on living with her grandma – although a little had disappeared since Matilda's death, she still weighed more than she had when she'd first left London. Perhaps Warren would forgive that for now because he'd know it had been down to comfort eating and her grandma wanting to look after her. It was too late to do anything about it now anyway, so whatever he thought, this curvier version of Esme was what he was getting. He said he loved her, and he'd love her regardless, wouldn't he? Perhaps this time he'd be less judgemental, just glad to have her back.

When all her clothes were packed, Esme sat on the bed and took stock of the little room that had been a sanctuary for the past few months. She'd miss the worn sheepskin rug and the floral wallpaper and the dressing table with patches of old blue nail varnish on it, and the way the door dragged on the carpet, even if sometimes she wondered if it had been good for her, being holed up here.

Her phone began to ring. She rushed to get it from the dresser and was surprised to see that instead of being Warren's, the number showing on the display was that of her parents' house.

'Hello?'

'Love, it's me.' Her mum's voice was brisk and clear on the line, full of purpose. 'Dad and I have been talking and we think you should come home. At least for Christmas. We know Matilda left the house for you to live in but we're not sure it's the best place for you to be right now.'

'But, Mum—'

'Esme, we're not trying to get you out of the cottage. We're more than happy to go along with Matilda's wishes in that respect and you can live in it for as long as you want, but you shouldn't be there alone right now—'

'Mum, I—'

'I know what you're going to say but I'll say again that we don't think you ought to be there alone. That's all.'

'But—'

'If you're worried about the house being empty you needn't be. We can pop in from time to time to check on things. In time, we'll decide together what to do with it – which, of course, means you living there if you want to. Your father did mention buying you out if you didn't want to stay there but I thought you might want to. For now, we really think it would be better if you were here with us.'

'But, Mum—'

'Dad's ready to come and pick you up whenever you like and your old bedroom's made up. I've got chicken in for tea if you want to come tonight.'

Esme sat on the bed and ran a hand through her hair. 'I'm sorry, Mum, but I'm going back to London.'

The line crackled and hissed.

'Mum… did you hear me?'

'Back to that man?'

'Don't…'

'But that's what you mean, isn't it?'

'He's changed. All that other stuff is out of the way now.'

'He tried to commit bigamy with you!'

'He knows it was wrong now and he's sorry.'

'It wasn't just wrong, it was illegal! He lied to you about his wife for all that time – and that's without the other things!'

'What other things?'

'The way you utterly changed when you met him.'

'Mum… I thought we were past all this. I know you don't particularly like him but—'

'Don't particularly like him? I hate him, and I reserve that word for people who truly deserve it. If he died tomorrow I'd jig on his grave and your dad feels the same.'

'Mum!'

There was another silence. Then: 'So you're determined you're going back?'

'Yes.'

'And what are you going to do with Matilda's house?'

'I don't know. I thought maybe Warren and me could live here.'

'Over my dead body!'

Esme pinched the bridge of her nose and squeezed her eyes shut. 'I don't know then – I haven't thought that far ahead really.'

Another pause. 'Please come here before you leave for London. At least talk to us before you go.'

'So you can try to change my mind?'

'So we can talk some sense into you.'

'Isn't that the same thing in your book?'

She heard her mother take a sharp breath. 'So you'd rather I pretend to be happy about this?'

'I want you to let me live my life the way I see fit.'

'But the way you see fit isn't good for you! If I saw you shooting drugs would you want me to stand by and not say a word?'

'Seriously, Mum? It's hardly the same.'

'He clicks his fingers and you run. He's no good for you, and yet you want him all the more for it. What does he have that's so irresistible?'

'It's not like that. He's leaving his wife and I love him – there's no reason for us to be apart now.'

'Even after you spent so long getting over him? And don't think we don't know what sort of state you turned up at Little Dove Morton in because Matilda did talk to us. We were desperate to intervene and the only reason we didn't was because she insisted it could be handled better her way.'

'But that was when I thought he was going to stay married to Shelly. I couldn't stay with him when he had a wife, could I?'

'So everything your grandmother did to help you means nothing either?'

'Mum, please... she'd understand.'

'I highly doubt that. But as she's no longer with us, we're never going to know.'

'She understood that I love him. She knew the only reason I left was because of Shelly. She'd never tell me what to do.'

'I should imagine this Shelly's throwing a party.'

'What's that supposed to mean?'

'She's had a lucky escape by the sounds of things.'

'Why do you need to say such mean things about Warren all the time? You barely know him.'

'That's true, I don't. But I know you. And I know that you've changed beyond recognition since you've been with him and not in a good way.'

'That's not true.'

'You didn't come up for your dad's special birthday, and in the past you would *never* have missed something as important as that. You didn't visit when he had his hernia operation; you said you'd come for your cousin's wedding and then let her down at the last minute. You stopped visiting your friends, you were thin as a rake and whenever we did manage to meet up all you did was look at your watch and fret about the time so you could be back for him... I could go on. What else am I supposed to think about that? He's a bad person. He lies and manipulates and controls, and he's made you a shadow of the girl you were. I can't believe we're having this conversation right now. I can't believe that you'd even think of going back to him.'

'People change, Mum. It's part of growing up. Just because I'm not the same wide-eyed little girl who lived with you doesn't mean the changes are for the worse, and it doesn't mean they're down to anyone else. Maybe it was nothing to do with Warren. Maybe *I* just changed.'

'Your grandma would have agreed with me.'

'Well, as you just said, Grandma isn't here, is she? We can hardly ask her.'

Esme bit her lip. Her retort had been harsh and it wasn't what she'd meant to say. But her mum was off again, attacking Warren at every opportunity, just like before, and it had just come out.

'Mum—'

'Fine,' her mum cut in. 'Go to him, but don't come crying to me when it all goes wrong again.'

The line went dead. Esme stared at the phone as the number disappeared and the screen went black. It looked as though she was going to need Warren more than ever because now there wasn't anyone else. She could only hope he wouldn't let her down this time.

Esme clicked the PAY NOW button, and the confirmation pinged through to her email. That was it – her train to London was booked and by tomorrow afternoon she'd be back there. Warren had arranged a day off work to collect her from the station and they were going for a drink at his local – what used to be *their* local – afterwards to celebrate. Esme's stomach groaned as she closed the lid on the laptop, and this time the feeling of hollow nausea that swept over her was too much to ignore. She went to the kitchen and picked up an apple from the fruit bowl, making a mental note as she did to clear the food from the pantry and the fridge before she went to the train station. Perhaps a local food bank or homeless charity would be grateful for it. The car she'd picked up cheap could stay here at Thimble Cottage – she'd have little need for it in London and it really was more of a hindrance there than anything else.

As she munched on her apple, she ran through an inventory in her head, trying to make sure she'd packed everything she was likely to need, in the short term at least. But it was hard, because her mind wouldn't stay on any of it. There were doubts, tapping away in the back of her head. Was she doing the right thing? Had Warren really changed? Would he really divorce Shelly for her? What if her mum was right – what if Warren really was bad for her? Sure, sometimes she'd thought him unreasonable and demanding, but nobody was perfect and no relationship was either. Everyone knew that love needed patience and tolerance and a bit of work if it was going to last. Hadn't her grandma said just that? She'd compromised for Granddad so many times and their marriage had been one of the strongest Esme had ever known. So Warren sometimes told her things she didn't want to hear and nagged her into things she didn't want to do, and she'd lost a few people along the way, but he did it because he thought he was doing the best for her and that proved he loved her, didn't it? She could make compromises for love, couldn't she? She could certainly do with a little love right now, even if that meant turning a blind eye to a few faults. In time, compromise would be as easy and natural as breathing.

Sometimes, when she was quiet and thoughtful and the skies beyond the windows had darkened, she could almost see Matilda sitting in the armchair, turning to her with a brisk smile.

'Time for supper and some brain exercise,' she'd say, surfing the channels for reruns of her favourite quiz shows while Esme went to fetch cake from the pantry. It had become a nightly ritual during their last weeks together, something Esme had grown to love, something that represented stability and order and emotional safety, as they tried to outwit and outscore each other on the questions and squabbled good-naturedly over the last bit of crumbly fruit cake.

Not tonight, though. Not any night now, ever again. Esme's eyes misted and she cleared them with an impatient thumb. Grandma would have said it was all tears for nothing and what was the use of crying for an old woman who'd had her time? And even though Esme would have to disagree, she couldn't deny the sense in it too. She had to look forward now, not back, to a new future. The engagement ring she'd once thrown at Warren was now back on her finger. It was a strange compulsion that had made her pick it up from where it had fallen the night she'd left London, but perhaps this moment had been in the divine plan all along. Her fingers ran over the smooth metal. Was it proper gold? What carat was it? She'd never even asked. She looked down at the diamond glinting at her. Was it even a diamond? Then again, did it even matter? It was a symbol of a commitment, nothing more, and did the authenticity of it even matter?

Esme shook herself. She had more packing to do and it was hardly going to happen with her standing around, pondering what might or might not be real.

Out of habit, she popped the apple core in the compost bin, just as her grandma would have done. Silly really, because it wasn't as if Esme was going to be putting compost on the garden any time soon; the bin was just another thing she'd have to empty and clean out before she left. She went upstairs to her bedroom and, even though she'd just told herself she had lots of practical things to do, she reached for Matilda's wedding photo – Granddad and Grandma as teenagers, smiling broadly, arms linked. Grandma clutched a glorious trailing bouquet of roses and Granddad wore his army uniform in shy pride. It was still in the old, broken frame, lying in the dust that had gathered on her dressing table. Esme turned it over, looking for the clasps that would undo the frame to get the photo out. Maybe she'd take it with her, slot it into a book to keep it safe until she could get a new frame that matched the décor of Warren's flat. Maybe Warren wouldn't mind it hanging on their wall too much – it was only an old photo, after all.

The fastenings were stiff with age and rust but after a bit of coaxing they came apart, one by one, with a faint ping. Esme slid the back off the frame to reveal the blank side of the photo and…

She frowned. Something else was lodged in there, slotted in behind the photo, out of sight. Esme pulled two rectangles of card out and peered at them. Plane tickets – old, by the looks of things. For a start, nobody even got plane tickets now – it was all electronic on your phone or print-at-home boarding passes. The tickets were in Grandma and Granddad's names. Esme's breath caught in her throat as she read the destination and the dates of travel. Heathrow to Helsinki, Helsinki to Rovaniemi, December 2008 – they were due to travel two months after Granddad had died.

The frame fell to the dressing table with a clatter and Esme lifted the tickets to her face, staring at them as if somehow the words printed on there might change if she looked hard enough. She reached into her memory. Wasn't Rovaniemi the place in Lapland Grandma had planned to take her? She could only draw one conclusion from her find – Granddad had planned to take Grandma to see the Northern Lights after all, to exactly the same place as Grandma had planned to take Esme. Had she known about it? Or had Granddad hidden the tickets behind the photo so she wouldn't find them and spoil the surprise? If Matilda had known then she'd never said, and clearly they never got to go because her husband had died in October of that year and she would never have gone without him. At least, not back then when the loss would have been sharp and raw. But if she didn't know, then it was one hell of a coincidence that Grandma had booked that same town for them to visit.

Esme shook her head. Silly – it was probably the most popular Lapland resort and the travel agent had probably just recommended it when Grandma asked. After all, it was the home of Santa Claus, and of course the travel agent would recommend it for a Christmas trip. Grandma would have gone in with a list of things they wanted to see and do and this place would have fitted the bill perfectly.

Esme took the tickets over to the bed and sat down, all thoughts of packing and old photos forgotten. What did it mean that they had shown themselves now, after all these years, at this precise moment? And despite trying to dismiss it, it *was* strange that the destination he'd chosen was exactly the same as the one

Grandma had booked for her and Esme. Did it have to mean anything at all or was it just a coincidence?

Her gaze was slack as a thousand scenarios ran through her head, and then she twitched, as if shaken from a trance, and got to her feet. Taking the photo and the tickets, she went over to her suitcase and tucked them into the front pocket to keep them safe.

Chapter Seven

Warren stood at the barriers to the train platform. In his arms he cradled a huge bouquet of cream and pink roses – they looked as if they'd cost a week's salary. He was as handsome as always – his ice-blue eyes stark against his tanned skin, teeth an expensive Hollywood white and a carefully put together outfit to maximise the whole effect. He'd always looked like a man who was going somewhere in life, and Esme had never stopped wondering what he saw in her. She'd always considered herself passably attractive and reasonably slim but no great beauty, with mousey, poker-straight hair that needed product to give it any kind of style more often than not. But he saw something and that was enough.

Even as Esme made her way over, suitcase wheels grinding across the pitted tarmac, she could see other women doing double takes in his direction, gazes unable to leave his perfectly chiselled features. His good looks attracted so much attention all the time that it was hardly surprising he'd found it hard to resist the temptation that had led him astray. But now he was promising to commit to Esme and it was her duty to be the best girlfriend she could be to make him so happy that he wouldn't be tempted to stray at all. Compromise, she kept telling herself – that was the secret. How hard could it be?

'Hi,' she said at the barriers, suddenly shy and awkward. It had been more of a jolt than she'd anticipated, seeing him again after so many difficult months apart.

He thrust the flowers at her. Esme took them with a grateful smile as he looked at her suitcase. 'Is that all you've got?'

'For now.'

'Right.' He leaned forward to kiss her.

'What's the matter?' Esme asked. Despite what the grand floral gesture would suggest, his kiss had been chaste and cold and not what she'd been expecting at all. Where was the passion, the lust, the thrill at being together again? Wasn't this what he'd wanted? Hadn't he been the one begging her to come home?

'Nothing,' he said. 'Let's get a cab – the queue will be a mile long when this train empties.'

Esme began to follow, the suitcase catching on divots in the worn concrete of the platform and the flowers weighing down her other arm. 'Are you sure? Because it feels like something is wrong.'

'Of course there isn't.'

'You've changed your mind? About me coming back? Things have changed with you and Shelly?'

'No,' he called, still striding ahead and not looking back. 'Don't be soft.'

'Warren… please!'

He turned now and they halted in the middle of the station concourse where a huge Victorian clock hung directly above them. Across the far side stood a fast-food stall, a vast queue snaking along the counter, and she tried to ignore the divine smell.

'You've cut your hair,' he said.

'Oh.' Esme smiled. She stopped and stood the suitcase up, putting a hand to her shoulder-length bob. 'Is that all?'

'You know I like it long.'

'Well, yes, but I fancied a change.'

'But I like it long.'

'Right. It will grow back in no time though. It grows really quickly, my hair…'

'Hmmm.' He turned and began to walk again and Esme followed. 'Shelly's got a mate who does extensions on the cheap.'

Esme frowned. 'You want to ask *Shelly's* mate to do *my* hair?'

'No, I want *you* to ask her. Obviously I can't ask her – that would be ridiculous.'

'Oh…' Esme panted, the suitcase getting heavier and more cumbersome by the minute as she concentrated on dodging the legs of a station full of commuters and balancing the bouquet. Who knew that flowers could be so heavy? 'But it's much easier to manage like this.'

'I expect it is. But anything worth having takes some effort, doesn't it?'

'Right. I suppose so,' Esme said, recalling that her own thoughts last night had led her to a similar conclusion when she'd questioned her decision to come back to London.

Outside the station he strode to the nearest cab waiting at the rank and knocked on the window. The driver got out and rushed to help Esme with her suitcase while Warren climbed into the car. With a brief thanks, Esme got in next to him and gave the cabbie the address. She laid the bouquet on the seat next to her, the cab filling with their scent.

'I've reinstated your gym membership for you,' Warren said.

'Oh. Thanks.'

'I thought you could go Mondays, Wednesdays and Fridays. Maybe Sunday mornings if you make an effort to get up early enough.'

'What about you?' Esme said, arching an eyebrow.

'I don't expect I'll have to go as often as you – I've kept my weight off, see? Still, I suppose if you need extra motivation I could come with you. Maybe hit the sauna or something while you're on the bike.'

The streets of London began to flash past – vibrant, noisy, chaotic, unpredictable – all the things her home in the Peaks was not. While she'd enjoyed living here before, now the excitement of being back was tempered by a sudden longing for what she'd left behind. To open the curtains to a quiet street overlooked by the majestic crags of the hills beyond, to go for hours without seeing a car pass, to look into the sky and see kestrels and sparrow hawks circling the fells, to receive a smile and a greeting from every resident you passed as you made the journey to the tiny shop in the village – it was funny how quickly Esme had got used to all that and how completely she'd calibrated to life at that pace. She gave herself a mental shake. Last night she was craving London and now she was craving Little Dove Morton. These days it felt as if she didn't have a clue who she was or what she wanted. It was no wonder people lost their patience with her.

'I'm surprised you kept the flat on,' she said, her thoughts turning back to their destination – her new-old home.

He gave a wry smile. 'I had a feeling you might be back. You and me, babe, we're meant to be. The sooner you understand it the sooner we can get on with our lives together.'

'You really want a life together then?'

'Would I be here if I didn't?'

Esme smiled, comforted by the thought, though still vaguely troubled without understanding why. 'It must have been a struggle to afford two rents.'

'Shelly's paying half the rent on the place I had with her. It's the least she can do now she's living there on her own – I'm not going to carry on paying for a place that's not mine, am I?'

'But you were living with her? While I was away?'

'Oh, yeah, but as soon as you said you were coming back I got the tenants out of our place and I'm back in there now.'

'Tenants?'

'I sublet it. Had to. Where else was I going to get the money to keep it going? Some Eastern European nurses or something. A bit fit, honestly, but couldn't understand a word they said.'

'So they've left?'

'Yeah.'

Esme was thoughtful for a moment. While she was happy to have the flat to go to, she was troubled by the idea that these women had been asked to move out at a moment's notice. 'Where did they go?'

He shrugged.

'Were they upset?'

'About what?'

'About the idea that they had to leave? They must have been nicely settled in after all.'

'People who rent round here expect to be thrown out at a moment's notice – it's how it works. I expect they've got sorted quick enough. I gave them their deposit back so they have something to put down on a new place.'

'It's not that easy to find a new place.'

'They can go to the agency – loads on the books there.'

'Not always suitable—'

'What is this?' Warren asked, his expression darkening. 'You want me to go and find them or something? Move them in with us? I'm not a bleeding charity. Life's life and business is business – it's my flat and I want it back. You want to be the one out searching for a place to live?'

'No,' Esme said, 'it's just…'

'Drop it, alright? I did it for you, babe, so you'd have a place when you came home. Everything I do is for you. I thought you'd be glad.'

Esme looked out of the window. If Warren had thrown out these poor women for her, it wasn't a gift she would have asked for. If he'd told her the situation in the first place she would have worked something else out. But, looking at his face now, perhaps it wasn't wise to push the argument.

'I know,' she said, 'and I am.'

'I thought we'd go to The Duke tonight,' he said, his expression lightening again. 'Have a few jars, see who's out.'

She turned to him with a vague smile. 'Sounds great.'

'Have you brought some decent clothes with you? You might need to go shopping for something before we go out.'

Esme looked at her watch, mentally running through the items she knew were in her suitcase. Maybe she'd have time to run to Oxford Street…

'About Shelly…' she began.

'That's all in hand – I told you.'

'And you're really going through with it? You're really going to divorce her?'

Warren glanced at the back of the driver's head. Between them and him was a thick layer of glass and it was unlikely he'd hear much, if any, of their conversation. Besides, he had his radio on, singing along to something that Esme didn't recognise.

'Do you really think this is the time to discuss it?' Warren asked.

'I don't know. I was just asking. Wondering. About what it might mean for us. I mean… do you still want to marry me?'

'You know I do. I wouldn't have asked before if I didn't.'

'Good.' Esme settled back in her seat. 'That's good.'

'I've been thinking about that actually,' Warren said. 'If you sell your half of that house up north it would pay for the wedding and a decent deposit on a place down here for us.'

'But my mum and dad would have to agree to the sale and I don't think—'

'But you could ask them, right? You could talk them round. After all, what good's half a house for anyone apart from the money tied up in it?'

'Well, yes, but I wondered if…'

Esme's reply died on her lips. Perhaps now wasn't the time to air her hopes that she and Warren might live in her grandma's house as a couple. She'd only just arrived back in London and they needed to get comfortable with each other again before she asked him to make big decisions like that. She'd need to plan the moment better, talk to him properly, introduce the idea slowly, make him think he had a stake in it…

'What?' he asked.

'It doesn't matter.'

'I've booked the day off work.'

'I know. It's good that we don't need to rush about for anything. I mean I had wondered if you still might want to get to the office but—'

The conversation was cut short by the swift motion of Warren's hand diving beneath Esme's skirt. She gasped as his fingers dug for her most intimate places, blood rushing to her face with shame and arousal in equal measure. His breath was hot next to her ear. 'Want to know what we'll be doing this afternoon?'

'Warren… the driver…'

'He's seen worse than this on a Saturday night.'

'But…'

'Haven't you missed me?'

'You know I have.' Esme clawed at his wrist but his fingers only dug in further.

'I bet you've missed this more,' he said. 'I bet you're practically dried up.'

'Warren, please!'

'You're not? Don't tell me you've been shagging someone else while you've been up north?'

There was danger in his expression again. Esme recognised the look and she knew it needed swift action to pull him from that place.

'Of course not!' She reached to kiss him, trying to ignore the pain his fingers were now causing her. 'It's only ever been you.'

It did the trick. With a lazy grin he pulled his hand away and relief flooded through her.

'I hope you're not thinking of unpacking when we get back to the flat,' he said, looking to the windows again, 'because we've got things to do first.'

*

Warren was in the bathroom taking a shower as Esme sat on the edge of the bed doing up her blouse. They'd been back for three hours but she hadn't yet had the chance to eat or drink and although she'd promised herself she'd manage until they went out later, after months of eating well with her grandma she wasn't used to going for such long periods without. She was light-headed now and her mouth was dry.

'I'm going to get a cup of tea,' she shouted through the bathroom door. 'Do you want one?'

Getting no reply, she called again, but getting none a second time decided that if Warren wanted one when he came out she'd just make another. But then her attention was drawn to his mobile, lying on the bedside cabinet. Without another thought, she reached for it. It was password protected, and she was relieved to see that he hadn't changed his password since she'd left. Not that he'd imagine he'd need to, she supposed – even when she'd lived with him before she was always too reverent and respectful to nosy at his phone, even when she wanted to. Perhaps it would have saved a lot of heartache a lot sooner if she'd ignored the instinct for politeness and the respect of boundaries that was entrenched in her. She certainly would have found out about Shelly a lot sooner. She scrolled through his text messages. It was strange, but while she expected to see lots of text messages from Shelly, back and forth about their relationship and their future, there was nothing. She couldn't even find an old thread for them about anything at all. What did that mean? Had Warren deleted all the old messages for some reason? Or did it mean there really hadn't been any?

She flicked onto the contacts and noticed Shelly's number. In a second she'd made the decision to note the number down, though she didn't even know why. She only felt compelled to do it, just in case she might need it one day. Pulling her own phone from the bag she'd dropped by the bed, she quickly tapped the number in, though she saved the contact as unknown. If Warren looked, hopefully he wouldn't know whose number it was and as it was the only unknown contact on her phone, she'd have no trouble remembering who it belonged to. Then she opened his photos and scrolled through. She'd expected to see lots of photos of herself but there weren't any. Neither were there any of Shelly. It was disappointing not to be able to see what she looked like, and she had to admit that it was a little odd. They'd had photos taken together before and she had to assume that he'd done so with Shelly. So where were they all? Had he deleted them to cover his tracks when he'd been trying to juggle both women?

Taking care to put the phone back in exactly the place he'd left it, she glanced up to see that the bathroom door was still closed and she could still hear the sounds of the shower running. So she made her way along the narrow hallway to the kitchen to get her drink. The tiny window, hardly more than a skylight really, that looked out onto the grey mass of the opposite apartment block only served to remind her of her grandma's house. She hadn't remembered the kitchen here being quite so dull and cramped before, but she'd got used to Matilda's airy, welcoming space, with its scrubbed wooden table and antique furniture and buttermilk paint on the walls. She switched the kettle on and wondered if Warren would let her paint this kitchen yellow. That was assuming they stayed put once they were married, of course, but she felt sure that once she explained the benefits of relocating to Derbyshire, how they'd be able to afford a whole house rather than a flat that was more like a coffin, how they'd have money to spare with no rent and how he'd be able to settle things financially with Shelly so he wouldn't have to keep up payments on her flat any more, he'd see things as Esme did and he might be willing to give it a go. After all, paying rent on two places in London for all these years must have been crippling him – it was no wonder he got moody from time to time trying to juggle all that.

As the kettle bubbled away her gaze fell on her suitcase, lying in the hall just beyond the kitchen doorway. Another thing that would need sorting – she just hoped that when she emptied it later there'd be something in there that Warren didn't mind her wearing to the pub because she was running out of time to go shopping now, they'd spent so long in bed. Absently, her fingers pressed against the bruises blooming on her thighs. Warren had been… *enthusiastic*. He'd missed her, he'd said, and he showed her just how much he'd missed her. They'd always had an energetic sex life, but this had been off the scale and she wasn't used to it. She wasn't even sure she'd enjoyed it like she'd thought she would. Still, Esme was certain things would calm down once she'd been home for a few weeks.

She trudged to the cupboard to reach for a mug. It was funny how quickly everything here became her normal again. She'd been gone since the autumn but she'd fallen back into her old life in a matter of hours. Once she got a job it would be like the time with her grandma had never happened. Except it had, and the memory of it now rushed at her. Hastily, she dragged a thumb beneath watery eyes and dropped a teabag into the mug before dousing it in boiling water. If she asked, perhaps Warren would agree to stay in tonight after all. The pub was fun and Warren was always in a good mood after a few drinks but exhaustion – both physical and emotional – was creeping over Esme, the sort of exhaustion that threatened to knock someone off their feet. She wanted to drink her tea and then she wanted to sleep, maybe grab a quick supper and sleep some more. Warren was sure to understand that she'd had a long and difficult day and they could go to the pub tomorrow night when she was settled in.

With tea in hand, she went to the living room to sit down. But she paused on the way through, rooting in the pocket of her suitcase and taking out her granddad's tickets for the trip to Lapland that had never happened, and her own – as yet unused and uncancelled – tickets and took them with her. She curled into the corner of an armchair as she mulled them over. Perhaps Warren would want to go with her, and that idea brightened her mood. She'd show him – they could have the most wonderful time that would get them in the mood for Christmas – romantic and fun, a real holiday to remember – and it would go some way to mending all that had gone wrong between them. And it was already paid for too – how could he possibly say no?

Esme set the tickets down on the coffee table with a small smile. She'd ask Warren, and if she managed to catch him in the right mood, he was sure to agree.

Chapter Eight

Perhaps it was because he hadn't drunk enough, or because he hadn't liked Esme's outfit – which he said made her look manly when teamed with her shorter hair – or because he'd run into Shelly's sister at the bar and they'd had to vacate The Duke to a pub he liked less, or simply because the wind was blowing from the east. Whatever the reason, the answer he gave was an emphatic no.

'But I have the tickets,' Esme reasoned, and to her it *was* a reasonable argument. 'They're paid for and it'd be crazy not to use them! We need a break away – it'd be good for us, give us time to get to know each other again as a couple.'

'They're not tickets bought for you and me.' Warren downed the last of his fifth pint. 'They're tickets bought to reward you for leaving me. Tickets to congratulate you on cutting me out of your life. Why would I want to use them? They're not even in our names.'

'I'd have to change Grandma's but I could do that easily enough – it wouldn't cost much.'

'But it would cost something – money better spent elsewhere. And it's expensive when you get there. Shelly's brother went with the kids – had to take out a bank loan. Said one beer there cost the price of five beers here. Why don't you get the money back and we'll use it on something we both want to do?'

'Like what?'

'I don't know. Just not freezing my bollocks off in the Arctic and paying over the odds for a pint.'

'It's too late to get the money back.'

'You should have tried sooner then. Won't they refund when they find out the old girl's dead? I thought they'd have to.'

Esme gazed across the pub, watching as the door opened and a couple walked in, hand in hand, heads bowed close together in shared laughter, shaking a light dusting of snow from their coats. The weather forecast had said it might snow that day but nobody had really expected it to. As the door closed shut again, a gust of icy wind roared through the stifling pub, freshening the air but lifting the gnarled old tinsel taped to the bar so it scraped and hissed as it settled again. The couple headed straight for the bar, almost dancing a salsa as they pushed through the crowd, laughing and kissing.

'Babe, if you really want to go away this Christmas I'll ask Gary for his caravan at Clacton. He'll let us have it for a hundred quid and we can get stocked up with cans and have our own private lock-in. And when we've had enough of drinking,' he added in a silky whisper, 'we won't have to walk very far for bed, will we…?'

'What?' Esme turned to him. 'Sorry, what did you say?'

'I know the stove won't be very good but I reckon there'll be a pub nearby to get Christmas dinner.'

'Where?'

'At Gary's place. What are you looking at?'

Esme shook herself. 'Nothing. Where's Gary's place? I thought he lived in Shoreditch?'

'His caravan, not his flat! In Clacton!'

Esme's gaze went to her drink.

'What's wrong with Clacton? Not posh enough for you?'

'Of course not.'

'Then what?'

'I'd just wanted to go to Lapland, that's all. Clacton's hardly the same.'

'But I thought it was the holiday you were bothered about. You said you wanted us to have a good time somewhere away from the flat.'

'Well, yes, but—'

'So Clacton's away from the flat. It's got the sea and decent pubs and some shops and it's a lot cheaper than sodding Christmas land.'

'I know. But I have Grandma's tickets.'

'I told you, get the money back. We could do some right damage in Clacton with it – live like kings for a couple of days.'

'It isn't as simple as that. It doesn't feel right. Can't you understand – this is kind of like the last thing she ever did for me? It'd be like throwing her Christmas gift back in her face.'

'Don't be daft.'

'I know it probably sounds over-sentimental.'

'A bit.'

'And it's not that I don't want to go to Clacton. In the summer it'd be fantastic to use Gary's caravan.'

'It's got central heating and double glazing.' He took a gulp from his pint. 'It's proper nice. It'd be warm enough even in the winter.'

'I know it would.'

'What's the face for then?'

'It's not a face.' Esme held back a sigh. How could she make Warren see what this trip meant to her? He'd never known her grandma and he'd never had the kind of relationship with her family that meant he had any charitable feelings towards any of them at all (and the feeling was mutual, she supposed, so perhaps it was no surprise). All of this meant it was hard for her to make him see how important the trip was. And when all was said and done, she really wanted to go. She might never get the opportunity to visit Lapland again and while she had this one, she wanted to seize it.

'Don't get moody on me,' Warren said. 'Your gran hated me so why am I going to pretend to be upset?'

Esme turned back to him. 'She never met you so how could she hate you?'

'All your family hate me – they've made that clear enough. If she's anything like the rest of them then she would have talked to me like I'd just puked on them. Makes me wonder what you tell them about me when I'm not there.'

'Nothing. I don't tell them anything.'

Warren looked at his watch. 'Time for one more if we're quick about it. In fact' – he handed Esme a twenty-pound note – 'get two for each of us so they can't chuck us out till we're done.'

Esme took the money and made her way to the bar – jostled and shoved and assaulted by beery laughter as she went – and her mind went back to fruit cake and quiz shows in her grandma's sitting room and if she'd been a less practical person she'd have wished for a time machine so she could be back there now.

'Sorry!'

She turned to see who'd almost knocked her flying, a reciprocal and totally unnecessary apology on her own lips, and found herself face-to-face with a man in his twenties. His soft grey eyes smiled at her – a little dopey, probably from whatever he'd been drinking – and his sandy hair was in some disarray. Still, he was good-looking and he had a happy face. Esme couldn't help but smile back.

'It's alright.'

'I mean, really, I am *so* sorry. Are you OK?'

'Oh, fine. No harm done.'

'Although…' He broke into an endearing grin. 'Wow. If my mate shoves me into beautiful women every time he falls over then I'm going to have to get him drunk more often.'

'Don't be daft.' Esme let out a little laugh, but even then her gaze flicked back to where she'd left Warren. She couldn't see him but…

'So, can I have your phone number now or do I have to fall for you all over again?'

'Oh… no… I…'

Then she heard Warren's voice behind her and she froze. *Please don't hit him; please don't make a scene…*

'Back off,' Warren said, and Esme turned to see him square his shoulders and puff out his chest. 'Unless you want to step outside.'

The man raised his arms in an immediate gesture of surrender. 'Mate – how was I supposed to know? No hard feelings, eh?'

Warren grunted, dragging Esme away with him.

'I didn't do anything, Warren, honest.'

'Weren't exactly fighting him off, were you?'

'But… he just bumped into me, that's all.'

'The oldest trick in the book. Next time a bloke bumps into you, walk away.'

Esme gave a weak nod. If he'd been reluctant to say yes to Lapland before, there was no way he was going to now.

The week had passed in a blur. While Esme couldn't say she was happy, she was at least beginning to settle. It was easy to slip back into old routines with Warren – easier than she'd ever imagined. She went to the gym on the three days they'd agreed, and she shopped and cleaned through the flat because the tenants Warren had been subletting the apartment to while she'd been in Derbyshire hadn't been the cleanest of people, and she made regular calls to her parents which always ended up with one of them hanging up as she tried, yet again, to defend the man she'd decided to spend her life with. But at least they weren't hanging up as soon as they discovered it was her on the other end of the line, so she considered that progress. She had yet to find a job, and although London was awash with coffee shops and bars and restaurants it wasn't proving to be as simple as she'd imagined to get employment at one of them. The place she'd worked at before she'd headed back to the Peaks had seemed the most promising – at least they'd promised to call her the minute they had an opening – having been pleased with her before she'd left them. Meanwhile, her savings were taking a battering now that she had half the costs of living with Warren to worry about again.

Contacting Shelly's hairdresser friend had hardly helped things – she'd had to pretend she'd found her details online so she could make an appointment for the hair extensions, which was bad enough, and then, when she'd found out the cost, she'd wanted to go even less. It felt like such a waste of money for hair that would grow back of its own accord if she just waited. But on Friday afternoon she went and sat patiently as the hairdresser weaved the lengths in – inwardly thankful that this particular friend of Shelly's didn't recognise Esme by sight and hadn't questioned the false name Esme had given, feeling faintly ridiculous about the fact she was using a false name, because who knew what she'd do to Esme's hair if she did?

Afterwards she caught the bus back to her flat feeling as if someone had sewn a ton of wet cotton onto her head, and by the time she got home her head was thumping. At least Warren would be pleased, but he wasn't in and she'd had to wait until 9 p.m. for him to appear. He'd been to see Shelly, he'd said, and he'd had to comfort her because she'd been upset about their split, and what kind of a man would he be to leave her in that state? Esme decided it probably explained the perfume on him and she went to make his supper. He didn't comment on her new hair, only to say that she looked like her old self again (apart from the weight but he'd help her to work on that so she could lose it faster) and that she should never have cut it in the first place.

Half an hour later Esme placed a tray of beans on toast in front of him as he flicked through the TV channels. Perhaps she dumped it on his lap just a little too forcefully as the beans slopped over the side of the plate and he looked sharply at her.

'Sorry,' she said, not feeling sorry at all.

'I've only just bought these trousers.'

'I said I was sorry. Anyway, nothing's spilt on your trousers, has it?'

'You're in a mood?'

'No.'

'Why are you acting like you are then? Got your period or something?'

Esme took a deep breath. 'No,' she replied through gritted teeth.

'Right.' Warren turned his attention back to his remote control and Esme had to remind herself that they were supposed to be trying for a reconciliation right now.

'I called at Gino's again today.'

'Yeah?' he asked, settling on a rugby match. 'Got your job back?'

'Not yet. I'm hopeful I'll get something soon. If not there then somewhere else. But Gino says he found me hard to replace and he really does want me to come back as soon as there's an opening. Says he'd have me back in a heartbeat.'

'If you'd never left in the first place you wouldn't be in this mess now.' Warren cut into his toast, his eyes never leaving the television.

'I mean, I'm OK for a bit.' Esme twiddled a length of unfamiliar hair. 'I don't want to burn too much of a hole in my savings – seeing as I was saving for a really good reason.'

'What reason?'

Esme stared at him. '*Our wedding…*'

'Oh, yeah, well, the divorce might be a while so it'll give you plenty of time to build your money up again. We don't need to rush either – the longer it takes the more money you can save and the better our wedding will be. Posh and Becks will be green with envy, right, babe? Although' – he scooped a forkful of beans into his mouth – 'I've already told you what I think.'

'About what?' Esme took a seat on the sofa across from his chair.

'Your place in… wherever that village is.'

'Little Dove Morton.'

'Yeah.'

'It's not my place.'

'There's a hell of a lot of cash tied up in it though. We could do a lot with that money.'

'But Grandma's place needs a lot of work to modernise it and prices up north aren't like they are down here. I don't think selling my half would fetch as much as you imagine. In fact… well, I thought we'd benefit more by other means…'

He looked up at her now, halted his chewing and waited.

He was going to say no. He'd already guessed what was coming and he was going to give her a flat refusal. Esme got up.

'I'd better wash the dishes.'

'Don't be long.' He turned to the television again, scooping more beans onto his fork. 'I've got to get up early tomorrow but I'm horny as hell and I could do with a bit of relief before I go to sleep.'

Esme nodded, though sex was the last thing on her mind. 'I'll be as quick as I can.'

The hold music was loud and distorted and Esme couldn't make out exactly what she was listening to but guessed it was some muzak version of 'Greensleeves' or something similar. Her gaze flicked to the door as she cradled the phone to her ear. Warren wasn't due in for hours but still she kept one eye out, half expecting him to burst in and demand to know what she was doing. Which was nothing, really, only a task she ought to have seen to weeks before – so why the guilt? Perhaps it was because while she'd phoned to do one thing, she really wanted to do another.

Finally, there was a voice on the line.

'I'm so sorry to have kept you waiting. I'm Clare, the manager. I understand you want a refund for a trip due to leave in a few days?'

'That's right. You see, my grandmother booked it for the two of us but she died suddenly.'

'I'm sorry to hear that. It's possible to claim on your holiday insurance, you know. I'm assuming you took insurance out?'

'I'm not sure, my grandma…'

'We can't refund it here.'

'But we can't possibly go! I mean, how could we…?'

'I know, I really am sorry but the insurance is the only way to do it. You'd need a copy of her death certificate. Do you have that?'

'I could get one, I suppose.'

'I'd be more than happy to help you complete the paperwork once you do.'

'There's no way around it?'

'Not really. You could transfer the trip to someone else. Is there anyone who might want to go in your place? There'd be costs associated with that, of course, but it's another option if you know someone who might be happy to pay them.'

'I thought my boyfriend might go but he's not keen.'

'Well, it was just a suggestion.'

'Right. Would it make any difference if I still went on the trip?'

'I thought you said you couldn't because of your grandmother.'

'I mean alone. Just use my ticket and not my grandma's.'

'Two tickets have been bought and paid for so I suppose there wouldn't be a need for a single-person supplement. I don't see why not.'

'Right.'

'Do you want to think about doing that?'

'Is there anything you'd need to do your end to enable me to travel?'

'I'd have to check with the tour company but I don't think so. There'd be no refund on the other ticket regardless.'

'Yes, I understand that. I wouldn't be looking for one.'

'If you're thinking about that option then you might be interested to know that this particular tour company are very good when it comes to solo travelling. They're keen on bringing everyone together and believe that if nobody is left out everyone has a better time. They've set up a Facebook group for people taking this trip alone – they do it for all their trips. We have regular customers who book with them just because of that.'

'People connect before they go? I've never heard of that.'

'It's a lovely idea though, don't you think? It can make the idea of travelling solo a lot less daunting, especially for someone like yourself who didn't originally plan to go on their own.'

'I suppose so.'

'If you like I could email the link to you.'

'Thanks.'

Esme gave her email address, all the while her mind working faster than she could keep up with.

'Brilliant,' Clare said. 'I'll let you have that in the next half hour and you can take a look, see what you think. Let me know if there's anything else I can help with too.'

'I will. Thanks so much.'

Esme ended the call and then immediately logged into her emails. Within minutes the message had come through and she clicked the link and requested to join the group. Someone was clearly paying close attention at the office of the tour operator too because only a few minutes after her request had been accepted she'd had a welcome message. She scanned the page, gleaning as much general information as she could, and then took a look at the list of other group members. Not so much of a list – just three names, which her own now made four: a lady named Hortense, an older gentleman called Brian and another guy named Zach. Zach's photo was a bit grainy but from what she could tell he was a good deal younger than the other two. They all looked nice but Esme wondered whether she'd have a great deal in common with any of them. Zach was perhaps the closest to her own age but it probably wouldn't be a good idea to strike up any kind of friendship. It wasn't like Warren was likely to find out, but he was always so insanely jealous when she so much as looked at another man that it was hard to get out of the habit of keeping her eyes shut. Against her better judgement, she clicked onto his profile anyway, too intrigued to find out what sort of man was travelling on his own. The other two were perhaps widowed and that would explain it, but someone younger... there was usually friends or family or a partner. Esme couldn't help but wonder why he didn't have any of those – at least any of them willing to travel with him. There wasn't a lot to go on though. His personal bio had a lot of blank spaces and most of his posts and photos were set to private.

She went back to the tour-group page, clicking through the gallery left there by the tour company. The photos were glorious and they made Esme's heart yearn for the glittering landscapes of frosted pink skies and endless banks of pristine snow, for valleys of iced trees and chalets tucked into hillsides, for cosy hotel interiors lit by roaring fires and lanterns and guests in thick jumpers warmed by their glow, for night skies alive with green and purple swathes of dancing lights. Her grandma would have loved this so much. Esme could picture them both by the fire at the hotel after a trip out into the frozen landscape, thawing slowly with hot chocolate and still dizzy with wonder at the spectacle they'd seen in the Arctic heavens.

But then her phone buzzed and Warren's name flashed on the screen. Hastily she closed the window on the computer. Stupid idea – the best thing to do now would be to get hold of Grandma's death certificate and get the money back for the trip. She didn't have to keep it – she could give it to her dad, who would then decide if it went back to the estate or whether he'd let Esme have it. She was sure that he'd do the latter because it had been intended as a gift to Esme in the first place. She opened the message from Warren.

Hey, babe, what are you doing? Have you been to the gym yet? Michael at the desk says he hasn't seen you.
She tapped out a reply.

I'm running late, things to do. Going there now.

With a sigh, Esme went to collect her gym gear from the laundry basket. It hadn't been washed since her last visit but what the hell – it wasn't like anyone there took any notice of her anyway.

Chapter Nine

Hi, I'm Zach and I thought I'd post here to introduce myself. I'm thirty-two and this is the first time I've travelled alone. I'll admit to being a bit apprehensive but I thought, what the heck, life is too short so... here I am. Anyway, it would be great to get to know you guys before we head off. Maybe we could even meet at the airport before we fly?

Esme read the post again. Both Hortense and Brian had replied to say they were keen to make friends before they left too. Since then there had been sporadic sharing and posts from all three – mostly of what they were hoping to see and do once they got to Lapland and how excited they were. Hortense and Brian seemed sweet, though not quite as engaged with the whole business of Facebook as Zach, as their misplaced posts and typos attested. Esme had yet to contribute to the page, preferring to stay in the background watching what the others were saying and doing.

That was, until this very newest post by Zach, in which she'd been tagged. Since then she'd been rereading his others, trying to decide whether she ought to reply or get the hell out of the group.

After all, she hadn't actually decided to travel to Lapland; it was just a crazy idea that she'd indulged with too much room to grow. But when all was said and done, it *was* crazy and she probably wouldn't go. If only Warren hadn't been so dismissive about the whole thing she wouldn't even be in this situation trying to weigh up complete strangers in the prospect of spending a week with them; instead, she and Warren would be looking forward to a fantastic, once-in-a-lifetime trip together. Esme knew that he'd have had a great time too if he'd just given in and decided to go, and it was only because he was feeling particularly stubborn about it for some reason that he hadn't said yes. Sometimes, it would be nice if he just thought about her for once, made a sacrifice or two, strived to give her things she wanted instead of her always being the one to compromise on everything.

She needed to call her mum to get a copy of Grandma's death certificate, however, if she wasn't going to take the trip, and that was one conversation she'd really rather not have. Warren had argued that as the trip had been a Christmas gift meant for Esme, the fact entitled her to any refund on it. Esme could see the logic in this, but she felt that as the money had come from Matilda's purse, and therefore her estate, which now belonged to Esme's dad, the refund really ought to go to him and she would offer it before she did anything else. Warren would have none of it, reminding her with some bile of the money they were getting through while she lived with him as an unemployed woman. But to phone her parents in the first place for help to get money that she may or may not be entitled to… that seemed like an insult too far in a situation that was already fraught with festering tension.

Esme turned to her phone again and unlocked it, the page for the solo travellers still open. Her eyes were drawn to Zach's latest post. It was perfectly innocuous, hardly anything to concern her:

Only a few days to go and really looking forward to meeting you all!
With: Hortense Williams, Brian De Santos, Esme Greenwood.

For just a moment she let herself imagine arriving at the airport and the little group waiting for her in the departure lounge, all chat and shy laughter and new beginnings. She imagined getting on the plane with them and arriving later in a new and magical place, the place of all her childhood dreams waiting to be explored and discovered with new friends. And she felt happy, for the first time in weeks. She'd thought coming back to Warren would fill the hole her grandma had left, that it would bring her happiness, but nothing with Warren had changed. She knew deep down she wasn't content and really he wasn't right for her. The trip to Lapland with a bunch of strangers was a nerve-wracking prospect, but then if she wasn't brave, nothing would change. And deep down she knew what Matilda would have wanted her to do.

Chapter Ten

Warren had left for work and even though he wasn't there, Esme still crept around the flat as she packed her suitcase. She could sense the impending explosion of anger already, and even though she'd be miles away and out of reach when it erupted, the idea of what it might look like still had her stomach twisted into anxious knots. Outside the street was grey, heavy with clouds that blocked the winter sun. Not that she could see much of it from the tiny bedroom window. It might be a white Christmas, Matilda's favourite DJ had said on the radio that morning, but didn't they say that every year? It hardly ever hit just right. In Lapland it was guaranteed. She'd put this to Warren in one last attempt to get him to agree to the trip, but he'd just laughed out loud and then turned up the volume on the TV. He'd never imagined she'd go alone. *She* hadn't even imagined it until last night.

When the cab for the airport arrived outside and the driver sounded his horn, Esme jumped, her instincts hurrying her to the window to shush him even though Warren wasn't there. The note she'd scribbled for Warren was a product of her chaotic thoughts – written in an unsteady hand, littered with mistakes and vague apologies for things she hadn't even done and things she would never do. She was still in shock herself, a decision made so quickly that she hadn't even managed to tell her parents about it yet. A quick phone call to them was another job she'd have to do once she landed in Lapland. At least she'd be able to talk to them without feeling the guilt like a boulder around her neck.

Esme hadn't decided that she was never coming back to the flat but, perhaps, in a way she had. The final thing she'd done was leave the carefully cut hair extensions in a drawer in the bedroom and she'd never felt freer in her life as she shook her neat hair out, hair that was now all natural and all hers.

By the time Warren got home she'd be thousands of miles away, and Esme didn't know whether to be thrilled or terrified. One thing she did know, Matilda would have been proud.

Zach had posted in the Facebook group that morning and Esme sat in the cab now reading it, her hands so numb and unsteady she could barely feel the phone in them. It was hard to know what was scarier – the thought of what she'd just done or what she was about to do.

> I'll be in Costa Coffee at departures from around ten. Feel free to come and say hello but if you'd rather not, that's fine too. There's no pressure for us to become best buddies or anything, and I understand some might want to keep things civil and nothing more, but I think it would be nice to see a friendly face at the airport. Otherwise, I really hope to see you around at the resort.

It looked as if neither Hortense nor Brian had seen the message yet – certainly neither of them had commented and they usually did – and Esme didn't know whether she ought to respond. A simple 'like' was a bit noncommittal but anything more obliged her to join Zach when she still didn't know how she felt about that. So she did nothing, only read the post again and made a mental note to look for Costa once she'd checked in her baggage and try to get a good look at him before she decided. If Zach in the flesh looked like an axe murderer she could steer well clear and hopefully he'd be none the wiser.

She reached down into her bag and ran her fingers against the thick edges of her granddad's old tickets and the wedding photo and then zipped it up again, satisfied that she had the most important things with her.

Once Esme had got through to departures, the little city of glitzy shops designed to rob you of your holiday money before you'd even got as far as the gates were strangely hard to resist, even though she needed none of the things they sold. And in one of them she caught sight of a lady, who looked very much like Hortense's Facebook photo, being doused in a cloud of cloying scent by an overenthusiastic sales assistant. Nobody had ever looked less like the sort of person who'd be interested in perfume than this woman (if indeed it was Hortense), with her square little glasses and stout boots and a thick winter coat. And yet she'd been drawn into the shop, answering the siren call that all flyers trapped in the airport inevitably answered, and now she couldn't escape, even though she looked desperate to.

With no thought for her own safety, Esme went in.

'Hi…' She tapped the customer on the shoulder. 'Sorry to interrupt but—'

'Esme Greenwood!' the woman cried, pulling her into a surprising hug. 'I'd recognise you anywhere – you really do look remarkably like your online photo!'

'Hortense?' Esme asked.

'The same! How the devil are you? Got here alright? I'm so happy you're here! I was beginning to think I'd be the only girl playing with the boys, so to speak. Not that I couldn't handle it, of course, but it's lovely to have some female company too.'

Hortense began to lead her away, Esme representing a welcome distraction. She lowered her voice as they went, sending a surreptitious glance towards the sales assistant who watched them go, frowning in disapproval.

'Seventy pounds for that bottle of perfume! I would have bought it too and I didn't even like it!'

Esme smiled. 'I know what you mean. They have a way of making you feel obliged to buy whatever it is they're selling.'

'It's some sort of voodoo magic if you ask me. Anyway perhaps we should scoot along to the coffee shop to see if young Zachary is there? At least that will force me to stay out of the way of seventy pounds of temptation!'

Esme nodded agreement. 'I suppose we ought to.'

'Splendid!' Hortense looped her arm around Esme's and pulled her close. 'Don't mind, do you?' she asked, angling her head at the contact. 'I wobble terribly when I walk – something to do with my inner ear. It's giving me the devil today. It helps to lean on someone.'

'Oh. Well, that's OK.'

'Not that I often hang onto complete strangers, of course, but I think we're friends already, aren't we?'

'I guess we soon will be if we're not already.'

'Considering we're already travelling companions,' Hortense continued.

'Yes.'

'It's a shame we couldn't have been a little more forward thinking from the start – we could have shared a bedroom and saved lots of money.'

'I didn't book to come alone originally.'

'No? Really?' Hortense tapped the side of her nose. 'A chap, was it? Let you down? Decided to stick it to him by coming without him?'

'No, my… someone who was coming with me couldn't. Not a man – nothing like that.'

'Quite right – none of my business, of course. Well, their loss is my gain, eh? We'll be just dandy together, won't we? Now, if we can find the rest of our group we'll be tickety-boo.'

'Perhaps Brian has already met up with Zach.'

'Now, there's a thought. Shall we toddle along and see?'

Esme nodded, though she had a feeling she'd have had very little choice in the matter even if she hadn't wanted to toddle along anywhere.

Hortense wobbled and gripped Esme's arm with a chuckle. 'See, there I go! Must take more water with that whisky, eh?'

'Is it a problem? I mean, does it cause you a lot of issues?'

'I've fallen over more times than I can count.' Hortense patted a hip. 'That's why I grew all this padding. It's not fat, you see, it's so I can bounce; no broken bones anymore!' She gave Esme a sideways look. 'If I were skinny like you I'd be smashed to smithereens the times I've fallen down the stairs at home.'

'Don't you have… like… I don't know… like disabled status or something?'

'Oh Lord, no! I couldn't be bothered with all that and no doubt those government assessors wouldn't look twice at me anyway. I'm perfectly mobile. It's just that my steering is shot.'

'But they'd have to give you some disability help if it affects your day-to-day living, wouldn't they? Benefits or equipment or something?'

'My dear child, people with genuine disabilities are being sent packing – you see it every day on the news. Mine's an inconvenient trifle. Most of the time I manage perfectly well with a helping hand and you're doing a marvellous job of that right now.'

Esme wondered vaguely how on earth Hortense was going to manage on snow and ice in Lapland if she couldn't manage on solid ground but she thought better of saying so. She assumed Hortense must have considered it at some point and decided it wasn't an issue.

Hortense hardly took a breath as she talked… and talked… and talked… and as the coffee shop appeared in front of them, Esme realised that although Hortense hadn't shut up the whole time she hadn't really said anything at all – at least, nothing of consequence.

'You must forgive me,' Hortense said, seeming to read Esme's thoughts. 'I'm alone at home and I take full advantage when I have the opportunity for a little social interaction. I'm not looking for the pity violins, of course, but I simply miss having someone in the house to talk to.'

'You live alone?'

'I looked after my mother for years, and by the time she died I was too old and spinsterly to go about getting a man.'

'What was the matter with your mum?'

'No idea,' Hortense said briskly. 'She just always seemed to want something or other. Barely put a toe out of bed during her last few years.'

'Oh… and your dad… I mean, did he die?'

'Oh dear Lord, no! Mummy threw him out – just like that. Some trifling affair but she had a temper like a sunburnt boar on her. Last I heard he was in Patagonia… Papua New Guinea…? Somewhere frightfully exotic and beginning with the letter P at any rate. I expect he breathed his last there too but I never heard about it.'

Esme tried to form a reply but what could she say to that?

'Ah!' Hortense exclaimed, nudging Esme. 'Looks like the eagle has landed. Two rather handsome eagles, in fact!'

Sitting at a table, engaged in easy conversation, Esme recognised Zach and Brian. Except that Brian had clearly been carefully selective of his online photo to show a rather more flattering version of himself that had to be at least ten years out of date, while Zach's had done him a grave disservice. In fact, Esme couldn't help a double take. It was the Zach she recognised from his online profile photo but about twenty times hotter. His dark hair, while flecked with the odd strand of grey, was thick and wavy, and his grey-blue eyes seemed to smile even when he didn't, and although his full mouth had a natural crookedness to it, something about that imperfection was perfectly adorable. It was hard to tell as he sat at the table but Esme would have bet a decent amount of money that he was tall too, and he filled his soft cotton shirt well.

'How lovely to see you at last!' Hortense called from across the coffee shop, and at least a dozen confused faces looked up from their own tables as Hortense trotted through them now, dragging Esme behind rather than leaning on her for support. Evidently, being excited meant she could walk without mishap.

Both Zach and Brian looked up at the same time and broke into broad smiles.

'We were just debating whether you two would come,' Brian said in a gruff voice with a northern accent that was hard to place. It could have been somewhere around Tyneside, and Esme resolved to ask when she knew him better.

'Dear boy, wild horses wouldn't keep us away,' Hortense said. 'Would they, Esme?' She patted her arm, smiling broadly at the assembled party as if she'd never been so overjoyed to see anyone in her life. 'Esme and I bumped into one another in the duty free,' she continued. 'I'd say she rather saved my bacon. Do you know how much the perfume that I almost bought was?'

'How much?' Zach asked.

'Hideously expensive!' Hortense cried. 'Really too much. I honestly don't know how these people justify it! A bit of dead old flowers and deer sweat and they want seventy pounds for it!'

'They don't need to justify it,' Zach said, shooting Esme a conspiratorial smile. It looked like he'd got the measure of Hortense already. 'Their brand is enough justification as far as they're concerned – it's all about conspicuous consumption, isn't it? Would you like something to drink?' he asked, gesturing for the newcomers to sit.

'I'll get them …' Esme began, but he waved away the offer.

'Honestly, it'd be my pleasure. I'm getting a fresh one anyway and we have a good hour before boarding.'

Esme relaxed into a smile. 'In that case a flat white would be lovely, thank you.'

'Black coffee for me,' Hortense said. 'The blacker the better. If it's so black light can't escape, that's perfect.'

Brian added a request to the order and Zach got up. Esme stood up too.

'I'll come and help you carry it all back to the table,' she said.

'Right, that'd be good – thanks.'

They left Hortense making herself comfortable with Brian and went to join the queue at the counter. Esme glanced back and could see them engaged in conversation now, getting to know each other, she supposed.

'I think Hortense is going to be a handful,' Zach said in a low voice.

Esme turned to him. 'I'm glad you've said it. She's absolutely lovely but a bit…'

'Full on?'

'I suppose so. But then it's better than being moody and miserable.'

'I don't doubt she's going to be hilarious but I think we might well need another holiday when we get home to recover from this one. Brian seems like a top bloke too. I'm glad you decided to come,' he added, pulling her back from her thoughts.

'I thought I ought to in the end.'

'But you weren't sure?'

Esme shook her head. 'I've never travelled alone before. I don't know what's been scarier – deciding to do the holiday alone or deciding to meet you guys instead.'

'And do you feel you've made the right choice?' His eyes were gently teasing, as if he was about to share the punchline of the best joke in the world.

Esme smiled at him. 'I hope so. Yes – I think so. I could hardly say anything else to you, could I? It'd be a great way to offend you before we'd even got on the plane.'

'It'd take a lot more than that to offend me.' He sunk his hands into his pockets and smiled down at her. Now that she was standing next to him she realised that her hunch had been right – he really was quite tall. A comforting sort of tall.

Around them china clinked on china and metal on metal and the low hum of conversation was overlaid by the sounds of the baristas shouting orders at each other and the coffee machines chugging and hissing. The air was spicy and warm and rich and sweet. It could have been a coffee shop in any town, apart from the televisions hanging from the walls listing the departures of various flights and the broad windows showing the runway where planes taxied to and fro. It was hot too, compared to the brisk wind outside the airport terminal, and Esme wished she'd taken off her coat before coming to the counter with Zach as her cheeks blazed. She wanted to ask why he was travelling alone. Did it mean he had no one? It seemed so unlikely talking to him now – so open, so agreeable. Not to mention handsome, although Esme was trying hard not to notice that aspect and her guilty thoughts quickly turned back to Warren, at his desk working hard and completely oblivious – for now – of her betrayal. It didn't feel quite like that to her, but in light of the conversations they'd had about this trip it was the way he'd see it once he discovered she'd gone anyway. So much for compromise, she thought wryly. She'd failed spectacularly there.

'Flat white you said?'

Zach's innocent question wrenched her back from the whirl-pool of guilt she was about to get sucked into.

'Please. And Hortense's was black.'

'Yes, how could I forget that?' He grinned.

He repeated the order to the barista who nodded and took payment before flitting off to prepare everything.

Zach leaned against the counter. 'I love the smell of fresh-ground coffee, don't you? I think if I lost my sense of smell then the smell of coffee would be the thing I'd miss most.'

'I've never really thought about it.'

'I must have about ten gallons a day when I'm working. I don't suppose it's doing me much good but I generally run out of adrenaline by ten in the morning so it has to be good strong coffee.'

'What do you do?'

'Theatre producer.'

Esme smiled. 'Wow! So you must meet loads of famous people?'

'It's not quite that glamorous,' he said with a soft laugh. 'It's more small-scale productions, niche stuff, provincial theatres, nationwide tours – that sort of thing. I'm hardly Cameron Mackintosh.'

'Still, it must be quite exciting.'

'It keeps you on your toes, that's for sure. And you do get a massive sense of pride when you finally see a production come together – that feeling never gets old. I must love it, but sometimes when I'm phoning people at one in the morning because some huge disaster has befallen us the day before opening night I have to wonder if I'm sane.'

'I'd love to do something like that.'

'What do you do?'

'Nothing right now. I'm between careers. Which means I don't know which minimum wage job I'm going to get next.'

'Oh. I suppose that might be quite worrying?'

Esme's mind went to all the other, far more pressing issues in her life right now, and she shook her head. 'It should be, but right now I'm not stressing about it. I'm sure I'll get something soon.'

'The philosophical approach. I generally find it's the best one to adopt. Enjoy your holiday and then worry about job hunting.'

'That's exactly what I intend to do.'

He folded his arms and regarded her with what appeared to be some amusement. 'Do you feel like running off yet?'

'Running off?'

'From here. Us lot. I only ask because this is probably your last chance – once we're on that plane together I reckon you're stuck with us. And I have a feeling it's going to get lively,' he added, angling his head across the coffee shop.

Esme looked over at Brian and Hortense. Their conversation had swiftly moved on from shy smiles and niceties and they now seemed to be embroiled in some heated debate. Esme and Zach had only left them alone for two minutes.

'Do you think they're arguing already?' Zach asked.

'It's hard to tell. If they are it doesn't look as if it's getting too violent yet.'

Zach laughed. 'We might have to keep an eye on them this week.'

'Like a pair of toddlers?'

'Something like that,' he agreed. 'I've only chatted to Brian for ten minutes or so, but I can tell from those ten minutes and what I've seen of Hortense so far that they're worlds apart. We might get a few more debates before the week is out.'

'As long as it doesn't get out of hand,' Esme said, still looking at them. 'Friendly banter is one thing, but I don't think I'd fancy refereeing an argument between those two.'

'I'm sure they can be adult about their differences.'

'You're right, though. We are a funny bunch to be hanging around together when you really think about it. All different ages and backgrounds that would never meet in normal life, and if we did, we probably wouldn't be more than passing acquaintances.'

'Do you think passing acquaintances can have a good time on holiday together?'

'Maybe. I hope so. I hope our funny bunch are more than that when the week is out. I'd like to think we could be friends.'

'So you think I'm funny?' he asked.

She glanced at Hortense and Brian again, and then back at Zach who constantly seemed to be sharing some private joke with only himself, and she shook her head.

'OK, maybe not you. Not yet I don't.'

'Give me time – I'll work on persuading you otherwise.'

Esme had to laugh.

'So, you're sure you don't want to run off and leave the funny bunch to it?'

'No, I don't think I'll run off just yet.'

'At least it's only seven days, eh?'

'That too,' Esme replied with a smile. 'If all else fails there's a big snowy wilderness to hide in.'

Zach grinned broadly at her. 'I'm glad you decided to come.'

Esme stopped laughing and another wave of heat rose to her face. She wanted to say that she was glad she'd come too. But Warren was at work and she pictured him getting home to a cold, empty flat and a note from her and she wasn't so sure after all.

Chapter Eleven

The flight had been delayed by two hours and while everyone had groaned and grumbled and stalked the departure gates restlessly, the delay had given Esme time to get to know her new travel companions better. She discovered that Hortense had never felt the need to marry and now raised chickens and sometimes sculpted, and Esme found herself rather envying her Bohemian lifestyle. Brian was an ex-headmaster at an inner-city comprehensive school whose wife had left him shortly before his retirement saying he was just too boring to spend her twilight years with and, since then, just to prove her wrong, he'd made every effort to be as far away from boring as it was possible to be. He sent her photos from each new adventure, just to make a point that he was having way more fun than she was. Esme liked Brian a lot, and she thought that his wife probably hadn't given him much of a chance to show her that life beyond retirement could be very different from a life that must have been characterised by long hours at work in a demanding job.

Zach, for all his apparent open friendliness, was harder to read. He volunteered very little personal information, other than providing funny anecdotes about various theatre productions he'd worked on, like the time one of his actors had got stuck in a lift and when the curtain opened, the only person who knew the missing thespian's lines and was available was Zach himself; an accidental debut that proved to be Zach's one and only terrifying foray into the world of acting – at least on stage rather than behind it. He briefly told them how he'd got into that world in the first place, as someone who hadn't really been interested in theatre at all but had been captivated during a summer break from college working with a lighting manager at his local rep, something a friend at the time had fixed him up with because he was struggling to find a part-time job and the theatre had been struggling to get someone who knew about electrics and would work for tea and biscuits. Zach, rather fortuitously, knew some basics about electrics because as a teenager his dad had taken him on as an assistant when he'd rewired their house, and the rest was, as the saying went, history. Zach had always planned on training to be a vet, but he'd had such a good time at the theatre that summer that the course of his future career had changed from that moment on. His parents had been horrified that he was turning away from a job that would pay handsomely to one where he'd be scraping to buy milk and bread most weeks, but then they'd seen how happy he was and how he was managing to make good-enough money, and eventually they'd come round.

He was content to tell his new companions all of this, but Esme got the impression there was so much more he was holding back, and that what he wasn't saying about his life was something so huge and painful that he simply couldn't say it, a hole that would swallow him if he dared to peer into it. Relationships past and present were barely touched upon, nor did he mention his current marital status, and while nobody was under any obligation to share such things, Brian and Hortense had both been happy to tell all. Esme didn't mind because she wasn't ready to share her personal information either, except for the part where her grandma had died before she'd had a chance to travel to Lapland with her as they'd intended, at which point Brian looked as if the information he'd just been given was a live hand grenade, Hortense rubbed Esme's back violently and Zach regarded her quietly with a look of such profound compassion and empathy that Esme wondered if something similar had happened to him too. It made Esme uncomfortable to be the focus of so much attention and she was glad when Hortense turned the conversation to how much she was hoping to take a trip out to visit a native Sami tribe to watch them hack a reindeer to death.

'It's only natural,' she concluded emphatically. 'After all, it's what our ancestors did. And they use every bit of the creature – nothing is wasted. It's a marvel really.'

'But now we have Sainsbury's for that sort of thing,' Brian said firmly.

'I'm with Brian,' Zach said. 'I might give the reindeer dismemberment a miss, if it's all the same to you.'

Esme simply smiled. Maybe a week with these people wouldn't be so bad. If she really tried hard, she even imagined she might be able to put Warren out of her mind for some of it, though she was certain he'd be doing his furious best to remind her of his existence at every opportunity. As if to labour the point, her phone pinged and she briefly checked it to see his name on the screen.

Don't forget it's your gym night tonight. Sorry I can't come and meet you there but I've got something on at work and have to stay over.

God, how she hated that bloody gym. She might have felt guilty about it, but there was a secret, slightly perverse pleasure in the idea that instead of going to a gym she hated and being bored out of her tree, she was about to get on a flight for the trip of a lifetime.

Eventually they'd been allowed to board the plane, where Esme had been separated from her new friends for a time due to their different seat allocations. She'd sat down, suddenly hit by an overwhelming sadness at the empty seat next to her. Sometimes she still couldn't quite take in that her grandma had gone, and it would take something like an empty seat to bring it all back with a force that knocked her flat. But she rallied now and reminded herself of why she'd chosen to come on this trip even though Matilda could not and she'd do her darndest to make the most of her grandma's last gift, if only to honour her memory.

The flight had been thankfully uneventful, and it was followed by a journey to their accommodation which took them through tiny snowbound villages of coloured wood and mellow lamplight that looked like clockwork toys trapped in snow globes, and mile upon mile of forests of majestic iced firs, stark against the blinding whiteness of the landscape in the low Arctic sun. Daylight here was a strange sort of dimness that was lit by the halo of the sun clinging to the horizon, saffron and magenta and lilacs bleeding into the indigo of the sky, and Esme realised that what she was looking at was something she'd read about before she'd come – the polar twilight. She recalled what she'd gleaned of the phenomenon now and that she hadn't really given it a lot of thought at the time, assuming that polar twilight just meant perpetual night. She never imagined it could look so beautiful. Occasionally they saw roaming deer weaving in and out of the shadows of the trees and birds swooping down from the kaleidoscope of the sky and even a pair of wolves peering at the bus from the safety of the forest edge. With every new and wondrous sight came the same thought – Matilda would have loved this.

Once, Esme turned to glance at Zach, who sat across the aisle of the bus next to Brian, and at once she knew the look on his face, because it said the same thing she knew hers did – he was thinking of someone dear too, wondering what they would have made of this magical place. He caught her eye, and quickly they both turned back to their windows, the place where both their thoughts were private.

An hour later the bus stopped outside their hotel. Esme's tummy flipped as she climbed down the steps and stood outside waiting for her suitcases. Her grandma had made a good call when she'd chosen this one – it was so perfectly traditional in every way. It was a sturdy wooden building with huge windows ranged along the outside walls to make the most of the spectacular polar sunsets, the main roof ascending into a tower with a clock embedded into it and a multitude of fairy lights strung from the eaves. It looked like something from Toy Town in the *Noddy* books that Matilda used to read to Esme when she was little and she half expected Martha Monkey to somersault out of the entrance and into her arms.

After a quick run-through of her passenger list, the tour representative led them all inside to get checked in with promises of mulled wine and hot food just as soon as they were settled.

'Isn't it marvellous?' Hortense said, grabbing Esme's hand to steady herself on the snow.

'It's lovely.' Esme smiled. 'I can't wait to get inside and get warmed up – I don't think I put enough layers on this morning.'

'One simply can't imagine how cold it could be,' Hortense agreed with a sage nod. 'We think it gets cold at home but this is something else.'

'I have a scarf here…' Zach interrupted from behind them. 'If it helps.'

Esme turned with a grateful smile. 'That's sweet of you but then you'd be cold.'

'I would, but I'd also feel very chivalrous about it.'

'And there's not much chivalry these days,' Hortense said. She turned to Esme. 'I wouldn't sniff at the offer if I were you.'

'I'm sure we'll be inside in no time,' Esme said. 'I can manage for a few minutes longer. But thank you anyway.'

'Lovely manners,' Hortense whispered. At least she probably thought it was a whisper, but Esme imagined that more or less everyone, including Zach, would have heard it. If he did, he showed no sign. Hortense was right, though, he did have lovely manners. She liked Zach very much already.

Esme was in her room now, unpacking and freshening up before heading down to dinner in the restaurant. She'd so far ignored three texts and another five calls from Warren, too tired and too worried to answer them. By now he would have found her note – presuming he'd gone straight home – and it wasn't like anything he'd have to say would be a shock. If she was honest, assuming that he now knew where she was, Esme was surprised his bombardment hadn't been more aggressive. Maybe that would come later. But now her phone screen lit up and her mother's number appeared. Esme snatched it from the bed and took the call.

'Esme! Are you alright?'

'Mum… what are you phoning for?'

'What do you mean, what am I phoning for? I'm phoning to ask what on earth's going on!'

'I didn't mean it like that; I meant I didn't expect to hear from you.'

'I can't phone my daughter now?'

'That's not what I meant either.' Esme let out a sigh. 'You don't sound happy. What's wrong?'

'That's what I'm trying to ask you.'

'There's nothing wrong with me.'

There was a pause. Then: 'Where are you?'

'Lapland.'

'Lapland?' her mother repeated in disbelief.

'On Grandma's trip. I said I might go.'

'Well, yes, I know, but I thought you'd changed your mind.'

'I know but I changed it again. Grandma went to a lot of trouble to book the trip and it didn't seem right to let it go to waste.'

'So who's with you?'

'Nobody.'

'So what did you do with Matilda's ticket?'

'Nothing.'

'What do you mean, nothing? You're all alone there? You haven't taken an old friend or anything?'

'No, no old friends. There's not really anyone I feel close enough to anymore, not since… Well, you know. But not exactly alone, either. There are other people on the tour with me but I'm alone in the room – nobody's staying with me.'

'So you're alright. Quite well… You haven't run off with some mystery lover?'

Esme wanted to laugh, but she swallowed it back. 'Who on earth would I run off with?'

'It's just… your boyfriend called us a moment ago…'

She said boyfriend as if the word might choke her.

'Oh,' Esme replied, her tone carefully neutral though her heart was thumping now. 'And what did he say?'

'That you'd either had a breakdown or you'd run off with a man but either way we needed to call you to find out what was happening and persuade you to come back because you wouldn't answer his calls for him to do it.'

'There's no breakdown.'

'I guessed as much. He can be quite… dramatic, can't he? Or is it all part of the show, the way he manipulates everyone so he gets his way?'

Esme ignored the comment. Whether he was or wasn't, getting into a conversation about Warren's perceived faults wasn't going to help her right now. Her mum wasn't about to let it drop that easily, though.

'Esme… have you left him?'

'For a week, yes.'

'Don't you think the fact that you're away now says something about the state of your relationship?'

'It might. I'm still working all that out.'

'There's a chance you might not feel quite the same as you did?'

'I suppose it would make life easier and calmer for us, wouldn't it?'

'That's not the reason I'm asking. You always think this is about me not liking him, but it's about knowing you're happy with someone who's stable and good for you.'

'I know. Right now I'm concentrating on this week. I think it will be good for me – clear my head.'

'I think so too.'

'Right. So you're not phoning to persuade me to come back?'

'No. I just wanted to make sure you're OK. I just wanted to make sure you weren't actually having a breakdown?'

'No, I'm not – not last time I checked.'

'And you're not with another man?'

'No.'

'Ah well… we can live in hope.'

Esme broke into a smile. 'I'm surprised you gave Warren the time of day so he could tell you all this.'

'What else could I do? He was livid, screaming like a lunatic, telling all sorts of tales. I had to find out for myself if any of it was true – your dad and I were worried sick.'

'You needn't have been. I'm OK. I'll have a nice little holiday and then I'll come back.'

'And then what? You can say it, you know.'

'I can't say it because I don't know. I suppose it will be back to normal life.'

'In London?'

'I don't know. Maybe.'

'With *him*?'

Esme paused. She wanted to make her own decisions in her own time and being here, away from everything, would help her to do that. She didn't know how she felt about Warren anymore; she only knew that she couldn't allow anyone else to influence her as she made up her mind.

'I think I'll have to at first,' she said finally.

'You have doubts?' her mother asked, her voice sharp and shrewd. 'Please, Esme, talk to me. You don't have to go through everything alone.'

'I can't right now, Mum, I'm sorry.'

'Could you talk to Dad if not me?'

Esme shook her head.

'Darling?'

'Sorry, Mum, but no. However, I do like that we're at *darling* again rather than pain in the neck.'

'You were never that, Esme. We simply couldn't stand to see you throw your life away on that man.'

'He's not that bad.'

'Darling, he almost committed bigamy with you.'

'He hasn't murdered anyone.'

'It's still against the law.'

'It's hardly the same.'

'No, but he's cunning and manipulative and I only wish you could see it all how we do. He's no good for you.'

Esme squeezed her eyes shut. 'Can we not talk about it now?'

'When *are* we going to talk about it?'

'Not now. I'm tired and I need to get ready for dinner.'

'Right… so you're on Matilda's trip after all? That's lovely. I'm glad you went.'

'Yes,' Esme replied, glad her mother had seen fit not to press the argument. 'I decided… Did you know that Grandma almost came here the year Granddad died? He'd booked it for her Christmas present – I found the tickets behind their wedding photo, stuffed into the frame.'

'I had no idea! I don't think your dad knew either. How strange. Did Matilda know? Because she never said a word to me or your dad.'

'I don't think she did, because we talked about coming here before she died and I brought up the times she'd asked Granddad to bring her and she never said a dicky bird about any tickets or a trip she'd never made.'

'What a terrible shame.'

'It is. So I thought it seemed right to come. Sort of for her, you know? Because she never got to.'

'I'm glad you did and I know your dad will be too. Esme, I realise that I haven't exactly been kind over the past few weeks – and indeed months and years – but unkind words were said with kind intentions. You do see that, don't you?'

'I do. So what are you going to tell Warren now you've spoken to me?'

'Nothing. You're going to have a lovely time and he'll have to mind his own business.'

'What if he calls you again?'

'Then I shan't pick up. How's that?'

'Perfect.' Esme gave a half-smile. While she could understand why Warren had gone to her parents (although she was a little surprised he'd had the nerve) she was annoyed that he'd dragged them into the situation. What was more, if he'd agreed to come to Lapland with her when she'd asked him he wouldn't have needed to worry about where she was or who she was with because it would have been with him.

There was a brisk knock at the door.

'Is someone with you?' her mum asked. 'I thought you were alone.'

'I think there's about to be.' Esme went to the spyhole in her door to see Hortense in the hall looking resplendent in something that might have resembled the national dress of some obscure Eastern European state. 'I met these people... other solo travellers.' She lowered her voice. 'One of them is an older lady and she's sort of taken me under her wing...'

'They're nice?'

'Very.'

'And you're happy? You feel safe?'

'Absolutely.'

'Then I'm glad. Phone me every day, won't you? Just so I know everything is alright.'

'I will.'

'Good, speak to you soon then.'

'Bye... Mum...'

'Yes?'

'Before you go...'

'What is it?'

'I love you.'

Esme could hear the smile in her mother's voice. 'I love you too – and I'm glad to be able to say that again.'

As she ended the call Esme wiped away a lone tear. At least this was a good tear, because there hadn't been many of those lately. Taking a deep breath and a moment to straighten her sweater, she fixed a smile to her face and went to meet Hortense for dinner.

The dining room was mostly constructed of soft wood, like most of the hotel and in keeping with much of the area's architecture. It was fragrant and cosy and dominated by large but slowly dripping ice sculptures depicting Santa and his reindeer. Waiting staff scuttled from table to table in smart black and white, while a band in the corner played what Esme presumed to be traditional Finnish songs on traditional Finnish instruments, and although it sounded slightly odd, there was a pleasing quality about it that added to the ambience of the room.

Everyone on their trip had been invited by the tour company to the welcome dinner and along with Esme, Zach, Brian and Hortense – who had a table of their own – there were perhaps two dozen others from their party sharing the feast. The choice of food on offer was dizzying – there was a wealth of traditional Finnish fare including sautéed reindeer with mashed potatoes and lingonberry jam (though it felt rather too much like eating one of Santa's helpers, especially with the ice versions looking mournfully in her direction every time Esme raised her head and so she gave this a miss), elk and black grouse and, of course, an array of fish dishes including salmon soup (Esme being reliably informed by a waitress that this was a particular local favourite). There was food to cater for faddy English tastes too, all of it whirling to and from the tables in a list of courses that Esme could barely keep count of. At Zach's persuasion Esme tried some of the local specialities but she was pretty sure the majority of them had been chosen as a culinary adventure for the holidaymakers because if she was forced to eat most of these dishes for any length of time she was sure she'd have no problem keeping the weight off.

'This fermented whatever it is certainly clears the system, doesn't it?' Hortense announced, chomping happily on a large mouthful of something that was a lurid green.

Brian grimaced while Zach looked vaguely alarmed, and Esme didn't know whether she wanted to laugh or gag.

'Hold on!' Brian reached for his iPad from the table and unlocked it. 'Squish in… that's it…'

He took a selfie, including Zach, Esme and Hortense and typed for a moment. Esme heard a whoosh and then he locked it again before setting it down to resume his meal.

'Another for the ex-wife?' Zach reached for his wine with a wry smile.

'You've got me already,' Brian said cheerily. 'I might even be persuaded to tell a few white lies – really get her going.'

'Tell her Esme's your holiday romance,' Zach said with a grin.

'My dear boy,' Hortense cut in through another mouthful of the unidentifiable lurid green fermented thing she was eating, 'nobody would believe that such a pretty young thing would be going out with an old chap like Brian.'

Brian looked sharply at her. 'What's that supposed to mean? A man can take offence, you know. I know I'm not exactly Burt Reynolds but I don't have one foot in the grave just yet.'

Esme looked up from her plate. 'Burt who?'

Hortense almost choked on her food. 'Oh Lord! She's too young to know who Burt Reynolds is and now I feel older than Methuselah himself!'

'Oh, it's me,' Esme said, deciding quickly against asking who Methuselah was too. 'I'm as dim as they come – never know who anyone famous is.'

'That doesn't make you dim,' Zach said. 'Just selective about what information you retain.'

'I don't retain any at all – that's the problem. Thick as… well, thick.'

Hortense clicked her tongue against the roof of her mouth. 'Nonsense!'

'Don't be daft!' Brian said. 'I can't tell you how many kids have passed through my school over the years and not a one of them that said they were thick actually were. Just because you don't know everything doesn't make you thick. Half these so-called boffins haven't got an ounce of common sense in their heads anyway.'

'Well, they must have some,' Hortense cut in. 'Otherwise they wouldn't be boffins.'

'Academic learning doesn't need common sense,' Brian insisted.

'I think you'll find it does,' Hortense replied airily.

'How's that then?' Brian asked.

'How is it not true?' Hortense countered. 'Please provide evidence for such an assertion.'

'I haven't got any bloody evidence,' Brian said irritably. 'How the bloody hell would I have evidence? It's what I've seen with my own eyes. I'm the one who's worked in education all my adult life.'

'I feel education per se would be very different from scientific research.'

'Who mentioned scientific research?'

'You did. You referred to boffins.'

Perhaps sensing a new heated debate between the two, Zach stepped in.

'All we're saying, Esme, is that you don't need to know who Burt Reynolds is to be intelligent.'

Their argument temporarily forgotten, Hortense and Brian made noises of agreement. But Esme knew they were just being kind because Warren was always having to explain things a dozen times, and she was always forgetting things he was supposed to have told her and it drove him mad. She gave a small, grateful smile. It was nice that they wanted to be nice to her. She liked this – sitting here with her three new friends. She barely knew them but already she felt easy in their company. But then the phone buzzed in her bag and her hand twitched to reach and pull it out. She resisted, knowing who it was likely to be and what the message was likely to say and not wanting to sour the mood at the table that was currently making her so happy. Instead she listened – at least she tried to – as Brian told an elaborate anecdote from his teaching days, though the persistent pinging of her phone as a new onslaught began kept distracting her.

Then she became aware of Zach studying her in silence. She turned to him.

'Are you OK?' he asked.

'Me?' Esme flushed. She looked across the table with a vague sense of panic that the others might have noticed her distraction too. But while she'd zoned out Hortense and Brian had embarked on a deep conversation of their own. 'Of course,' she added, forcing a smile.

'You're tired? It's been a long day, hasn't it?'

Esme was about to reply when her phone pinged again and somehow this one seemed louder than all the others, as if Warren's frustration was racing, silent and angry and invisible, across continents to reach her. Zach frowned.

'Is that your phone?'

'I don't think so.'

'Are you sure? It doesn't sound like mine. Brian's is on the table and I don't think Hortense has one.'

'I expect it's something and nothing. It will wait.'

'You don't want to check? None of my business, of course, but someone really wants your attention by the sound of things – it's been going off all night.'

Esme took her phone out and switched the sound off. 'Oh, it's a silly notification. I get a lot of them.'

Zach studied her in silence again. Then he nodded.

'It's pretty late,' Esme added, her desire for company evaporating. 'Maybe I'll skip dessert and head to my room.'

'It's not something I said, is it? I didn't mean to be nosy about your phone, I only meant—'

'It's not that – you're right; it's been a long day.'

'I understand. It's a shame, though; we'll miss you being here.'

Esme flushed again. They'd miss her? Would they really? It was such a throwaway comment but it brought a strange kind of pleasure. 'I expect you'll see more than enough of me over the next few days. So much you'll soon be sick of me.'

'I already know that couldn't happen.' He gave one of his easy smiles that already she recognised and almost craved. When he smiled that way, it was like golden hour, like the sun rising and filling the room with light. It made her feel…

She pushed the feeling down, way down, out of harm's way.

'So… I'll be off,' she said. 'Goodnight.'

'See you tomorrow, I hope. I'm looking forward to our first day in Rovaniemi.'

Esme smiled. 'Me too.' Her chair scraped the floor as she pushed it from the table and now Hortense and Brian looked up from their conversation, which had been turning into lively debate again. But Zach would have to referee this time, because Esme was exhausted.

'I'm sorry but I'm going to excuse myself,' she said in answer to their questioning looks. 'Long day and all that.'

'My dear girl, no need to explain,' Hortense said. 'Early start tomorrow too. Have you booked onto the snowmobile safari?'

'Against my better judgement,' she said with a laugh. 'I'm sure I'll end up head first in a snowdrift as soon as we leave the compound.'

'Not to worry!' Hortense said briskly. 'I never pass up the opportunity of a little adventure! We've come all this way after all, no point in spending every day sitting in the hotel!'

'I can't wait,' Zach said. 'And I for one am really glad you're coming with us.'

Esme flushed and turned her attention to fiddling with the zip of her handbag so it wouldn't show. Then she dared one more glance at Zach before tearing her gaze away and offering the table as a whole a final apology.

'I expect I'll see you all in the morning either way.'

Hortense pushed her own chair from the table and toddled round to give Esme a firm hug. 'Now, do you need one of our gentlemen here to escort you to your room?'

Esme gave a grateful smile. 'Unless I'm going to run into a polar bear on the landing I expect I'll be alright.'

Hortense gave an emphatic nod. 'Righto. Goodnight then, dear girl.'

'Goodnight.'

Esme left the dining room and she could feel the eyes of the other three on her as she went. It was obvious they all wondered about her, that they guessed she was keeping parts of her life back in England secret. Even she wasn't sure why – she only wished she could tell them. And she wanted to stay at the dinner table and get to know them all better but how could she, knowing what was happening at home right now?

In the lift she took out her phone and noted the five new messages to add to the ones Warren had sent earlier. She'd have to read them eventually, of course, but not now. Now she wanted to fall into bed and sleep and not think about any of that until the morning.

Chapter Twelve

Their guide was Niko – an endlessly enthusiastic and gregarious twenty-something with blond dreads and a nose piercing, a hot accent and eyes as blue as the clear Arctic skies above them. He flirted outrageously with Esme as he showed her the controls of the snowmobile but later when she heard peals of laughter coming from Hortense, she realised that Niko flirted outrageously with everyone.

It had been a short drive on a minibus to get them from their hotel to the snowmobile station. Esme had expected to sit on the bus with Hortense, but as it ploughed through fresh snow to stop in the hotel car park, she could barely restrain a raised eyebrow as Hortense made a beeline for Brian and clung to his arm.

'You'll be sitting with me?' she asked.

Brian looked down at her and gave a bright, warm smile. 'Of course – I wouldn't have it any other way.'

'That's marvellous. I'm so excited for today. You'll have to take care of me.'

'I'll be your Lancelot, my lady,' he said.

Esme almost let out a guffaw. Hortense was one woman who did not need taking care of – Lancelot or not.

As Esme stared after them, Zach's voice spun her around.

'You missed the entertainment last night,' he said carelessly.

'Entertainment?'

'Hortense and Brian. Getting it on. Slow dancing at the post-meal disco. They were both legless. Then they disappeared together mumbling something about being tired and going to bed. Whose bed is anyone's guess but I bet that's one bit of the holiday Brian won't be photographing to send to the ex.'

Esme stared in amazement at Brian and Hortense. If their tryst had been fuelled by alcohol then they must still have been drunk because Brian had his arm around Hortense now and she didn't look like she minded a bit. In fact, just to show him how little she minded, Hortense's hand slid down to Brian's backside and gave it a cheeky squeeze. Esme turned back to Zach.

'Oh my God!'

'My thoughts exactly. Didn't take them long, did it?'

'I thought…'

'That we might be breaking up a fight by the end of the week? Me too. Looks like we might be breaking up something very different at some point.'

'Is that…? Are we…?' Esme's mouth opened and closed again and she didn't know how to articulate the questions filling her head. 'I just don't understand.'

'If you worked for a dating agency, you'd never put them together, that's for sure.'

'Maybe not.' Esme laughed. 'So what did you do?'

'Last night?'

Esme nodded.

He shrugged. 'Had another drink, got talking to a couple from Cleveland for a bit and went to bed myself.'

'Oh. I'm sorry.'

'What for?'

'That you got left alone.'

'It was hardly your fault. Honestly, I'm not bothered. Good luck to Brian and Hortense – if they find romance this week then I'd say that's a pretty good result. Doesn't sound like either of them get much of that these days, and doesn't everyone deserve something good from time to time?'

Esme gave a vague smile. Her thoughts had returned to the barrage of messages from Warren that she'd finally dared to read that morning. The experience had stressed her out so much she'd barely been able to face more than a black coffee at breakfast. Still, she hadn't replied – they'd mostly been ranting and impossible to reply to – and because of that she knew there'd be more. Zach, as if reading her thoughts (about the food at least), brought it up.

'Did you get anything to eat? I didn't see you have much at breakfast.'

'I'm not so hungry in the mornings.'

'There's a stop about halfway through the day to cook sausages and marshmallows on an open fire. Maybe you'll be hungry by then.'

'If it's more reindeer sausages then I doubt it.'

Zach grinned. 'I'm glad you decided to come today – I didn't think you would.'

'What makes you say that?'

'Nothing in particular. Perhaps I was just preparing myself for disappointment.'

'Why? Would you have been very disappointed if I hadn't come?'

'It would have been manageable, I suppose. You know, like finding the wrong burger in your order after you've left the drive-thru.'

Esme laughed. 'Lucky for you that I did come.' She angled her head in the direction of Hortense and Brian, who were sneaking kisses behind a spreading fir like a couple who'd just discovered what their mouths were really for. 'You'd have been a proper gooseberry.'

'You could be right there.'

Their conversation had been cut short by the tour company representative ushering everyone onto the bus, and Esme had sat next to Zach instead of Hortense, trying to ignore the heat of his leg as it pressed against hers and wishing she could think about something else.

They stood waiting now at the snowmobile station as Niko worked his way through the party to make final safety checks before giving the go ahead to hit the snow. Esme stamped her feet to stave off the biting cold. Even in her borrowed snowsuit and thick gloves it crept into every gap in every line of stitching and her toes were numb. Every time she took a breath it was like ice filling her lungs and her throat ached. Hortense was right when she'd said it was difficult to imagine cold like this until you'd experienced it. Once she was back at home basking in a British winter, she'd never complain she was cold ever again.

'Wishing you hadn't come after all?' Zach leaned in and lowered his voice.

'How did you know?'

'Because I'm freezing too,' he said with a smile. 'Right now that open fire back at the hotel seems very tempting.'

'And the hot chocolate.'

'That too.'

'Maybe this wasn't such a great idea.'

'Come on – it's cold but it's not that bad. Just like being in an ice bar. A great big outdoor, perpetually freezing ice bar.'

'I've never been in an ice bar.'

'I have. Many. One of those things that… well, let's just say I've been in a lot.'

'Doesn't seem much point to me. Just go to a regular bar and get ice in your drinks.'

'That's what I used to say.'

'You like them now?'

'Yeah, I like them now. Good memories.'

'It's not just the cold,' Esme said, not wanting to talk about ice bars any more. She had a feeling there was something significant about ice bars and she was scared to ask. 'I'm nervous too.'

'About what? This?'

'Well, driving the snowmobile. The only thing I've ever driven is a car.'

'This is way easier – that's why they let us take them out with very little instruction.'

'You've been on one before?'

'Yeah.'

'Where did you do that?'

'Here…'

'Here? In Lapland? So you've been before?'

'Yes.'

Esme waited for more information but none came. It was obvious there was something he didn't want to tell her. And maybe they hadn't really known each other long enough for Esme to push it.

'And you're still here to tell the tale,' she said instead, trying to keep the situation light even though she was beginning to see darkness in it.

'Exactly.'

'OK. So what if I lose the party? If I go off course I could end up really lost.'

'You won't. It's really hard to get lost.'

'But what if I do?'

'Don't worry. I'll stick with you, so if you go off course, then so will I. At least we'll be off course together.'

Esme shook her head. 'Maybe I should ride with Niko on his snowmobile. He said anyone who felt nervous could.'

'Or how about you ride on mine with me?'

Esme blinked.

'Only if you wanted to, of course,' he added quickly. 'With me you'd have my full attention but Niko has the whole group to worry about.'

'I…' Esme glanced across at where Niko was high-fiving a teenage boy. Niko was very young – which was a ridiculous thing for her to think considering she herself was probably only a few years older. But his carefree, bohemian manner made him seem *too* young. And a little too carefree. Niko didn't look like he'd catch you if you fell, rather sit back and watch with a wry chuckle. But Zach… Zach looked like someone who'd be there no matter what. Maybe she would be safer with Zach. At least physically she'd be safer. Emotionally… she tried again to dismiss that pull when she looked at him. He was a travelling companion, nothing more, and she had Warren waiting at home. Sort of. Though she hadn't exactly decided how she felt about going back to Warren, she hadn't exactly finished things with him either. But then she looked up again at Zach and he smiled and her heart melted just a little.

'OK. As long as I'm not holding you back I'll ride with you.'

Zach grinned. 'So, the next question is do you feel confident enough to drive? Or do you want to go piggyback with me?'

'I'll let you drive.'

He gave a short nod. 'I guess you could always have a go coming back. If you feel up to it.'

'You'd trust me to drive with you riding pillion?'

'Of course. Why not?'

'I don't know. My…'

Esme wanted to say boyfriend but the word wouldn't come out. Why couldn't she mention Warren? What was the use in hiding his existence from everyone?

'I'm not the best driver, that's all,' she finished lamely.

'Even if we did come off – which we won't – we'd hardly hurt ourselves with all this snow to cushion the landing.'

Esme's pulse quickened. She waited for the *but*. There was none. He really did believe she could do this. He looked at her like she was valid, like she had worth.

'I don't think so,' she said, despite this. 'I think I'd feel better if you drove.'

'I will, but I bet you change your mind when you see how easy it is.'

She smiled, but she didn't say anything more because it might commit her to a course of action she wasn't ready for.

'I'd better have a word with Niko,' he said. 'Let him know the plan.'

Esme watched him go. She tried not to watch him but despite the snow glittering in the pink half-light of a polar noon and the plumes of breath curling like ice sculptures into the cleanest air she'd ever seen, and the infectious excitement and anticipation of her fellow travellers infusing the cold with a subtle warmth, she couldn't watch anything else.

It's nothing, she told herself firmly. *It's a silly crush because you're in a weird emotional state right now and he's being kind to you and in any other situation you wouldn't look twice.* And she wondered whether the guilt and the desire showed on her face as he made his way back, blowing into his palms to warm them.

'Niko's going to get someone to put the spare snowmobile away and he's cool with us going together.'

Esme caught a wink from Hortense and wondered what to make of it. Then she watched as Hortense straddled her vehicle as if it was a bucking bronco and she'd been a cow wrangler all her life, swatting away any assistance that Brian looked set to offer. She opened the throttle before Niko had even thought about telling everyone to start up. As the sound of her engine cracked the iced air he shot her a look of vague annoyance that looked oddly incongruous on his serene and happy features, and Esme wondered if he'd suddenly realised that his day might have just got that little bit less chilled with Hortense in his charge. Esme would bet a large chunk of money that her new friend wasn't very good at taking instruction or orders or advice of any kind meant to keep her safe. If someone handed her a live grenade and told her to throw it, Hortense would probably juggle it for a while first as she whistled a jaunty tune, just to see if she could. To see her now, so bold and enthusiastic, made Esme smile, but it made her a little sad at the same time, because she couldn't help but reflect on how much her grandma would have liked Hortense. She would have liked Brian too, who was now watching Hortense with fondness but also with the ghost of a wry smile. He was probably thinking much the same as Esme – that he didn't fancy Niko's chances trying to keep the indomitable Hortense in line. In fact, her grandma would have got along famously with everyone.

'Ready?'

Zach's voice brought her back to reality but it also stirred another emotion in her that was hardly helping to steady the ship.

'As I'll ever be.'

'Don't worry – I've got you.'

The famous line from the *Superman* film came to mind, where Lois Lane is swept into Superman's arms and asks that if he has her, who has him. But looking at Zach now, Esme realised that nobody needed to have him because he was the sort of man who just coped with anything that life threw at him and never even broke a sweat. Her throat was tight and the cold air burned her lungs, but she swallowed it in and climbed onto the back of the snowmobile. A moment later it roared into life.

'I feel like James Bond,' he called behind. 'And don't reply to that – let me keep my little fantasy that I look like James Bond too!'

Esme wouldn't have replied. He didn't look like James Bond – his features were far too gentle and thoughtful to be that steely. Not that he didn't have the bone structure or the well-sculpted torso or the thick wavy hair, but the whole package was more approachable, more down to earth. Like a James Bond that normal women could actually date without feeling woefully inadequate. Perhaps it was a strange way to think of him, and she had to smile at her odd notion. She almost told Zach about it, but then the sound of the other snowmobiles coming to life one by one filled the air and Zach wouldn't have heard it even if she'd been silly enough to let it slip.

Niko was at the front of the pack. He raised his arm above his head and pointed to a barely visible track, which Esme had to assume was what passed for a road in these parts, and everyone began to follow as he picked up speed. The engine vibrated through Esme's chest and she wrapped her arms around Zach's waist. His coat was thick and padded and there was no warmth for her as she pressed her cheek to his back, but there was heat from his legs as hers slotted behind them and she was cosy enough in her own snowsuit to be content as the frosted landscape began to flash by. Their shadows were long and grainy on the snow and already the blue moment – as the locals called it – was fast approaching where the skies were lilac and rose and forget-me-not and just about the most beautiful thing Esme had ever seen.

'OK back there?' Zach called.

Esme nodded, forgetting her voice.

'Esme?'

'Oh… I'm fine.'

'Isn't this just amazing?'

'Yes… amazing.'

'Doesn't it feel like the adventure of a lifetime already?'

'Yes.'

Zach paused. Then: 'You know…'

His voice faded. Esme waited.

'Zach?'

She felt the wobble as he shook his head.

'Nothing,' he said, and for the first time since they'd met there was something in his voice – a note of defeat or perhaps pain. There was a fleeting spark of recognition, and Esme knew instantly that whatever he'd wanted to say, he'd boxed it up again. She didn't push the conversation; she simply laid her head against his back and watched the landscape flash by once more.

The box that Zach had metaphorically shut was still secure. After ten minutes of silence, broken only by the thrum of their engines sounding like a thousand really angry bees, the occasional shouted instruction from Niko, which could have been instruction or could have been simple expressions of joy – it was hard to tell – and the snow spraying from beneath them, Zach spoke again. One word.

'Elk.'

Esme whipped round and then she saw it, black against the bank of snow, watching the party whiz by with lazy interest. They passed within seconds, but she was left with the impression of a shaggy creature of enormous size and strength, something that had taken her completely by surprise. She'd imagined an elk in the wild to be more like a deer but this was something far more alarming, frightening even.

A short time later, as the clouds began to crowd the pastel skies, Niko gave the signal to stop.

'We will eat now,' he said as the engines stopped one by one.

Zach turned to Esme with that easy smile. 'A bit early for dinner – somebody must have the munchies.'

It was good to see him amenable and charming again, but at the same time it troubled Esme because some unnameable instinct told her now that all his agreeability came at a cost. But it was probably none of her business, even if it was anything at all. Maybe it was just an overactive imagination on her part and she dismissed the idea. After all, he seemed OK now.

Niko set to work in a sheltered clearing, shovelling the snow aside to reveal earth blackened with the marks of many fires before the one he was building now. He gave instructions to various members of the party for assistance while he showed some of the children what he planned to do, explaining to them in gentle tones the origin of every ingredient of the meal they were going to eat and the Finnish ethos of taking care of every resource so there would always be food to eat in the future. Niko was good with kids – less cocky and more approachable – and every one of them was now entranced by his husky voice with its accent sharp enough to cut leather and his dancing blue eyes. There were questions and he answered each one without judgement, no matter how silly they might seem or how similar to the one before. Esme forgot she was cold as she watched them.

'He's a cool customer, eh?'

Esme turned to see Zach watching too.

'Oh God, yes.'

'And good-looking too.'

'That's an indisputable fact.'

'I shouldn't say it but it makes me feel quite inadequate. I should become a monk or something rather than trying to compete.'

Esme studied him. 'Why would you need to compete?'

'I don't. I was just saying…'

Zach seemed flustered. The second surprising discovery of the day: Zach got flustered.

'I just meant… he's a pretty tough yardstick for the rest of us men.'

'You have different qualities,' Esme said. 'Just as valuable.'

'Well, thank you, I think.'

'At least Hortense doesn't seem too concerned about Niko. And Brian's certainly not feeling inadequate.' Esme angled her head to where Brian and Hortense were engaged in some sort of Eskimo kissing, their noses smudged together and their arms wrapped around each other's padded torsos. 'It looks like the foursome has now become a couple of twosomes.'

'It does,' Zach said, and left Esme wondering how he felt about that. She turned to the landscape, pristine and white for miles apart from the dark shadows of trees and the odd distant dwelling. She'd once thought the beloved peaks of her home could be uninviting and bleak, but even amongst all this beauty, how inhospitable, how hard must life be here? Was there ever a day when the inhabitants of Rovaniemi didn't risk death from hypothermia just by walking out through their front door?

When she looked again, Niko and his helpers had the fire going. It seemed strange to see a fire in the middle of so much snow but there it was. The kids of the party were full of excited chatter as they helped Niko unpack the food they were going to cook. Esme almost wished she could join in, but this was a task for them to enjoy and she wouldn't dream of taking these memories from any of them. He then pulled pots and pans from the luggage box on his snowmobile and gathered them round to issue a few safety instructions before they began to prepare lunch.

She'd been determined not to eat too much either, an inevitable hangover from the diet she'd been on for Warren, but when the sausages began to cook, the rich smell of them on the frosty air was so incredible that, reindeer or not, Esme had to try them. So she sat on a log cleared by Zach and he sat next to her and the whole group fell silent as they devoured a hot lunch that felt all the more welcome in the searing cold of their surroundings.

Reindeer sausage was unexpectedly good too, though Esme tried not to think about Santa's helpers as they ate. Perhaps if she ate enough of them this week she'd stop thinking about Rudolph at all. As Hortense had reminded her when she'd said so, it was only what the Arctic people had instead of cows and it was silly to be so sentimental about it – although Hortense had a way of saying so that made Esme feel sillier still. It was sort of like someone had taken beef and given it flavour steroids – very intense and dark and almost earthy. Esme looked around – some of the children were staring mournfully at their plates and picking at the berry accompaniment to the meal and Esme guessed they were finding it a little harder to separate their dinner from Donner, Dasher, Blitzen and co.

Then Niko served up hot, strong coffee to wash it down, and as soon as everyone was warmed through they washed up and packed up and got ready to start on the trail back to the snowmobile station. By now dusk had fallen and the pockets of sky in the gathering clouds were deep indigo, dusted with stars.

'Do you think we'll see the Northern Lights?' someone asked Niko.

'The solar activity is low,' Niko said. 'Perhaps, but I would not place a bet on it for today.'

Zach stared up as he fastened his crash helmet. He looked disappointed by what they'd just heard, perhaps more than he ought to be. After all, they had a week to see the Lights so perhaps it wasn't time to be *too* disappointed just yet.

'But we have the Lights chase tomorrow night,' Esme reminded him. 'We're bound to see them eventually.'

He sniffed, unimpressed, or perhaps more disappointed than he could articulate.

'And don't forget the weather changes quickly here,' she added. 'The sky might not be clear now but it might change later.'

Esme and Zach both turned to see Brian behind them, looking up at the clouds too. Zach's disappointment lifted and he grinned.

'Good of you to join us, Brian.'

Brian's grin in return was rather more sheepish. 'Hortense and I…'

'You hooked up,' Zach said. 'It's great – don't worry about it.'

'You don't feel abandoned by us?'

Zach looked at Esme. 'We're all grownups – I'm sure we'll survive it somehow.'

Brian looked over to where Hortense was already astride her snowmobile like the Amazonian queen that the legends forgot to mention. 'She's one on her own that woman.'

'She is that,' Zach agreed.

'At the airport I had my doubts that we wouldn't throttle one another before the week is out – she's a bit too much like the ex, if truth be told.' He gave a small smile. 'It's funny how your feelings can change, isn't it? I never thought I had a "type" but it looks like I might have after all.'

'It is. I hope you two have a great time together now that you've decided no throttling is necessary. Just remember to say hello every now and again, eh?'

'Of course!' Brian said. 'We wouldn't leave you two!'

'Good.' Zach nodded towards Niko, who'd raised his arms for attention. 'Looks like he's ready to move.'

'Oh, right... I should...' Brian began to wade through the snow back to his own vehicle, the overgrown hair poking from beneath his woolly hat almost as white as the landscape.

'See you later, Brian.'

'Yes!' Brian lifted his hand in farewell as he struggled forward. 'See you at the hotel!'

Esme and Zach watched him go, silent for a few short moments before Zach spoke quietly.

'Just goes to show there's hope for all of us, doesn't it?'

Esme turned to him. She wanted to ask what that meant but she didn't know how so she climbed on the back of the snowmobile and left it at that.

Chapter Thirteen

'Mum, I'm so sorry.'

Esme sat on her bed, wrapped in a fluffy hotel robe while the feeling slowly returned to her tingling toes and fingers. She'd arrived back from the safari exhausted and exhilarated. Zach had been so patient and encouraging, she'd even been persuaded to take the controls of the snowmobile for the last fifteen or so minutes of the journey back, and it had been the most exciting thing she'd ever done – she'd felt almost invincible. They'd parted at the hotel lobby with grins on both sides. But the feeling hadn't lasted long – two minutes on the phone to her mum had brought her hurtling back to earth.

'I don't want you to apologise,' Esme's mum said firmly. 'We can handle Warren – don't you worry about that.'

'But you shouldn't have to… this is my fault.'

'Nonsense. It's that silly man's fault for making a pest of himself.'

'My phone was dead…' she continued. 'The battery… Zach says phone batteries don't like extreme cold; they shut down.'

'It doesn't matter, darling,' her mum insisted.

'I didn't realise he'd keep calling you, but I should have done.'

'Well, I'm glad he couldn't call *you*.' Her mum's tone was stoic, defiant. 'I'm glad the cold got your battery. I don't want you dealing with it – I just needed to tell you what happened.'

Esme pulled the robe tighter and wrapped her arms around herself. 'I should call him.'

'No! That man has ruined enough things for you! Esme...' Her mother's voice softened. 'I realise I can't tell you how to live your life now, but I can tell you what I think about it. Sometimes you might want to listen to what I have to say.'

'I know, and I already know how you feel about Warren. It's not as simple as me listening to you – he needs me, that's why he's stressing out with me gone. I never should have left him.'

'He's not a puppy being left while you go out to work. He's a grown man. I'm sure he can manage a few days without you.'

'But he's very... well, he gets dependent on people.'

'I'd say it's more that he likes to control people. I think it's you who's grown dependent.'

'But you don't understand our relationship, Mum—'

'No, I'm afraid I don't. All I see is a man who pulled the wool over your eyes, pretending he was free to marry when he wasn't. Not only that, he tells you what to do and who to see. Look at what happened to us—'

'That bit wasn't entirely his fault.'

Her mum let out a long sigh. 'Perhaps not, but your father and I were forced into the action we took.'

'Look, I don't want to keep laying blame and I don't want to rake up bad feelings from that time again. I'm glad we're OK now, Mum, and I don't want things to go back to that.'

'I feel the same; I just can't stand by and let you get hoodwinked by that man again.'

'I won't be, I just—'

'Don't you dare think about going home early! Give in to him now and you'll be giving in forever. He can spend time with his wife if he's feeling lonely…'

'You don't know him like I do. He'll keep calling you.'

'And we'll keep telling him the same thing.'

Esme paused as something occurred to her. 'Has he asked exactly where I am?'

'Yes.'

'But you didn't tell him?'

'He already knows you're in Lapland and he knows the resort. I'm assuming you told him that much.'

Esme gave a silent nod. She had, hadn't she? She'd asked Warren to come and she'd even shown him the hotel online in a bid to persuade him. She stared at the opposite wall. He wouldn't come here, would he? Surely that would be an extreme course of action, even for Warren?

'Esme?'

'Sorry, Mum. I was just thinking about something I need to do.'

'You're going to call him?'

'I think I have to. Just to settle things. I think it will get much worse if I don't.'

'You don't need to phone him on our account – I told you, your dad and I can handle it.'

'It's not just that.' Esme squeezed her eyes shut. 'I just need to talk to him. And it's not to give in or anything. It's just to clear things up. Do you see what I mean?'

'I can't say I do. Just don't let him talk you into anything you don't want to do.'

'I won't.'

'You say that but I'm afraid you will.'

'Mum, I can't have him hassling you and Dad and that's that.' There was also the notion that he might even go as far as tracking her down in Rovaniemi, and that would be a whole new mess, but Esme didn't mention that for fear of giving her parents something new to worry about. If they thought that, they might just get on a plane and come to her themselves, to be on hand in case he did. The idea of Warren flying out was perhaps a bit extreme, but crazy as it was she couldn't rule it out –sometimes Warren had been known to do extreme things.

'It doesn't bother us,' her mum insisted.

'I know, but it bothers me.'

Her mother gave a loud sniff. Esme could picture the look of disapproval on her face.

'Who's Zach?' she asked.

'What?'

'You mentioned someone named Zach.'

'Oh, he's one of the solo travellers. We went out today – I mean lots of us did. Together. Not just me and him.'

'You had a good day?'

'The best. We went on a snowmobile safari. Honestly, it was just the most incredible thing.'

'So this Zach…'

'No, Mum…'

'I'm just asking. I can ask, can't I? I'm your mum, after all.'

'Yes, but no. Whatever you're thinking. And I have a feeling I know what that is.'

'Alright then.'

Esme heard a rare chuckle. Her mother was always so serious that the sound took Esme quite by surprise, especially as she didn't see what there was to laugh about. It wasn't often that Esme sought advice from her mum, particularly as they'd fallen out so spectacularly over the past few years, but she was gripped by a sudden urge to ask for help. She'd had her grandma before, always saying just the right thing to settle Esme's mind, but she was gone now and Esme missed her counsel. In some ways, perhaps Matilda's death had contributed to the fact that Esme and her mother were getting along now, and as Esme was finding herself more and more confused about her feelings, she was taken by a hope that perhaps her mum would know the right thing to say.

'Mum… what do I do about Warren?'

'Nothing. I've told you, we're more than happy to fend him off.'

'I don't just mean this week.'

Her mother sighed. 'That I can't tell you,' she said, her tone soft again now. 'I think you know my opinion but I can't force you to act on it – I think the past few years have taught us that much. The only opinion that really counts in that regard is your own. It's the only one you'll listen to.'

'I'm ready to listen to yours now.'

'I don't think that's quite true yet. If it was you wouldn't even need to ask me that question.'

There was a brief silence.

'Mum?'

'I'm still here.'

Esme opened her mouth to speak but then closed it again. Her mother was right – perhaps Esme wasn't ready yet. Her mother's perspective on the situation wasn't the catch-all solution she'd been hoping for, but it was probably wiser than Esme might at first give credit for.

'Goodnight,' she said instead.

'You're going to bed already? What time is it there?'

'It feels late because it's dark. It sort of makes you tired all the time. Until you get used to it I suppose.'

'Not because you're perhaps feeling low? Sleep is always appealing as the refuge of someone who doesn't have the strength to face the world.'

'I know, but I'm just tired. It's hard to get used to the constant night-time here. Do you know the sun was only above the horizon for two hours today?'

'Sounds depressing.'

'But they have this polar twilight – it's so beautiful. The sky is all sorts of colours you wouldn't expect. Not really like darkness at all. I wish Grandma could have seen it.'

'Me too.'

Coral had never been great friends with her mother-in-law, but Esme knew that when her mother said that she meant it. She'd done her best with Matilda, even when she'd disagreed with her – which had been over many things – simply because she knew how much Esme's dad loved his mother and because of how much she herself loved him.

'All the more reason for you to make the most of your time there and not worry about home,' her mum added. 'Promise me you'll try.'

'I will.'

'I'd better go. Your dad will call tomorrow to check in. I think he'd really like a chat with you.'

'He could have one now.'

'He could but that would mean me peeling his face from the newspaper he's fallen asleep into.'

Esme couldn't help but laugh at the image. 'I love you, Mum. And I'm so glad we're friends again.'

'I love you too, darling. Goodnight.'

Esme watched as the screen of her phone went black. She'd promised not to worry about home and she'd said she wouldn't call Warren, but how could she leave it? How could she leave him to keep bothering her parents without trying to stop it?

She stared at the phone for a moment before she put it to one side. Not now. Tomorrow was the Northern Lights chase – the reason she'd come. If she only got to see them she could be happy to go back to England and deal with whatever was going on there. One more day – that was all she needed.

She was about to climb into bed and turn out the light when there was a thud at her door.

Hortense stood in the view of her spyhole, a vast silk dress of deep scarlet stretched across her bosom and her hair pinned up with chopsticks. Esme opened the door.

'Sorry for the commotion, dear girl, fell into your door. The old wobbles, you know.'

Esme stared. 'You look…'

'Stunning.' Brian stepped into view and took Hortense's arm. 'Doesn't she look the dog's—' Brian gave an apologetic cough. 'I mean, the bee's knees?'

Esme smiled. Brian and Hortense – it looked as if it was becoming a real holiday romance.

'You're not dressed.' Hortense threw a critical eye over Esme's bathrobe. 'Aren't you coming to dinner?'

'I'm a bit tired.'

'You'll starve to death! I've barely seen you eat more than a sausage today and I'm not convinced you ate all of that!'

Esme laughed. 'I promise you I did.'

'You simply must come to dinner.'

'But…'

'I wouldn't sleep a wink if I thought you'd gone to bed on an empty stomach.'

Esme's glance switched to Brian and the way he was gazing soppily at Hortense she suspected he had his own plans for sleep deprivation and they had very little to do with Esme's food intake.

'You really don't need to worry about me,' she insisted.

'I don't need to worry about a great many things but I do,' Hortense said. 'Please come. Zachary is already at our table saving you a seat and I think it would be a terribly uneven arrangement, just the three of us without you.'

Brian nodded in agreement. 'I think he'd appreciate your company. I mean, we all would.'

Esme tried not to narrow her eyes. It suddenly occurred to her that some kind of double date was being engineered here. Even Hortense and Brian couldn't be that obtuse, could they? However, Esme could see that it might be awkward and uncomfortable for Zach to sit alone with them.

'Give me ten minutes and I'll meet you down there,' she said.

'Marvellous! We'll be waiting!'

They left, Brian propping Hortense up as she wobbled into him. He looked back, beaming, as if he had Miss World on his arm. It was sweet. Had Warren ever looked like that with Esme? Had he ever been so evidently proud of her, proud to be seen with her, flaws and all?

She closed her bedroom door and went to the wardrobe to find some clothes. It wouldn't be a spectacular Chinese silk dress but whatever it was, it would have to do.

*

When Esme arrived in the dining room thirty minutes later the first course of dinner was already under way. Hortense waved from the table where she sat with Brian, but Zach was nowhere to be seen.

'My dear girl, you've just missed him,' Hortense announced as Esme sat down.

'Zach? He's finished dinner already?'

'Out. Niko has stolen him away.'

'What?'

Brian shook his head. 'I never saw that coming.'

'What coming?' Esme asked, wishing that their sentences could be a little less cryptic so she could catch up.

'He looked like he was batting for our side to me,' Brian continued. 'Not that I have any issue with it, of course. What a man chooses to do in his private life is no business of mine.'

'But you could have guessed Niko was.' Hortense nodded sagely. 'And Zachary *does* work in theatre.'

'That doesn't make a man gay.'

'No, but it certainly narrows the odds.'

'I don't agree with that! I thought you were supposed to be broad-minded!'

'You don't have to agree, but I'm almost certainly right. Take it from me, I have a wealth of experience in this field.'

Esme had to wonder what kind of experience Hortense was talking about, but she was too confounded by the direction of the current conversation to find out.

'I don't doubt you do,' Brian said. 'I must walk around with my eyes closed. Theatre or not, I wouldn't have had a clue if not for whatshername at the bar. You know, the one with the long hair.'

'Inari,' Hortense said, heaving her bosom onto the table as if to remind him that while Inari might have long hair, she had the chest to end all chests.

'Yes, that's the one. Well, if she hadn't said…'

'I wonder where they've gone,' Hortense said. 'I bet it's fabulous – these places always are.'

'I wouldn't have even imagined they had places like that here. It *is* Santa's home after all.'

'Like what?' Hortense asked.

'Well… gay clubs.'

'I'm not sure what us being at Santa's home has to do with anything,' Hortense said. 'Are you insinuating there are no gay people in Santa's homeland? Are you saying that there shouldn't be places for gay people to meet here – that there might be something unsavoury about it…?'

'Of course not, I just meant—'

Esme held up a hand, wary of them descending into another of their lively debates. They might have been dating but that hadn't meant undergoing personality transplants. She wouldn't get any sense out of anyone then. 'Hold on! I'm confused. Zach's gone somewhere with Niko? Our snowmobile guide Niko, from today?'

Hortense nodded. 'He was just chatting to us and he said he knew a great place to get a drink and would Zach like to go. Actually, he asked us all but I rather think he was hoping Brian and I would say no and he'd get Zach all to himself. And we thought you weren't coming down to dinner after all because you were such a long time—'

'So Zach said he'd go,' Brian finished.

'I suspect he thought he'd give us some privacy,' Hortense continued, 'but still, Niko's a good-looking chap.'

Brian shook his head. 'You say it's a date but, honestly, I don't know what to think.'

Esme looked from Brian to Hortense and back again. 'They've gone on a *date*?'

Brian took a sip of his water. 'So Hortense keeps saying. Not that I have any problem whatsoever with that if it's true.'

'Oh, Brian, do shut up, there's a good chap.' Hortense patted his hand. 'Anyone would think you're a raging closet case the way you keep denying your opposition. We don't know what Zachary's preferences are but there's no harm in a little experimentation. Stops one getting bored. Take it from me – I know.'

Brian flushed, but far from feeling chastised, Esme suspected Hortense's not so subtle reminder of her wild past had probably given him an inappropriate little gift. She half expected to see the dinner table start to rise in front of them. As for Zach – the news that he was gay was as big a shock to her as anyone. Not that she was an expert on the signals, but evidently she was much worse at reading them than even she herself had realised.

'You're sure that's what happened?' Esme poured herself a glass of water. 'They're on an actual date?'

'They looked very friendly when they left,' Brian said.

'How friendly?'

'Niko had his arm around him.'

Esme was silent. She'd already noticed that Niko was a tactile sort of man. Having his arm around someone didn't necessarily mean anything. She had to wonder if Zach had guessed what was on the agenda when Niko had asked him to go for a drink. What did it mean that Zach had said yes? Could it be that Hortense was right about this?

Esme's own face flushed now. All this time she'd imagined some chemistry between them – at least on her part. Although now she thought about it he'd been reserved in that regard. Very sweet and friendly, of course. Chivalrous. Massively encouraging and interested in her. But perhaps a bit too polite and courteous. In the past, when a man had been interested in her in a romantic way they'd let her know in no uncertain terms. Maybe it was just the sort of men she attracted, but Zach hadn't shown any of that obvious lust.

She didn't know whether to feel like an idiot or to feel relieved knowing that it had all been in her head. There was an upside to the revelation, however – she could spend time with Zach guilt-free. He was no threat to Warren and no threat to her conscience. She could tell Warren that, in fact, and he'd probably be happy that Esme was spending her time away with a very nice, caring man who wasn't remotely interested in her in any romantic capacity.

While it solved one problem, however, it did leave Esme with a more immediate issue. While she'd been silently turning things over, Brian and Hortense were making serious eyes at each other once again. Any minute now things were going to get amorous and it didn't matter that Zach might be gay, because she wasn't going to thank him for leaving her with Taylor and Burton slobbering over each other while she tried to eat mashed potato and pretend she hadn't noticed.

When she looked again, they'd already started. *Great*, she thought. *Perfect*.

There were many things she'd planned to do on this trip, but watching Brian and Hortense court wasn't one of them. She glanced over at the far side of the room where the now-infamous Inari stood behind the bar, polishing wine glasses and looking quite bored. Maybe Esme could go and get a drink, try and engage her in some conversation. Inari might be able to tell her a little more about Niko, and maybe finding out more about Niko would tell her more about the situation with him and Zach. If there was a situation. She'd miss dinner, of course, but she could probably get room service later if she got hungry.

Looking back at her companions and realising that they wouldn't notice if she disappeared for half an hour or so, Esme made up her mind to do just that and went to the bar.

Inari looked faintly surprised to see her there as Esme cleared her throat in a subtle attempt to get noticed.

'Your waiter can get drinks for you,' she said.

'I know, but I'm not eating,' Esme replied, perching on a stool.

'You would like a drink?'

'I'd love a beer.'

'Which one?' Inari gestured to the choice of bottles in a fridge and Esme shrugged.

'I'll take a recommendation from you.'

Without another word, Inari reached into the fridge and took out a bottle with an illustration of a bear on it. After opening it, she placed it on the counter and went over to the till, turning back to Esme with an expectant look.

'Oh, please charge it to room one-twenty,' Esme said.

As Inari keyed in the details, Esme took a sip of her drink. It was cold, a bit tart. Rather like a special Danish beer she'd once tried at a festival, though the name of that one escaped her now.

'It's not too busy for you tonight?' Esme asked.

Inari went back to polishing the glasses that didn't look as if they needed polishing at all.

'It's very quiet. It will get busier when dinner is over.'

'People want drinks with their meals.'

'Yes, but they drink them more slowly. Later they're drinking only and much faster.'

'You like your job here?'

'Yes.'

'Do you do anything else?'

Inari gave a vague frown.

'Studying or anything?' Esme clarified.

'No, this is my job.'

'I bet you get to know everyone else who works around here really well, don't you?'

'Quite well.'

'Especially when they come in here a lot… for the tourists, you know.'

'Yes. Sometimes I help tourists to find tour and activity guides and it helps the guides find work.' She smiled. 'Do you want me to help you? I know all the good people.'

'Maybe, when I've decided what I want to do for the rest of the week. I've already been snowmobiling and that was fantastic.'

'Ah. With Niko?'

'Yes,' Esme said, inwardly marvelling at how easy that conversational segue had been. 'He's lovely.'

'He's very good. A lot of fun.'

'And he's… easy on the eye too.'

Inari frowned again.

'Good-looking,' Esme said with a little laugh.

Inari gave a knowing smile. 'Everyone thinks so.'

'I bet he gets a lot of phone numbers from the ladies.'

'Yes.'

'And I'll bet he calls quite a few of them too.'

'I don't think so.'

Esme took a swig of her beer. Though the conversation had been easy to steer in this direction Inari wasn't giving a lot away now that they were here. She supposed that was understandable when she hardly knew Esme, but it was disappointing. She decided to go out on a limb. It might very well backfire in a glorious fashion, but if what Hortense had told her was right, then the gamble might just tell her what she needed to know.

'Although, I suppose a man that good-looking would already have a girlfriend…'

'He's not into girls.'

'Oh,' Esme said.

Inari gave an apologetic shrug. 'Sorry to give you disappointing news.'

'Oh, no, it's OK. It was just idle conversation, you know. So, I expect he has a very handsome boyfriend then.'

'His partner left Rovaniemi in the spring. He has gone to work in Stockholm and I don't think he will ever come back.'

'Oh. Niko doesn't seem too sad, though.'

'Why would he cry in front of tourists?' Inari asked with genuine surprise, as if she couldn't quite believe that Esme could ask such a foolish question. Perhaps it was a foolish question ordinarily, but it wasn't really Niko Esme was trying to find out about.

'I suppose not. Silly of me – it's just that he seemed so cheery and full of fun when we met him – you know? It's hard to imagine how someone can keep sadness that well hidden.'

'He is looking for new love,' Inari said, holding a glass up to the light to inspect. 'In fact, he has gone to a club with someone tonight.'

'On a date?'

Inari put the glass on a shelf. 'I don't know. I think maybe. I can tell Niko likes him.'

'Does he like Niko?'

Inari turned to her with a slight smile. 'It is impossible not to like Niko.'

Esme returned the smile, though it was tinged by a vague disappointment that she couldn't quite understand. 'Yes, I suppose it is.'

Chapter Fourteen

Zach was at breakfast. He drank coffee and didn't eat and held his head a lot.

'Nice hangover?' Esme smiled sweetly as she sipped her own coffee. She'd slept in late and hadn't expected to see anyone else as she caught the last half hour in the dining room before they cleared breakfast away, but he'd shuffled in ten minutes after her looking like an extra from a zombie movie. Her minor annoyance about being abandoned with Hortense and Brian the night before evaporated as he made a beeline for her table with a sheepish – if a little spaced out – grin. Whatever had happened the night before, she couldn't help but feel instantly happier at the sight of him, even though the feeling annoyed her and was mixed with a sense of awkwardness, and left her not quite sure of herself. She was still smarting from what might have been a huge misinterpretation of his intentions and feelings towards her, and although she was hoping that everyone was wrong about Zach and Niko, the more she'd thought about it the night before, the more she'd convinced herself they were all right.

The smile he returned now was rather less bright than hers. 'Card game.'

'Really?'

'With Niko. Shots of something… I don't know what but it explains why everyone who lives here doesn't freeze to death. Anyone with that amount of alcohol in their veins couldn't freeze even if they were on Pluto.'

'So I suppose you're heading straight back to bed after breakfast?'

'I haven't been to bed yet.'

Esme stared at him.

'I mean I've been back here for a few hours but I haven't slept. We raided the minibar in my room. Niko's up there now sleeping it off.'

'He's in your bedroom?'

'Yep.' Zach swallowed a large mouthful of coffee. 'I'm never getting talked into that again.'

'Right. Sounds like a good idea.'

'Where's Romeo and Juliet?'

'They haven't come down yet. I expect they haven't been to sleep yet either. I'm beginning to feel very boring with you lot around.'

Zach's cup rattled in his saucer as he put it down. 'That's one thing you're definitely not. Anyway, I'd take boring over this headache right now.'

Even in his delicate state, he gave her that smile, the one she already loved, and she had to remind herself that now he wasn't just off limits, but not even in her marketplace.

'What are you doing today?' he asked.

'We've got the Northern Lights chase.'

'Not until eight-thirty this evening. We've got a whole day to fill until then.'

'I don't know yet. I suppose you're going to sleep.'

'If I can get Niko out of my bed. He didn't seem very amenable to that earlier on.'

'You could use mine. For an hour if you needed to – I wouldn't mind.'

'But it's your bed. Wouldn't that be…?'

'There are twin beds in my room and I'm only using one.'

'Oh God, I forgot. Your grandma. I'm so sorry, Esme…'

'Don't be daft. All I mean is that it's no imposition at all.'

Zach looked torn. 'What about you?'

'I'll probably go for a walk. I meant to go yesterday before I got press-ganged into the snowmobile thing. At home I walk all the time and I get itchy feet when I can't get out.'

'It'd just be for an hour or so.'

'I know. Go, you look like death so take as long as you need.' She fished in her pocket. 'I have a spare key – you take it and let yourself in. I'll see you later.'

Zach took the key from her and offered a grateful smile in return. 'You're amazing – you know that?'

'It's just a key.' Esme laughed. 'Now go and get some sleep and learn your lesson for next time.'

'Already learned, ma'am,' he said, getting up from the table. 'An hour, tops. I'll set my alarm.'

'As long as you need,' Esme reminded him. 'It honestly makes no difference to me.'

People didn't care about the cold in Rovaniemi. At least, nobody was complaining. Every face wore a smile spread across rosy cheeks and topped with a cherry-red nose, and eyes that peered out from beneath woolly hats with wonder at every corner of Santa's home town. Here, it was easy to believe that Father Christmas was real, and Esme was quite sure that at least ninety-nine per cent of the population that lived here all year believed that too. As for the tourists, young or old they were sold on the idea. You couldn't set foot in Rovaniemi and not be.

Esme decided to do a small circuit of the town. The pavements had been cleared that morning and she hadn't needed the snowshoes that the hotel loaned out. It was Finnish Lapland's capital, but that didn't make it any less quaint, and it was hardly the size of anything more than a market town back in England. The architecture in the main shopping area was a strange mix of low sixties blocks and more traditional wooden housing, while the town-hall square had grand terraced buildings that looked perhaps Victorian – there was even a modern mall with a slick glass tower – but blanketed in fresh snow, everything looked utterly charming regardless. Fairy lights were strung across the streets in a dazzling display and every building was festooned in tinsel and yet more lights. There seemed to be music everywhere too, and a general thrum of excitement that appeared to resonate on every street.

She noticed a huge queue outside a wooden lodge and she heard someone say they were waiting to see Santa. Suddenly she was five again, waiting at the tinselled curtains of the department-store grotto of her childhood, hand enveloped in her dad's, giddy with excitement, and for a moment she almost joined this queue. But she'd look silly, a grown woman waiting to see Santa by herself. Instead, she moved on, relishing the memories of Christmases past.

There were gift shops galore. She'd already bought the few gifts she'd needed to get for family before deciding she was coming here, but they were too cute to walk past. There were shops selling traditional sweets and candies – peppermint sticks, cough sweets, sugared almonds and candied fruit. She spent a while savouring the multicoloured displays, wondering what her mum and dad might like, but in the end decided it wasn't worth trying to get it all home and, besides, she'd already bought enough Christmas chocolates to go with their gifts to sink a schooner, so she bought a bag of chocolate-coated raisins for herself and moved on. They were succulent and moreish, and she quickly lost any sense of guilt she might have had for the calories in them.

There was a little shop full of jewellery and trinkets, and Esme spent some time here looking at bits for various friends and family back home but, again, jewellery was such a personal gift that it was hard to know what people would wear, even when she knew them well. They didn't really have anything that looked typical of the region either, and if she was going to buy something like this for herself then she wanted it to be something that would remind her of Rovaniemi. So, tempting as it was to stay here a while, Esme tore herself away from this store too.

Then the idea struck her that it might be nice to buy something for her new friends. It was Christmas, after all, and they'd all been so kind to her and so welcoming that it would be nice to show her appreciation. After all, this week felt significant somehow, like when she looked back on it she'd see it as a turning point in her life, and the people she was sharing it with would play their part, she was certain. It only needed to be a token gift, and Esme didn't need any more of an excuse to continue shopping.

Half a block away she came across the perfect store. A Christmas-cum-general souvenir store. Some of it was tacky – there was no getting away from that. But some of the goods on display inside were locally produced artisan crafty bits – at least, they were labelled in such a way to convince the tourists. But, as Esme inspected some heavy woollen mittens and thick, hand-knitted socks adorned with geometric designs and drawstrings around the top, they looked rustic enough. They looked useful too, and her eye was drawn to a pair of leather, fur-lined slippers – they looked wacky and ethnic enough that Hortense would probably love them. Until she saw the price and quickly plumped for the socks instead. She was sure Hortense would love these too and they wouldn't bankrupt her.

On a stand next to them were some men's sizes, and Esme wondered if it might be cute to buy Hortense and Brian matching his and hers. Was that a little presumptuous of their relationship status? Did it assume they'd stay together long enough to appreci-ate the suitability of matching his and hers socks? Maybe, but still she thought if anyone would have a sense of humour about it, Brian and Hortense would. She decided they'd have a giggle and picked up the men's pair too.

Which just left Zach. Zach, who was so difficult to read, whom she'd seemed to have gotten so wrong so far. If she'd bought gifts for Hortense and Brian then it was only fair not to leave Zach out, but what would he make of it? What could she buy for a man she barely knew? She wandered round and round the displays, socks clutched to her chest as she studied everything from money boxes featuring Santa to encourage saving for Christmas to paring knives made from deer antler. Nothing seemed right.

'Can I help you?'

Esme looked round to see a lady wearing a leather apron with the name of the shop on the front smiling at her.

'Oh. I'm looking for a gift.'

'Anything in particular?'

'Well, that's just the problem. It's for… well, someone I don't know that well. We're here on holiday together. Not together, actually, but with each other. In the same tour party. And we've only just met but we've become friends. So I wanted to buy something to remind him of our holiday together. With each other, I mean. On the tour…'

Esme took a breath and felt the heat rise to her face. She was rambling and she knew it. But she probably sounded crazy buying a gift for a person she'd just met on holiday. If the woman thought so, however, she didn't show it.

'That's a lovely thought,' she said. 'And everyone knows it's the thought that matters. I'm sure he will be touched by whatever you decide to buy. Do you have a budget? I could perhaps make some suggestions.'

The dreaded question. She'd either sound like a cheapskate or someone who was spending far too much money on a person she didn't know and might never see again. However, she *did* want the perfect gift. For some reason it mattered to her.

'I'm not really sure. I think if I find the right thing then I'll consider the price. I don't want to restrict myself by settling on a price because I might miss something perfect that's out of budget.'

'That's a good idea. I see you already have some of our traditionally made garments. Are they for him too?'

'Oh, they're for some other friends on the tour. I don't think these would be his sort of thing at all.'

The woman nodded. 'Does he like sports? Or games? We have some traditional board games for sale.'

'I don't know. He hasn't really said, but I don't think I'll risk it.'

'What about his dress? Perhaps he wears smart shirts and would like some cufflinks?'

'A bit personal, to be honest. I don't really know if I'd get his taste right.'

The woman nodded.

'You're very patient,' Esme said.

She smiled. 'It's my job to help customers find the right gift. After all, here in the home of Father Christmas it's more important than anywhere.'

'I suppose so,' Esme said with a smile. 'I was thinking maybe something to remind him of his trip here.'

'A souvenir?'

'Yes, but…' Esme's gaze went to a display of garish T-shirts and baseball caps. Would it be rude to point them out as a perfect example of what she *didn't* want?

'You would like to look at the souvenir items there?'

'Actually, no. I don't think they're his sort of thing at all. Maybe if you have something more… subtle. More of a keepsake.'

The woman was thoughtful for a minute. Then she said, 'I have something. Please follow me.'

She led Esme to a shelf behind the counter and took something down, winding it in her hands for a few seconds before placing it in Esme's palm. A broad smile lit Esme's face as the snow globe began to turn, playing a tinkling classical tune that seemed to sound like gentle snowfall. Inside the globe there was a perfect model of Rovaniemi, complete with houses and trees and hills all in silver and glitter swirling in the water, settling on the tiny town.

'You like it?' the woman said.

'It's lovely,' Esme said, gazing at it as the music began to slow. Then it stopped and she handed it back. 'I don't know. Does it seem a bit…?'

'I can show you more things?' the woman said.

Esme nodded. 'If you don't mind.'

So they went to look at more souvenirs, but nothing she saw could erase the enchanting vision of the little snow globe and the music that seemed to capture the very essence of Lapland, and the more she thought about it, the more she didn't care if it was the right thing to buy Zach or not. It probably wasn't, but it somehow felt like the right thing – though she couldn't explain why. But then, what would he make of it? Would he think she was a little crazy buying him a gift when she hardly knew him? Brian and Hortense was one thing, but would a gift for Zach be seen to come with subtext? Would he see it as a romantic come-on?

'I'm sorry but I really can't decide about this. I'll just take the socks for now and I might come back when I'm sure.'

The woman nodded. 'No problem – I will wrap the other things for you now.'

Esme had spent a lot longer than she'd planned shopping, but she was happy with her purchases as she left the souvenir store. Out of habit, however, she looked at her phone. It had crashed again in the sub-zero temperatures outside but she'd felt strangely calm about its uselessness this morning. No phone meant no stress from Warren, no hyperventilating over angry messages, nothing to feel guilty about. She was almost back to her old self, the self she'd found living with her grandma. She put it away again and her attention was caught by the bright window of a bakery, with row upon row of lavishly iced cakes, comforting puddings and delicate pastries, and they looked too good to resist. Despite the big bag of raisins she'd devoured earlier, trudging around the shops on icy pavements had been harder than she could have imagined and she'd worked up a serious appetite. Not to mention that she could take comfort in the nugget of wisdom that Niko had cheerfully imparted to them on the snowmobile safari – he'd said that it was a known scientific fact that the human body burned calories faster in colder climates in an attempt to create more heat. If it was good enough for Niko, then it was good enough for her, even if it had been a little white lie designed to get the kids eating the reindeer sausages. So she went in and bought a cinnamon bun and a traditional gingerbread cookie called a *piparkakku*, and ate both outside on the frozen pavement, one hand gradually going numb without its glove, and she felt a more delicious guilt than she had over the raisins in the amount of calories that had slipped down so easily.

Eventually her nose was dripping and she'd lost the feeling in her lips and her thoughts turned to Zach. Maybe she ought to check he was OK and get warm back at the hotel in the process. After all, he'd looked pretty rough and he'd had *a lot* to drink the night before. And if he was OK, then she could entertain herself by teasing him mercilessly for his folly.

She took a moment to get her bearings and had to ask for directions before she finally headed back. Snow was falling again, drifts growing fat on the pavements as fast as they'd been cleared, hampering her progress.

At the hotel, she fumbled with the key in the lock, weighed down by outdoor clothes and shopping, and the door creaked open. The room was in darkness and she felt her way to the lamp, a small halo of light spreading into the shadowed corners. Zach was still sleeping on the spare bed, his breathing deep and regular and his expression content. He looked as if he'd barely stirred at all and he'd clearly forgotten to set his alarm as he'd said he would. She could wake him, but it felt like a mean thing to do when he was so peacefully asleep. She could save her ribbing for later.

She sat on her own bed and pulled off her boots and coat before stowing her shopping bag beneath it, her eyes never leaving him. He was shirtless and the covers had worked their way down. His perfectly sculpted chest had always been buried under layers of thick sweaters and brushed cotton shirts, and she'd never really appreciated just how pleasing it was. There was a scar at his shoulder, faintly visible, a neat straight line and a series of tiny dots. Some sort of surgery, perhaps? Esme reached out to touch it but then yanked her hand back, nursing it as if she'd burnt it, her face flushed.

The hotel kept the heating running at a high temperature and it meant that whenever she stepped inside her outdoor clothes were immediately too big and clumsy. Already she felt sticky. Maybe she'd kill a bit of time by quietly freshening up so he could rest a while longer.

Pulling a clean top from the wardrobe, she unravelled her scarf and flung it onto her bed, followed by her jumper and thermal vest. In her bra, she crept into the bathroom and splashed some cool water over her face and neck before burying herself in the soft hotel towel.

As she lifted her face from it, the bathroom door opened and a bleary-eyed Zach stumbled in. But his eyes widened instantly as he saw her standing there.

'Oh God, I'm so sorry! I didn't realise you were back!'

Esme blushed, pulling the towel around her bra. She gave a nervous laugh as Zach turned and rushed out.

'It's OK!' she called. When he didn't come back she went through to the bedroom. 'You need the bathroom?'

'I was… I'll go in my own room.'

'Don't be silly – that's on the next floor! Use mine.'

'But you're…'

'I was just getting changed but I can do it while you're in the bathroom.'

Zach looked as if he might argue but then he nodded. 'I'm so sorry,' he said again as he passed her.

Esme smiled as he closed the door behind him. She heard the tap running and the sounds of splashing water and guessed he'd been getting a little overheated too. There was something quite liberating about standing in front of a man half naked and not having him size you up. If he was embarrassed about the situation, that was sweet, but it wasn't necessary for him to feel awkward when there was no sexual temptation. She wondered how best to relay that to him without making things even more awkward but eventually decided that the best course of action might be to let things blow over in their own time and not mention the incident again.

'Are you decent now?' he called.

'Perfectly,' she said, tugging her top down.

He emerged from the bathroom with a towel draped around his neck, his hair dripping.

'I think we might be on our own a lot now that Brian and Hortense are an item.' He rubbed at the nape of his neck with the towel. 'In fact, I think in the circumstances, that might be less painful for us two.'

'It is a bit awkward to be around them,' Esme agreed. 'Last night at the table it was like the outtakes from *9½ Weeks*.'

Zach chuckled. 'I can imagine. Listen, I'm sorry I dropped you in it. I only said yes to Niko because I thought you weren't coming to dinner.'

Esme held up a hand. 'It's OK, I understand.'

'Right. So you're not mad at me?'

'Why would I be mad? Seriously, it's OK. Just warn me next time so I can make other plans too.'

'There won't be a next time.' Zach sat on the end of the bed. 'I can't keep up with Niko.'

Esme shook her head. Being OK with Zach and Niko was one thing but she didn't need gory details – she'd had enough of those sitting with Hortense and Brian.

'It might sound silly,' she said, changing the subject, 'but I had this hankering to go and see Santa. That's silly, right?'

Zach's smile faded and his expression was ghosted with pain. It was fleeting, and Esme wondered if she'd even seen it at all.

'That's not one bit silly,' he said, his voice low. 'Don't ever think that.'

'But I'm a grown woman.'

'Doesn't matter. You were once a little girl. You want to see Santa, see Santa. Life's too short to care what other people think about it.'

Esme took a steadying breath. 'Would you come? I understand if you think it's too silly for you but—'

'Of course I will.' His smile was strained and not like the one she'd come to know so well already. 'Give me half an hour and I'll meet you in reception. You want to see Santa then that's what we'll do.'

The snow had lightened again but it didn't look as if it would be stopping any time soon. As they stood outside the building where the queues for Santa had been earlier Zach leaned in and lowered his voice.

'This is not the real deal you know.'

Esme looked up at him, stamping her feet to get some feeling back in them. 'It's not?'

'The real Santa is out on Highway Four. We could get a bus.'

She looked back at the building. 'So who's this guy?'

'Some chancer – there's hundreds of them all over the world at this time of the year, don't you know? Even here.'

Esme grinned. 'And there was me thinking he just had a really fast bike.'

'You want the real Santa,' Zach continued, 'you have to go to Santa Claus village.'

'Do you have to book ahead?' she asked doubtfully.

'Santa's never too busy to see anyone no matter when they drop by.' He started to lead the way to a nearby bus stop. 'Come on.'

Esme trotted after him. 'How do you know so much?'

'I've been before.'

'You never said.'

'I didn't think it mattered.'

'Well, no. But I would have asked you loads about it if I'd known.'

'Like what?'

'I don't know. Is that the time you learned to drive a snow-mobile too?'

'Yes. Last time we…'

'What?'

'Doesn't matter.'

'Did you go sledding too?'

'Went out with huskies.'

'Is that fun?'

'Yeah, you want to try it out?'

'Would it involve Niko again?'

Zach laughed. 'Does he scare you?'

'He's a bit… full on.'

'Tell me about it. My head's still pounding.'

'So we're getting the bus now?'

He arched an eyebrow. 'Is there somewhere else you need to be?'

'No.' Esme laughed. 'Will it take long?'

'Don't worry, we'll be back in plenty of time for the Northern Lights chase.'

'OK then.'

Zach led them to the bus stop with ease and they joined a queue of mostly families with small children speaking lots of different languages, and the noon began to swiftly turn to night. It was almost impossible to imagine how it could be any colder, but as they waited for the bus to arrive Esme felt the temperature drop by degrees. She began to shiver.

'You're cold?' Zach asked.

'I'll be OK when the bus arrives.'

'It's got colder for sure.' He took both her arms and rubbed his hands vigorously up and down them. 'Better?'

'A little.'

He frowned. 'No, it's not – you're still shivering.'

'A little.'

'Do you stop talking when you're cold?'

'My tongue's seized up.'

'I can't have you silent the whole trip – I'll be bored to death. Not to mention it'll be a serious disability when you try to tell Santa your Christmas wishes.' He looked at her with mock solemnity. 'You do *have* a Christmas wish, don't you?'

'I thought you just asked for presents.'

'Doesn't it amount to the same thing? It just so happens that most kids want toys so that's what they wish for. But we can wish for anything.'

'Sounds a bit suspect to me. Is this *actually* true?'

'Of course!'

'It sounds silly to me. I think you've just made it up.'

'On my honour.'

'OK, so what do you wish for?'

In a moment his expression had changed and his voice was flat. 'Some things are too big, even for Santa.'

Esme would have teased and cajoled him into a proper reply but the slump of his shoulders told her not to.

'I'd ask for a faster metabolism,' she said, trying to rescue the moment.

He raised his eyebrows. 'That's not what I was expecting. Why?'

'Isn't it obvious? So I could keep the weight off.'

'You've got no weight on you!'

'It's hidden under all these jumpers.'

'Don't forget I've seen you without the jumpers,' he said. And although Esme blushed she was pleased to see him laughing again. She didn't even know why she was blushing because it didn't matter if Zach saw her in her bra.

'That could have been very awkward,' she said.

'You don't need to worry about your weight,' he said. 'Even if you were twice the size you are now you'd still look lovely.'

'That's not what Warren says.'

Zach's eyebrows went skyward again. 'Ah, so this is the mysterious boyfriend you've been careful not to mention.'

'How did you…?'

'It was obvious really.'

It was strange, but Esme felt stupid now for keeping Warren a secret from Zach. After all, there was no reason why she needed to.

'Have you been together long?'

'Sort of. Three years, a gap, and we've just got back together again.'

'So you split for a while?'

'Yeah.'

'How come?'

Esme frowned.

'Sorry – none of my business,' he said quickly. 'Forget I asked.'

'It's OK – I just don't want to rake all that up again. You understand?'

'Of course. My mistake. So you're happy now that you've made it up?'

'Yes.'

'Good,' Zach said, though he didn't sound convinced.

'Well, when I say happy… I suppose we're still trying to get past all that. It's hard to go back to how it was before the split.'

'Is he good to you?'

There was a pause. 'Yes,' she said finally. Was Warren good to her? She was constantly defending him but she was beginning to wonder why.

'If he's telling you you're fat,' Zach continued, 'then he's an idiot. Sorry, but there it is.'

'It's not like that… he's thinking of me… you know, my health and all that.'

'So I suppose this guy is some sort of Adonis?'

Esme shrugged. 'Honestly, he kind of is.'

'Well then, that makes everything he says gospel, doesn't it? Beautiful people get to tell other people how to look just because they're beautiful. It's written into the constitution.'

'Do I detect some sarcasm there?'

'I'm just saying he's wrong. And even if he wasn't he has no right to tell you how to look.'

'Easy for you to say – you're pretty good-looking too.'

Zach blinked.

Esme laughed. 'It can't have escaped your attention.'

A sudden gust of wind rushed them, picking up a cloud of powdery snow and dumping it over them. Esme gave another shudder.

'Seriously, your lips are blue,' Zach said.

'I'm OK.'

'Here… I know it's probably inappropriate but…' He held his arms open. Esme hesitated. 'Come on,' he said. 'It's just a medical emergency hug.'

'There's such a thing?' Esme asked as she stepped into it. He pulled her close.

'Judge for yourself. Don't you feel better already?'

Esme closed her eyes. It *was* better. She was warmer and she felt… she felt safe. Safe and calm and content. It had been a long time since she'd had a hug like this. Warren never hugged – he just wasn't that sort of a man. He pawed and kissed and clung on when they made love but he didn't hug, and he especially didn't hug when there was no chance of sex at the end of it. Zach was a good hugger. And he smelt good too – like cedar wood and fresh soap and clean air.

'I have to admit, that *is* better,' she said into his chest. God, his chest was comfy. Broad and lean and yet soft in all the right places. Even through all those layers of clothing she could hear his steady heartbeat, like an emotional metronome. If it's true about Zach and Niko, then lucky Niko, she thought, closing her eyes again.

They lapsed into silence while Esme breathed and emptied her mind and thought only vaguely of how good and right she felt in Zach's embrace. Suddenly nothing else mattered – not Warren or her grandma's house or not having a job. This was a place she could stay forever.

Zach's voice broke the spell. 'Have you fallen asleep in there?'

'Not quite,' she murmured.

'Only, if there's sleeping to be done, I think it ought to be me. I'm the one with the hangover, after all.'

Esme lifted her head to look at him. 'You get no sympathy because it's self-inflicted. This is different – it's not my fault I'm susceptible to the cold.'

'If you had more meat on your bones you wouldn't get cold.'

'Now you sound just like my grandma.'

'Sorry. I didn't mean to bring back painful memories.'

'It's OK. I miss her but I do like to think of her. It doesn't bother me to be reminded.'

He gave a short nod, seemingly satisfied that he hadn't caused her any great distress.

'So, tell me, now that the great secret has been revealed, why isn't the boyfriend here keeping you warm? Warren, is it?'

Esme's contentment evaporated at the sound of his name. Being able to mention him to Zach was one thing, but she didn't want to talk about him at any length, and especially when it would mean discussing all the ways he'd tried to stop her from coming on her grandma's trip.

'He was too busy to come.'

'Too busy to help his grieving girlfriend get over the loss of a grandmother who was supposed to be taking this trip with her? He was happy to let you come alone? I take it you asked him to come?'

'We were on our break when Grandma booked it.'

'That doesn't excuse anything.'

'He… my family… they don't see eye to eye. He felt like it was a trip that had been booked to reward me for breaking up with him. So I suppose it kind of irked him. I can understand why.'

'But you think it's OK that he left you to come alone, knowing what you'd been through? It doesn't matter why the trip was booked, you needed his support. I'm right? You wanted him to come?'

'No… I don't know. Maybe…' Esme let out a long breath. 'God, I can't believe I'm telling a total stranger all this.'

'I hope we're not strangers now. I've slept in your room, seen you in your bra and you're currently leeching all my body heat from me.'

'You offered yourself as a willing sacrifice.'

He gave a warm chuckle. 'Did you call him back?'

'Warren?'

'I take it he was the one texting you like mad.'

'No. I mean, yes, it was him, but no, I didn't call.'

'You don't want to?'

'I don't know how to.'

'It's not that hard. You pick up the phone and—'

'You know what I mean.' Esme gave his arm a playful slap.

'Ow. Leeching my body heat and now assaulting me. What next?'

'Shut up, baby.'

'It hurt!'

Esme smiled. 'So I take it you're single at the moment.'

'I thought we were talking about you.'

'I changed the rules.'

He was silent. Esme stepped out from his arms to see him squinting into the blinding distance.

'I think our bus is here,' he said.

Chapter Fifteen

The bus was packed and they'd been forced to stand. Esme loved the way Zach reached to steady her with every jolt and slide with a gentle hand to her back or arm, and she had to keep reminding herself that there was nothing romantic in it, especially in light of what Inari had told her. But the bare honesty of earlier had turned to banter again. Zach's box was still sealed tight shut, even if Esme had allowed him to peek into hers. Her own openness had shocked her more than anything – how comfortable and easy she suddenly felt with him now that the angst of repressed sexual tension could be put to one side. At least, the sexual tension she'd clearly imagined because she'd got that situation a whole heap wrong and then some.

Darkness fell quickly, like a cloak thrown over the town as they travelled. It was so hard to get used to the idea that the sun set almost as soon as it had risen here. It should have been a depressing thought, but it wasn't – it just made everything about this place even more magical.

Zach nudged her. 'We've just crossed into the Arctic Circle.'

'Seriously?'

'You're at the North Pole. How does that feel?'

'Weird. Unbelievable. Weird, unbelievable and cold.'

Zach laughed. 'We'll save that review for TripAdvisor.'

Esme smiled. She liked that Zach found her silly, mixed up thoughts funny instead of annoying.

'I feel as if there ought to be some ceremony,' she said.

'For what?'

'Crossing into the Arctic Circle. Like a special certificate or something.'

'I think you can buy those.'

Esme blinked.

'Honestly,' he said, laughing. 'I'm not joking. I think you can get them at Santa's village. We'll look for one if you like, so you can show the folks back home.'

'I don't think it would get them all that excited.'

'No? I guess not all of them. Your boyfriend sounds like a real laugh a minute for a start,' he said, and his smile had gone now.

'I didn't mean just Warren,' she said.

'Sorry, it's just…' He shook his head. 'Ignore me – none of my business.'

'You don't need to apologise. He can be grumpy but it's not his fault. He's got a lot on his plate. Money troubles and everything.'

What she neglected to mention was the reason why Warren had money troubles. But if Zach didn't think much of him now, the revelation that he'd been funding a double life, sharing a flat with both her and his wife Shelly in two separate locations would certainly not help Zach to change his mind. Not that it mattered what Zach thought of Warren, of course. Though, now that she thought about how it might sound if she said it out loud, she could see why Zach might not have approved. It *did* sound pretty bad. And, if she was honest, his opinion mattered. Not about Warren, but about Esme putting up with it. About how she'd forgiven the unforgivable even though everyone had told her she was crazy. It mattered what Zach thought about that, more than she cared to admit, even though she didn't know why.

'Looks like we're here,' he said.

Esme looked through the window to see a large complex of buildings buried in a thick blanket of snow and festooned with bright lights. There was a ripple of excitement along the whole bus as everyone else saw it too. Her morose thoughts gave way to a sudden sense of childlike wonder and anticipation.

'Oh, it's so cute!'

'Isn't it?' Zach grinned, evidently gripped by the same giddiness too. 'Wait till you get inside – it's like every Christmas film you've ever seen times a thousand.'

The bus came to a halt and emptied and they were swept along with the throng to the gates of Santa's village. Instinctively, she reached out her hand and, without looking, Zach caught it and held tight. It was funny how much braver he made her feel whenever he was there.

At the gates, Esme pulled back.

He turned to her. 'What?'

'I don't want to go in,' she said.

'Seriously?'

'I do, but I don't want to go in yet. Once we're in, all the anticipation is over and that's the most exciting part.' She gazed up at the gates, trying to drink in every detail, trying to capture the moment so time would never dull the memory. 'I want to save this in my brain. I don't ever want to forget it. And I want to remember my grandma because I wouldn't be here if it weren't for her.'

When she looked back at him, his smile had faded. He was staring up at the gates too, but there was no happiness in his eyes, no excitement now, only pain.

'I'm sorry,' she said hastily. 'I suppose I'm being morbid.'

He shook his head. 'No, you're not. It's just…'

He looked down and suddenly seemed to realise he had his hand wrapped around Esme's. He let it go, and, somehow, in that instant, Esme felt the temperature around her drop.

'Are you OK?' she asked. 'If you want to go back to the hotel…'

He smiled, but it seemed as if he'd forced it just for her. 'I'm still feeling a bit ropey from all the drinking last night. You want to see Santa and I promised – I'll be fine once we're in there.'

'You're sure?'

'Positive. After what you've just told me do you really think I'm going to make you turn around and go back to the hotel?' He began to walk. After a few paces he turned to her again, a shadow backlit by the lights of the village. 'Are you ready now?' he asked, his voice unexpectedly cheery once more, as if the moment had never happened.

Esme nodded. She didn't know what to think but he seemed OK after all; perhaps she'd imagined his distress. 'Ready,' she said.

'Right then – let's go.'

The Christmas village really was a village. There was everything from gift shops to cafés, from the post office that sorted the mail sent to Santa from all over the world and from where you could send postcards back home, to the distribution depot that could dispatch gifts on your behalf to loved ones, right down to a workshop where Santa and his helpers were based. All of this was like no village Esme had ever seen, where it was hyper bright and colourful, cheerful and noisy and happy. There were probably a thousand, rather less happy scenarios behind the scenes – it was easy to forget in all the spectacle that the people smiling and nodding in Santa's service were real people with real lives away from here, with all the pain and hardship that real lives sometimes suffered by. But every street corner featured a choir or a show, lights and tinsel, cheery music blasting through loud speakers. Merry Christmases were wished a hundred times a minute, and Esme wondered how people's faces didn't crack from smiling so hard.

They'd just finished what had to be the best hot chocolate Esme had ever tasted when Zach leaned back and studied her.

'I suppose we ought to go find the main event.'

'Santa?'

'Well, he is the reason we came, isn't he?'

'And you're sure you don't mind? You don't think it's silly?'

'Of course it's silly. That's part of the fun though. Whoever went to see Santa thinking it would be like taking a course in accountancy?'

Esme had to laugh. 'You might have a point there. It's just…'

'We don't have kids with us? I don't know why you're getting so hung up on what other people think. So we don't have kids with us – we've as much right to see Santa as anyone else. We've come all this way for a reason.'

'To see the Northern Lights,' Esme reminded him.

'Well, yes. But this is a pretty good perk on the side, right?'

'I guess.'

'Then stop second-guessing all the time and learn to live for the moment. You won't see any of these people again after this week so who cares what they think?'

Esme smiled. He had a way of arguing things that made it difficult to argue back. Where had Zach been all her life when she'd needed a friend like this? Why couldn't she have found him years ago?

He held out a hand and she took it, and it was as natural as breathing.

'Come on,' he said, pointing to an elaborate signpost. 'It's this way.'

Esme followed where he led, and even though there were signposts at every corner she still couldn't help wondering how he found the way so easily. Then she recalled he'd been before, and then she fell to wondering who he'd been there with. He'd never told her, and because he'd never told her she was too scared to ask. Maybe not so much scared of his reaction but scared of reminding him, of turning his thoughts to something that might upset him. She liked Zach happy, and that was the way she wanted to keep him, especially now in this most happiest of places on earth. Maybe she'd ask him eventually and maybe he'd tell her, just not now.

'I feel like I'm waiting to see a rock star or something,' Esme whispered as they stood in the antechamber of Santa's office. It wasn't a grotto, like it was in department stores and shopping malls back home; it was known as Santa's office, as if he ran the whole concern like a little business and Santa was the CEO. There was even a bank of desks, with elves busily working like secretaries, only they were filing Christmas lists into good children and not so good children, though Esme noticed that there was nothing in the basket for naughty children at all. Maybe this Santa was a fair and tolerant Santa who strived for rehabilitation with kindness rather than punishment and believed in the inherent goodness of all children. Or maybe Esme was just a nut for even looking into it that deeply. The idea of this made her giggle to herself, and Zach turned to her with a raised eyebrow.

'What?' he asked.

'Nothing.' Esme smiled up at him. 'It's just… all this. It's funny.'

'Good. That's the general idea.'

'I'm glad we came.'

'Me too.'

He said it, but Esme wondered whether it was entirely true. His smile held that shadow of sadness again, the one she caught every so often.

He leaned in and lowered his voice to an amused whisper. 'Are you going to ask for his autograph?'

'Hey, don't laugh – I might!'

'I bet it wouldn't be the first time he's been asked.'

'I'm going to get a selfie too.'

At this Zach leaned back and scanned the room. There were a handful of other people waiting in there with them, but the real queue stretched down the corridor beyond the office. 'I think they make you buy an official photo with him.'

'Oh, OK. Then you're going to be on it too?'

'Me? Why do you want me on it?'

'So I can remember how much fun we've had here together.'

'I'm sure your boyfriend will love that.'

'Well,' Esme said, feeling suddenly belligerent about it, 'he doesn't need to look if he doesn't like it.' Why did Zach have to keep bringing Warren up?

'Remind me not to let you have my home address, just in case he feels the need to come after me.'

'You'd have to go into witness protection if he thought you were a threat. Luckily, you don't need to worry about that.'

'He wouldn't think I'm a threat? I don't know how to feel about that.'

'I'd feel relieved if I were you.'

'You know,' Zach said, a wry smile about his lips, 'you're painting this guy to be a real charmer. So he likes to beat people up in his spare time? I like him more and more the more you tell me.'

Esme laughed. She'd never thought of how ridiculous Warren's jealous rages were before but now Zach had put it like that, they *were* ridiculous. Childish and petty and completely unnecessary. Perhaps there was an upside to Zach bringing him up in conversation. Perhaps an outsider's view of things could make Esme see her relationship with Warren in a whole new way. She had to admit that it might not be a bad thing.

'I think he's insecure,' she said, still defending him even though she knew it was a lame defence and even despite what she'd just thought.

'I thought you said he was an Adonis.'

'He is. But I suppose you can still get insecure, even if you're good-looking.'

'If you say so.'

'That's unfair. Even you must be able to see that.'

'What do you mean – even me?'

'Well, I don't suppose you've ever felt insecure about yourself.'

'How would you know?'

'I don't. I'm just guessing. On account of the fact that you're quite handsome. If you like that sort of thing,' she added quickly, blushing, even though she didn't know why.

'Wow, that is some compliment. Still, as you said, anyone can feel insecure for any number of reasons that are not always apparent to onlookers. You're exhibit A.'

Esme prodded her own chest. 'Me?'

'Well, you're not exactly Lurch's ugly sister and yet I've never seen you at ease with the way you look. Or anything else about yourself for that matter. In fact, I find it frustrating that you don't like yourself a little more.'

Esme's mouth fell open. Was this a compliment, an insult or merely a life hack? What was he trying to say? More to the point, what gave him the right to say it?

'Don't look so shocked,' he said with a wry smile. 'I'm only saying that if you could see yourself how we all see you, you'd love what you saw. That's all.'

'I think that's a compliment, then?' she asked uncertainly.

'Of course it is. Please take it as just that. I'm not expecting it to change anything for you overnight, but perhaps, from time to time, you might remember it and when you feel like being down on yourself, you might be a little kinder.'

'Well, what sort of things do you mean? Give me specifics.'

'I can't, because that would make you focus on them and probably in a negative way.'

'You can't leave it like that! I need to know. How am I supposed to change if I don't know what you want changing?'

He let out a sigh. 'There you go – wanting to change to order. That's exactly what I'm talking about. How about just being you, regardless of what you think anyone else might want. You'll probably find that just you, exactly the way you are, is what they *do* want. Be you, warts and all. If they don't like the warts, then ditch the people and not the warts. Find someone who does like the warts.'

'Everybody has something about them that irritates somebody else.'

'Precisely. So why bother trying to be all things to everyone? Why not just be you and roll with the punches? If they like you, great, if they don't, let them go and find someone who suits them better.'

Esme was silent for a moment. 'So,' she said finally, 'is this about Warren in particular?'

'It's about whatever or whoever you think it's about. I think you already know all this – you just don't want to see it.'

She fell to brooding again. Sometimes Zach could be funny, sometimes inexplicably morose and sometimes just plain annoying. But perhaps the annoying bit was only because, in her heart, she knew the truth of what he was saying but she wasn't ready to admit it yet.

'Anyway,' he said. 'Maybe this is not the time to discuss it.'

The need for a reply was saved by a cheery elf wearing long, blonde plaits who waved their group through. Esme had wanted to know more, and for a moment had almost wished they'd been sitting somewhere quiet and private in a little corner of the hotel bar. But now, the need was replaced by a sudden kick of excitement as they were ushered into Santa's room and she was finally face-to-face with him.

'Oh my God, he looks exactly like Santa!' she squeaked, unable to contain herself.

Zach grinned and replied in a low voice behind his hand. 'He *is* Santa, that's why.'

Esme elbowed him in the ribs. 'Yeah, of course.'

'Don't you believe me?'

'Yes.'

'No you don't.'

'No, but I'm happy to play along.'

His grin spread. 'Now that's what I'm talking about!'

Esme wasn't sure what time Santa's village closed – if it ever closed at all. But there seemed to be a steady flow of people coming away from it now, heading for the same bus stop as them. Zach was quiet as they waited for the bus back to the town centre. His mood had become steadily more subdued throughout the visit, and it worried and annoyed Esme in equal measure. She'd tried to ignore it, but she couldn't. It had begun just as they'd started to talk to Santa, where she'd seen it visibly dip, and had become more and more noticeable as they'd progressed through the village. If only she could get to the root of things, find out what it was that set the melancholy off, maybe she could find a way to nip it in the bud before it took hold. She was quickly understanding that an unhappy Zach meant an unhappy Esme, his mood affecting her in ways she couldn't understand herself.

'I thought getting to see Santa Claus was supposed to be an uplifting and happy experience,' she said.

'It is.'

'You don't look happy.'

'I am.'

She looked up at him. He certainly didn't look like someone who was happy, or even just happy inside. Her gaze went to the warm glow of the buildings they'd left behind. She wasn't getting any further with her current conversation, that much was obvious. 'It's cold again, isn't it?'

'We're at the North Pole.'

'I know, but it's colder now the sun has gone down.'

'I'm not sure the sun was warming much when it was up.'

'I could do with one of your magic hugs.'

On autopilot, he pulled her into his arms but it wasn't the same as before. He didn't mean it, and she didn't feel safe and content, she only felt tricked and confused and wondered where the Zach she liked had gone. She stared out from the folds of his perfunctory embrace, watching families stream out from the gates of the village with excited kids, and couples of all ages giggling, arms locked and kisses stolen as they relived their youth.

'You came here before with someone you loved, didn't you?' she said. 'Someone who meant a lot to you?'

She'd asked the question but somehow, though it had only just occurred to her, she already knew the answer. She waited.

'I wonder what's on the menu for dinner tonight?' he said. 'I don't know about you but I'm getting hungry. I hope they're serving early enough for us to get something before we catch our Northern Lights bus.'

Esme gave a noncommittal reply. Her mind was far from the dinner menu. Zach had been here before and being here again had made him sad. Why come then? Why offer to bring her? He must have known it would make him sad. But when they'd arrived he'd been full of good humour, even lecturing her on letting go and living a little. Whatever it was that could turn his mood on a dime, he wasn't letting that go, and Esme wondered if it was stopping him from truly living.

She turned her eyes to the road and willed the bus to arrive. Whatever had made him sad made her sad too, and she wanted to be away from it so they could get proper Zach again, the one whose smile rivalled Santa's city of lights and made everyone laugh and gave hugs to melt the iciest of hearts.

At 8 p.m. Esme was standing in the car park of their hotel. It was dark, the lights of the vast dining room windows throwing a warm glow across compacted snow and illuminating breath that rose on the icy air. It was bitterly cold, and Esme was almost tempted to head back inside to sit by the fire and drink warm cocoa. She gave herself a mental slap and asked herself what else she'd expected at what was a stone's throw from the North Pole.

They'd returned from Santa's village a couple of hours previously with a muted farewell. Zach had tried to be cheerful, and Esme had tried to be grateful for the day out, but things were somewhat more subdued than they had been when they'd started out that afternoon. Esme had skipped dinner and eaten an apple in her room after Zach had seen her to the door and then gone to find out what sort of state Niko had left his own room in. He hadn't yet arrived back in the car park as they'd arranged, and given the mood she'd left him in, Esme wondered if he was even coming at all. She'd understood that it hadn't been about her or directed at her, but somehow she still felt partially responsible. He'd been happy, and then she'd brought up his past when she'd vowed not to and ruined all that. She could be such an idiot.

Hortense and Brian were already there waiting for the tour bus.

'Isn't young Zachary with you?' Hortense asked, extricating herself from Brian's arms as she realised Esme was there. Brian looked suitably embarrassed as he straightened the shock of white hair peeking from beneath his hat, although, in truth, there was nothing on earth that could straighten that mop. More than once Esme had considered the fact that if someone stuck a convincing enough beard on Brian, he might make a pretty good double for Santa if the man himself fancied a day off. 'As neither of you came down to dinner I'd assumed you'd spent the time together.'

'Well, we had… I mean, not all of it. We went to Santa Claus Village but we didn't stay together. He didn't come down to dinner either?'

'No. I thought perhaps you'd both decided to eat elsewhere.'

'No.'

'But he is supposed to be coming with us tonight?' Brian asked.

Esme nodded. 'Yes. I mean, that was the plan. But he went back to his room to see whether Niko was still there and I haven't seen him since so maybe he's changed his mind.'

'What on earth would make him do that?' Hortense asked. 'He'd been absolutely set on seeing the Lights.'

'That's what he'd said to me,' Brian agreed. 'This was the number one activity on his list.'

Esme shrugged. She wondered whether to mention to them that Zach's mood seemed a little... unstable. They might know something about it. But then, if they hadn't noticed then perhaps it said more about her than it did about Zach. What if it was all in her head? What if she was just being paranoid and there was really nothing wrong at all apart from what she imagined? He'd already told her that she spent too long worrying about what other people thought of her. Perhaps she was doing just that – being hypersensitive to an issue that really wasn't there. He could have been tired or still hung-over – a delayed reaction to his raucous night out – and she'd simply read too much into it. Quickly, she decided that she wouldn't mention it and wait to see whether Brian or Hortense said anything first.

Brian jammed his woolly hat back on and scanned the crowd waiting to do the Northern Lights trip with them. 'If he doesn't get a move on he's going to miss it whether he wants to or not. Does anyone have his phone number?'

'Don't look at me,' Hortense scoffed. 'I wouldn't have one of the blasted things if you paid me. I'm available as and when I decide, and I rather like it that way.'

'I don't have it either. I suppose one of us ought to swap numbers with him at some point so we can avoid this happening again.' Esme glanced at the tour guide, who had started checking people onto the bus. 'Do you think we can get them to wait for him?' she asked, her gaze still trained on the young man.

'I don't think they'd hold things up for too long,' Brian said doubtfully. 'Schedule to keep to and all that. It might take a while to find the right bit of sky too so they'll want to get away on time.'

Esme turned back to them. 'I'll go and see if he's in his room. It won't take me a minute.'

She didn't get far. Zach emerged before she'd crossed half of the car park and Niko was with him. It looked as if they'd spent the hours he'd been back from Santa's village together. She was beset by a sudden pang of jealousy.

'I'll miss your company tonight,' Esme heard Niko say as he clapped him on the back. 'But I understand – the Lights are calling and you do not want to miss them.'

Zach fixed him a look full of gratitude. 'I appreciate it.'

'Any time, man. You come and look for me.'

Esme began to back away. She didn't know what this conversation was but she had a feeling it wasn't for her ears. Had Niko waited for Zach in his room all the time she and Zach had been out? Or had he been hanging around at the hotel anyway? Maybe it was simply a coincidence that they'd run into each other again. But it didn't seem that way. What was the deal with those two? She tried to work out the body language but somehow the signals were all mixed up.

Niko gave a brisk nod. 'Take care, man.'

'I will. And thanks again.'

Niko turned to leave, but then he caught sight of Esme and gave her one of his megawatt smiles. Sort of like one of Zach's smiles, except that where Zach's was like the sun, Niko's was more of an electric light bulb – less natural and seeming as though it had required a lot more effort to produce. This was the version of Niko reserved for the tourists – flirting and pretending to be everyone's best friend. What Esme had just seen with Zach – she had no doubt that was the real Niko.

'Hey – going to the Lights chase?' he asked.

Esme nodded. 'That's if the clouds move – they look pretty thick tonight.'

'Your driver knows the best places. If there are Lights tonight he'll find them.'

He threw her a wink and then sauntered off, hands buried in the pockets of his thick downy jacket. Esme turned to see Zach watch him go before giving her his full attention.

'I didn't know if you were coming,' she said.

'That makes two of us.' For a moment it looked as if melancholic Zach had returned. But then he smiled and that Zach was banished again. 'But I wouldn't miss it for the world. It's really the reason we're all here in Lapland, isn't it?'

'That's what I just said,' Brian cut in cheerily.

Esme wasn't sure that was true for any of them – not really. There were many personal reasons for each traveller – she was beginning to see that now – and she felt a lot of them had very little to do with the Northern Lights when you really got down to it. Certainly her own reasons were more complicated than that. 'I thought Niko had tempted you away again, that's all.'

'God no, he's too wild for me. Finished me off last night – I still feel like my blood is fifty per cent alcohol.'

Brian's voice came from behind them. 'Come on, mate, you'll cause a riot if you hold the bus up any longer. We've got an aurora borealis to chase!'

Zach threw him a grin. 'OK, OK, I'm getting on the bus now!'

*

Their guide followed weather reports from all over the neighbouring territories, and while the driver followed the satellite navigation system across the snowy terrain, the guide recalibrated from time to time to give them the best chance of a gap in the clouds. They drove for miles searching, but despite the weather remaining largely dry and the best efforts of the tour team, everyone was left disappointed. The fickle Northern Lights weren't showing their colours to anyone tonight. They'd been told it was something to do with solar activity (or a lack of it) and so even though the weather hadn't been a total loss, the solar activity that made the Lights dance had. It was often like this, their guide said, and anything worth having was worth a patient wait.

So, sometime in the early hours of the morning they conceded defeat. There was a collective groan from the passengers, a disappointment so huge and palpable it almost buckled the walls of the bus, only tempered by the fact that everyone was tired now and ready for a warm bed, and their guide had promised that they'd try again the following night. The weather forecast wasn't perfect but he was hopeful that luck would be on their side.

Esme's head rested on Zach's shoulder as the bus bumped and jolted them back to the hotel, and in a half-slumber she almost fancied she could disappear into his arms and curl herself around him like a cat to sleep. She liked the idea that he'd keep her safe and warm for as long as she slept. When she dreamed those vague half-dreams of someone only dozing, she dreamed his face, the face of a friend she could rely on, someone she hoped she could keep in her life forever. She dreamed of days in the future where they'd be sharing a meal or a lazy coffee or a walk in the hills, of days where he'd meet her at some train station and smile his wonderful smile and her heart would leap at the sight of it. They'd share jokes and laugh, and sometimes they'd share woes and comfort each other, and he might even share the thing that made him sad, and she'd be able to help him so she would never have to see that sadness again.

She snapped awake at the sound of her phone and the dream popped like a soap bubble.

'Are you going to answer that?' Zach asked.

Esme nodded as she fumbled in her pocket. She looked at the screen and turned it off with a groan.

'The boyfriend?'

She nodded again.

'Heck of a time to be calling. He really does want to talk to you. You ought to put him out of his misery.'

'He probably just got back from the pub,' was all she could offer as an explanation.

Zach's glance went to the large digital clock at the front of the bus. 'At this hour?'

'Lock-in. His local. They do it from time to time.'

'Still, he could have safely assumed you'd be in bed asleep, even if *he* wasn't.'

Esme thought back to all the times Warren had returned from a late night/early morning at his local and woke her for a cheese toastie or to clean up his sick or simply because the beer had made him horny. Sometimes she wouldn't see him till late morning or even early afternoon, but she'd been up anyway, worrying to death about where he might be, trying his phone over and over. He'd get home and tell her he couldn't remember where he'd been because he'd been so drunk, or that he'd crashed at a friend's house, or he'd had to walk home because he'd run out of money for a cab. After she'd discovered Shelly's existence, that fateful night when Shelly's friend had seen her and Warren out on the town together and had set the events in motion that would see Esme running back to the hills of Derbyshire, she'd wondered if he'd really chosen to go back to Shelly's place all those times instead. Perhaps she'd done the cheese toastie or cleaned up his sick or cured his horniness. She had to suppose that had been the case, although she had to admit that his new promises to her when she'd returned had meant that his visits to Shelly would have become a thing of the past. Wouldn't it? Not for the first time she thought about the phone number she had for Shelly and she wondered how weird it would be to call her and ask her what had really been going on. Had Warren ever been straight with her about any of it? What was he telling Shelly about his relationship with Esme? Was he being straight with either of them, even now?

'He probably forgot what time it was,' she said.

'Inconsiderate is what I'd call it.'

'I suppose he's a bit worse for wear and hasn't realised what he's doing.'

'Even drunk he must have some sense of consideration for others,' he said. 'Unless there was never any in the first place.'

'He's…' Esme paused. 'I don't know.'

Zach was silent for a moment. But then he spoke again and all trace of humour was gone. 'Tell me again what's so great about this guy?'

Esme turned away from him and laid her head against the seat.

'It's none of my business,' Zach said quickly. 'I'm sorry.'

Esme stared down the aisle of the bus, where the lights of the instruments on the dashboard pricked the gloom, and she didn't say anything. What could she say when she didn't know the answer to that question herself?

Chapter Sixteen

On balance, neither of their outings together had ended the way they'd begun. Esme had parted from Zach after the trip to Santa's village in a weird mood, and returning from the Northern Lights chase had seen her fall into bed in an even weirder one. On the face of it they got along so well – at least they ought to – but something was always in the way. Perhaps it was the things that neither of them would say, rather than the things they did say. Although Esme had opened up a little, she was frustrated that Zach wouldn't give an inch, and perhaps he felt that even the inch she hoped for was just too much.

In bed in her room, as she drifted to sleep, she wondered if Niko might have some answers – he and Zach had seemed pally as they'd parted the night before at the bus. Although, if they *had* slept together then she guessed that pally was the least they ought to be. Somehow, though, she was beginning to doubt that the true nature of their relationship was quite as cut and dry as Hortense would have Esme believe. It just didn't stack up.

But the train of thought had ended there with Esme falling asleep. She slept so soundly that she couldn't even recall a single second of anything she might have dreamed and she woke at eight the following morning for breakfast, wishing that the hotel would serve it a lot later. But having skipped dinner meant she'd barely eaten anything the evening before and even she couldn't manage to wait for lunch, so she hauled herself out of bed and into the shower.

As the impressive force of her luxury showerhead massaged life and reason back into her, Esme's thoughts drifted back to the things they'd said the previous night. Or rather, things Zach had said. As usual, it had all been concentrated on what he thought she needed to hear and there was very little about what made him tick. Nevertheless, there had been so much to ponder, and all of it leading back to the fact that, sooner or later, she needed to face Warren with an awful truth that she hadn't yet been able to face herself. Did she really want a future with him? It was a truth that had been niggling, creeping up on her. In fact, it wasn't even that subtle – she'd known it but she wasn't ready to admit yet that her life might be better without him.

She wondered if they'd see Zach today, and if he'd want to spend time with her again. Had she put him off? He might decide she just wasn't worth the hard work and she wouldn't have blamed him. She hoped not, because if so, it might be a lonely few days before she went home.

Given that they'd been virtually inseparable for the last two days, it was a shock to see Brian and Hortense sitting at different tables and at opposite ends of the room when Esme turned up for breakfast. Hortense was throwing black looks at a mournful-looking Brian, who stared into his coffee and tried not to quail under the ferocity of them. There was no sign of Zach, and Esme didn't know who she ought to go and sit with.

'Esme!' Hortense hissed, and the decision was made. Esme liked Brian but she wouldn't dare cross Hortense, not for anything.

'Why aren't you…?' she began as she took a seat at Hortense's table.

'That man,' Hortense replied with all the drama of a Shakespearean actor, 'is a… *pig*.'

'What did he do?'

Hortense gave an exaggerated shudder. 'My dear girl, I couldn't possibly talk about it.'

'Oh. OK.'

'His wife,' Hortense said, clearly forgetting that she couldn't possibly talk about it.

'*Ex*-wife,' Esme corrected, immediately regretting the impulse. Hortense looked as if she might explode.

'So he says. In name only, it would appear.'

'What? What has she done?'

'She doesn't stop phoning him! And last night we were… well, let's just say it was a delicate situation to interrupt. And do you know what that *pig* did?'

'What?'

'He answered the phone! Left me there like…'

'Perhaps Brian was worried it was an emergency,' Esme interrupted hastily.

'*Nothing* could be that important! She's his ex-wife, and she should be phoning somebody else for her emergencies!'

'It does sound as if they're actually still quite close.'

'Doesn't it just!' Hortense slapped a hand on the table. 'It sounds as if they still want to be married!'

'I'm sure it's not like that. I suppose they've just stayed friends. After all, I don't think the only reason Brian sends her all those photos is to rub her face in their divorce because I don't think he's really like that. I think he just says it to look as if he doesn't care, you know? I think he sends her photos because they actually still share quite a lot of their lives. As friends,' she added hastily, seeing Hortense's expression darken further still.

'I'm not playing second fiddle to any wife! I have all his attention or not at all!'

Esme didn't doubt for a minute that Hortense could claim anyone's full attention in any situation, but she had to sympathise with Brian. He seemed like the sort of man who'd find it hard to stop caring about someone he'd once shared his life with, even if they weren't still together, and if she was in trouble he'd want to help. Assuming that *was* the reason his ex-wife was calling. Maybe she'd thought his Facebook page showed him having just a little bit too much fun without her and she'd decided she ought to put a stop to it. 'So you're making Brian sweat a little?'

'Oh more than that! We're entirely over!'

Esme blinked. 'Just like that?'

'I threw his clothes at him right there and then. Off he went back to his own room, tail between his legs.'

Again, too much information for Esme. That was one image she didn't want invading her thoughts. 'You're not going to give him an opportunity to explain? A chance to make it up to you?'

'When you get to my age you'll realise that life is too short to waste on anyone who doesn't completely worship you.' Hortense rammed half a buttered croissant into her mouth and

Esme glanced across at Brian, who was chewing mournfully on a corner of toast.

'I think he does worship you,' Esme said. 'He looks pretty sorry at any rate.'

Hortense swallowed. 'It's too little too late.'

'You won't even *consider* giving him a second chance?'

'Life's too short for—'

'Second chances, I know.'

Hortense turned her attention to a Danish pastry and folded it into her mouth, washing it down with a great glug of black coffee.

'What are you doing today?' she asked when she'd finished chewing.

'I hadn't really decided.'

Esme had wondered whether it would be worth seeking out Zach or whether it would just get weird again. She'd also wondered whether she might finally broach the subject of his emotional state with Hortense and Brian to see what they thought. But that had been before the new Hortense and Brian situation and she had a feeling that Hortense might be about to hijack her non-existent plans. She also had a feeling that the only thing they'd be talking about was how much of a pig Brian was. Hortense, despite her insults, clearly still liked him. In fact, it was precisely because of the insults Esme knew Hortense still liked him.

'Why don't you come to the sauna with me?' she asked. 'That lovely girl, Inari, at the bar recommended a place to me. I thought I might try it. Do come along!'

Esme poured herself a glass of orange juice from the jug at the table. 'I don't know… I'm not really into that sort of thing.'

'My dear girl, you'll love it!'

'Will it take long?' Esme asked doubtfully.

'As long as you like. We could stay there all day if you wanted to. It's wonderful – the Finns adore them!'

Esme thought about the boring, hot cramped cubicles at Warren's gym packed with high-cheeked women with perfect eyebrows who didn't speak to her. If the Finns adored saunas then they were a weird race.

'It'll do wonders for your skin,' Hortense insisted. 'You'll positively glow! You could certainly use a pick-me-up.'

Esme looked over her glass as she took a sip of juice. 'Thanks. Has it occurred to you that I might just look like this because I've been up half the night driving around Lapland?'

Hortense laughed. 'There's no need to be offended. There's always room for improvement, even for a ravishing little flower like yourself.'

'Thanks, again, I think.'

'Not at all. So you'll come?'

'I'm not promising anything,' Esme said carefully. She needed a get-out clause, just in case it turned out to be the worst idea ever. 'Where do we need to go?'

'It's not far away. We can go directly after breakfast. Apparently they do the most wonderful lunches there and you don't even need to get dressed to eat.'

Esme hesitated. She didn't suppose she had anything else planned but somehow going out with Hortense felt like irrevocably breaking up their little gang, like she was picking sides. If she did this now, it felt like a point of no return, like they could never go back to the foursome from the start of the holiday – and she'd quite liked the foursome they'd had at the start of the holiday. She might have known a relationship in the group would mess things up – they invariably did. 'What about the others?'

Hortense sniffed. 'They can do whatever they like. Brian is perfectly at liberty to visit the sauna or whatever else he wants to do. I won't be doing any of it with him. And I suspect young Zachary is sleeping late after his busy day yesterday, what with all night partying and then staying out late again the following night to chase the Northern Lights. Perhaps he wouldn't worry too much about missing our sauna day.'

'Had you mentioned it to him at any point?'

'I didn't know I was going until this morning. Besides, it's not my job. I'm not the events coordinator, you know.'

Esme was tempted to point out that Hortense usually took great pleasure in organising their activities, but she thought better of it. Her new friend was in a strange and unpredictable mood today, and Esme wasn't sure how she felt about being consigned to the same lonely metaphorical table as Brian. She supposed at least they'd have each other, but still. And as for Zach, while she didn't want to leave him out of anything either, she didn't want to be the one going to his room to ask him out to the sauna. For a start she might wake him. There was also the possibility he might have Niko in there with him, and as if those two reasons weren't enough, the way they'd parted the night before she wasn't sure at that moment where their friendship stood.

In the end Esme decided against waking Zach and waited instead to see if he appeared for breakfast. But an hour passed and there was still no sign, and Esme had to resign herself to a day in Hortense's company. She could have gone out by herself, of course, but as Hortense told her more about the sauna and she realised it wasn't going to be a bit like the one at Warren's gym, the more she wanted to try it out. After all, wasn't it for new experiences that she'd come here? If she'd travelled all this way she might as well fit as many in as possible. Maybe Zach would keep Brian company when he finally emerged from his room. Though she still felt guilty about leaving Brian on his own, she tried to take comfort in the fact that Zach was so nice he probably would.

Because Esme had taken almost all her clothes from Warren's flat when she'd packed for her trip, by chance her swimsuit was with her. It was lucky, because if she'd packed with any actual plan she would never have imagined she'd need it and she certainly wouldn't have put it in. Hortense had insisted that she wouldn't have needed it anyway, but Esme wasn't getting naked in a wooden box full of strangers for anything. The sauna was a short taxi out of town, which Hortense had arranged as this was a jaunt not included on the list of excursions run by their tour company.

They were dropped at a log cabin. It sat on the banks of a frozen lake, surrounded by snowy woodland, and from somewhere they could hear squeals and peals of laughter. Inside they were greeted by a stunning receptionist (Esme had noticed that nearly all the Finns she'd met were exceptionally good-looking and concluded that it must be something to do with all the fresh air and snow sports) who provided them with towels and slippers and showed them to a small room bordered by high wooden benches and a stack of hot stones smoking at its centre. Esme noted a man in an extremely low-slung towel ladling water onto the stones from a bucket, which evaporated on contact with a crack and a hiss, and she hesitated.

'Unisex,' Hortense said briskly, shoving Esme in. 'Nobody cares here.'

In now whether she wanted to be or not, Esme gave a mental shrug. People were definitely less uptight here – perhaps it wouldn't be such a bad thing for some of that to rub off on her. She'd got so used to self-regulating her contact with the opposite sex – mostly in fear of Warren's jealous rages – that it was difficult to stop, but when she really thought about it she realised just how silly this was.

After a brief struggle, Hortense managed to haul herself onto the high bench. Esme sat next to her. There were half a dozen other people in there with them, and Esme guessed they were all locals given that they conversed easily in what sounded like Finnish. Not that she knew for sure. She took a breath and tried to settle. The steam smelt like when her dad used to bring the Christmas tree home, freshly felled from the farm, and the house would be filled with the scent of Christmas. The scent on the air here, though, was overlaid by something heavier and smokier. It was pleasant enough, and as Hortense closed her eyes with a contented sigh, the tension left Esme's shoulders and she did the same. The saunas she'd been to back home had always felt suffocating, but this, though hot, was a gentle heat, a fragrant balm for troubled bodies and minds. Now she understood why every house in Finland had one, and it was no wonder everyone here seemed so happy and relaxed.

A minute later a grunting sound coming from Hortense made Esme open her eyes again. There was a stifled giggle from across the room.

'Your friend is enjoying the sauna,' the woman said, and Esme realised that Hortense was snoring. She smiled.

'We've had a long night – trying to see the Northern Lights.'

The woman leaned forward. Esme would have said she was about fifty, but she looked amazing – toned and clear skinned. 'Ah! You are on vacation?'

'Yes.'

'How are you finding Rovaniemi?'

Esme wiped perspiration from her brow. 'Fantastic. I love it.'

And as she said it, Esme realised that for the first time she sincerely meant it. The place had a magic about it – and not just because it was the focal point for a million childish hopes and dreams. She loved the people and the landscape; it was like nowhere else she'd ever been and, again, as they often did, her thoughts strayed to her grandma, and she only wished Matilda could have shared all these wonderful experiences with her. 'You're so lucky to live here,' she said.

'Oh, but we live in Helsinki,' the woman said. 'We're on vacation too. I am Ansa and this is Milla.' She gestured to her companion – as toned and healthy-looking as her – who smiled and nodded before closing her eyes again, unconcerned with the need to contribute anything more to the conversation.

'You've come here for vacation? Doesn't it snow enough in Helsinki?'

'Yes.' Ansa laughed. 'But sometimes we like to look at new snow.'

'I would have thought you'd want to go somewhere warm if you had snow all the time.'

'In Helsinki the summers are actually quite hot and the days are very long. We've travelled Europe twice over – I have seen enough sun for now. We thought it was time to discover more of our own country.' She stood up, and instinctively Milla opened her eyes and stood up too. 'Would you like to swim with us?' she asked Esme.

'Swim? Where?'

'In the lake – it's just outside.'

'But it's frozen solid!'

'There will be a hole in the ice. It is good.'

Esme doubted that. She looked at Hortense, who was out for the count.

'We sit, we swim,' Ansa said. 'We come back, we sit a while longer and then we swim again. It is the way we do it.'

It *was* getting hot. Perhaps a cool dip might be nice, though Esme still wasn't convinced that a sub-zero dip wasn't a little bit extreme. But then she stood up. Hadn't she promised herself she'd try new things? Didn't she owe it to her grandma to try as much of what Rovaniemi had to offer as she could fit in?

'We won't be long?' she asked. 'My friend…'

'It's quite impossible to stay in the water for long. Don't worry, your friend will not even notice you are gone.'

Esme smiled. 'What the hell! Let's do it!'

Ansa returned the smile. 'This is the best way to do sauna.'

Esme loved the way Ansa said *sauna*, all crisp consonants and stretched out vowels, and she wished that her own accent was half so exotic and pleasing.

Outside, the cold air hit them like a slap. This was supposed to be good for you? Esme shivered as she raced across the snow in pursuit of Ansa and Milla, and in a matter of seconds they stood at the hole in the surface of the frozen lake, the water black and sluggish with icy slush.

'We swim in *that*?' Esme asked.

Ansa took Esme's hand with an easy smile. 'You must do it quickly. We will stay with you.'

Before she had a chance to argue, Ansa and Milla had jumped and Esme had jumped with them. There was an almighty crash, the icy water closing over her head, and then Esme fought her way to the surface, spluttering and laughing and shocked, all at the same time, hardly able to draw breath.

'It's freezing!' she yelped, although she couldn't help but remark that although it *was* cold, it wasn't as cold as she'd been expecting. Perhaps being so hot in the sauna had mitigated some of the more extreme effects. But the surprise didn't last long and within seconds the cold began to bite with more ferocity.

She gestured to a helpful ladder built into the ice, presumably to assist with getting out. 'I should…'

Ansa nodded. She and Milla followed and all three raced back to the sauna and Esme wondered whether this might be the most fun she'd ever had with two complete strangers.

It was almost supper time when Hortense and Esme arrived back at the hotel. Esme couldn't believe they'd spent most of the day laughing and chatting with their new Finnish friends. Once Hortense had woken things had got really raucous as she regaled them with stories that Esme had already heard but was happy to listen to again, and they became a new wide-eyed audience. Hortense had been right – saunas here were nothing like the ones back at Warren's gym. They were a place to relax and socialise and recharge the batteries, and the day had flown by. Esme had even swapped numbers with Ansa and Milla and had promised to visit them in Helsinki with Hortense.

Now, she hurried up to her hotel room to change and fix her sauna-ravaged hair, ready for a bite to eat. The sauna staff had cooked for them around midday – salmon on an open fire served with bread and salad, which they ate wrapped in fluffy, warm towels and cosy slippers – and it had been incredible. Esme had eaten her fill – more than she'd eaten in months, but despite this she was ravenous again and looking forward to seeing what was on the menu. Maybe she'd even be able to catch up with Zach's day. Hopefully he and Brian had found something equally fun to do, and Hortense, being so relaxed and pampered, might be in a more forgiving mood. While Hortense and Brian as a couple was excruciatingly awkward at times for their companions, Hortense and Brian apart was far worse.

When she came down again, Brian and Zach were at the bar. Esme hurried over and while Brian greeted her as warmly as ever, Zach was rather colder. It was clear she'd done something to annoy him. Surely he wasn't still sulking about the way they'd parted the night before? Had she really been that insufferable?

'Is Hortense…?' Brian began hopefully.

'She's getting changed for dinner,' Esme said. 'At least I think she is. She's in a good mood, though, if that helps.'

Brian gave a grateful smile. 'You spent the day together then?'

'We went to a sauna. It was actually really incredible. And we met—'

Esme stopped, distracted by a look of distaste from Zach that took her by surprise.

'We met,' she continued, more hesitantly than before, 'some lovely women on holiday from Helsinki. We swapped numbers with them and everything. We might even go to Helsinki to stay with them. Perhaps you could come along.'

'That's good,' Brian said, wearing the smile of the boy who was no stranger to being picked last for his school football team but wanted more than anything to show how much he still loved them. 'I'm glad you enjoyed it.'

Esme glanced between the two of them. 'What did you get up to?' she asked carefully.

'Oh, I mostly pottered about here,' Brian said. 'I was a bit tired, to be honest, so it did me good to have an easy day.'

'And I didn't know you'd gone anywhere,' Zach cut in. 'Because nobody told me.'

Esme frowned. Was there some rule that they had to go everywhere together? Was there a law that said she had to tell him everything she did? She'd thought about going to knock on his room, but she hadn't done out of courtesy to him and surely he could see that.

'So you didn't go anywhere either?' she asked, choosing not to respond to his pointed remark.

'No.'

'But you could have…' Esme flushed. Suddenly, she got it. Zach had felt duty-bound to stay with Brian. But that was his choice and she wasn't going to feel guilty about hers. Except that really, she did. 'I'm going to find Hortense. We'll probably go out somewhere in the town for dinner tonight. The atmosphere here… well, I could do with a change of scenery.'

'Oh.' Brian looked downcast and Zach even more annoyed, but it only filled Esme with a greater belligerence.

'Maybe we'll see you later,' she said, trying to temper it. 'For the extra Northern Lights trip they promised us. I expect you're both going to go along and try again?'

'I expect so,' Brian said with forced cheer.

Esme tried to smile but nothing happened. Instead, she couldn't decide whether she wanted to hurl something at Zach's head or burst into tears. She held the mask well, though, and she was composed as she turned to leave them.

She'd barely made it out of the dining room when she felt a hand close around her arm and spun round to see Zach's face close to hers.

'I can't believe you of all people did that,' he said.

'Did what?'

'Left Brian all alone. I thought the point of our group was that nobody would have to be alone.'

'Me? But you—'

'You went off with Hortense!'

'Because I knew you'd take care of Brian!'

'Right…' Zach's jaw tightened. 'And did you actually know that for sure?'

'Well, you weren't around to ask. But I assumed—'

'Exactly! You assumed! I came in this afternoon to find him propping up the bar looking as miserable as sin.'

'They had a bust-up.'

'So that means you had to take her side?'

'I wasn't taking anyone's side!'

'But you went out with her.'

'Because I thought you'd be here.'

'Well, I wasn't. He was on his own.'

Esme frowned. 'So where were you?'

'Does it matter?'

The heat rushed to Esme's face again. 'No. I just thought you'd be here for him. Just like you thought Hortense and Brian would be here for me when you went off with Niko the other night.' She pursed her lips and tried to imitate him. 'I thought the point of our group was that nobody was left alone.'

Zach flushed now. 'That was different!'

'Different how?'

'Esme…'

'And where were you this morning? Out with Niko again, assuming that Brian and Hortense would be taking care of Esme the gooseberry?'

As soon as it was out, Esme wished she could take the comment back.

Zach's expression darkened. 'I needed to go somewhere.'

'Yeah? Well, so did I.'

He stared at her, and for a moment Esme thought he might tell her where he'd been that morning. Not that he was under any obligation, but it was clear he'd been missing for reasons more complicated than a morning in bed. But he clammed up again. Without another word, he stalked off to join Brian at the bar once more. Fighting back tears, Esme made her way back to her room. Why did Zach have to be so bloody infuriating?

Chapter Seventeen

'So you're coming home now, right?' Warren's question was more of an expectation than a query. In fact, it sounded more like a demand. Esme's resolve was already in danger of crumbling and they'd barely been speaking for more than ten minutes. One day some scientist would quantify it and classify it and label it The Warren Effect.

'I would but it's not so easy.'

'You can get a flight – I checked online.'

'I know I can get a flight but—'

'Come home now before it all gets out of hand. If you're worried I won't forgive you for running off, don't be – as soon as you get back we'll sort it.'

'But I haven't even seen the Northern Lights yet. And it's only a couple more days until I can get back on the scheduled flight. What's the point in paying more for another one?'

'Because you left me here on my own. You abandoned me—'

'You said you didn't want to come. I asked you.'

'I said I didn't want *us* to go. We'd agreed to cash in the holiday and have the money! Is your memory that bad?'

'No, of course not. I'm sorry. I needed to… I just needed to do this. I explained it in the note. I needed to get it out of my system. Grandma left this for me and I can't tell you why but I feel like it's all happened for a reason.'

'A reason? You've gone nuts! What kind of bullshit is that?'

'I know it sounds crazy – it sounds crazy to me.'

'Has this miraculous thing happened yet?'

'Well, no, but…'

'For God's sake, Esme! I've told Shelly I'm leaving her and then you go and do this! Is that any way to repay me for choosing you over her?'

'*Leaving?* So you haven't left her yet? I thought—'

'Where am I supposed to go with you missing?'

'We have the flat.'

'Nobody's there to look after me at the flat because you're in sodding Christmas Land! I've had to stay at Shelly's, haven't I?'

'What the hell…?'

'You don't get to sound indignant about this!'

'But you're supposed to be divorcing her! It's hardly giving out the right message when you're still there! I feel sorry for her!'

'I've got to get fed somehow! Anyway, what do you care where I am? You proved you didn't care when you took off on holiday without me! I told you we could have gone to Clacton but you just went off on your own selfish way anyway!'

'I do care! I didn't want to go to bloody Clacton – that was your idea!' Esme let out a sigh. They were going round in circles, and something told her that they would continue to go round in circles until she caved in and gave Warren what he wanted. She was beginning to wish she'd carried on ignoring his calls. 'Look, it's probably better if we talk when I get back.'

'Talk? What does that mean? What are we talking about?'

'This. Us.'

'Us? What's there to talk about?'

Esme looked out of the window, where fresh snow was gently falling. She shivered, even though she was warm in her room, propped up on fat pillows as she sat curled on the bed.

'You're dumping me?' he yelped without a reply. '*Again?*'

'No, no, of course not. But there are things—'

'What things?'

'I can't explain it properly now. Not like this, not on the phone.'

'Explain what?' He paused, and Esme could almost hear the gears grinding. 'You've met a bloke there?'

'No!'

'Then what's there to talk about?'

Esme was silent again, her gaze still fixed on a sky full of billowing snow clouds beyond her window.

'You're at Shelly's for a start. I thought you were supposed to be leaving her.'

'I've told you – maybe if you were here I wouldn't have to be at Shelly's.'

'I know and I've said I'm sorry.' Esme's voice rose with her building frustration. God, she'd forgotten just how infuriating and unreasonable and sometimes downright intimidating Warren could be when he didn't get his own way. 'But it doesn't mean you get to break your promise to leave her the minute my back is turned.'

'I told you I was leaving her when I thought you would be here for me.'

'I *was* there for you – I gave up my family and friends for you! All I wanted was this one favour in return. Just one time when I get something I want, one time when you compromise.'

'I never make you compromise.'

Esme held in a groan of frustration. 'I'm always compromising.'

'OK, so I won't ask you to compromise anymore.'

'You can't help it. I don't even think you know when you're doing it. Anyway, I'm not saying I never want to compromise – I just want us to be give and take, like normal couples. Right now it's me giving and you taking all the time.'

'I'll change.'

'You've said that before.'

'I will this time. Now stop dicking around and come home. Then I'll prove it to you.'

'I've already told you I can't come home early.'

'You keep saying that but I know you can.'

'I can't afford it.'

'You could find the money if you really wanted to.'

'From where?'

'You're spending money there? So you must have some.'

'Well, yes, of course, but not enough for a flight.'

'Then ring your mum and dad and ask them. They're loaded.'

Esme bristled. 'They're not, and I wouldn't phone them for that even if they were.'

'No… of course you wouldn't,' he sneered. 'I expect they're happy as Larry about this. I bet they've been telling you not to come back to me. In fact, I'll bet they're behind all this. Them two and your gran… I bet they cooked this up together to get rid of me—'

'We had already split up when Grandma booked this! And please stop phoning my parents – they have nothing to do with this and they don't need the stress!'

'What about *my* stress?'

'Warren – it's just a couple more days. Then we'll talk.'

'Babe… you don't really want it to end like this, do you?'

'Nothing's ending like anything.'

'But we're good together, aren't we? Think about all the good times we've had together, all the laughs we've had on nights out, all the daytrips, all the steamy nights in…'

'I'm sure you've had lots of those with Shelly too. I'm surprised you can remember which fun nights out you've had with which one of us.'

'That hurts. I was confused and I was out of order and I know that now – I've learned my lesson. I only want you now, babe.'

'You want whoever is free at that moment.'

'That's not fair.'

'It's true.'

'It's bollocks.'

'Then why are you at Shelly's now?'

'There's nothing in it – she's just putting me up. I was lonely without you, and Shelly and me are friends now. She's just helping a friend out.'

'How can I believe that? You have to see it from my point of view – how can I believe that's true after what happened?'

'I thought we'd sorted that; I thought we were straight now. I am leaving her, promise. Just come home and we'll—'

Esme cut the call. She couldn't do this anymore. But within seconds Warren's name appeared on the phone display again. She rejected it. They'd talked and talked but said nothing, just as she'd suspected they would. There were things, important things, she should have told him, and in the midst of the noise, her courage had failed her. Because while she was still mixed up over a lot of things in her life, one thing had become clear to her today. She had to leave Warren. And this time she had to mean it.

When she'd first arrived in Rovaniemi she'd been uptight and nervous, but as the town had worked its magic, despite hiccups and mishaps, she'd come to see that life could be so different. And part of what was keeping her from that new life was Warren. She shouldn't have returned when her grandma had worked so hard to cure her of her weird addiction to him, to loosen the strange hold he had on her. She'd come so far only to end up right back where she'd started. Perhaps here, in Rovaniemi, was the final piece of the puzzle and somehow Matilda had known that. Esme wasn't sure about anything, but she knew she owed her grandma at least this – to start anew in a life that would make her happy no matter how scary that might be. It was what her grandma would have wanted more than anything.

And even though it was truly what she wanted too, Esme began to cry.

She was still on her bed and it was dark outside. She'd thought once or twice about changing out of her outdoor clothes, but in the end she just hadn't had the energy. She could have gone to find Hortense, but that would mean opening up about her life back home and perhaps Hortense wasn't the person for that right now. As for Zach, that was a definite no, and Brian would be about as useful as a paper dishcloth in his current state. She'd thought about phoning her mum for advice, but she didn't want to give her parents anything more to worry about than they already had. In the end, Esme didn't have to make the decision because the phone rang and she picked it up from the bed to hear her dad's voice.

'Alright, love? We hadn't heard from you today and your mum said I should ring – you know what she's like.'

Esme couldn't help a smile. She knew exactly what her mum was like and she never wanted it to change.

'Have you had a good day?' her dad asked.

'Yes, not too bad.'

'And there's nothing to report?'

'No, nothing to report.'

'Right… good.'

Esme's dad had never been one for small talk in the flesh, and on the phone the problem was magnified by a thousand. At least it was a problem for anyone else, because he didn't seem to think it was an issue that none of his conversations ever lasted longer than three minutes. Practical to the last, just like Esme's grandma – his mother – he didn't say anything that didn't need saying. This wasn't an issue when he was fixing an engine or putting up shelves, but not so good when you wanted to touch base. That was why Esme's mum usually did all the phoning.

'I'll tell your mum you're alright then,' he said.

'You can. Thanks, Dad.'

'Alright, love.'

'Dad…' Esme added before he had time to hang up. 'There've been no more phone calls from…'

'Warren? No, love.'

'Are you telling me the truth?'

'Well, I am in as much as he's phoning but we're not picking up. So technically there have been no more phone calls because we haven't actually answered any of them.'

Esme laughed. 'OK, that's fair enough.'

'Would you rather we picked up? Would it be better? Do you need us to tell him anything?'

'No. If anything needs saying then I have to be the one to do it.'

'Does that mean you have something significant to say to him?'

Esme was quite sure she could guess what her dad was hoping she might need to say to Warren, but she didn't want to get embroiled in that conversation when she was so far away from home. Her parents would worry, and she wouldn't be able to reassure them as she'd want to. 'I'm not sure. I'll speak to you soon, Dad.'

'Goodnight, love.'

Esme locked her phone and the screen went black. She stared at it. And then she took a breath, before unlocking it to find a number, a number she'd wrestled with the temptation to dial. But she dialled it now.

'Hello?'

Esme hesitated. It was the first time they'd ever actually spoken, woman to woman, and Shelly's voice was not as she'd expected. It was a bit husky, confident and emphatic. It didn't sound like the sort of voice that belonged to a woman who'd allow herself to be messed around.

'That's Shelly?'

'Yes. Who is this?'

'I'm…'

Esme looked at the phone. She was a millisecond away from ending the call but then Shelly spoke again.

'Is this… Esme?'

'Yes,' Esme said, putting the phone to her ear again.

'What the hell do you want?'

'I… I don't really know. To talk to you.'

'Why on earth would you think I have anything to say to you?'

'It's more what I want to say to you. I wanted to say… I wanted to say I'm sorry.'

'For taking Warren from me? Honestly, you did me a favour. I've finally seen the light, thanks to you.'

'But I do feel terrible about what happened. I didn't know, you know. I didn't have a clue about you.'

'That's what they *all* say.'

'All?'

'You think you're the first? He's done this twice before since we got married, and those are just the times I know about.'

Esme's eyes widened.

'He can't help himself.'

'But…' Esme thought back to the promises. He was still pursuing her, even now. He'd never stopped pursuing her, even when she'd first left him and gone back to Little Dove Morton. Why would he do that if she was just another in a long line of conquests? Why go to all that trouble if she was no different from the rest? It had to mean something, didn't it? But what?

'So, are you two… are you back together?' Esme asked.

Shelly laughed. 'Why the hell would we be back together? Do you think I'm that stupid?'

'But he's with you now? He's staying with you?'

'Warren? No he bloody well isn't!'

'You're sure?'

'Are you soft in the head or something? I'll just go and have a look, see if he's under the cooker, shall I?'

So if Warren wasn't staying with Shelly after all, why would he say he was? Esme's head was spinning. Nothing that Shelly said made any sense and yet she had no reason to lie.

'So where is he?'

'Don't know and don't care. Is there anything else because I have a kettle boiling in the kitchen and frankly that's more important than this conversation.'

'So Warren's not paying half the rent on your flat?'

'Oh, that he is. Do you think I'm going to let the stupid bastard get away with that after all he's done? He's the one who left me with this place and he can keep me here until I'm ready to move on.'

'But he's not staying with you? Not even just for a couple of weeks over Christmas?'

'For the last time, no! Christ, I know he said you were a bit dim but I never realised he was telling the truth!'

'He said that?'

'What do you think? I know him better than anyone. We might not be together but he still tells me things.' There was a heartbeat's pause. 'So how come you don't know where he is?' Shelly asked.

'I…'

'He's left you?'

'No.'

'You've left him?'

'No. I…'

'On second thoughts, perhaps I don't care enough to know. If you want him, he's all yours. Good luck if you take him on, though. Take it from me – you'll need it.'

Before Esme could reply, the line went dead.

Warren had made up the whole thing about staying with Shelly, but it made no sense. What on earth did he have to gain from telling her that? But though it was perplexing, was there any reason it should change how she felt about him now? Should it affect the decisions she was making about her future? She'd barely had time to consider it when there was a soft tap at her door. She went to the spyhole and looked out.

Zach.

Was he ready for round two, because Esme wasn't in the mood. She opened the door.

'I just wanted to apologise,' he said before she could speak. 'I was out of order earlier.'

Esme could have cried with relief. She was confused enough by what she'd just heard from Shelly and the last thing she needed was to continue an argument with Zach. She shook her head. 'No – you were right. We shouldn't have left Brian.'

'But you had a point about Niko too. It's just that he and I—'

'It's OK.' Esme pulled her cardigan tighter and folded her arms. 'I understand.'

'But that doesn't make it right.' He looked up and down the empty corridor before turning back to her. 'Truce?'

'Absolutely.'

Zach paused. 'What are you doing now?'

'I don't know. I suppose it depends if the Lights chase is on again.'

'They've been called off – it's snowing like crazy out there – can't see a thing. I'm surprised you haven't had a phone call from the tour company yet.'

'Perhaps they did call – I've been on the line…'

Esme turned to check the window. What had been light snow had become fat flakes, driving against the glass. She'd been so preoccupied with her thoughts the fact had barely registered.

'Are you OK?' he asked.

'Yes, I'm…' Esme sighed. 'No. I don't know, if I'm honest.'

'Would it help to talk about it?'

'I'm not sure about that either.'

He produced a bottle from behind his back. 'I have lakka – want to share?'

'What's that?'

'I have no idea but it tastes good and makes everything look better.'

She arched an eyebrow. 'Is this the thing you got smashed on with Niko?'

Zach grinned. 'Don't worry – I'll know when to stop this time. It's a sure-fire way to forget your troubles though – trust me, I know.'

Esme stepped back to let him in. 'I've only got the toothbrush glasses in the bathroom.'

'That's all we need.'

'You don't mix it with anything?'

'I don't know. Niko drank it neat.'

'Niko would.'

'What does that mean?'

'Nothing. He's just a bit…'

'Unpredictable?'

'I guess you could call it that.'

'He's a good guy. Kind. There if you ever want to talk. He's not what you think he is.'

Esme went to fetch the glasses from the bathroom. She didn't want to talk about Niko, and it suddenly occurred to her that she was jealous. Returning to the bedroom, she dismissed the ludicrous idea and held out the tumblers for Zach to fill.

The first went straight down. It was sweeter than she'd been expecting but it was potent and it went directly to her limbs.

'That's the stuff.' Zach gave the bottle an approving examination before holding it up to her. 'Another?'

'What is this muck?'

Zach looked at the label. 'It's all in Finnish. I think Niko said it was made from cloudberries.'

'What are cloudberries?'

'I don't know but they make good liquor.'

'Only in Lapland would I be drinking something made from cloudberries.'

'It is a strange and wonderful place.'

Esme grinned, holding up the glass he'd just refilled. 'It is that. Here's to cloudberries!'

She drank that one, then Zach refilled and as that went down, his phone rang from his pocket. He pulled it out and looked at the screen before answering.

'Niko… sorry, man, something has just come up. A friend in need – I know you understand, don't you?' He paused as Niko replied. 'Thanks; I knew you would. Another night, eh? We'll do it again before I leave, promise.'

'You had plans?' Esme asked as he put his phone away.

'Not set in stone.'

'You could have gone, you know.'

'I could have done, but right now I have a feeling I'm needed here. He's OK with it, and it's not like he's short of friends.'

Esme smiled. He'd put Niko off for her, and the thought warmed her more than the lakka.

Esme opened her eyes. For a second she stared at Zach, sleeping on the bed beside her. His arm was draped across her collarbone and his shirt was partially unbuttoned in a failed attempt to remove it. Esme craned to look down at herself and was relieved to see that she was fully clothed and that they'd both slept on top of the bedcovers. She looked at Zach again. There was no denying that his breath had smelt better, but still, he looked…

She pushed the feeling away – no good could come of it. And while she could have happily watched him sleep all day, Mother Nature had other ideas, and she suddenly realised that if she didn't get to the bathroom soon they'd have more immediate problems than the aftermath of getting inappropriately drunk. Delicately, she tried to move his arm and, managing to do it without waking him, sat up.

OK, so there was the headache – cracking across her skull as she changed her position. If this was the same hangover Zach had been blessed with after his night with Niko then no wonder he'd needed time in a dark room to recover.

Sliding from the bed she padded through to the bathroom, clicking the door gently shut. After doing the necessary, she leaned on the sink and, while she waited for it to fill, inspected her reflection. The same as yesterday, but different. Almost certainly rougher, but that wasn't the only change, though she couldn't pinpoint what the change was. Shaking her head, she turned off the taps and plunged her face into the water. As she dried herself, there was a knock on the bathroom door.

'Esme, I need to…'

Esme opened up and before she'd had time to move he squeezed past, straight to the toilet where he dropped to his knees and hugged the bowl. Not wanting or needing to see any more for fear of a chain reaction, Esme hurried out and tried not to listen.

When Zach came out again his face and hair were wet and he gave her a weak smile.

'I'm sorry, I just… you know.'

'Honestly, I'm amazed it wasn't me. I must have a high tolerance to cloudberries or something because I'm usually always sick when I've drank too much.'

'I have to say I'm impressed.'

'Don't be – it's hardly a talent at all.'

'What time is it?' he asked, massaging a hand through his hair.

'Breakfast time.'

Zach sat on the bed. 'Oh God – don't mention food to me.'

'Not even a nice bowl of pickled herring?'

'Please!' Zach held up a hand and Esme giggled. From her toiletry bag she produced a blister pack of aspirins, and after taking two she handed him the same.

'Always prepared,' she said as he gave her a grateful look.

By the time she'd returned with a glass of aired water from the bathroom tap Zach had already swallowed his straight down.

'Thanks.' Esme swallowed down her pills with the water.

'For giving you a hangover or for letting you see me in all my barfing glory?'

'For staying with me. I don't think you'll ever understand how much I needed last night.'

'Then I'm glad to have been of service. So, do you know what you're doing?'

'Maybe.'

Esme couldn't quite recall how much detail she'd shared with Zach the previous night. Past their fourth shot of lakka it had all got a bit fuzzy. She seemed to recall laughing a lot, crying once or twice, and Zach almost telling her something that he then seemed to think better of. He mentioned his last visit to Lapland a few times and being here with someone else who was no longer in his life. Just like all the other times he'd hinted at something big, something not good, Esme's courage had failed and she hadn't dared to ask him. Then the conversation had got too drunk to be anything but silly and at some point she now had no recollection of, they must have decided to sleep together. Literally. As in just going to bed and sleeping. It must have been nice because Esme hadn't felt weird or guilty about it, and there had been no regrets on waking up. In fact, his arms looked rather inviting right now and she wondered how he'd react if she asked to go back to bed. To sleep. So she did.

He smiled, and he opened his arms, and they snuggled down, this time under the covers, and before she knew it, Esme had drifted off, listening to his heartbeat.

Chapter Eighteen

'Hello, sleepy.'

Esme opened her eyes and took a moment to focus. Yep, Zach was still there, arms wrapped around her. With a contented sigh, she nuzzled into him and felt something…

In the next instant he leapt up and made for the bathroom. Esme wondered if he was going to be sick again, but she didn't hear anything other than the tap running and a minute later he came back out.

'We should probably see about getting some lunch,' he said, grabbing his sweater and pulling it over his head. 'We've missed breakfast by a mile I expect.'

Esme gave a lazy stretch. She didn't much feel like going anywhere right now, though her stomach growled as if to argue the point.

'That's you?' Zach asked briskly.

'I'm afraid so. But it can wait.'

'What for? For you to waste away? Come on, you need to eat something. What do you want?'

'I want to stay in bed.'

'In that case I'll go for food and bring it back.'

'Room service will do. Unless you've a hankering to go for a walk in sub-zero temperatures.'

'Actually, I have,' he said, although it all seemed rather sudden. Esme would have been happy to lie in bed with him all day and let food come to them when absolutely necessary. It would be a bit like being on honeymoon. Except without all the sex and certainty of disappointment in the years to come.

'I could do with some air,' he said, lacing up his boots. 'It's hot in here. Absolutely roasting. Ridiculous really.'

'It's toasty.' Esme settled into the pillow again and pulled the covers over her shoulder. She was still dressed beneath them in the same clothes she'd worn the previous evening, but if it didn't bother Zach then it certainly didn't bother her. 'Maybe I *will* get a pastry or something,' she added. 'If you insist on foraging.'

'That's all you want?'

'And a coffee. Flat—'

'Flat white – I know.' He smiled.

'You don't mind, do you?'

'I wouldn't have offered if I did.'

'There's money on my dresser.'

'Don't worry – I think I can stretch to a pastry.' He headed for the door. 'I'll be half an hour, tops.'

True to his word, half an hour later there was a knock at the door and Esme found Zach in the hallway laden with bags.

'There's almost certainly more than one pastry in there,' she said, eyeing them.

'I got carried away.' He stepped in with a grin. 'So now you'll have to help me eat it all or it will go to waste.'

'Everyone's obsessed with feeding me up,' Esme said, closing the door after him.

'Maybe that's because we all think you don't eat enough.'

'Maybe that's because I just don't have a big appetite.'

'I know that's not true because you wished for a faster metabolism from Santa.' He began to lay out packs of sandwiches and cakes on the dressing table. 'Which means you have to work at staying thin and that you deliberately avoid eating enough.'

'God, you've got an answer for everything!'

'It's annoying as hell, isn't it?'

Esme reached for a sandwich. It was something or other on dark rye but now that she was faced with all these goodies she realised that she was so hungry she didn't actually care what was on it. Taking a bite, she discovered it was smoked salmon and let out a sigh of contentment.

'Better than sex,' she said.

Zach raised his eyebrows as he unwrapped a pack of sandwiches for himself.

'But then most things are,' Esme added.

Zach coughed. 'Maybe you just haven't had the right sex,' he said.

Esme let out a giggle. 'What's the right sex?'

'I don't know. The *right* sex. I mean, you just know when it's right, don't you? Usually it's right when it's with someone you love and who loves you.'

She shrugged and reached for her coffee, peeling back the plastic lid to let it cool. 'Are you suggesting I've never been in love?'

'I'm not suggesting anything of the sort. Perhaps you're drawing that conclusion all by yourself. I just meant that, in my humble opinion, sex ought to be making love.'

'And occasionally making babies.'

Zach sipped his coffee and didn't reply, and Esme sensed that strange, odd dip in his mood that sometimes plagued him at the most unexpected moments. She never quite knew when she'd say the wrong thing. Either she'd have to stop talking completely or learn to leave it be when she had said something wrong and let him work through his moods by himself.

'What's in the other bags?' she asked in a bid to lighten things again.

'It might be easier to ask what isn't. Everything looked so good and I was getting a bit hungry myself. Bad idea, going for food on an empty stomach.'

'Where did you get it?' Esme peered into a paper bag to see an almond-topped bun.

'A little bakery café place near that fake Santa building you saw the other day.'

'Oooh, the cakes are good there – I had a couple. What can I have out of these bags, then?'

'Anything you like. I'm not fussy – I'll hoover up the stuff you don't like.'

'That won't leave much for you then.' Her mouth was full of the last corner of her sandwich as she added, 'I wonder what Brian and Hortense are doing. You know… I hope they're not both alone and fed up.'

Zach looked sheepish, probably recalling the argument he'd had with Esme about Brian being abandoned by her and Hortense.

'I ran into Brian actually,' he said. 'When I went out to get this stuff. I think they've made it up – at least he said he was taking her to lunch. He asked about you.'

'Probably thought I'd fallen into a hole.'

'Something like that. I told him you were having a lie-in. I also made it clear there was no… you know. Between us.'

'I wouldn't have thought he'd have any worries on that score,' Esme said cheerfully, and Zach's forehead creased into a vague frown as he took another bite of his sandwich.

'Maybe we should all have taken each other's mobile numbers,' he said. 'At the start – although of course we couldn't get one for Hortense. But it might have saved a lot of this worrying about where people are and if they're OK.'

'I said that myself. Were they worried then?'

'A bit.'

Esme smiled. 'That's quite sweet.'

'It is but it's also awkward. You said that too – do you come and look for people when they miss breakfast or whatever, or do you assume they're doing their own thing and leave it? A quick text would answer that.'

'I suppose so. You could have my number now.'

'It's a start. Hang on.'

He reached into his pocket and unlocked his mobile. Esme relayed her number and he keyed it into his contacts. Then her phone rang, the screen showing unknown.

'That's me,' he said. 'Now you can save it.'

'Now you're stuck with me forever.' Esme laughed as she unlocked her own phone and saved the contact.

Zach smiled. 'I'd like that. Though I don't think your boyfriend would.'

Esme stopped chewing. It had been so easy to forget Warren with Zach around, but he was still there, a real presence in her life, and sooner or later she'd have to face up to that.

'He'd be alright with you,' she said.

'Really?'

'Yes, because we're not… well, you don't fancy me. So he's got nothing to worry about.'

Zach reached for his coffee and took a great gulp. 'Esme…'

'What?'

He paused, held her for a second in a gaze that was now serious. 'It doesn't matter. You're feeling better with some food inside you?'

'A million times better. Thank you – you're the best friend ever.'

'I'm glad. I meant what I said too – I'd love it if you called me when we got back to England. I could show you around my home town some time.'

'Which is… Dorchester?' Esme asked, trying to recall information that was given to her at their very first meeting.

'Bang on.'

'I've never been there. It sounds nice.'

'Well, I've never been to Derbyshire so we're even.'

Then it struck her. She'd told them she lived in Derbyshire and not London, a strange slip to make, like she'd tried to wipe out that part of her life. Just like she'd struggled to mention

Warren to them. Perhaps it was something she ought to have taken more notice of before.

'You'd love it,' she said warmly. 'I can't describe how beautiful it is there. Sort of rugged and hard, but beautiful.'

'I can't wait to see it then. That's if I'm invited, of course.'

'Oh God, yes! You are most definitely invited!'

'Looks like you're going to be busy next year,' he said, 'what with me and Brian and Hortense and your new friends from Helsinki. You'll have to start a travel blog or something with all these places you'll be visiting.'

'I think I'd quite like that.'

'I think you more than deserve it too.'

Esme tried not to think about what he might mean by that remark and wished she could recall more of what she'd told him about her life the night before. Her gaze went to the window.

'Do you think we'll go on that Northern Lights trip tonight? I'm beginning to think it won't happen at all.'

'I really hope so. That's the one thing I absolutely want to see before we go home.'

'Me too, but everyone keeps telling us to be prepared for the fact that we might not get to see them. Or at least, if we do they might actually be a bit rubbish.'

'They could never be rubbish.'

'They could if all we see are wispy bits of grey. I bet the tour company still classes that as a sighting and considers their end of the bargain fulfilled.'

Zach bit into one of the almond pastries. 'If that happens then I'll book another one. I'll pay for it as often as I need to; I just want to see them. Properly.'

'That's all very well if you can afford it.'

'It doesn't matter to me. If I have to beg, steal or borrow, then I will. It's what I came to do.'

'What about all the other stuff?'

'Happy extras,' he said with a small smile.

Don't you dare go to misery town on me again, Esme thought, sensing a change in the mood. Sometimes, Zach really did feel like hard work. 'Like these amazing cakes,' she said. 'It was worth travelling to Lapland just for these.'

'Agreed – they are pretty good.'

'Pretty good? They're amazing! All I can say is if you know a better cake shop in Dorchester then you'll have to take me to it.'

'What about your slow metabolism and your non-existent appetite?'

'I'd have to get round it all somehow.' She laughed. She couldn't help it, because everything that she'd ever said to Zach seemed to be faintly ridiculous right now. Who was she kidding – she loved food! One of the things she'd loved most about being back with her grandma was the home-cooked dinners and stodgy puddings and the fact that the only gym she needed to work the calories off was out in the hills and dales of her home, where she walked many evenings as the sun set, making peace with the world. And she suddenly missed that life, more than she could say, and she was seized with a sharp and desperate desire to get it back. But she could never have it back now – at least not as it was with her grandma.

'What's wrong?' Zach dropped his cake back into the paper bag and ran to pull her into a hug.

She shook her head. She hadn't even realised that she was crying until a tear tracked her cheek. She'd been so determined that she wouldn't allow Zach to get melancholy on her again and yet she'd done just that herself. 'Ignore me – I'm being silly. I was just thinking about my grandma. I suppose it was the cakes.'

'Hey,' he said, his voice soft and low, 'never apologise. You miss her – of course you do. You wouldn't be human if you didn't.'

'I know but… I'm not the first to lose someone, am I? And nobody else goes on like this.'

'How do you know that? Just because they hide it better? Because they might deal with it in a way that's invisible to everyone else? I understand, and I'm here if you need to talk about it. Never feel that you can't because I will always listen, as many times as you need.'

Esme buried her face into his chest and breathed him in. There was no aftershave, no soap, just him. It was warm and calm and safe, and she could have stayed there with him filling her head all day.

'Thank you,' she whispered.

'Don't thank me,' he said. 'Isn't it what any decent person would do?'

Yes, she thought, *it is*. So how come he was the first person who actually had?

*

There was a distinct feeling of déjà vu as Esme stood in the hotel car park waiting to board the minibus that would take them out for their second attempt to find the Northern Lights. There was a pause in the snow that had been sporadically falling all day but the clouds still looked as if they were out to spoil the party. This time, Zach stood with Esme, and after their almost twenty-four hours together doing more or less nothing she felt closer to him than ever. For better or worse, he was quickly becoming her touchstone, and whenever the thought of all the problems waiting back in England for her got too much to bear, she'd only have to look at him, see his smile or hear his voice and she'd be strong again. Right now, she didn't want to think about how much she was going to miss his presence when they all went their separate ways.

He was studying the clouds as these thoughts ran through her mind. 'It's not looking very hopeful.'

Esme looked up at him, recalling their earlier conversation and how much seeing the Lights meant to him. It meant a lot to her too, but she was relaxed about it, for the first time since she'd arrived in Rovaniemi, and she suddenly realised that although she'd done this for her grandma, if she never saw them it didn't seem to matter anymore. She'd gained so much more from this trip, and perhaps those things were the really important ones to take home. She had a feeling they'd be things her grandma would have approved of.

'I don't know,' she said with a lazy smile. 'I have a good feeling about tonight.'

'You do? And this is based on…?'

'Nothing in particular. Just do.'

'So you're psychic now?'

'I wish.' Esme laughed. 'If I was there's a whole heap of things I wouldn't have done over the years. Maybe I'm just in a good mood today.'

'Even though you've spent the whole day stuck in with me?'

'*Because* I've spent the whole day stuck in with you.'

'That's not the usual reaction I get.'

'Maybe you've been spending your days with the wrong people then.'

He smiled. 'I'm glad you've enjoyed it. I've enjoyed it too.'

'Now, hang on – don't get ahead of yourself. Let's face it – it was sort of your fault we were both too hung-over to do much else even if we wanted to. I think *enjoyed* is stretching things a bit. I'd say more like *not completely awful*.'

Zach chuckled and blew into his hands.

'Where are your gloves?' Esme asked.

'I must have dropped them somewhere – can't find them.'

'Maybe we ought to go and look because you're going to get frostbite.'

He shook his head. 'I don't want to miss this trip. If there's the tiniest chance we might see the Lights then I want to be there.'

'I hope we do too – it would definitely be a highlight. You're probably sick of hearing me say this, but Grandma would have loved all this. Even if we hadn't got to see the Northern Lights she would have loved visiting this place. She'd have loved the anticipation and the hope for something magical to happen. She'd have loved the food and the people and the cold and snow – she'd have been asking for recipes and knitwear patterns wherever we went. And she'd have loved having a legitimate excuse to lecture me about wearing thermal underwear.'

Zach smiled down at her. He reached to tuck a stray hair behind her ear, and it was like an instinct, as if he hadn't even noticed he'd done it. Momentarily, she closed her eyes, the contact sending a faint shiver of pleasure through her, making her wish that it could have been as much of a throwaway gesture for her as it seemed to be for him. But when she opened them again she saw that he'd turned his attention to the bus, now pulling into the car park, its headlights illuminating the snow.

'Mostly, though,' Esme said, 'she would have loved that she'd been able to give all this to me.'

'She sounds as if she was amazing,' he said quietly, eyes still trained on the bus.

'She was. My one sadness is that she can't be here now.'

He tipped his face to the sky again and he was silent. Esme could almost see the shape of his thoughts, printed on his features. Around them there was a ripple of activity, people gathering travelling companions and belongings ready for their trip. With his gaze still trained upwards, Zach took a breath. Then he began: 'Esme... there's something—'

There was a loud clap from the doorway of the bus. Esme looked across to see that the tour guide was ready to check them all on and get moving. She turned back to Zach.

'Looks like we're ready to go. We'd better get lined up.'

Hortense hailed them as she hurried from the doorway of the hotel, Brian bringing up the rear, arms outstretched comically, almost like a goalie waiting to catch an errant cross. However, she didn't look in much danger of one of her infamous tumbles as she rushed to meet them.

'Talk about last minute,' Zach said.

Esme grinned. 'I expect they were snogging behind the sleigh shed.'

'Honestly, I don't know what's worse – Hortense and Brian happily together or Hortense and Brian at loggerheads.'

'I do – I'd rather have them together and just look away than have the terrible situation we had when they fell out. At least you can be friends with both of them again now.'

'True. It was a bit awkward.'

'And it made us fall out too,' Esme said. 'That's the thing about these situations, they drag everyone else in too.'

He looked at her. 'Sometimes you're quite wise.'

'Only sometimes?' she asked as they walked to meet Brian and Hortense.

'Yep.'

'When am I not wise?'

'Do you really want me to answer that?'

'Maybe not.'

'Good, because I would hate to put you in a bad mood before we leave.'

'Quick, say something nice then or I'll dwell on it.'

'That *was* my nice thing.'

'Oh, great. That's it?'

He laughed. 'OK, I'll try to think of something else as we travel. Think of it as your Christmas gift.'

At the mention of Christmas gifts, Esme remembered that she actually did have gifts for all of them back in her room. Tonight would have been the perfect time to hand them out, but with everything else going on that day she hadn't given it a thought. Not that she'd have had the time or privacy to wrap them with Zach around for most of it. She'd have to find another perfect opportunity now, but with their days together numbered, she'd have to find it pretty quickly.

'Anyway,' she said, her thoughts returning to the evening to come. 'What was that you were just about to tell me before the bus arrived?'

He gave a small smile. 'Nothing,' he said quietly. 'It doesn't really matter.'

*

They had a different guide tonight. She couldn't have been more than eighteen or nineteen (at least she looked like that to Esme, who was feeling all of her twenty-eight years tonight as she continued to struggle with the after-effects of her excesses the night before) and spoke English with an accent that suggested she'd learned it in America rather than in England.

'Good evening everyone!' she announced over the microphone. 'My name is Twain and I am very pleased to be your guide today. I am letting you know that we have been working very hard to find the best place to see the Lights tonight and with our detective skills, your driver and I have decided that we will drive to Saariselkä to look.'

'What's the name of the place?' someone shouted.

'Saariselkä,' the guide repeated patiently.

'Where's that?'

'Um…' She turned to the driver and they had a brief conversation in rapid Finnish.

'Never mind!' the someone shouted up again. 'Surprise us!'

'Oh, we do like a magical mystery tour,' someone else shouted, and there was a ripple of laughter from that section of the bus. Twain looked as if she was wondering if her passengers were going to be something of a handful and Esme had to agree. Some of them sounded a little tipsy and she'd seen some of them sneak bottles of alcohol onto the bus. Perhaps they were ready to party in the tundra, or perhaps they thought it would help to keep their body temperatures up. Either way, it certainly didn't promise to be conducive to good behaviour.

'Do you know where that is?' Esme asked Zach.

'How should I know?'

'Well, you've been before.'

'I know, but I haven't been to that place before, so not a clue I'm afraid. Hang on though – if I can still get on the hotel Wi-Fi from here I can find out.'

It took a few attempts to look for it on Google because while the guide had, of course, pronounced it perfectly, spelling it perfectly was a different matter entirely.

'I feel as if it should have more Ks,' Esme said, looking over his shoulder.

'Probably about twenty,' Zach agreed and Esme giggled.

'And no vowels,' she added. 'What is it with this language and their aversion to vowels?'

'They probably think we have far too many. Ah… here we go!' He turned his phone for Esme to see.

'Oh, it looks pretty.'

'Doesn't it?'

'And a little further away than I'd expected.'

'I suppose they have to go where the weather will be kind. I don't mind – it's not like we've got anywhere else to be.'

Esme smiled as the bus engine started and they began to pull out of the hotel car park. 'I'm so excited to see the Lights. I really hope we do this time.'

'Me too.'

'I know it means a lot to you but will you be *very* disappointed if we don't see anything tonight?' Esme's mind went back to their previous failed attempt to view the Northern Lights, which had left them barely speaking. She didn't want that to happen again and was determined to take all dangerous variables out of the equation if she possibly could. It really did seem massively important to him too – hadn't he said he'd go to any lengths he could to achieve the one thing he'd come to Rovaniemi for? And anything that important to him felt important to her. Although it wasn't helping her to live the moment when, even with her phone on silent, she could still feel it vibrating in her pocket, and two or three good guesses would tell her exactly who was calling.

He closed down the map function on his phone and looked up at her. 'Will you be disappointed?'

'A bit. When I first arrived I thought that was the most important part of the trip, the only reason to come that mattered because it was the thing Grandma had wanted to see. But now… I almost think it's the least important bit. I mean, I want to see them, but I won't be heartbroken if we don't. I've seen so many other wonderful things and I've had just the best time, so it would be OK. Grandma could be happy that her gift had been everything she'd hoped for.'

'I understand,' he said, giving her a fond smile that made her want to smile too. 'It's helped that I've got to share all this with the best people too.'

'Even she who must not be named?' Esme arched an eyebrow and lowered her voice. Hortense and Brian were friends again, which meant their interactions were verging on the wrong side of socially acceptable again.

'I know we've been taking the mickey, but I'm actually glad for them. At least they've found something good,' Zach said. 'I really hope it works out for them.'

'Beyond this week? Do you think it will carry on when we all get back to England?'

'I don't see why not if that's what they want. They seem pretty into each other, don't you think?'

'I suppose so. I guess Hortense wouldn't have got quite so upset about Brian's ex-wife if she didn't care about him.'

'Exactly. So maybe they've got a chance for something long term.'

Esme nudged him. 'You pretend you don't care but really you're a soppy old romantic at heart.'

'I pretend I don't care? Is that what you think?'

'I was just saying—'

'Esme, I care. I care too much – that's the problem. If not I'd…'

'You'd what?'

He let out a slow breath. 'I'd be able to share my true feelings with someone I've grown very fond of over the last few days.'

Esme smiled. 'Have you arranged to see Niko before you leave? For another night out, I mean?'

'Niko?' Zach frowned. 'Nothing concrete,' he said uncertainly. 'I expect we'll run into one another – he's often hanging out at the hotel. I think he gets a lot of his bookings from there.'

'Yes, he is,' Esme agreed, wondering if there was another reason Niko spent so much time at their hotel. 'I think he's very fond of you.'

'We're friends. He's been good to talk to. Understanding.'

'He's not bad to look at either,' Esme said, nudging him again.

'Well, yes, but…'

Zach gave his head a tiny shake. By now the bus had left the lights of Rovaniemi behind and they were heading out into the countryside where the streetlamps were few and far between. Zach turned to stare out of the window, though all there was to see was blackness. Esme could see his reflection in the glass and it was pensive, sulky almost. She sensed that dip in mood again was imminent.

'You like Niko?' she asked.

'Not as much as you, apparently.'

'What?'

Once again, he offered no reply, and Esme was left frustrated that she had completely lost control of the conversation. What the hell had she said wrong this time?

Time passed. Esme was quietly straining to see what was out of the window and wondering what she could say to Zach that wouldn't cause another misunderstanding. Brian called across the aisle of the bus.

'Esme… Zach! Do you know how much further this place is on your map?'

'Not sure.' Esme glanced at Zach, who simply checked his phone again.

'I'd say about ten minutes,' he replied after a brief gap. 'Why?'

'Hortense wants—'

'A pee!' Hortense leaned across Brian and there was no shame, judging by the volume of her voice. 'Every bump is agony!'

'I doubt there'd be public loos out there,' Esme began, but Hortense gave her head a firm shake.

'As nature intended will do. There's nothing wrong with finding a snow bank.'

'I suppose needs must,' Esme said with a smile, though she wasn't sure she'd be so enthusiastic about pulling her trousers down in temperatures of minus twenty.

No sooner had Hortense spoken than there was a loud squeal from further up the bus.

'I see it! Did you just see it? There! A gap in the clouds… just there!'

Half a dozen people raced to the woman's seat and craned to get a look out of the window.

'Oh my God, yes!' someone else cooed. 'It's amazing!'

'Please!' the guide said into her microphone. 'Please sit. We will stop in only a couple of minutes and take a look outside together.'

Reluctantly, the rogue passengers returned to their seats. Zach was sitting nearest to the window on their row and he peered out-wards and upwards. Then he turned to Esme with a broad smile.

'It's only a little,' he said, allowing her to lean over and guiding her gaze. 'There… you see?'

It was only the tiniest pocket of clear sky but Esme saw it: a ripple of vibrant green.

'Oh God!' she breathed. She watched as it ebbed and flowed like brilliant waves on a celestial sea. But then the clouds moved in and swallowed the Lights once more. Esme sat back in her seat.

'They've gone already.'

She sounded like a petulant child, but she couldn't help it. Most people never got to see them once in their lives, and she already had one up on them. But she wanted to see them again. The moment had been so unexpected and fantastical that it was hard to believe it had actually happened at all. Zach sat back in his seat too.

'At least we can say we've seen them, even if that's all we get.'

He was right, of course, and Esme rallied, particularly when the sentiment had come from him, knowing how he'd longed to see them. 'I suppose so. Weren't they beautiful? It's funny, even though I've seen endless photos I never imagined them to look like that in real life.'

Zach smiled, and it seemed an infinite thing that could never fall short of happiness to fuel it. And yet, even in the midst of the joy there was sadness. Though she couldn't say how, Esme sensed it was there. It was like, over the past few days, she'd become subtly attuned to his moods on some unconscious level. It was strange, something that had never happened with anyone else before. Perhaps that was why she felt such a strong connection to him now, why she felt so desperate to retain some kind of friendship with him when all this was over. She only hoped he felt the same.

The bus slowed and then finally halted.

'Now we can find a place to stop and get out,' their guide announced.

A moment later everyone climbed out, eyes immediately heavenwards, apart from Hortense, whose eyes turned towards the nearest broad tree. She made a dash for it, leaning on Brian for support so she wouldn't fall in the snow, and Esme couldn't help but giggle at the loud sigh of profound relief that came from their direction. At least she hoped it was relief – surely even Brian and Hortense could control themselves for this particular excursion.

When they emerged they rejoined the tour party, Hortense looking very pleased with herself… Brian not so much. The clouds were patchy, and although there were decent stretches of sky it was now lit only by stars. They were beautiful enough, despite not being what they'd come for, dazzling and multitudinous away from the light pollution of the city. They even caught a shooting star, streaking towards the horizon. Instinctively, Esme glanced at Zach and made a wish. Would they always be friends now? She hoped and wished it, more than anything. She'd never had a friend like Zach and now that she'd found him she couldn't imagine her life without him. She realised, with a sudden quiet epiphany, that her life had always been poorer for it.

'Did you see the meteor?' he asked as they watched the clouds roll and part, only to tumble back across one another again.

'Yes.'

'You made a wish, right?'

'Of course – what do you take me for?' She grinned. 'You think I'm going to pass up on the opportunity of a divine favour?'

Zach gave a warm laugh. 'I couldn't have put it better myself.'

'Did you?'

'What?'

'Make a wish?'

His smile was teasing. 'I did. But obviously I can't tell you what it is.'

'Obviously, I know the rules. Can you give me a ballpark?'

'No.' He laughed. 'I don't want to anger the Wish Pixies.'

Esme snorted. 'Wish Pixies!'

'Well, whatever it is that sorts out your wish – wish pixies, fairies, elves, stars, God, Santa…'

'You know, that's a good point well made. Who *does* listen to your wishes? I've never actually thought about it before.'

'I'd say that's time sensibly spent doing other things,' he said.

'I don't know what then, because currently I have no job, half a house and even less of a boyfriend.'

Zach stopped smiling. 'He's still partly boyfriend then?'

'I suppose he is. Technically.'

'Can I say something that you might not want to hear?'

'Depends what it is.'

'It's about your boyfriend. I think you might have a good idea of what it's going to be…'

'There!' someone in the group squealed and pointed. A strip of sky, low on the horizon cleared and a glorious dancing display of greens and pinks erupted.

Esme's mouth fell open. She couldn't help it. She forgot that she was cold, that Zach had been about to say something he knew she wouldn't like and that she'd wanted to hear it anyway.

'Oh my God,' she whispered, letting out the breath she hadn't even realised she'd been holding. There was a silence, more complete and profound than Esme had ever encountered before. Everyone watched as the sky shimmered and dazzled and walls of colour snaked across it and everyone was as silent and awestruck as her.

The stillness was broken by the sound of someone clapping and the applause began to ripple through the group. Some whooped and cheered and Esme laughed, filled to the brim with an indescribable kind of euphoria, and she felt oddly like a single-celled creature staring into the face of an infinitely complex universe that was all at once beautiful but also bewildering and terrifying. Zach turned to her with a grin, and in the heat of this one incredible, life-changing moment, she kissed him.

He didn't pull away. Instead, he pulled her closer, cupping her face gently in his hands. Everything around them faded – there was only this: his cold hands and warm lips. And when they finally parted to take a breath, his eyes locked onto hers, he didn't say a word.

What had she done? It had come from nowhere and she wouldn't have been able to stop it no matter what – how could she have stopped something she'd had no idea she was going to do? His expression was unreadable in the half-light and she wanted him to say something, to tell her what he felt about what had just happened. But there was nothing. He simply turned back to the skies. And then he moved away – an inch at most, but Esme didn't miss the action. It wasn't what she'd been hoping for.

It was done and there was no going back and Esme didn't know what to say to fix it. She didn't want to apologise because saying sorry would imply that she'd done something wrong and, despite everything, it had felt so very right. Had it been worth it, though? Had it been worth throwing away a friendship for? Zach still said nothing and still didn't look at her, and surely something needed to be said? What was he thinking? Did his silence mean that in one foolish, impulsive moment she'd lost him?

She glanced behind her to see Hortense, not looking at the sky like everyone else, but looking at her, mouth open. It was obvious from her face that she'd seen the whole thing.

Esme tried not to acknowledge the look on Hortense's face that begged for an immediate explanation. Instead, she turned her eyes heavenward again, though the joy she'd first felt as the Lights danced and cracked had died. Her eyes were heavenward not to enjoy the celestial display, but to offer a silent prayer to whoever might be listening – wish pixies, fairies, God, Santa – that she hadn't screwed everything up.

Chapter Nineteen

'Esme!' Hortense grabbed her arm and hauled her away from the group. It was strange how her wobble was non-existent in times of extreme excitement. Like right now, though Esme didn't see what there was to get excited about. Everyone else was still gazing at the sky in wonder but Hortense, apparently, had other ideas. Esme glanced back to see Zach still staring upwards, though he must have noticed Esme had left his side. Was he trying to pretend the kiss hadn't happened? Esme had already accepted quickly there was no point. It wasn't that easy. You could pretend that a farcical bra-exposure incident hadn't happened, but some things were simply too big to ignore.

'You didn't tell me!' Hortense's whisper wasn't really quiet enough to qualify as a whisper at all, though it was probably about as discreet as she'd ever been.

'Tell you what?'

'That business with Zach! Why didn't you tell me you were together?'

'There's no business and we're not,' Esme said, vainly hoping but knowing in her heart that she wouldn't put Hortense off the scent so easily.

'But I saw you!'

'Hortense, please…' Esme screwed her eyes up and sighed. 'Please don't make anything of this. It was a silly, impulsive mistake. The Lights… I got carried away, excited, that's all. I feel just terrible about it and I don't think Zach knows how to tell me I was out of line. I just hope he's not too offended.'

'Dear girl, he looked far from offended to me.'

'He's kind like that – probably didn't want to make me feel worse than I already do.'

Hortense shook her head. 'Nonsense.'

'Do you think *everyone* saw?'

'Most of us were looking upwards; I shouldn't think so. I don't know why you'd want to worry about it anyway.'

Esme nodded, her shoulders relaxing a little. 'That's something. I'd be mortified to think everyone had.'

'I'm sure they've all seen kissing before. You were hardly doing the dance of the seven veils.'

'I know.' Esme couldn't help a small smile. 'But it would have been embarrassing. For Zach too. I suppose it still is. After all…'

Esme closed her eyes again, as if by closing them for long enough she might finally open them again to find time had rewound and she could stop herself from perpetrating the kiss in the first place.

'I still say he rather looked to be enjoying himself,' Hortense said archly.

'But still,' Esme replied, not wanting to acknowledge the new and complicated emotions that notion stirred in her. She shook her head. 'It doesn't excuse anything. He's my friend, and now I've ruined everything… I don't know how we can get past this.'

'I think you're reading too much into it, dear girl.' Hortense gave a sage nod. 'There's no great love affair.'

'What do you mean?'

'I think he's perfectly available. And it's not as if kissing someone is asking to marry them, is it?'

'What about Niko?'

'You must stop worrying. It was just a little kiss. All this lamenting is hardly going to help. If it was in the heat of the moment, tell him so and I'm sure you'll both be able to laugh about it come tomorrow morning.'

But Esme knew she wouldn't laugh. Not tomorrow or any morning. She'd been coming to a slow realisation since that impetuous kiss. It hadn't been just the heat of the moment that had made her do it. She could no longer deny her attraction to Zach, despite their friendship and whatever he might have with Niko. She'd even go so far as to say, in another, less complicated situation, she might be falling for him. But how could that be?

As these thoughts raced through her head, Esme became aware of the world darkening by degrees, and she realised that the clouds had moved in again, obscuring their view of the light display. Hortense seemed to notice it at the same time.

'That's a shame,' she said, although she hadn't been watching with any great interest as far as Esme could tell. Instead, she'd noticed just about everything else that was going on around her, including the things she wasn't supposed to have seen. 'I was rather enjoying the spectacle. And now I shan't be able to see a thing when we walk back to the bus; probably break my ankle… *again*.'

'I'll help you back,' Esme said. 'Would you mind if I sat with you too?'

Hortense turned with a look of surprise. 'On the bus?'

'Yes. When we drive back to the hotel. If Brian doesn't mind, of course.'

'My dear Esme, I'm sure he wouldn't, but don't you think that would look rather obvious?'

'What do you mean?'

'I'm assuming this change of heart has something to do with your recent moment of indiscretion?'

'Well, yes, but—'

'Then surely it's better to pretend your kiss meant nothing and that you couldn't care less if you want it to blow over. If you avoid Zachary now it will just seem to be something more than it was.' She paused and held Esme in a shrewd gaze. 'Or am I missing something?'

'No,' Esme said quickly. 'You're right – it will seem more of a thing if I avoid him. Of course, I should act like nothing happened. Like I don't care.'

'Quite. Take it from someone who is rather practised in the art of pretending not to care.'

Esme stared at Hortense. Was this, for the first time, a glimpse into the real Hortense? Had she just let her guard down for the tiniest moment to allow Esme to see that Hortense – seemingly outspoken and stoic and endlessly unsentimental – had actually been deeply hurt in her past? It wasn't such a leap of the imagination when she thought about it – hadn't most people experienced some kind of emotional pain at some point in their lives? But it was just that Hortense appeared to be so bulletproof, so strong and resilient and endlessly blasé that the idea had simply never occurred to Esme before.

Hortense clapped her hands together. 'Righto. Now that's all sorted, perhaps we ought to go and find our chaps.'

The moment had been and gone, and perhaps it was a good thing that Esme hadn't been given the opportunity to delve any further. Hortense probably wouldn't have given her anything else anyway. Esme suddenly saw, through that tiny window into Hortense's life, that she wore her practicality like a suit of armour. She wasn't opening it up to anyone, not even an inch. She couldn't help but wonder if Brian had been allowed to breach it yet, or whether he ever would be. How close did someone have to get before they saw a real, vulnerable, human Hortense?

'I suppose we should,' Esme said, not relishing the idea of facing Zach again. Perhaps he'd take her in his arms and tell her how the kiss had made him discover new feelings for her, but she doubted it. More likely he'd feel as awkward and uncertain as she was right now. Perhaps he'd already had a similar conversation with Brian as she'd had with Hortense and had asked to swap places on the bus so he could sit with him, away from Esme and away from any pretending-nothing-had-happened scenario.

Just then, there was another burst from the skies, once again streaked with green and pink. Despite everything, Esme couldn't help but stare up in wonder. It was an incredible phenomenon. When she thought about all the people in the world who apparently had this sight on their bucket list, what amazed her more than the fact that she was one of the lucky ones, here now to see it in all its dazzling glory, was that nobody could truly appreciate the majesty of it until they were staring up at it. You could look at all the photos and videos you wanted, long for it, imagine it, but you could never dream what it might really be like to experience this. Wrapping her arms tight around herself against the cold, once more she was overwhelmed at the sight.

'What do you think, Grandma?' she whispered to the sky. 'Not bad, eh?'

The lights seemed to flicker and then burn brighter still, filling the heavens with intense, rippling colour.

'Yep.' Esme smiled. 'That's what I thought too.'

Chapter Twenty

Hortense wasn't about to drop her new favourite topic of conversation. At breakfast the following morning she accosted Esme at the hot buffet.

'I wonder,' she began, leaving Esme wishing Hortense's voice came in a register that wasn't loud or extremely loud, 'if we haven't got the situation with young Zachary entirely wrong.'

'What situation?'

'You know... *the* situation.'

As Esme ladled porridge into a bowl she wondered how to respond to this. It was the same train of thought that had kept her awake for most of the night as she'd replayed their kiss over and over. After all, it had only been conjecture on Hortense's part, so why had Esme been so quick to go along with the notion that Zach and Niko were an item? Esme had been forced to question that too and she couldn't come up with a solution, except for perhaps it being the only way she was able to feel so completely comfortable with Zach. Because, strangely, the idea of him being interested only in Niko had made being with him so much easier for Esme. There'd been no complication, no trying to read subtext or worrying over hidden agendas – they'd just got along, loving each other's company. And even though there had been nothing sexual about it, she'd loved the emotional connection, perhaps more than she ought to have done. Perhaps that alone said so much more about her feelings for Zach than she'd been willing to admit.

He'd been awkward as they'd journeyed home, and neither of them had addressed the incident, and yet there had been passion in that kiss from both sides.

They'd parted at the hotel and gone their separate ways with only the barest courtesy; he'd been distant and strained and Esme couldn't understand how so much heat had cooled so quickly – she only knew that it saddened her. She'd woken with him on her mind and had sent him a text to say she'd see him down in the breakfast room, but so far he hadn't replied and he hadn't shown up. Did that mean he was avoiding her? It seemed the most obvious explanation.

'I don't know what to think,' Esme said.

'Ah! So you do like him. I wouldn't blame you – he's rather handsome and really rather sweet. There's clearly some huge trauma in his past, but aren't we all a little damaged by the time we reach adulthood? I'm sure it's nothing that can't be exorcised. You'd be well-suited, I think.'

Esme stared at Hortense as she gave her impromptu analysis while scooping three sugary pastries onto her plate, emptying the tray they'd occupied.

'I'd take the direct approach,' she continued. 'Straight out with it. You don't get anywhere pussyfooting around.'

'Straight out with what?'

'Ask him if he's gay.'

'OK,' Esme said slowly. 'And if he says yes, what then?'

'Then, dear girl, you needn't give it another thought. Carry on regardless, enjoy the rest of your holiday and put it all down to experience. Have a laugh about what a ghastly mess it all was.'

'It's not that simple. I have…' She was about to say boyfriend again, but she didn't even know if she did have one of those anymore, at least, not in her own mind. Maybe her inability to make Warren's existence public didn't matter anymore regardless. 'What about Niko?' she asked lamely instead.

'Precisely my point. In my experience it's always sensible to take the direct approach so everyone knows where they stand. Just ask him.'

Esme shook her head. 'I couldn't. I wouldn't even know where to start.'

Hortense clicked her tongue on the roof of her mouth as they moved towards the tiny pots of butter and she grabbed a handful. 'Perhaps *I* ought to do it.'

'No!' Esme glanced around and lowered her voice. 'No. Thank you, but that would be worse. I'll talk to him.'

Hortense shrugged. 'It may seem awkward now, but at least you'll know whether it's worth losing sleep over. No point in ruining the rest of your holiday over nothing. Now… what plans do you have for today?'

'I don't really know yet. I just thought…'

What had she thought? That she'd hide in her room all day, rendered useless by her own sense of mortification? Waste her last opportunity to put things right with Zach? Even worse, waste the last precious hours of a holiday that had been gifted with so much love from her grandma? Then again, if she was going to be a grown-up and finally take control of her life, perhaps what she ought to be doing was flying home to talk Warren through all the reasons that meant she could now never go back to him. Over the last few days she'd come to the creeping realisation that there were many more of them than she'd ever imagined.

'There's a carol concert in the town,' Hortense said. 'All the local children will be singing. And afterwards Christmas fireworks. You'll come, won't you?'

'It does sound nice. But—'

Hortense patted her hand. 'Of course it does. That's settled then.'

They began to walk back to their table. What was the point in trying to argue – Hortense would only have an answer for everything anyway. And if she didn't, there was always the danger she'd take matters into her own hands and cause mischief. It was probably better to stick close to her today after all, where Esme could keep an eye on what she might be up to.

As they sat down, Brian came into the dining room, forfeiting the hot breakfast buffet and heading straight for their table.

'Have you sorted everything?' he asked, looking from one to the other.

Esme suppressed a groan. Of course Hortense had told him what she'd seen the previous night and what she'd planned to do about it. And yet, Esme had hoped that, for what she imagined would be the first time in her life, Hortense could have practised a little discretion.

'She simply refuses to talk to him,' Hortense said, dipping a cinnamon roll into her coffee before stuffing it into her mouth.

'I can't say I blame her,' he replied.

Hortense glared at him. 'That is not what you said last night! And just because you're emotionally stunted,' she huffed, 'doesn't mean that's the way we all deal with these things.'

'It doesn't make me emotionally stunted. Sometimes these things iron themselves out if you leave them to breathe.'

Hortense folded her arms. 'When did that ever happen in the history of the world? Woman ignores problem, problem goes away? Perhaps if a man ignored it he might imagine it had gone away, but women are far too practical to imagine that avoidance is any kind of solution.'

'Give the man some space and he might come to talk to her…' He turned to Esme. 'I mean *you*, pet. He might come and talk to *you*. It wasn't meant to be rude.'

Esme smiled. 'I know you did, and I didn't think you were being rude.'

'Rot,' Hortense said. 'I keep telling you, Esme, the direct approach. It's the only way. Churchill didn't win the war by waiting for Hitler to come and talk to him.'

Esme exchanged a look of confusion with Brian. She wasn't sure what it had to do with Churchill and Hitler and she guessed he didn't either.

'Perhaps you could talk to him, Brian,' Hortense said. 'On Esme's behalf.'

Esme bit back a cry of frustration. 'No! Thank you both, but there's no point in stirring things up and I get the feeling Zach wouldn't want to talk about it. I'd quite like to forget about it too.'

'But—'

'I thought you'd just agreed to go and see him,' Hortense said with a look of faint surprise.

'I did, but on balance I'm not sure it's the best idea.'

'But, my dear girl—'

'I appreciate everyone's concern,' Esme cut in, 'but, really, I'd rather leave it be.'

Brian exchanged a glance with Hortense, where he was obviously feeling vaguely triumphant and she was more irked by him than ever. Then he gave a cheerful shrug.

'I'll go and get my breakfast then.'

Hortense watched him go, swirling the last corner of her cinnamon bun in her coffee. 'Don't you think you might come to regret your decision?' she said mildly.

'Maybe, but if it spares any further difficulties between me and Zach then I'll live with the consequences.'

'What if it creates more?'

'I don't see how it can.'

Hortense turned to her with a vague shrug. Clearly, for possibly the first time in her life, she was holding back on something she really wanted to say. So much for the direct approach.

It was as she was getting ready to go out to the fireworks that evening that Esme's mobile phone rang and she noted, with mild surprise, an unknown number showing on the screen.

Shelly?

Her suspicions were confirmed as she took the call.

'Is that Esme?'

'Shelly?'

'Look, this doesn't mean we're friends or anything, but I thought you might want to know that Warren came round here last night – just after you phoned me. Trying to worm his way back into the flat, telling me we're meant to be together and all that bullshit. I don't know what's changed but something has, and he was doing his persuasive best to move me this time.'

Esme was thoughtful for a moment. 'I take it you've told him no?'

'Told him to sling his hook. What's the situation with you two now? Be straight with me – it's the least I deserve.'

'You're right – it is, but I can't tell you. Not because I don't want to but because I don't really know. It's complicated.'

'Isn't it always? You don't need to tell me about complicated – it's all Warren and me have ever been. So you're not living together now? Or you are and he's bored? It doesn't take him long to start wandering and he usually ends up back here. Probably because I'm stupid enough to take him back.'

'I thought you didn't want to know what was going on with Warren and me,' Esme replied with a wry smile.

'That was before he turned up here with flowers and wine. I always know something's amiss when there's flowers and wine. Good wine too, so I know for sure he's after something.'

'Oh, yes. And the flowers. The bigger the bouquet the more trouble he's trying to fix.'

'Oh God. You should have seen the size of them when he first messed me around. Julie, her name was. I think he'd cleaned out Kew Gardens. Silly bloody moo I am forgave him too. Back then I thought big flowers meant big remorse. What an idiot.'

'You're not. If you're an idiot then I think there are quite a few of us around.'

'So you've chucked him out?'

'Not exactly.'

'You've left his other flat?'

'I'm not even in England right now.'

'Not in England? I know he can be a pain but that's a long way to run.'

'I suppose it is. It's a holiday, though.'

'I've got to hand it to you – dump Warren and go on holiday. Cool as you like.'

'Not even that,' Esme said, and she couldn't help a little laugh at the notion. 'It was booked by my grandma for me as a Christmas present.'

'So she's with you?'

'No. She died before the trip. I had wanted Warren to go but he didn't fancy it.'

'I suppose he had to pay for the ticket?'

'No, he could have had my grandma's. I asked him but he said no.'

'Bloody hell – there's a turn up. He's not one to pass up on free. He'll even take cut price. We've been on some shit holidays because he's had the accommodation cheap. His mate's caravan… ugh!'

'Is that in Clacton, by any chance?'

'Yeah. Gary's place. Don't tell me you've been there?'

'He wanted to take me there instead of this holiday.'

'Oh God, you've had a lucky escape. It's a shithole! Doesn't get cleaned from one month to the next – used condoms down the side of the bed, food left rotting in the fridge…'

Esme smiled. It was funny, but she was warming to Shelly already now that they were able to talk properly, and she got the impression that the feeling was mutual.

'When Warren didn't come home, where did you think he was?' Esme asked.

'Where did *you* think he was? He must have been doing the same to you when he came home to me. Or whoever it was that week.'

'Away on training courses—'

'Oh, yeah, that was one of his favourites.'

'He did use that one a lot. Sometimes he said he'd been at a lock-in and he'd stayed there all night or crashed with a mate. It's funny because I sort of didn't mind. It almost felt like a break when he didn't come home. Sometimes he said he'd got a conference with an overnight stay.'

'I had all those. I know what you mean about a break too. I think on some level I knew he was lying, but I didn't want to think about it because I enjoyed the peace too much when he wasn't here. I didn't have to tread on eggshells all the time and constantly think about whether he was pleased with me or not.'

Esme blinked. 'You felt like that?' Shelly seemed so confident to Esme, so mature and collected. She couldn't imagine that Warren would make her feel just the way he made Esme herself feel – like nothing she ever did really pleased him.

'He has a way of making you feel shit. Like you're an essay and he's a teacher who never marks it with anything but red pen no matter how hard you try. You can study and you can revise and you can research all you like, but it will never be good enough for him.'

'But we don't leave him, even though he makes us feel like that.'

'It's because he makes us feel like that we don't leave him. It took me a long time to realise it. He makes us feel like we're not worthy, and then he lets us believe he's making this huge sacrifice to be with us, how we'd never be good enough for anyone else and so staying with him is saving us from a life of loneliness. He puts up with all our imperfect crap as a favour and we ought to be grateful he's there at all.' Shelly paused. 'Sound familiar?'

'And yet you kept taking him back...'

'You did too – right?'

'I suppose I did.'

'Took us both for mugs then, didn't he?'

'Yeah.' Esme sat on the bed and stared at the wall. 'How stupid do I feel?'

'However stupid it is, you can bet I've been there.'

'Not anymore though?'

'Do you know what I did yesterday?'

'What?'

'I went for coffee with a boy I knew at school. We'd been mates all those years ago, and he'd been off round the world on a cruise ship doing shows. Every time he came back to England for leave he'd message me to ask if I wanted to meet up for coffee and I'd always said no.'

'Because Warren was jealous?'

'Because Warren likes to control the contact you have with other people. He likes to decide who you see and don't see, and it usually ends up being his friends you see – not yours. I told him time and time again he had no need to worry about my mate Danny – he's gay for a start. But Warren just wouldn't have it. Once I said I was going anyway and he went mental, threatened to lock me in the flat. In the end it was just easier to make excuses to Danny and not go. But yesterday, I got to decide who I saw and where I went, and I walked into that coffee shop and I met Danny and I felt properly free for the first time in years. I can't tell you how valuable that is and I'm not giving it up again. I've wasted too much of my life already trying to please a man who can't be pleased. It's about time I pleased myself.'

Esme was silent as she took in all that Shelly had told her. It was time to be brutally honest – hadn't she already seen all of this for herself in her own relationship with Warren? Hadn't she lost her friends and her family because he'd made it just too difficult to stay in contact? She'd persuaded herself it was a reaction to their dislike of him, but perhaps it was about control.

'Am I describing your life with Warren too?' Shelly said into the gap.

'Yes.'

'Do you want some advice from an old discarded wife?'

'You're not any of that.'

'I still feel like it. I think that feeling will take a long time to go. Still, my advice is this – and I don't owe you anything so let's make that clear; this is just my altruistic side coming to the surface – get out. Get away from him before he wears you away so completely you can barely see yourself when you look in the mirror.'

It was almost certainly the coldest evening Esme had endured so far, but she wasn't going to let that stop her from watching the fireworks. So she stamped her feet and shivered and wished that she had some mountaineering thermals or whatever it was that Hortense said she was wearing that kept her happily impervious to the chill.

Despite this, however, the Christmas carols had lifted Esme's mood. The children in the choir had been adorable, and the whole thing had been surprisingly moving, so it had been quite impossible not to feel uplifted by the end of it. The fact that Zach hadn't shown up had been something of a relief in the end too. Out of sight, out of mind, her grandma used to say, and although he wasn't exactly out of mind, the emotional turmoil had been put to one side for a while at least. She'd have to address what it all meant at some point, if only in her own mind, but not now. Then again, they were going home tomorrow. By sending the text before breakfast she considered that she'd made the first move. She'd made it clear she was available and willing to discuss things. If Zach didn't come to her today and talk things through then she could only assume he didn't want to talk – not now or ever, and that he wanted her to leave him alone. As much as the notion stung, she'd have to respect his wishes all the same. It was all very well adopting Hortense's direct approach if you were exactly like Hortense – strong and resilient enough to take whatever consequences may result from it, but Esme wasn't like Hortense and it just wasn't an option.

That wasn't the only thing that had Esme's head in a whirl. Snippets of her conversation with Shelly kept replaying in her head, along with the warning Shelly had left her with. In many ways, everything looked clear for the first time since she'd met Warren, but in so many ways Shelly's insights led to more questions than they answered. Most importantly, why had Esme herself been so utterly taken in by him? For that matter, why had Shelly been taken in? Esme felt she'd got a pretty good measure of Warren's wife now and she didn't come across as a fragile flower who'd be that easy to hoodwink or control, and yet he'd done both those things to her for a number of years. One thing Esme did know, Warren needed to be stamped with a government health warning. It didn't seem fair to set him loose on the female population without one.

For once, perhaps out of respect for delicate feelings, Brian and Hortense kept a respectful distance from each other – merely holding hands as they waited for the show to begin, and every so often one of them would fire a knowing look at Esme, or at her and then each other. Esme didn't know whether she wanted to scream with impatience or throw her arms around them both for being so concerned for her welfare. She certainly couldn't argue that they didn't care.

'Oh dear. There's still no sign of him,' Hortense said. She looked at Esme like Esme ought to ask who she meant but, of course, Esme didn't need to.

'He missed the carols too,' Brian said, perhaps a slightly unnecessary observation in the circumstances. They were all well aware Zach had missed the carol concert because they had all been at the carol concert. 'That's a real shame.'

'Oh, it is a shame,' Hortense agreed. 'I don't suppose you went to talk to him after all,' she added. 'As you said you might this morning…'

'I thought you told me not to,' he replied. 'And Esme made it clear she didn't want me to.'

'Thank you,' Esme said, giving him a grateful smile. While their situation troubled her, the only people she wanted to involve in it were her and Zach – any more would only complicate things.

'Although I did go to his room while you waited in that big queue for chestnuts,' Brian announced, and this time Esme turned sharply. 'Only because he's part of our gang and I didn't want him to think we'd forgotten him or that we weren't bothered. He told me he felt under the weather but he'd try to join us later.'

'How did he look?' Esme asked, unable to stop herself. She was doing her best to look as if she didn't care but was beginning to resign herself to the fact that she was probably fooling no one.

'Alright. Not very talkative.'

'But he looked OK?'

'Right enough.'

'Not ill?'

'Not really.'

'Right… good.'

Esme didn't know what to make of the information. What was she supposed to do?

'Don't give it another thought, dear girl,' Hortense said. Esme tried to smile.

'I just feel bad about how it all wound up. I feel as if it's ruined the holiday for everyone.'

'Nonsense! I've had the most marvellous time! It's been a pleasure spending it with you. I hope I've made a rather wonderful friend for life.' Hortense turned to Brian. 'Don't you agree?'

Brian nodded. 'Oh, yes. We'll have to meet up again back in England sometime.'

Esme wasn't sure Zach would be quite as keen for that, but she liked that Hortense and Brian were. At least that was something. And despite all their obvious differences in age and background, she had become very fond of them both. Like Zach, she harboured a secret hope that Hortense and Brian would stay together once the holiday was over, and looking at them now, she had a feeling they just might. It looked as if Esme, however, would have to be content with that and with the memories of the good bits with Zach. Maybe she'd try to see him once more before their flight tomorrow, give it one more shot, once the fireworks were over. That was assuming he didn't show up at all tonight, and that was looking increasingly likely right now.

'I'd like that,' she said in answer to Brian's offer. 'And when I get settled in my new house you're welcome to come and stay with me.'

Hortense raised her eyebrows. 'You never said you were buying a property! Congratulations! When are you able to move in?'

'No.' Esme smiled. 'I'm not. It's my grandma's house. At least, it used to be. I suppose it's mine now.'

'Ah. I hadn't realised. Did she leave it for you in her will?'

'Something like that. I must admit I'd been a bit hesitant to live in it but now...'

'Oh, you simply must live in it. It's a wonderful thing to be able to keep it in the family for the next generation. You must fill it full of new memories – it's the best way to honour your grandmother's memory.'

'I never thought about it like that. I just got... well, I got a little lonely there. I mean, I lived there for a few weeks after she died but...'

'It was bound to be strange at first. Have you tried redecorating?'

'I can't say I've given it much thought. I was so busy holding on to her stuff... I suppose to try and hold on to her. Trying to hold on to the last few months with her. They were the happiest I've been in a long time and…'

Hortense rushed to give Esme a hug. 'Oh, dear one, you simply must let these emotions out. There's no shame in grief. When Mummy died I cried and cried for weeks.'

Esme shook her head and smiled through her tears. 'It's OK, I'm not ashamed. Not with you and Brian. It's just… I'm angry with myself. I'm angry that I threw away what I'd achieved in that time with my grandma and I'd let myself slide back into a life I hadn't wanted, a life I'd tried to run away from.'

Hortense threw Brian a puzzled glance. 'I don't want to pry but if you need to talk about it…'

'I don't, not really. But I do need to remember it because I have a lot to sort out when I go home tomorrow. I need to hold onto this feeling I have now, and I need to remember how much I love Grandma's house so I can stay strong enough to resist the temptation to take the easy path again. Sometimes I'll get lonely but I have to remember it's OK.'

'You need never be lonely now – I'm only ever a phone call away. Say the word and I'll hop in my little car and be with you before you can blink.'

'Too right,' Brian said. 'That goes for both of us.'

Their kindness filled Esme's eyes with fresh tears and she blinked them back. On a practical level it was far too cold for crying – if she carried on like this her tears would be freezing right on her face. And it was just plain silly too. With people like Hortense and Brian in her life, what reason did she have to cry?

'Thank you – that means a lot to me.'

'It will be our pleasure. We've both become quite fond of you this week. As you know, I don't have a daughter of my own but if I did, I'd be jolly happy if she was like you.'

'Oh God, don't!' Esme laughed through her tears. 'Don't make me worse! Listen,' she said, sniffing, 'I was going to leave this until later but, well… now seems like a good time in the circumstances.' Esme unfastened her rucksack. 'I just… well…' She lifted three gifts wrapped in metallic paper and finished with bows and tags from her rucksack and peered at the labels of each. 'They're only small. Just, you know, because it's Christmas and I wanted to say how much better you've made this trip for me. In fact, I'm sure I'd have had a miserable time without you.'

She handed one to Hortense and one to Brian. Then she looked at the label of the third again with regret before putting it back in her bag. She didn't suppose she'd have the opportunity to give Zach's to him now and she didn't know how appropriate it would be in the circumstances, even if she did.

'I'm sure that's not true at all,' Hortense said, turning over the parcel in her hands. She pulled off a mitten and tore at the sticky tape sealing it. 'I feel dreadful that I haven't bought anything for you.'

'I didn't buy to receive. I just wanted you to know that your company has meant a lot to me this week. Plus, I really like Christmas shopping, especially here. In fact, it's absolutely mind-blowing here!'

'Oh, dearest girl, they're marvellous!' Hortense held up her knitted booties for Brian. 'Aren't they marvellous, Brian?'

Brian nodded as he opened his and showed Hortense and she laughed to see he had a matching pair.

'Well, that can only mean one thing,' he said, laughing too. 'It means we have to live together, Hortense.'

'What a fabulous idea!' she said, laughing harder now. 'I'll be over next week with my trunk, dear boy!'

'Bloody hell, woman, we'd kill each other inside a week!'

Esme giggled. Though something told her that if Brian had agreed, even in jest, Hortense would probably take him at his word and might well pack up and head north to his house. And maybe that wouldn't be a bad thing for two people who seemed so happy and natural in each other's company. For a fleeting moment there was a tug of envy. What a wonderful ending for their story. If only there could have been an ending like that for Esme. But she shook the thought away. Perhaps the best she could hope for now, the best outcome she could strive for was to be happy on her own in a new life, and perhaps, if luck was on her side, the rest, one day, would follow. She was young enough and she had time, and perhaps all she really needed to make peace with was the notion that settling for nothing at all was sometimes better than settling for second best.

'Thank you, Esme,' Brian said.

'Yes, it's terribly kind of you,' Hortense agreed. 'Thank you.' She reached to give Esme a kiss on the cheek. Then her gaze went to the rucksack. 'I suppose the third gift…'

Esme nodded. 'I suppose I could keep hold of it. Maybe I can give it to him if he comes tonight.'

'Of course, dear girl. Quite.'

'And if he doesn't, I suppose I'll just take it home with me. I do quite like it anyway so it would be a nice souvenir of my time here.'

'Not much time to go and get a refund now, eh?' Brian said.

'I don't think I'd want to,' Esme said. 'It wouldn't feel right somehow.'

'I quite understand,' Hortense said with a sage nod.

'Do you think…' Esme began, but then the public address system burst into life and cut short her question. The assembled crowd (which had swelled considerably as Esme had waited in the cold) turned expectantly towards the stage, and Esme had to put all other thoughts to one side – for a while at least. There was an announcement, much cheering and then Santa Claus arrived with his elves – direct from their village, as the announcer said – and then even more cheering as they wished the crowd a merry Christmas. It wasn't quite Christmas yet but nobody cared. The elves danced under flashing disco lights and whooped and looked more like lithe extras from a seventies dance troupe than fabled woodland-dwelling, gift-constructing creatures with a peculiar unexplained loyalty to a fat red-coated man.

Esme couldn't help but smile. Despite everything, there was something about Santa's home town that was utterly enchanting, whatever your age. How could anybody be unhappy for long in a place like this?

Half an hour later the first fireworks exploded across the sky. Not quite as rare a sight as the aurora borealis but every bit as magical. Blue, green, gold and silver, scarlet and orange, they popped and fizzed and rained down to rapturous applause. There was music and narration too, and everything was choreographed to a theme that told of the various global beliefs around Christmas, tales and traditions of the festive season from around the world. They told the story of the Christmas log in Spain, the Yule Lads from Iceland and, of course, the Finns had to have a festive sauna! Esme had been to some impressive firework displays in her time but none so thoughtfully planned as these. From time to time she'd glance around the crowd and everywhere were little children, beside themselves with excitement, and parents not much better. Even though the temperatures were enough to keep her freezer ticking over back at home, the sheer numbers in the crowd massed around her and the swell of happiness was enough to keep her toasty warm.

She gave a broad smile as Hortense grabbed her and pulled her into such a determined hug that she might fall over when she let go. In fact, Esme was ready with an arm to catch her, just in case.

'Isn't it all marvellous!' Hortense cried. 'There'd be no wars at all if all the generals came along to see this!'

Esme laughed. 'That's true.'

'Merry Christmas, dear girl!'

'You too,' Esme said. 'It's honestly been wonderful getting to know you and I do hope we can stay in touch.'

'Just try to keep me away!'

It was then that Brian turned to see the outpourings. He looked rather uncomfortable, as if he wasn't quite sure if he ought to join in. That was the thing about Brian – he never quite looked as if he was certain he ought to join in and yet he was always welcome. Perhaps an after-effect of his marriage, but if he stayed with Hortense, Esme was pretty sure he'd soon lose that particular trait. She leaned in to give him a light kiss on the cheek.

'Merry Christmas to you too, Brian.'

'Absolutely,' he said. 'Thank you. I mean, merry Christmas.'

Another flash of scarlet burst across the sky and then rained down fiery sparks.

'Oh, that was a good one!' Hortense cried, bursting into spontaneous applause.

Then there was a hand on Esme's shoulder. She spun around, heart suddenly, inexplicably thumping, half expecting to see Zach behind her. Instead, it was Niko. Instinctively, she looked beyond him, scanning the crowds.

'You are looking for Zach?' Niko asked.

Esme blinked. Was it that obvious to everyone?

'Oh, I'm sorry… Hello, Niko.'

Niko gave a perfunctory smile. 'He's not with me. Sorry.'

Esme hesitated. What was Niko trying to tell her? Was it anything at all? 'Have you seen him today?' she asked.

'Yes.'

'He's alright?'

'Not completely.'

'Oh.' Esme didn't know what to say to that and she didn't really understand what it meant either. 'Is he planning to catch the rest of the fireworks?' she asked as another burst of magenta sparks rained down from the sky, accompanied by more applause from the audience.

'He will try.'

Esme forced a smile. In a strange way she felt they had been rivals for Zach's affections all week, and yet neither of them had ever made it so. 'You like him a lot, don't you?'

'Yes.' He gave a wry smile. 'You think we are lovers?'

Esme stared at him. 'Well, Brian and Hortense… they said…'

But she never got to finish the sentence because a girl Esme instantly recognised as one of their snowmobiling party spotted Niko and pushed through the crowd to grab him.

'Merry Christmas!' she cried.

Esme watched as Niko fell into easy small talk with the girl. The way he switched it on and off was really quite incredible, and to see him now it was as if the brief revelation he'd shared with Esme had never happened

But Esme knew that she needed to know, once and for all, how Zach felt about her, about Niko – about everything – and it was now or never. This was their last night in Rovaniemi, her last chance to get it right, to mend a broken friendship or coax it into something more. She'd got so close to Zach she couldn't lose him, not without a fight. However that played out – whether they left as friends or (and the hope now grew in her) something more than friends, she had to see him one last time at least. Besides, she had a gift for him – the perfect excuse to search him out and an innocent enough lead into a more meaningful dialogue.

Tuning into the conversation between Niko and the girl again, she listened for an opportunity to grab Niko's attention. She needed to hear more of what she was certain he'd been about to tell her and she somehow knew that it was important for her and Zach. All the while she kept one eye on the crowd, hoping to see Zach himself arrive.

The hoped for lull in their chat didn't materialise, but a few minutes later she saw Zach across the crowd. Her heart did that strange leap again, and she wanted to run to him, but there were so many bodies in the way she hadn't a hope of reaching him at all, let alone running. He didn't seem too concerned with reaching them either as he watched the skies, and Esme wondered whether perhaps he hadn't seen them. Pulling out her phone she sent a text. With all the noise of the fireworks and the music he probably wouldn't even hear the notification – all she could hope was that he'd notice her message at some point and come to find her.

Then she heard Niko's voice close to her ear.

'Come… we need a quiet place.'

Brian and Hortense were watching the fireworks and there was now no sign of the girl who had been talking to Niko. Zach was still stranded in the crowd – so close and yet so hopelessly out of reach.

'I think you will be glad to talk to me,' Niko insisted.

Another moment's hesitation, and then Esme gave a short nod. Whatever it was, she felt certain it was going to shed some much needed light on whatever the hell was going on here.

The temperature dropped noticeably as the crowd began to thin and soon they were standing on a street corner, away from the bustle but with the fireworks still cracking and popping above them in a blaze of colour, the odour of gunpowder strong on the icy air.

'Will you walk?' Niko asked. He seemed agitated, uncertain. Esme could hardly say she knew him well but she had never imagined that these emotions were even possible for him. It made her feel uncertain too. She didn't want to leave the safety of the crowds and the fireworks, but she nodded anyway and followed as he led the way, taking her along the road that led back to her hotel.

'Zach is my friend,' he said, picking up where they'd left off.

'I guessed that. He seems to like you. I hope he's a friend to all of us – me and Hortense and Brian. We're all very fond of him.'

'He's dear to me.'

Esme hesitated. What was that Hortense was always saying about the direct approach? From what Niko had said earlier, perhaps that direct approach wouldn't be as difficult as she'd imagined – at least with him. 'You like him as much more than a friend?'

Niko nodded slowly. 'I think… you do too.'

Esme flushed. 'I suppose I do.'

'Then we are the same.'

'But you two…' she offered uncertainly. *Come on, the direct approach*, she reminded herself before beginning again. 'You spent the night together.'

'Sleeping,' Niko said, in a voice that spoke of weariness at people's assumptions. 'I took the bed and Zach slept on the floor. We were drunk.'

Esme's cheeks flared hotter still. Hadn't she and Zach done exactly the same and managed it perfectly well without having sex? 'I'm sorry, I thought…'

'It doesn't matter. I suppose it would be easy to imagine something else.'

'I guess,' she said with a self-conscious smile.

Niko nodded this time and faced the path ahead once more, seemingly content with the explanation. Or perhaps just not that interested after all. Then he spoke again.

'He has been to Rovaniemi before. He told you this?'

'He mentioned it.'

'Did he tell you what happened?'

'No. I only know he wasn't here alone like he is this time.'

'He came with his wife.'

Esme stopped dead. Niko was a few paces on before he turned to see her standing on the pavement staring at him and walked back to join her. He didn't speak; he just waited for her to say something, but she didn't know what to say. All she could do was run two words over and over in her head, unable to compute them.

His wife?

How could she have been so stupid? How could she have been taken in a second time? Did she have *mug* tattooed on her forehead? First Warren and Shelly and now Zach. How many more before she learned her lesson?

'Well,' she said coldly, beginning to walk again. 'Thanks for telling me. He never mentioned his wife.'

'It pains him to talk of her.'

At this the anger subsided almost as quickly as it had fired up. 'Why?' she asked after a pause.

'I didn't remember them at first,' Niko continued. 'But when you both arrived for your snowmobile lessons this week he came to talk to me. I see so many people come and go on their vacations… but then I remembered them because it had been their honeymoon and I'd shared a drink with them in their hotel after their lesson. They were nice and very much in love.'

'So, where is she now?'

Niko turned to face her and they both came to a halt again, this time at his instigation. 'She's dead.'

Esme suddenly felt sick. All this time she'd sensed something was off but she'd never imagined it could be something so massive.

'How…?' Her throat was dry as she tried to get the question out. 'How long has she been dead?'

'I think for two years.'

'So their original visit was a long time ago?'

'Three years ago.'

'Oh God!'

Esme's eyes filled with tears. How could she have got this so wrong? She wanted to run and find Zach and fold her arms around him. She wanted to tell him it would be alright. But it wouldn't be, would it? For Zach there would never be an alright. How did you move on from a loss like that? How did anyone help you?

'So they were only married for a year? Do you know how…?'

Niko shook his head. 'I did not ask too much. He wanted to talk and I was happy to listen.'

'And I kissed him,' she said, hardly realising that the words she'd run through her head had come out of her mouth.

'He told me.'

Esme looked at him. 'What did he say?'

'He was angry.'

'I know that much – he hasn't spoken to me since.'

'No, you misunderstand. He was angry with himself.'

'With himself? Why would he be angry with himself? He didn't do anything wrong – it was my fault…'

But Niko suddenly looked at a spot over her shoulder, his eyes wide. Esme turned, half expecting to see a furious Zach wanting to know why they'd been discussing him, but instead she saw a hooded figure and a fist fly past her. Niko swerved, simultaneously pulling her from harm's way. The hooded man skidded on the icy pavement, thrown off balance by his miss, and when he turned to face Niko again for another try and she finally caught a glimpse of his face, Esme's heart stopped.

His name frozen in her throat, she could only watch in numb shock as he swung for Niko again. It seemed, however, that Niko's attacker hadn't banked on a super-fit snowmobile instructor who was also a lot younger than him. The next thing Esme saw was Niko duck another punch, and then his own fist connecting squarely with his attacker's jaw, sending him crashing to the ground.

Instinctively, Esme ran to the man now groaning on the floor. 'Warren!'

Warren pushed himself to sit, glaring at Niko. Esme knelt on the snow beside him.

'What… what are you doing here?' She was incredulous, but somewhere beyond the shock of seeing him she'd always known he was capable of this. She just didn't know how to feel about it.

'I came to take you home,' he said, struggling to get purchase on the ice and get back on his feet. But he slipped again.

'But I'm coming home tomorrow anyway!' Esme squeaked. 'That's ridiculous!'

'Isn't it a good thing I came?' he said, ignoring her. 'Now I see what's been going on.'

'No!' Esme said quickly following Warren's train of thought. She threw an anxious glance at Niko, who was still standing a couple of feet away, eyeing them warily. 'It's not like that!'

'There had to be a reason you were being so cagey, and now I know,' Warren said, his own darker glance settling on Niko.

'No.' Esme shook her head. 'You've got it wrong! Niko's just my friend!'

'Yes, I can see that. Friendly is one way to describe it…'

'Warren, please, you've got it wrong—'

Warren leapt to his feet this time, slipping and sliding but managing finally. He waved a dismissive hand at Esme to silence her, and Niko put his fists up in a defensive stance. Warren eyed him up, clearly appraising how he'd fare if he took another swing at him. Then Niko spoke to Esme, never taking his eyes from Warren.

'You know this man?'

'He's my…'

'Fiancé,' Warren finished for her. 'That's the word you're having so much trouble with.' He looked back at Niko. 'She's mine.'

This time Niko looked at Esme when he spoke and in his expression there was a note of utter disbelief. 'You are marrying *him*?'

'No… yes…at least I was. It's sort of complicated.'

Now Warren turned to stare at her in disbelief. 'Is it?'

'Warren, I…' She hesitated. Why couldn't she just say it? What was she so scared of? Nothing would be settled until she did and nobody could move on while they stayed in this limbo – least of all her. But then, perhaps this – here and now – this wasn't the time or place to do it. Nobody deserved that sort of humiliation. She needed to get him somewhere private.

'Warren, we need—'

Throwing Niko a look of pure loathing, Warren grabbed Esme by the wrist. She cried out in surprise. Niko made an uncertain move towards them but then stepped back at Esme's pleading look. She didn't need him to antagonise Warren any further. Niko might have survived one onslaught and he might yet survive another, but Warren was fit and strong from hours spent at the gym and she couldn't take the chance that Niko might get injured.

'We're going home,' Warren said, starting to walk and dragging Esme with him. But she dug her heels into the snow and held back. He rounded on her.

'What it is now?'

'Warren, we need to talk…'

'We can talk all you like at home.'

'Warren—'

Niko took a step towards them now, as if he might intervene, and Esme shot him another pleading look that she hoped he'd understand. This was a quarrel only she could resolve and she had to do it alone. He halted, tensed and he looked ready to step in at any moment, and Esme could only hope that he wouldn't.

'Stop messing around!' Warren said, trying to walk again.

'No!'

Her voice was steady and clear but her stomach churned and her legs shook.

'You want to stay here with "your friend"?' Warren stopped and turned to her now. 'You think he'd still be that pretty if I rearranged his features? Would you still want to be "friends" then?'

'We are not…' Niko put in, but Warren silenced him with a look.

'Niko's not my boyfriend, if that's what you're getting at,' Esme said, giving Niko a look that said she was grateful he'd had the sense to be quiet again. 'Why can't you ever just listen to me?'

'You looked cosy enough to me.'

'How can you say that – you didn't see anything!'

'I saw enough.'

'That's the trouble with you,' Esme said, 'you only see what you want to.'

He stared at her now, confused. 'I saw my woman getting a bit too friendly with another bloke.'

'I'm not yours! I'm not your property! I can talk to another human being if I want to!'

'Yeah?' He reached for her wrist again. 'Well, you can talk to me on the plane.'

'No!' Esme yanked her arm free again. 'I'm not coming.'

'Esme, stop pissing about. It's cost me an arm and a leg to come and fetch you and now you tell me you're not coming back with me?'

'*Tomorrow*, Warren. I'm coming back tomorrow, just like I'm supposed to. Not until then.'

He looked even more confused. 'What am I supposed to do?'

'You could wait until tomorrow if you're so determined to travel with me.'

'How the hell am I supposed to do that?'

'I don't know. I suppose you'll just have to wait until the morning.'

'Wait? Where?'

'Have you booked a hotel?'

'Why would I book a hotel?'

'You thought I'd come straight back with you like a good, obedient girl? You thought I wouldn't even question it?' In days gone by Warren could have made such an assumption safely. He'd have told her to jump and she would have got a pad to write down his height requirements. But not anymore.

'You're not coming then?' he asked, looking as if the conversation was rapidly losing him. Perhaps it was – Warren wasn't used to people telling him no.

Esme turned to Niko now. 'Know any good hotels?'

'Plenty,' Niko said with a wry smile of his own. 'But with vacancies tonight – I would be very doubtful of that.'

Esme chewed on her lip for a moment. Then she turned to Warren. 'If you want to travel with me tomorrow then you'll have to stay with me tonight. In the spare bed in my room,' she added quickly. 'I suppose it would give us time to talk anyway.'

'What about the flight I booked for us?'

'What about it?'

'We'll miss it.'

'I've told you – catch yours if you want to, but mine's wasted money, I'm afraid, because I intend to keep my original booking. Perhaps the airline will let you change yours if you want to stay the night. Perhaps they'll let you have a refund for mine. If you're not happy with any of that, there's not a lot I can do about it. The offer of a bed is there, but if you really feel strongly that you want to go back tonight then I'm not going to stop you.'

'You'd let me fly alone?'

'I don't know how you expected anything else. I did tell you on the phone that I wouldn't come home early.'

Warren opened his mouth to speak but then clamped it shut again. He glowered at her, a look of fury that would have had her changing her mind in days gone by. But she wasn't backing down tonight. Wasn't she Matilda Greenwood's granddaughter? Esme had no idea where that girl had been hiding for the past few years but she was here now and things were going to be different.

'I can't afford another ticket for tomorrow!' Warren whined, changing tack to try to persuade Esme to back down. 'I've spent everything I have getting here already!'

'I'm sorry, but I can't help with that. Maybe you should have taken more notice of what I'd said on the phone before you made the booking.'

Esme began to walk. She'd wanted to hear more from Niko about Zach, and then she'd wanted to find Zach and hear it all in his words and maybe set things straight between the two of them, armed with a new understanding of all he'd been through. But now Warren was here and she couldn't do any of that. All she could do was try to sort one mess at a time, starting with the one that was currently watching her leave, stubbornly refusing to accept a version of her that he'd never known.

'I'll walk with you!' Niko called. He jogged to catch up, and that was enough to have Warren dashing to her other side.

'Back off!' he growled.

'Warren…' Esme turned to him. 'I can assure you that Niko is not remotely interested in me.'

'What makes you so sure?'

'I might be interested in you, however,' Niko said with a mocking smile.

'If you weren't making yourself look like such an arse right now,' Esme added.

Niko's smile became a grin, showing a flash of that old, carefree charm again, while Warren looked confused and then horrified. He was such an alpha male it was almost laughable.

'Niko…' Esme said gently. 'While I appreciate the sentiment, I really need to talk to Warren. Alone. So you don't need to worry about me – go back to the fireworks and enjoy the last hour.'

'But—'

'I'll be fine – honestly. There's no need to worry.'

'Where are you going?' Niko asked, throwing a look of deepest distrust at Warren.

'The simplest thing would be to go back to my hotel for a bit of quiet. And maybe a glass or two of lakka.'

Niko grinned again. 'Zach said you liked it.'

Warren's expression had eased as Esme had talked of taking him back to the hotel, but then it tensed again.

'Who's Zach?'

'My lover,' Niko said, and Esme gave a grateful smile for the white lie that had perhaps come just a little too easily to him. He turned back to Esme, who nodded to reassure him that she'd be OK. Then, with a last glance at Warren, he turned on his heel and started back to the fireworks party. She and Warren headed in the opposite direction, and as they walked she half imagined that every few yards Niko would turn and check on her, but she didn't look back to see.

Chapter Twenty-One

'Why are you doing this?' Warren's voice cut through the silence. Esme was still thinking about Zach and what Niko had told her and she was finding it hard to focus on the more immediate problem of Warren's arrival. In reality, while it was rotten timing, it had only served to hasten a moment she'd gradually realised had been coming for some time. Perhaps it was a blessing after all. She just had to keep it together now and stay strong to take advantage of it.

'I don't know what you mean. I'm doing my best to help you out here.'

'You're hurting me. You're making me look like a mug.'

'I don't mean to. The flight problem – that's your mess.'

'I don't mean the flights. I don't give a shit about the flights.'

'Then what do you mean?'

'I love you, babe. I came all this way to get you – and I haven't even got a proper coat. How can you throw it back in my face like this?'

'I know you think you love me…'

'You don't think I do? Why would I fly all this way to get you if I didn't love you?'

'If you loved me you'd have flown all this way with me in the first place. Not just to take me back because it was annoying you that I'm not doing what you want, but because you wanted to be with me. You knew how much this trip meant to me and you knew why. It wasn't a case of me being unreasonable, demanding, spoilt. It was because of what it represented – that was why I wanted to come.'

'You think the only reason I'm here now is because you were annoying me?'

'Isn't it? You and I both know the truth. Perhaps I didn't quite phrase it right – you're here now not really because you're annoyed at me, because annoyance is too mild. The reason you're here now is because you're proud and you hate to lose. You love to call the shots. Usually you do – with me, with Shelly… but this time you can't and you don't know how to deal with that.'

'What the hell does that mean?'

'It's a battle of wills. It's always been about control for you. You always win, but just this once you were scared you might not. So you pull out all the stops – fly over here, take me home, get me settled in the flat again, pile on the guilt for what I'd done to you, make certain I don't ever want to do it again and preserve your unbroken record of wins over Esme.'

'You're not making any sense.'

'For the first time in a long time I *am* making sense.'

'So you're not coming home with me?'

Esme turned her face to the heavens, clinging onto the scream of frustration building in her throat. How many times did she have to explain this?

'I've told you already that I'll come back when I'm supposed to.' She turned once more to the road ahead. 'When did you arrive in Rovaniemi?'

'This morning.'

'This morning? So what on earth have you been doing all day?'

'Trying to find you,' he said, a new tone of accusation in his voice. 'You weren't at the hotel you said you'd be at and I went there at least four times to look for you.'

She turned to him. 'Didn't it occur to you that I'm on holiday and that being on holiday might mean leaving the hotel occasionally?'

'You were gone all day.'

'I was with some friends.'

'Who? That bloke I just saw you with?'

'No. And it was nobody who might be a threat to you, if that's what you're thinking. Even then, you've no right to lecture me when you've been trying to get back with Shelly!' She paused, tried to even out her tone again.

His mouth turned into a perfect O of shock, but Esme waved an impatient hand at him.

'Don't think I don't know about that.'

'But, babe—'

'Don't bother; I don't need your excuses. When's your flight out?'

'What does it matter if you're not coming?'

'I'm just trying to work out what we need to do if you want to be on it. I'm assuming you do want to be on it, as you said you couldn't afford another and you don't seem all that keen to organise anything else with the airline.'

'They wouldn't let me organise anything else.'

'You're not even interested in asking, are you? Still convinced that I'm going to change my mind and come with you. I'm right, aren't I?'

'I don't see what difference it makes to you anyway. Tonight, tomorrow... it's nearly the end of your holiday and you said you're supposed to be flying out in the morning anyway.'

'But maybe there are people I want to see before I go.'

'Like who?'

'My friends.'

Warren sniffed. 'I don't see why these friends you've only just met are so important.'

'I know – you wouldn't. Nobody's important to you. Except you, of course.'

'What does that mean? What's happened to you? Why are you being like this?'

Esme shook her head. 'So what time is your flight supposed to be? The one you've got booked?'

'Midnight,' Warren replied, sounding like a sulky teen.

Peeling back a mitten she checked her watch. 'It doesn't leave you much time to get back to the airport if you're going to catch it.'

'I don't understand why you're being like this,' he said, ignoring her warning. 'Just tell me what's happened. It's got to be another bloke!'

'Nothing's happened and it's not another bloke.'

'I knew I shouldn't have let you come here.'

Esme turned to him, incredulous. 'You didn't!'

'I couldn't stop you, could I? You came anyway after I told you I didn't want to. I didn't expect you to come on your own.'

'Exactly – you had the option to come with me. I never once said you couldn't – in fact, I wanted you to. You knew how much this trip meant to me and it would have cost you nothing to come. But still you said no. You can hardly blame me for coming without you. Why shouldn't I?'

'Yeah, well, I'm here now – freezing my balls off. This was why I never wanted to come in the first place.'

'Yes, you're here to take me home early.' Esme stopped walking and inclined her head at a brightly lit building. 'This is my hotel.'

'Yeah. I know – remember. I've spent all day hanging around it waiting to see you.'

'I didn't ask you to.'

'Well, I did. That should mean something to you.'

'Should I call a taxi for you? To take you to the airport?'

'Babe… Don't do this…'

'Or you can come into the hotel and stay with me until tomorrow and we'll see about getting you on a flight then. Of course, there's no guarantee that there'll be room on my flight so we might have to make it the next one they have, but there's not a lot I can do about that now. So it's your choice really whether you stay tonight and take that risk or whether you go now on your own.'

'Please…'

Her glance went to the hotel windows. She half expected to see Niko in there waiting for her, perhaps having raced down a shortcut to head them off. Or maybe even Zach. But the brightly lit bar was almost empty, apart from a member of staff cleaning tables and a couple on a corner sofa wrapped in each other's arms. It was hard not to be disappointed by the absence of an ally, but she couldn't think of that now, and, in reality, either one of those men being at the hotel waiting for her might only complicate things again. Perhaps it was better that she was on her own with this after all, as the reason she was in this mess that only she could sort out was because she'd never grown the backbone she'd needed to deal with Warren long before now.

She turned back to him and held him in a frank gaze. 'Warren…' she began slowly, 'what do you think of my hair?'

'What?'

'My hair. It's short again. I took the extensions out.'

'But you can put them back in, can't you?'

'I don't think I want to.'

'Oh.'

'And I've put on a little padding this week.'

'What do you mean?'

'I've eaten like a pig. Cakes morning, noon and night. Probably put on about half a stone. What do you think of that?'

He smiled, letting out a long breath of relief. 'If that's all you're worried about, babe, we can get it fixed. Extra gym for the next few weeks, a low-carb detox and you'll be back to your normal size again.'

'Only it's not my normal size – it's the size *you* want me to be.'

'You look good that size.'

'*You* think I look good that size.'

'But you do.'

'Why?'

'You—'

'I don't want to be that size. It makes me miserable trying to stay that size. And I bloody hate your gym. I don't want to see it ever again. I don't want to wear that horrible itchy underwear you love so much, and I don't want to spend half my life on Oxford Street trying to guess what clothes you'd like to see me in, and I don't want to be woken up at three in the morning for a cheese toastie when you've had one too many at The Duke.'

'What are you saying?'

Esme shook her head. 'I think you already know, and that's why I won't be coming home with you tonight.'

She was sitting at the bar of the hotel. For a while she and Warren had been able to hear the fireworks display, even from this many blocks away, but in the last half hour it had become silent, apart from the low strains of easy-listening music being piped in through the bar's sound system and the low hum of conversation of a few other guests who, like her, had returned from the show early. Inari was on duty at the bar. Esme hadn't really talked to her since their chat at the start of the holiday when she'd grilled the barmaid about Niko. Inari brought a fresh coffee over and placed it in front of Esme with a courteous smile.

'Would you like that charged to your room?'

'Yes, thank you.'

'You are checking out tomorrow?'

Esme nodded. 'I'll be sorry to leave.'

'Perhaps you'll come back?'

'I hope so. One day.' Esme gave her a grateful smile; Inari nodded, smiled in return and moved on.

Esme took a sip of her coffee. It was hot and fresh and she needed the caffeine. She wanted a clear head tonight. She wanted to say exactly the right thing in the right way and alcohol was not going to help.

Esme watched Inari walk away with her used cup. She could have gone back to her room with Warren but she wouldn't have felt comfortable in there with him now that she really thought about it. Besides, down here in the bar she could keep an eye on the hotel foyer. Zach hadn't replied to her message from earlier and she couldn't help but think he was ignoring it on purpose.

Her phone lay now on the bar top, next to her coffee. Despite everything that had happened, Warren was still on her mind too. He'd come a long way to be disappointed and she felt guilty about it – some old habits were going to be harder to break than others. Unlocking the phone, she began to type.

I'm sorry.

Her finger hovered over the button that would send it to his phone. But then she deleted it and locked her phone again. A message like that might only complicate again what she'd hoped was now sorted. And what did she really have to be sorry about? She'd made mistakes, she'd handled some things badly – everyone did from time to time. But at least her mistakes had been genuine ones. Warren's had been deceit, lies and manipulation dressed up as mistakes. He'd wanted it all and he'd been willing to do anything to get it. Everyone but her had been able to see it all along. She pushed her phone away, afraid she'd succumb to temptation if it was close to hand.

Since the day she'd met him, Warren had been subtly and insidiously reshaping her into someone who suited his needs, crushing everything that had made her attractive to him in the first place. She supposed, looking back on it all now, she had been a challenge he couldn't resist. He'd always been a game player, and she'd been the ultimate contest of wills. He'd almost won too, and she couldn't help but wonder if Shelly had once been like her. Had Warren reshaped her, discarding her when he'd finally got what he'd wanted to start again on a new project? Was that what he would have done to Esme if she'd let him? One day she might have woken up to find herself replaced in the way she herself had replaced Shelly – but would she have had the good fortune to find out before the bombshell had landed, as Shelly had done?

Just to be certain that she wouldn't pick up her phone, Esme wrapped her hands around the coffee cup, savouring the warmth beneath her curled fingers. It wasn't particularly cold in the bar but there was something comforting about cradling a hot cup when snow was driving against the windows.

As she gazed at the window and sipped her drink, Esme gradually became aware of a commotion in the foyer, racing footsteps and raised voices. Placing her coffee back on the bar, she made to get up to investigate, but then Zach burst into the bar. He rushed over.

'Are you alright?' His eyes were all over her, as if looking for signs of distress or injury. 'Where is he? You're not going home

with him? Niko told me… no, don't answer; there's something…
let me tell you this…'

Esme shook her head. Her heart was pounding again; she felt
sick with nerves – excited and hopeful and yet despondent all at
the same time. She'd become a stronger person in the last hour,
but there was no trial that could make her ready for this. She took
a breath, and although her voice was measured and calm, it was
nothing like the emotions under the surface. 'There's something
I need to tell you and I really need to do it first.'

Zach dragged a hand through hair that had been flattened
by a woolly hat. He stared at her. 'Can't I… please? If I don't say
this now I might never…' He looked pained, like the words he
needed to say were barbed, lodged inside. They were painful to
keep in, but even more painful to get out. 'Are you going home
with him?' he asked. 'Because you can't. You might hate me, but
I have to say this because I care about you—'

'Zach—'

'Please, Esme… just let me finish. He's not the man for you.'
He took a gulp of air, wringing his hat in his hands. 'I know he's
not the man for you. I know this because… well, because… I
could be. The man, I mean. The right one.'

Esme stared as Zach took the stool next to her, holding her
in a pleading gaze.

'I know I've been a top wanker and you must have wondered
what the hell I've been playing at,' he said. 'And I know there are
things I should have explained. I couldn't…'

'Your wife,' Esme said.

Zach nodded, relief evident in the way his features relaxed.
'Niko told you, I guess.'

'Some. I don't think he told me everything. We were interrupted. That bit you already know about.'

'Your boyfriend…'

'Warren.'

'He's here? In the hotel?' Zach glanced around the bar. 'In your room? Niko said—'

Esme shook her head. 'On his way to the airport. It's over – for good this time.'

'He's OK with that?'

'I wouldn't go that far. But I told him straight and I don't think even he would try to argue this time.' She gave a small smile. 'He'll be OK… he can go home to his wife.'

'His wife?'

'Long story.'

'Right. But you're OK?'

'Depends on your definition of OK. I'm dealing with it and I'm relieved it's over, if I'm honest. At least I hope it's over. I should have done it long ago. I know you were trying to tell me as much that night on the bus. In fact, a lot of times. I was listening, you know. I was just scared.'

'It was nothing to do with me and I should have kept my mouth shut. It was just…'

'It's alright. It's done now, either way.'

'So you're…?' He made a move towards her but then shrank back. 'Presumptuous of me… You're single – it means nothing, of course. It's just that—'

'Has he told you yet?' a new voice rang across the bar. The few customers sitting in quiet corners enjoying a peaceful drink whipped round to see Hortense gripping the doorframe. She was panting, and a second later Brian brought up the rear as she began to march over.

Esme opened her mouth to reply and then closed it again. Her gaze switched from Hortense and Brian and then back to Zach and she wasn't quite sure what was going on here. She'd thought Zach about to tell her something important, maybe the thing she longed to hear, but now... Then she was drawn to the doorway again as Niko arrived too, following Hortense and Brian in.

'I hope you've sent that animal packing!' Hortense continued. Despite fighting for breath it seemed she'd rather become hypoxic than let a moment of drama pass by without her input.

'What? Warren? How did you...?' Esme saw that Niko looked a bit too sheepish and it didn't take much to guess the rest.

'I'm sorry,' he said. 'I was worried about you and I did not know who else to tell. Things seemed a little... dangerous.'

'He's all bark and no bite,' Esme said with a wry smile. 'Warren likes to think he's dangerous but it's all a show.'

Niko narrowed his eyes. 'It did not look that way to me. It didn't feel that way when he hit me either.'

Esme flushed. 'Oh God, I'm sorry. I didn't mean to make light of that, I only meant...'

'I'm not hurt,' Niko said. He gave a small smile. 'Perhaps my pride, a little.'

'I do feel bad that you got involved, though,' Esme said. 'If I'd known things would get that out of hand I would never have—'

'You could not have prevented that. Men like him know only one language,' Niko said. 'It's not the first time I've been hit.'

'But you're alright? No permanent damage?' Esme asked.

Niko shook his head. 'Don't worry.'

'What a monster!' Hortense put in. 'And he flew all this way to drag you home?' she added, folding her arms tight across her bosom as she looked at Esme.

'I'm afraid so. It sounds a bit silly now, though, saying it like that.'

'There's nothing silly about physical violence,' Hortense said. 'Is he a terrible brute? Has he done this sort of thing before?'

'Never to me,' Esme said quickly. Warren might be many things but at least he'd never hit her. 'He's been known to get into the odd fight outside a bar and he's got a jealous, possessive streak a mile wide. But it's all for show really – he's not as tough as he likes to make out.'

'Hmmm,' Hortense said, looking at Brian, Niko and Zach in turn.

'You can all relax now anyway,' Esme said. 'Because he's gone.'

'And you're not going back to live with him?' Hortense asked, though it was evidently a rhetorical question because Esme was certain that if she'd given any other reply than a negative one Hortense would have restrained her and refused to let her leave Rovaniemi. Just to reinforce her intent, she started forward, but she wobbled so violently that Brian had to race to catch her.

'No,' Esme said. 'I'm not. I have a little house in Derbyshire that needs some TLC. It's missing life within its walls and it's not used to being cold and empty. I think I'll go and live there for a bit. I think my grandma would like that. It's been a weird day,' she continued, looking at them all. 'Who am I kidding – it's been a bloody weird week! Would it be very rude of me to say thank you for coming to my rescue but I might just need my bed right now?'

'If it had been anyone else I'd have considered it rather ungrateful,' Hortense said with a smile. 'I'm glad to see you finally came to your senses, dear girl. I said to Brian there was a man at home, even though you hadn't told us. I said he was trouble too. Didn't I say it, Brian?'

Brian nodded. 'You did.'

Hortense barely gave his answer a moment. 'I'm seldom wrong about these things.'

'I'm sorry I didn't say anything before,' Esme said. 'I just... I suppose I thought if I didn't mention him I could pretend all that trouble at home wasn't going on.'

'Absolutely,' Hortense said. 'A brief escape.'

'Sort of.' Esme turned to her coffee and wrapped a hand around the cup. It was almost cold and she wondered vaguely whether there was any point in ordering a new one. It wasn't like she needed much help to keep her awake tonight, but perhaps more caffeine might not help in that regard.

'If you're quite alright then we won't keep you,' Hortense said. Esme looked up with a grateful smile. Brian took Hortense's hand and nodded towards the door. For a moment she looked as if she might say something more to Esme, but then relented and leaned into him.

'Goodnight then,' Brian said to Esme. 'Sleep well.'

'Thanks,' Esme said. 'You too.'

Esme thought about the few hours now remaining between her and a return to her life back in England – which was almost certainly messier than it had ever been for all her efforts to tidy it up. Warren was gone but there was still a lot to sort out. Her flight home was tomorrow, but what was waiting for her at the other end? The fact was, she no longer had anything in particular to rush home for. The idea was oddly appealing though. What if she just rebelled? What if she refused to follow the rules? Where was the rule that said she had to go home anyway? What if she just stayed here in Lapland? She could do it, and the notion was deliciously full of the promise of adventure. Would it be so hard to get work and a place to stay? Perhaps Niko could help. What if she phoned her parents tonight and told them? She was sure they'd take care of her grandma's house for a while. How long was a while? Three months… six months? There was no denying it would be the adventure of a lifetime. Although, now that she thought about it, she wasn't entirely sure she hadn't already had one of those in the week she'd been here – it had certainly been eventful.

'Goodnight, dear girl,' Hortense said. She bid the same to Zach and Niko and then leaned on Brian as they made their way to the lifts. As they disappeared into the lift Esme turned to Niko.

'Thank you for looking out for me. I appreciate it.'

'I would not have done anything else.'

'I don't doubt it for a minute. You're a lovely person.'

He smiled and nodded, and then he clapped Zach on the back. 'Take care, man.'

It sounded as if Niko had already decided they wouldn't be seeing him again. Perhaps he was their Mary Poppins or Nanny McPhee – when they no longer needed him, he simply disappeared over the blue Arctic horizon. Although what he'd fixed for them, Esme still wasn't entirely sure. She wasn't sure anything was fixed as far as her and Zach were concerned, because she wasn't even sure what did or didn't need fixing.

'You too,' Zach said, and then Niko was gone. Not with an umbrella or a walking stick, but with an airy wave that took him out of the bar.

Which just left Esme and Zach. He stood and looked at her, and it seemed he was in no hurry to go anywhere, despite what she'd said about being tired. She could understand why – they needed to talk and she knew that, but the truth was she didn't feel strong enough right now. The future was all new and untested and she needed to understand how she felt about that before she could make promises of any other kind.

'We need to talk,' he said.

'I know. But everything's happening at once and I don't know if the answers I might give you at this moment are the right ones. They'd be instinctive, not measured enough.'

'What if I promise not to ask questions of you? What if you just let me talk?'

She shook her head. 'I can't. I might speak from my heart and not my head and I might give answers whether you're asking questions or not.'

Zach stepped forward. He placed his hat on the bar and took her hand in both of his. 'You say that like it's a bad thing.'

She couldn't deny the pull of his eyes and the heat of his skin, and she had to tear her gaze away, even though she couldn't bring herself to relinquish the feel of his hand closed over hers. Her heart was screaming for him, and yet her head was telling her to beware. For once, she was going to listen to her head because her heart had got her into enough trouble. 'I need time,' she said. 'Sorry.'

'OK.' He let her hand drop and retook his stool. 'At least let me explain some things. Then you can sleep on it – tell me in the morning what you think.'

Esme nodded and braced herself for the full story. To see him pained would cause her pain too but he needed to tell it and she needed to know.

'You know about Libby,' he said.

'Your wife?'

'Yes.'

'Niko told me she died a couple of years back. He said you hadn't been married long.'

'A year. We were in that first blush, trying for a baby, getting the house perfect. She used to say our life was like a fairy tale. It wasn't – nobody's is. We had bills and worries like everyone else, but it was OK because we had each other. She was the best, the most amazing woman. Whenever we were together all we did was laugh.'

'So what happened?'

'She had this… this heart defect. All along this ticking bomb in her chest. We didn't know – nobody knew. Why would we? She collapsed one day at work. Died on the floor of her office. They told me it would have been quick – instant. She wouldn't have known anything about it.'

'Oh God. I'm—'

'Sorry, I know. What else can you say?'

'It's been hard?'

'Yeah, but I think… sometimes I think I'm over the worst of it and that makes me feel guilty. I shouldn't be moving on, because Libby can't move on, can she? I feel like I owe her grief for the rest of my life.'

'She doesn't sound like the sort of person who would have wished that on you.'

'She wasn't. I'm being weird about it, but that's how grief gets you. You think weird things. I mean, isn't it awful that my first thought when I heard the news had been thank God we hadn't had that baby we'd wanted?'

Esme put a hand out, but then drew it back. How did you comfort someone for a loss such as that? No gesture felt big enough. She wanted to pull him into her arms and kiss away his sadness, but that was her heart, misbehaving again. Her head told her to sit and listen.

'It's the shock that gets you at first,' he continued. 'I didn't even believe it – for days I kept expecting her to walk in, throw her bag down, ask for a foot massage or a cup of tea, tell me something funny that had happened during her day.' He gave a small smile, his gaze somewhere in a perfect past. 'She was a real live wire – full of energy and endless enthusiasm – like a big kid. That's what made it really hard to believe. How could someone with such vitality and spirit have this fatal weakness all along? How could someone so completely alive suddenly be dead? If we'd known perhaps I could have told her to slow down, look after herself. Not that she would have listened. Life was for living, she used to say, and she lived it well, even if it wasn't for long.'

'You came here with her?'

He nodded. 'She loved Christmas – like, seriously adored it. She'd always wanted to meet "the proper Santa". We had the most incredible time here – huskies, snowmobiles, cross-country skiing… did it all.

But as we flew home she was still disappointed that we hadn't managed to see the Northern Lights – the weather hadn't been quite right – so I promised her we'd save up and try again the following year and she was so excited she'd marked a date on the calendar – we hadn't even booked it at that point. She said it ought to be our annual Christmas trip, and when we had kids we could take them every year too.' He gave a short laugh. 'Not sure where she was expecting the money to come from, but I would have tried. God knows I would have tried to get it for her. I'd have done anything for her.'

'But you never made that second year?'

'She died in the September.'

They were silent for a moment, Esme taking it all in and Zach lost in his own past.

'I don't know what to say,' she said finally.

'Whatever you might think of, you can bet it's all been said already anyway. I don't need you to say anything; I just wanted you to understand why sometimes I was a bit…'

'I know. Why did you come back alone? Wasn't it a painful thing to put yourself through?'

'This year I just decided… I don't really know why. For some reason I just needed to come back and see those lights. To go home to Libby's grave and tell her all about it.' He looked up at Esme, finally back in the room. 'I suppose that sounds morbid,' he said, his expression one of self-conscious awareness for the first time since he began the story.

Esme shook her head. 'No, not one bit. I understand it more than you realise. Like you said to me, we deal with grief the best way we know how and sometimes it makes us weird – at least to other people. Who am I to judge how you handle yours?'

'So when we were out the other night,' he continued. 'On the Northern Lights chase… and I finally got to see the Lights and then…'

Esme flushed, the memories of that impetuous kiss barrelling into her. There were many things she'd wished undone in her life, but right now that topped the list. She shook her head. 'I'm so sorry… it was a silly impulse. If I'd known—'

'Of course you didn't know. I was the idiot for not telling you, so if it's anyone's fault it's mine. And the truth is I liked it. I mean, I *really* liked it. I like you, Esme, but…'

She could only imagine what kind of pain and guilt that must have caused him. To be on what amounted to a pilgrimage to honour the memory of his dead wife and yet, at the moment he'd made the focus of that memory, he'd found himself kissing another woman. It was no wonder he'd been avoiding Esme – he must have been going through emotional torture. More than ever she wanted to reach for him. But was this explanation his way of saying that even though he liked her there were still barriers they couldn't hope to overcome? Wasn't she doing the same by holding back and trying to listen to reason where her own feelings were concerned? There was an indisputable attraction, there might even be the beginnings of love, but was it enough?

'It's OK,' she said. 'I suppose it's just bad timing for both of us. Maybe if we'd met at a different time or place…' She shrugged. 'Who knows?'

His smile was bleak, the smile of a man accepting the inevitable.

'Bad timing,' he repeated. 'Seems to be the story of my life.'

Esme rifled in her rucksack and drew out his gift. This might be the last opportunity she had to give it to him. It might be the last time she ever saw him at all – at least alone. She slid it across the bar towards him.

'What's this?' he asked.

'I didn't think I'd see you tonight to give it. Maybe not even at all, considering… But you might as well have it now.'

'It's for me?'

'That's why I gave it to you,' Esme said with a small smile.

'What's it for?' he asked, taking the gift and turning it over in his hand.

'Christmas.'

He pulled at the sticky tape. 'I didn't get you anything.'

'I didn't buy it to get something back. I wanted to show you how much I've appreciated your friendship this week. It could have been a very different trip without you, Brian and Hortense.'

'I'm not sure I really deserve this,' he said. 'I would imagine I've given you as much annoyance as I have pleasure.'

'Not really. Well, not often, anyway.'

He briefly looked up and she smiled. Then he turned back to the present and tore away the paper to reveal the snow globe inside. He shook it, and then stood it on the bar.

'I love it,' he said, gazing into its depths as the silver snow began to settle on the tiny replica of Rovaniemi. 'It's perfect.'

'It plays music too,' she said, taking it and twisting the base. She looked up to see him smiling as the tinkling tune began.

'I thought maybe it would be a nice souvenir,' she continued. 'You know, remind you of the holiday. Maybe even a little of me.'

'I don't need a replica of Santa's village to remember you,' he said softly. 'I'll never forget you.'

Esme forced a smile that didn't care. But she ached to reach for him, to feel his arms around her as she had before, to feel his lips on hers. Things had changed since then, though. It wouldn't be smart or right to rush into something that, ultimately, neither of them was ready for. There was too much at stake, too much that could go wrong and, in the end, they might hurt each other more. Friends – that was the best outcome now. They couldn't go wrong as friends, could they? They could love each other as friends, couldn't they?

'I think I ought to call it a night,' she said. 'We've got an early start, haven't we, and I'm exhausted.'

'But you're OK?'

'As OK as I can be considering the night I've had. Maybe not the best I've ever been but I'm sure a few weeks will cure that.'

'A few weeks at your grandma's house? Not back in the flat with Warren?'

She shook her head. 'Not back with Warren. I've learned my lesson this time. I'm looking forward to some quiet time at my grandma's house… *my* house, I suppose now.'

'I'm glad.'

'Me too. What's waiting for you when you get back to England?'

'Christmas with my sister and her brood. It's not as bad as it sounds though.'

'Honestly, it sounds pretty nice to me.'

'Will you stay for one more drink?' he asked. 'A lakka, for old times' sake?'

Esme almost said no. But something stopped her. 'Just one?'

'Cross my heart. We've all got to get up tomorrow, and even I don't fancy a hangover on an early-morning flight.'

'OK, just one. That'd be nice.'

He nodded at Inari and she began to walk down the bar to them. He ordered their drinks. 'What I said earlier,' he began slowly as he watched Inari go to get them.

'Which thing,' Esme asked, though she already knew.

'About…' He turned to her. 'Don't make me say it again. I just want to know… is there a chance?'

'I want to say yes, but I honestly don't know. Everything's a mess right now.'

'I understand. I'm sorry I asked.'

'Please, don't be. Please just be patient. It doesn't mean we can't keep in touch. In fact, I'd really like that.'

'Me too. I don't want to hassle you—'

'You'd never be hassling me. In fact, I might be very disappointed if you didn't hassle me a little bit.'

'Friends, then. I can deal with friends.'

'Friends. Thank you.'

'I should be thanking you.'

'What on earth for?'

Esme looked up as Inari placed their drinks on the bar in front of them.

'Your room?' Inari asked Zach, who nodded.

He continued as she left them alone again. 'I think it's no exaggeration to say you might just have saved me. I'd been so wrapped up in my loss for all this time, thinking I could never move on from Libby, and you showed me that wasn't true. You showed me without even trying, and you made it feel so natural and easy that it's not this *thing* anymore, this mountain I can't climb. There is an end in sight now to all that grief. It doesn't mean I can ever forget Libby, and I wouldn't want to, but it does mean I can start to pick up the pieces, get my life on track again. Maybe even find love again.'

Esme smiled as she picked up her glass. If she'd done all that, then she was glad, but maybe it would end up benefiting some other woman, not her. Maybe she'd paved the way for Zach to find happiness with someone else. Only time would tell.

Chapter Twenty-Two

In the corner of the kitchen Matilda's old wind-up radio played Christmas carols while her favourite DJ interjected every so often to interview people about what their Christmas Day plans looked like. Esme smiled as a seven-year-old boy said he intended to spend the entire day with his new toy racetrack and he didn't care about his mum's turkey dinner because everyone said it was always dry anyway but they didn't dare tell her. Esme could picture the mad backtracking of various family members trying to placate a disgruntled cook who'd been serving up their traditional roast every year to barefaced lies of smiling gratitude and traitorous sounds of enjoyment.

In the year she'd been back at Little Dove Morton there had been many changes. Most of them had been made to her grandma's old house, which now boasted proper central heating and windows that didn't rattle with every thunderstorm, paid for with what had been left of Esme's wedding fund. She didn't see that she'd need money to get married for a very long time to come, but that was just fine. The décor still needed a lot of updating, but in many ways Esme was in no rush to erase the last traces of her grandma from the old cottage. In fact, she'd decided, for now, to tell people it was extremely shabby-chic retro and they'd all be installing fringed lamps and pasting up faded flock wallpaper soon enough.

It had been a good year – a time of new beginnings, of rediscovering who she really was and what she was capable of. There had been peace and calm amongst the hills and valleys of her beloved Peak District and she'd savoured every moment. Of course, there had been times when she'd been lonely too, but as many times as she'd felt lost and isolated she'd also been content. It was impossible to be lonely for long when she had new and wonderful friends at the farm shop where she now worked and regular visits from Brian and Hortense, who'd told her at their last one that they'd just booked to go to Crete and get married. They'd invited her, of course, and, of course, she'd said yes. It was another wonderful thing to look forward to, and it reminded her that although she was often alone she had no need to be lonely.

Putting the finishing touches to a turkey that was so small it was really more of a sparrow, she put it into the oven and closed the door. Compared to the time her grandma would have begun cooking on a Christmas morning, it was late in the day. It didn't matter because a couple of hours would have it all ready and Esme didn't see the point in rushing. Potatoes were peeled and soaking, Christmas cake had been made weeks before, prepared following the meticulous notes in her grandma's old handwritten recipe book, and there was a glass of good sherry sitting on the side, which Esme visited every now and again as she worked and hummed along to the radio. Life was good right now, and even when this Christmas morning brought back memories of Christmases past that hadn't been so good, she was able to reflect with courage and know that things had moved on, and that she had the power to stop them from ever getting that bad again. She'd had it all along; she just hadn't ever seen it before.

Sometimes she'd wonder what Warren was doing. Not because she longed to be with him, but just because she didn't have it in her to hate him and she wanted him to be happy, despite the bad times they'd been through together. And perhaps it hadn't all been completely bad. The last official report she'd heard he'd attempted another reconciliation with Shelly, and she'd told him where to go. There was no huge surprise there. Shelly and Esme still spoke from time to time, bonded now by the man who'd been a trial in both their lives, and Shelly had told Esme she'd heard rumours of a fling with a nursery teacher – a young, impressionable, sweet girl who gave him everything he wanted. It all sounded depressingly familiar and Esme would have loved nothing more than to find out where this girl lived and impart the benefit of her wisdom and experience. But, as Esme had, she would have to work it all out for herself. Esme hadn't listened to anyone else's advice in that regard, and there was no reason to suppose Warren's new girlfriend would either, even if Esme could track her down and get to see her. It would all look like sour grapes anyway, despite Esme's good intentions.

In the living room, her phone rang. Wiping her hands on a dishcloth, Esme dashed through to get it.

'Mum! Merry Christmas! Are you and Dad having a nice time in Scotland?'

'Oh yes! It's freezing and your dad's made a new friend. All they talk about is fishing. So, as you can imagine, I'm having the most wonderful time.'

Esme laughed. 'I'm sure it's not that bad. I bet the scenery is gorgeous and the hotel too.'

'I suppose it'll do. I'm taking full advantage of the spa and cordon-bleu meals. How are you coping?'

'I'm fine. Just getting dinner on.'

'All by yourself?'

'I am capable, you know,' Esme said with a chuckle.

'I know, I know. I just meant…'

'I'm fine. I'm managing perfectly well and actually really enjoying a quiet hour – well, an hour with just me and the radio, anyway.'

'I'm still not happy about leaving you today.'

'Mum, I wouldn't have said it was OK if it wasn't. You have absolutely nothing to worry about – I'm happy as Larry here. I've got my turkey, a glass of sherry on the go, a nice bottle of white in the fridge – not that I'm drowning any sorrows, just in case you're thinking that – a box of chocolates for the big film on telly later… Nothing to worry about.'

'That all sounds quite nice, to be honest. I might just drive home and join you, leave your dad to his fishing.'

'Don't you dare! You and Dad have been talking about Hogmanay for years and you deserve a nice long break. You know how I feel about doing things you've always wanted to do before it's too late. I learned all I need to learn about that last Christmas and my opinion hasn't changed one bit. Let the staff at that swanky hotel pamper you and be sure to enjoy it, and don't let me see you darken this door until after the New Year!'

'I suppose it will be back to dishwashing and ironing and everything else after next week.'

'Exactly. I'm a big girl now and you don't need to worry.'

'I know. But it's Christmas.'

'I noticed.'

'There's no need to be sarcastic.'

'I'm not.' Esme smiled. 'I'm trying to tell you that there's no need to beat yourself up on my account. I love you.'

'I love you too. Does that mean you're trying to get me off the phone?'

'Sorry, but sort of.'

'I thought so. In that case I can take a hint.'

Esme smiled. 'But I'll speak to you later. That's if you're not too busy.'

'That'd be lovely. Phone after nine, darling – there's a big Christmas show in the cabaret lounge and your dad wants to see it, so we won't be able to hear you call.'

'After nine – will do.'

'Bye. Have a lovely day.'

'You too. Bye, Mum.'

Esme took the phone through to the kitchen and placed it on the windowsill, out of the way of spraying pans but close by, just in case. The clock on the chimney breast said 11 a.m. and she'd planned lunch for 1.30 p.m. Pulling a bag of sprouts from the fridge she began the laborious task of peeling them. As a kid, peeling the sprouts had always been her job and while she was little she'd loved being a part of the preparations for Christmas lunch. It was only as she'd got older she'd realised that the job had been given to her because everyone else knew what a fiddly pain in the arse it was. She smiled to herself as she began to pull back their little green jackets, putting the ones she'd done into a pan of water. Matilda had had a special way of cooking sprouts, and Esme must have been the only child at primary school who'd actually looked forward to that mound of everyone else's least popular vegetables on the side of her plate. She tried to recall now what method her grandma had once explained to her – back when she'd been a sulky teen who'd only half wanted to listen. How she'd often wished since that she'd listened more to everything her grandma had wanted to teach her. Now that Matilda was gone, Esme realised that with her had gone so much knowledge and wisdom – some that could have been Esme's if she'd taken more notice. But somehow, she'd always imagined her grandma would be around forever and she'd never been able to countenance a day when that hole would appear in her life.

In a photo album in her drawer upstairs Esme had put her grandma's wedding photo, along with her granddad's tickets for Lapland and Esme's own from her trip the previous year. Just to show Matilda that she'd done it, that she'd seen the Northern Lights for her. The trip had changed everything, and there was barely a day that went by when Esme didn't wish she could tell her grandma, face-to-face over a cup of tea and a slice of home-made fruit cake, just how much. She'd had to be content with weekly trips to the graveyard with fresh flowers and a one-sided chat, but that was OK. Everybody suffered losses and everybody had sadness. Even so, life went on, as Matilda had often remarked herself, and nobody was ever gone, not truly, while their loved ones remained.

The sedate sounds of the carol concert on the radio came to an end and a new announcer launched straight into Slade's 'Merry Xmas Everybody'. Esme had no issue with the Slade song – she liked it as well as anyone – but she crossed the kitchen to turn it off. Somehow, it didn't fit with the serene, contemplative mood of the house right now. In silence, she worked to finish preparing the vegetables and by the time she looked up at the clock again it was 11.30 a.m. The sight of a bag of seed in the pantry as she searched in there for some flour to thicken the gravy reminded her that the bird feeder needed topping up. The birds her grandma had cared for had disappeared while Esme had been away in London and Lapland, but once she'd returned, so had they, and she made certain now to keep the feeder full so they'd stay. Then there was just time to water the Christmas tree, sweep up the needles it had shed overnight and change into something a little more presentable before the knock at the front door she'd been waiting for.

Esme raced down the stairs to open up, and there was that smile she'd grown to love, the smile that lifted her above the clouds and made her believe she could touch the sky. The smile that made her feel anything was possible. Most of all, it made her believe in love for the first time in her life.

Zach stepped over the threshold and pulled her into a passionate kiss. He had snow on his coat and his lips were cold, but they warmed as they pressed against hers.

'Merry Christmas,' he said, his voice husky as he gazed down at her. Her stomach did a flip. God, how she loved to hear him speak when he was all gravelly and seductive. She'd often joked that he could get her into bed reading the shopping list when he talked like that, and just to be certain, he'd start to reel off the contents of his fridge at home. Sure enough, they'd usually be in bed by the time he'd finished.

Esme pouted now, but it was only a half-hearted attempt at being annoyed. 'I thought you'd never get here.'

'I didn't think I was all that late.'

'No, you're not that late. I'm *that* impatient.'

He kissed her again. 'Something smells good.'

'I just put the turkey in.'

'Not the turkey – you. Come here…'

Esme giggled and gave his arm a playful slap. 'There's time for that nonsense later – although not at nine o'clock.'

'What's happening at nine?' He took off his coat and hung it on the peg in the hallway, then followed Esme through to the kitchen.

'I have to phone my mum.'

'Why – what's happening to your mum at nine o'clock?'

'Nothing.' Esme laughed. 'At least nothing earth-shattering. They've got some show to see, that's all. I did promise I'd ring her once it was done.'

'Well, I suppose I can spare you for a few minutes.'

'How very noble of you.'

He sat at the table with a grin.

Esme reached for another glass from the cupboard and poured an extra sherry. Zach raised his eyebrows as she placed it in front of him.

'What am I, a geriatric?'

'You have to have sherry on Christmas morning – it's the rules.'

'Not my rules.'

'Have you ever even tried sherry?'

'What do you think?'

'I bet you like it more than you think you will. And after the first three or four it goes down nicely and you don't even notice that it tastes like Victorian cough syrup.'

Zach's grin spread as he reached for the glass. 'I suppose it could be worse. I have a surprise for later, though I probably ought to save it until we've finished cooking because I don't want any drunken accidents.'

'What kind of surprise?'

'Niko sent a bottle of lakka.'

Esme smiled. 'How is he?'

'Good, I think. Busy with his snowmobile tours – says he's booked out this year. I think he's happy. He says to say hello, by the way.'

'Oh, OK…' Esme leaned over to press her lips onto his. 'Hello then…'

'Steady.' Zach grinned, kissing her again despite his warning. 'I'm not sure that's entirely the kind of greeting Niko had in mind when he said it.'

Esme giggled and took a seat across from him. 'How was the drive up?'

'There wasn't much on the roads. I suppose most people have got more sense than to be on the motorway on Christmas morning.'

'I suppose so. I wished you could have come up last night instead.'

'Me too but…'

Esme reached for his hand to tell him it was OK. She didn't need him to explain that this would be the first Christmas Day he wouldn't be visiting his wife's grave, and she understood that it was probably what he'd been doing on Christmas Eve this year instead. He was here now, and she couldn't have asked more of him.

'You've got your toothbrush?' she asked instead.

'Yes, ma'am. But I forgot my pyjamas.'

'That's OK, I think I have an old nightie you can borrow.'

'I was kind of hoping I wouldn't need my pyjamas.'

'I know. That's why I'm going to find an old nightie for you.'

'I was kind of hoping you wouldn't need your nightie either.'

Esme looked serious for a moment, as if she was considering his statement. 'It might get awful cold. We'd need hot-water bottles.'

Zach laughed, and then winced as he took a sip of his sherry. 'Wow! That's an acquired taste. And I thought lakka was hard work!'

'Remember when we got slaughtered last Christmas in Lapland?'

'And then I ended up in your bed. We were supposed to be in this chaste friendship and I couldn't... well, you know... the wee fella down there wouldn't behave. I was mortified.'

Esme's eyes widened, but then she started to laugh. 'You never said!'

'I didn't think I needed to say – I'm surprised you couldn't tell! Why do you think I dashed out for food?'

'I thought you were hungry!'

'Well, I was,' he said with a sheepish grin. 'But it was also the closest I could get to a cold shower to calm down.'

Esme leaned over him and gave a flirty look. 'So you did fancy me even though you weren't supposed to?'

'Of course I did.'

She lowered her voice into a teasing lilt. 'And now that you have free rein to do whatever you want, is it still as exciting?'

'You know it is,' he said, kissing her gently. Then again, and again, until they were locked together.

She was giggling as she pushed him away. 'That wee fella never behaves. Down boy – we have carrots to chop!'

'Can't the dinner wait? We can work up an appetite…'

'No. It's Christmas and we have to do it properly.'

'Bloody conventions,' Zach said, pretending to be annoyed.

Esme placed a paring knife and a bag of carrots in front of him. 'Earn your keep. You can have your Christmas present later.'

He opened the bag. But then he stopped and his smile faded as he gazed up at her.

'What?' she asked, suddenly wrong-footed.

He got up. And then he sat down. He stood up again and went to the window, his back to her. Outside it was snowing. Not like the snow they'd seen in Lapland the previous year, which felt like a heavy blanket of frozen whiteness, but soft wet snow that melted almost as soon as it landed. Esme had spent the morning watching it stop and start as she got lunch ready.

'Zach. Sit down, for God's sake. You're making me nervous.'

'*You're* nervous? God, Esme…'

'If you have something to tell me, you know you can. I'm sure whatever it is we can work it out.'

He turned and came back to the table, his foot tapping a drumbeat on the old stone floor.

She sat next to him. 'So, what is it?'

He shook his head. 'It's nothing.'

'It's not nothing. A minute ago you're all frisky and now I have Mr Angst. We've been dating for a year now and I might not see you that often with two hundred miles between us but I can still tell by now when you're agitated.'

'I'm not agitated.'

'Really? Then why is your foot currently displaying the characteristics of a pneumatic drill and trying to dig through my floor?'

He stopped tapping and reached for his sherry, taking a gulp. 'That's just it,' he said. 'We don't see each other often.'

'But we make the best of every opportunity, don't we?'

'Yes, I suppose we do. But I don't like it.'

'You don't like seeing me?'

'No – that's not what I meant! Stop being silly!'

'I'm not the one who's making no sense.'

'Sorry, I know.'

'So are you going to tell me what this is really about?'

'I don't know…'

'Please. Bad or good, I can take it.'

'It's about us.'

'You have doubts? We're moving too fast? It's OK, you can say it.'

'It's not that at all. It's…'

Esme swallowed her impatience. She noticed the potatoes were boiling over on the stove and she rushed to turn them off. When she turned back, Zach was studying her. It was unnerving, because he didn't look like himself. He looked like a version of Zach she hadn't seen for a long time now – uncertain, vulnerable. She'd hoped never to see that Zach again.

'Whatever it is,' she said gently, 'you know we can work it out. We've come this far. I've got all the time in the world – we can do things as slow or as quick as you like. I understand about… Well, you know I do.'

'While I was driving here this morning, I realised I don't want to keep doing this journey every month or few weeks or whenever we can get a precious few days. I don't want to arrive back home to an empty house exhausted and bereft.'

Esme sat across from him again and frowned.

'OK… What are you trying to say? Are you finishing with me?' Her heart was thumping, but she would be strong. If this was what Zach needed then she'd be strong for him, because she knew he loved her and she'd always known there were many obstacles that would be in their way, no matter how much love they had.

'No!' Zach looked horrified. 'God, no! Of course not!' He paused and then downed the last of his sherry. 'I've been thinking about something all the way here. A solution. And I think I have one. I was going to wait until after dinner to do this but…'

Esme stared as he dropped to one knee and pulled a velvet box from his pocket. The fabric was worn and faded around the edges. He opened it up to reveal a heavily engraved gold ring set with a stunning heart-shaped emerald and a halo of tiny diamonds.

'Esme Greenwood… Marry me!'

'What?' Esme shook her head. Where had this come from? Where had he even got a ring on Christmas Day? But then, unwittingly, he provided the answer.

'I know it's perhaps not to your taste, and maybe it won't quite fit,' he said, holding the box higher for her to inspect. 'But I had to make a last-minute dash to my mum's to see if she still had my grandmother's old engagement ring. It's why I was late. She couldn't find it for a while… And the dresser was locked and then Dad couldn't find the key… Turns out it was in the cupboard under the stairs with the keys to a front door we don't even have now. God knows what it was doing in there. They both say hi, by the way,' he continued, and Esme realised that a babbling Zach was probably a nervous-as-hell Zach. It only made her love him more. He gave an awkward shrug. 'In a way I thought it was quite fitting really too,' he added, 'since it's my grandmother's ring, and it's thanks to your grandmother that we ever met at all.'

Esme took the box and stared at the ring. 'It's gorgeous. Perfect.'

She looked at him, staring up at her, waiting on her answer as if she could bring his whole world down upon him with one word. There was a whole mess of logistics to consider: would they live in Dorchester or Little Dove Morton? How would they cope with life together all the time? Could Esme live with the spectre of Libby's tragic death as a constant of their relationship? Would he want kids and how soon? Did she even want kids? Where would the money come from for their wedding now that Esme's previous fund was upstairs and currently pumping heat around her house…?

They'd have all that to think about and more, but right now, none of it mattered. She loved Zach and he loved her. There was no way she was going to give any other answer.

'Yes,' she said. 'I'll marry you.'

She didn't even get time to put the ring on her finger. Zach jumped up and pulled her into his arms. She drew a breath, safe and warm in his embrace, and she knew then that she never wanted to be anywhere else.

'I love you, Esme Greenwood,' he said, kissing her. 'I loved you from the moment I bought you a flat white in a coffee shop at the airport. I promise, if you'll let me, I'll make you the happiest woman in the world.'

She smiled through her tears. 'You already have.'

Zach kissed her again, and in that moment there was hope. This old house had seen loss over the years, as many houses had, but mostly it had been filled with joy and love. Perhaps, finally, this was Esme's chance to fill it with love once more. The old place certainly needed it. Perhaps this was her chance to build on the love planted by her grandma and granddad, the love that had seen her through the darkest days of her life. And when the old place was full to the brim, Esme and Zach would be ready to pass it on to the next generation, and Esme couldn't think of a more perfect ending than that.

A Letter From Tilly

Wow, I can't believe I've just released my third Christmas novel for Bookouture! Where the heck are the years going? The last few have been a whirlwind of publishing deadlines and I've been so proud to share every new book with my lovely readers. I really hope you've enjoyed reading *The Christmas Wish* as much as I enjoyed writing it (even though it was during the longest heatwave we've had for years!). If you've enjoyed Esme's story then I'd be hugely grateful if you could spread the word or leave a quick review. The more people who hear about it, then the more we can share the love.

If you ever want to catch up with me on social media, you can find me on Twitter @TillyTenWriter or Facebook.

So, thank you for reading my little book; as always I'm so grateful for your support. And please look out for my next book, which I'm currently working feverishly on and will be with you in spring of 2019.

Lots of love and heartfelt wishes to you and yours this Christmas,

Tilly x

www.tillytennant.com

TillyTennant

@TillyTenWriter

Acknowledgements

The list of people who have offered help and encouragement on my writing journey so far must be truly endless, and it would take a novel in itself to mention them all. However, my heartfelt gratitude goes out to each and every one of you, whose involvement, whether small or large, has been invaluable and appreciated more than I can say.

There are a few people that I must mention. Obviously, my family – the people who put up with my whining and self-doubt on a daily basis are top of the list. My mum and, posthumously, my dad, who brought me up to believe that anything is possible if you want it enough, no matter how crazy or unlikely it seems. My ex-colleagues at the Royal Stoke University Hospital, who let me lead a double life for far longer than is acceptable and have given me so many ideas for future books! The lecturers at Staffordshire University English and Creative Writing Department, who saw a talent worth nurturing in me and continue to support me still, long after they finished getting paid for it. They are not only tutors but friends as well. I have to thank the team at Bookouture for their continued support, patience and amazing publishing flair, particularly Lydia Vassar-Smith, Kim Nash, Noelle Holten, Peta Nightingale, Lauren Finger and Jessie Botterill. Their belief, able assistance and encouragement means the world to me. I truly believe I have the best team an author could ask for.

My friend Kath Hickton always gets a mention for putting up with me since primary school. Louise Coquio also gets an honourable mention for getting me through university and suffering me ever since, likewise her lovely family. And thanks go to Storm Constantine for giving me my first break in publishing. I also have to thank Mel Sherratt and Holly Martin, fellow writers and amazing friends who have both been incredibly supportive over the years and have been my shoulders to cry on in the darker moments. Thanks to Tracy Bloom, Emma Davies, Jack Croxall, Clare Davidson, Angie Marsons, Christie Barlow and Jaimie Admans: not only brilliant authors in their own right but hugely supportive of others. My Bookouture colleagues are all incredible, of course, unfailing and generous in their support of fellow authors – life would be a lot duller without the gang! I have to thank all the brilliant and dedicated book bloggers (there are so many of you but you know who you are!) and readers, and anyone else who has championed my work, reviewed it, shared it or simply told me that they liked it. Every one of those actions is priceless and you are all very special people. Some of you I am even proud to call friends now.

Read on for an extract of Tilly Tennant's feel-good romantic comedy,
The Little Village Bakery

Chapter One

On the hottest day of the year so far, the sprinklers on the green of the tiny village of Honeybourne made miniature rainbows in the shimmering air. Jasmine Green's triplets, Rebecca, Rachel and Reuben, squealed as they raced backwards and forwards through the water, while Jasmine folded the last of the bunting from her stall of homemade crafts and furnishings.

'It's been a fabulous day for it,' she commented cheerily to the vicar as he wandered over.

'Certainly has,' he agreed, looking round at the other stalls lined up around the perimeter of the green, their owners also packing away. 'I love the fête, the one day of the summer when the whole village comes together to have fun.'

'The children have certainly enjoyed it this year.' She looked fondly over at her offspring, now soaked through but grinning all over their faces.

'Some of the adults have had a good time too,' he replied, angling his head to where Jasmine's husband, Rich, was sitting on a deckchair looking distinctly sunburnt despite his dark hair and complexion, grinning drunkenly and staring into space.

She blew a ringlet the colour of candyfloss from her damp forehead and giggled. 'I told him to be careful with Frank Stephenson's scrumpy.'

340

'Who's got scrumpy?' Rich asked, now squinting up at them.

'No more for you today,' Jasmine scolded, but only half-heartedly. He pouted like a little boy and she smiled indulgently. 'If you can manage to walk in a straight line, how about you gather the kids up and help me get this stock back to the van?' She folded her arms. 'I suppose I'm driving home too as you've lost the ability to coordinate your limbs properly?'

He pushed himself up from the chair and made a move to take her into his arms. 'Who can't coordinate his limbs? You wait till later, my gorgeous little hippy chick,' he said, wrapping her in his strong embrace. 'I'll show you how to coordinate limbs.'

'*Richard Green*, the vicar is standing right there!' Jasmine giggled.

'Don't mind me,' the vicar said amiably, 'I'll just peruse the lovely items you have left on your stall here. Honestly, this metalwork is quite spectacular.' He picked up a pendant and turned it over in his fingers. 'You have lots of special things here, Mrs Green, but in the main a remarkable talent for making unusual jewellery.'

'Take something home for Mrs Vicar,' Rich said with a grin. 'Pretty trinkets always work on the missus.'

'Not when the missus has made them herself, they don't,' Jasmine said with a mock scowl.

'Fair point.' Rich hiccupped. He was a good foot taller than Jasmine and she had to stretch up to kiss him.

'Go and get your children, there's a good boy,' she laughed.

He let go of her and staggered off. But when Jasmine looked up again, he was chasing the children through the sprinklers, making monster noises as he went, sending them scattering and squealing with delight. Some of the other villagers had joined in with their children. Jasmine stopped her packing for a moment and watched them all play their elaborate game.

'You know, Vicar,' she said in a voice full of lazy contentment, 'I really don't think there is a happier place to live on Earth than here.'

In her kitchen, a hundred miles to the north of where Jasmine Green was ushering her reluctant family into a van, Millicent Hopkin – Millie to the handful of people who dared get close enough – was sobbing. It felt like she did little else these days, though she was always careful to save it for when she was alone. Some would take great satisfaction in her pain. She probably deserved it, but that still didn't give anyone the right to victimise her.

The car had been the last straw. She'd spent the last three hours trying to scrub away the vile words. Whoever wrote the old rhyme about sticks and stones was wrong. The smashed windows, the faeces shoved through her letterbox, the mysterious taxis and pizza deliveries in the early hours that she had ended up having to pay for when they insisted she'd ordered them – she'd borne it all with a quiet fortitude. But the words... Words had magic, they had power – the power to heal, to hurt, to make things happen, and the ones she'd failed to remove from her car, even though she'd rubbed and rubbed until her hands were raw, had hurt her as much as any stick or stone could. She'd had enough.

Drying her tears, she tried to concentrate on the task in front of her. The only constant in her life now was her creativity, and baking was the one creative thing she could still do that brought pleasure to others. Although these days she didn't know who she could share this one with when the people she had once called friends had all turned against her. She had tried to be a good person, to set things right, but in the end it had meant nothing. Turning her attention to the mixing bowl in front of her, she added ingredients to the mix – cinnamon and nutmeg, vanilla, a pound of dried fruit, a sprinkle of heartsease, her unintentional tears – and thought about how she needed a new start, somewhere far away where people didn't know her. Somewhere people wouldn't judge her or hurt her or blame her for everything that had gone before.

She focused on the thought, on the photo of a tumbledown old building on a property website that had captured her imagination, four walls in an adorably named village that might just be the new start she'd been searching for. She closed her eyes, pictured the bakery – *her* bakery – and tried to imagine the sweet smells, the bright colours of the cakes, the chatter of customers, opening the shutters on every new day and welcoming it in; she tried to remember what happiness felt like, how it was to want to live. She longed for it with every fibre of her being. In less than a week, if the universe was finally smiling on her, maybe she would find out.

When the mix was done, she poured it into a tin and whispered a last wish before she put it into the oven. She needed a new start. Perhaps the cake would make it so.

'Who's that?' Rich nudged Jasmine as he watched a woman stagger into the old bakery under the weight of a huge box she had just pulled from the back of a van bearing the name 'Countrywide Vehicle Hire'. She was slim and looked to be in her late twenties to early thirties, with sleek black hair cut into a cute bob and a feline beauty that made you want to stare.

At least, it was making Rich stare.

'Perhaps,' Jasmine replied, giving her husband a wry smile, 'you might want to roll your tongue in and ask her if she needs any help…'

'I could,' he said, 'but I don't want to make you jealous.'

'I think I'll survive,' she replied, raising her eyes heavenward as he walked backwards across the deserted road, grinning at her all the while.

'Hello!' Rich whipped himself back round and called to the woman as she emerged from the shop door, wiping a hand across her brow. 'Are you moving in?'

The woman looked at him. There was something wary in her eyes and he faltered for a moment. 'I'm Rich,' he said, collecting himself and sticking out a friendly hand.

The woman took it in a loose grip and shook. 'Millicent…'

'You're taking over the bakery?' he asked, nodding at the building. Before Millicent could reply, Jasmine had joined them, slipping an arm through her husband's. 'Oh, this is my wife, Jasmine.'

Millicent's smile for Jasmine was warmer. 'Pleased to meet you,' she said.

'And you… Millicent did you say?'

'Call me Millie. Millicent makes me sound like someone's great-aunt.'

'Are you doing all this alone?' Jasmine asked, glancing at the open doors of the van.

'Sadly, yes.'

'We'd be happy to help. Rich and I have a couple of hours to spare before we go to get the terrors from school.'

'Terrors?' Millie asked.

Rich grinned. 'Otherwise known as the Green children. They're probably not as bad as people tell us, but the teachers have all been given standard-issue canisters of tear gas and riot gear, just in case.'

Jasmine elbowed him in the ribs with a giggle.

'Help would be most welcome, in that case,' Millie said, relaxing into a smile. 'When I started to pack all this stuff, it didn't look like much. It's not until you're on your twentieth box with no sign of stopping that you realise just how much you own.'

'We found that when we moved from our tiny cottage into where we live now. You wouldn't believe what you can fit into a one-bedroom house.' Jasmine pushed a stray curl back from her forehead. 'And we still have boxes in the loft that we've never unpacked, even years later.'

'Just goes to show how much we needed the stuff,' Rich grinned.

'Or how lazy you are,' Jasmine replied with a smirk.

'Hey, I have a highly demanding job!'

'Don't listen to a word he says,' Jasmine said to Millie in a loud stage whisper. 'He sits on his backside all day tinkering in a home recording studio and he calls that work.'

'You're a musician?' Millie asked, looking at Rich with obvious awe.

'Some might argue that point,' he laughed, 'but that's how I make my living.'

'So… you're taking on the old bakery?' Jasmine asked.

'It's going to take a lot of work, I know,' Millie said, resting her hands on her hips as she turned her gaze to the building. 'But I hope to get it back to its former glory and trading again.'

'The village could certainly do with it,' Jasmine said. 'It used to be a lovely place to meet people and stop for something yummy. We have the supermarket about five miles away, and a general store that sells allsorts, but it's not the same as a proper cake shop.'

'Where did you say you'd moved from?' Rich asked, shoving his hands into his pockets with an amiable smile.

'I didn't.' Millie's expression suddenly darkened. Rich threw an uncertain glance at Jasmine, but the moment quickly passed.

'Ignore him,' Jasmine said. 'No concept of social boundaries – size elevens straight in every time.'

'Well,' Rich said with a self-conscious laugh. 'I suppose you could tell us where you want these boxes and we'll crack on.'

'I can always get the kids myself if we don't finish here,' Jasmine told Rich. 'And you could carry on moving Millie's stuff.'

'I can't ask you to drop everything and carry my boxes all afternoon,' Millie said, looking mortified by the idea. 'I'm sure you must have plans.'

'Nothing that can't wait,' Jasmine said with a smile. 'And as we both work for ourselves, the bosses are pretty lenient about time off.'

'You write music too?'

'God no! I have a craft business. I make jewellery and homey knick-knacks.'

'Is that one of your pieces?' Millie glanced appreciatively at a burnished silver pendant hanging around Jasmine's neck.

'Oh yes,' Jasmine said, running a hand over the piece to remind herself which one it was.

'It's beautiful.' Millie stepped forward and took it gently in her fingers. She looked up at Jasmine with a bright smile. 'You know this is a Celtic symbol?'

'Is it?' Jasmine laughed. 'I got it out of a book.'

'Yes, a very apt one too, in your case. It's the symbol for inspiration and creativity.'

'Wow. You seem to know a lot about it,' Rich said.

Millie shrugged and let the pendant go, the darkness crossing her features again. 'A little. I read a lot of mythology.' She turned to Jasmine again, the storm clearing from her eyes as quickly as it had come. 'Your hair looks amazing too. I noticed as soon as I saw you across the road.'

'It's kind of hard to miss, I suppose.' Jasmine twisted a pink ringlet self-consciously. Her hair was pinned up, an explosion of sugary curls piled on her head, the odd corkscrew escaping to frame her face.

'I wish I was brave enough to colour my hair like that.'

'Why would you do that? Yours is glorious as it is.'

'But sometimes you just feel like you need a huge change, do something completely different... you know what I mean?'

Their conversation was interrupted by Rich clearing his throat. 'I suppose we really should get these boxes in.'

'You're right,' said Millie. 'The van will have to go back soon.'

'In that case we're at your service.' Rich saluted. 'So tell us where you want everything.'